More praise for
FOOL'S PUZZLE
and Earlene Fowler . . .

"A Quadruple Irish Chain" is a quilt pattern consisting of
one-inch squares set in a stair-step design. Its traditional
colors of green, white, black, and gray make a striking finished quilt . . . if one has the perseverance to stitch together
the numerous pieces of the whole.

IRISH CHAIN

EARLENE FOWLER

BERKLEY PRIME CRIME, NEW YORK

THE BERKLEY PUBLISHING GROUP
Published by the Penguin Group
Penguin Group (USA) Inc.
375 Hudson Street, New York, New York 10014, USA
Penguin Group (Canada), 90 Eglinton Avenue East, Suite 700, Toronto, Ontario M4P 2Y3, Canada
(a division of Pearson Penguin Canada Inc.)
Penguin Books Ltd., 80 Strand, London WC2R 0RL, England
Penguin Group Ireland, 25 St. Stephen's Green, Dublin 2, Ireland (a division of Penguin Books Ltd.)
Penguin Group (Australia), 250 Camberwell Road, Camberwell, Victoria 3124, Australia
(a division of Pearson Australia Group Pty. Ltd.)
Penguin Books India Pvt. Ltd., 11 Community Centre, Panchsheel Park, New Delhi—110 017, India
Penguin Group (NZ), Cnr. Airborne and Rosedale Roads, Albany, Auckland 1310, New Zealand
(a division of Pearson New Zealand Ltd.)
Penguin Books (South Africa) (Pty.) Ltd., 24 Sturdee Avenue, Rosebank, Johannesburg 2196,
South Africa

Penguin Books Ltd., Registered Offices: 80 Strand, London WC2R 0RL, England

This is a work of fiction. Names, characters, places, and incidents either are the product of the author's imagination or are used fictitiously, and any resemblance to actual persons, living or dead, business establishments, events, or locales is entirely coincidental. The publisher does not have any control over and does not assume any responsibility for author or third-party websites or their content.

IRISH CHAIN

A Berkley Prime Crime Book / published by arrangement with the author

PRINTING HISTORY
Berkley Prime Crime hardcover edition / March 1995
Berkley Prime Crime mass-market edition / February 1996

Copyright © 1995 by Earlene Fowler.
The Edgar® name is a registered service mark of the Mystery Writers of America, Inc.

ISBN: 0-425-15137-9

BERKLEY® PRIME CRIME
Berkley Prime Crime Books are published by The Berkley Publishing Group,
a division of Penguin Group (USA) Inc.,
375 Hudson Street, New York, New York 10014.
The name BERKLEY PRIME CRIME and the BERKLEY PRIME CRIME design
are trademarks belonging to Penguin Group (USA) Inc.

PRINTED IN THE UNITED STATES OF AMERICA

27 26 25 24 23 22 21 20

To Mama and Daddy,
who gave me
Southern roots and Western wings

and

To my Grammas,
Edith Bennett Worley and Muriel Webb Phillips,
who taught me what being a "tough old broad"
was all about

ACKNOWLEDGMENTS

My deepest thanks to:

The Lord God—Your grace is always sufficient

Mary Atkinson and Ann Lee for their attention to detail and moral support

My agent, Deborah Schneider, who continues to support and believe in my work; and my editor, Melinda Metz, for her generous efficiency and cheerful spirit

Jose Padilla and Veronica Carillo, *muchas gracias* for their good-natured answers to all my crazy questions

Farideh Naeim-Ebadolahi for her help and for introducing me to the joys of Persian food

Helen May and the rest of the ladies at Oakview Convalescent Home. You all taught me much more than I could ever teach you

And, with love, to my husband, Allen. If I could save time in a bottle . . .

IRISH CHAIN:

The origin of the Irish Chain quilt pattern is unknown, but it is very old, rumored to go back as far as Colonial times. The color arrangement of the fabric pieces creates the "chain" effect. The single chain is made with two contrasting colors or prints, but can also be expanded to make a double, triple, or quadruple chain. The color combinations become more varied and the pattern more complex as chains are added. The chain can go on and on, making a quilt as large as desired. It is only stopped when the quilter decides to end it.

1

"I'M GOING TO snatch you baldheaded, Benni Harper, if you don't haul your butt over here right now," Gramma Dove said, her voice as raspy as the old Hank Williams records she loves. All the orphan calves on the Ramsey Ranch had been milk-fed and soothed to sleep by her gritty-voiced renditions of "I Saw The Light," and "I'm So Lonesome I Could Cry." For that matter, so had I.

"I was just walking out the door," I lied amicably, sitting behind the counter of the small gift shop in the empty folk art museum. An earsplitting click answered me when she hung up the phone. She hadn't called me "young lady" yet. That meant I still had time. My stomach rumbled, reminding me I'd forgotten to eat breakfast again. I knew Dove though, and she never came down from the ranch without bringing something to eat, determined to bring me back up to what she called "fighting hen weight." I'd lost ten pounds when my husband, Jack, was killed a year ago when his Jeep flipped over on a lonely stretch of old Highway One, and I'd never regained it. Dove worries about that as she does every minuscule detail of my life. A born "heel snapper," she is a determined cattle dog of a woman and, according to her, I remain her most unmanageable calf. Her constant interference in my life is a good-natured but continual bone of contention between us. Hope and anticipation for her heart-melting sweet potato biscuits caused my stomach to growl again.

Ignoring my hunger, I turned back to the oak-framed cross-stitch sampler I was logging into the inventory book. "The Best Things Come But Once in a Lifetime."

Stitched in a dashing sweep of blues ranging from robin's egg to deep, lustrous navy, each letter was outlined in black, causing the sentiment to almost jump out at me. It was one of the over two hundred samplers we'd received at the museum in response to our newspaper ad requesting cross-stitched and embroidered samplers for our newest exhibit. As curator of the Josiah Sinclair Folk Art Museum, I was responsible for choosing the hundred or so we actually had room to display. To be fair, I had tried to select a wide variety of styles, ages and degrees of craftsmanship but especially ones with heart, ones that appeared to mean something special to each artist when they created it. What I had in mind was for the exhibit to tell its own story, about the individual artists, about our town and about the wider community of man. The success of the show was important to me. Though proud of my last exhibit of antique quilts and of the five newspaper articles written about the museum, I couldn't overlook the fact that the publicity had more to do with the murders that took place on the premises rather than my expertise as a curator. A reporter for the travel section of the L.A. *Times* had contacted me two weeks ago wanting to do a small piece on our new museum and she didn't even mention the murders. That made it essential for this exhibit to shine.

"The Best Things Come But Once in a Lifetime." I studied the daisy and lily-of-the-valley border, the fancy script, the blue and purple peacocks gracing each corner before writing down the name and address of the sampler's owner. The age-faded embroidered words stitched by K. G. Drusell in 1924 struck a melancholy chord in me. At thirty-four and, in less than a week, widowed a year, I was beginning to wonder if this lady might be right. My relationship with Jack had definitely been the best thing I ever had—though being married to him since the age of nineteen, I didn't have much to compare it with. Until now, that is.

Gabriel Ortiz. I'd met him, sparred with him and grudgingly allowed him to weasel his way into my life when murder was a major contributor to the museum's exhibit of antique quilts almost three months ago. His qualifications were listed in my head in a permanent resumé. San Celina's temporary chief of police. Olive-skinned Hispanic-Anglo native of Derby, Kansas with a twenty-some-odd-year stopover in Los Angeles. Long, sinewy, half-miler's legs. A thick black mustache with touches of silver hiding a sensuously full lower lip that disappeared when he was tense or angry. Blue-gray eyes the color of the Pacific Ocean in January. And, for want of a better description, my steady companion these last few months. Was it love, loneliness or just an incredible physical attraction? That was the question of the hour. One I didn't have an answer for on an empty stomach so early on a Saturday morning. I glanced at the Daffy Duck watch on my wrist—a present from Gabe, who declared, in his husky, sardonic voice, that Daffy and I shared similar characteristics. I'm still trying to decide how to take that one.

I closed and locked the heavy Spanish door of the old Sinclair Hacienda, now the Josiah Sinclair Folk Art Museum and Artists' Co-op, thanks to the generosity of our rich benefactress, Constance Sinclair. When I reached my old red Chevy pickup with "Harper's Herefords" still stenciled on the doors, I turned and surveyed the newly painted two-story adobe house and stables with a bit of a proprietary air. Two weekends ago the entire co-op had banded together and whitewashed the outside walls, restained the rough wood posts supporting the front porch and planted the huge brick-colored clay pots in front with flowers native to San Celina County—tiny purple Shooting Stars, yellow Bermuda Buttercups, and exotic Leopard Lilies with their long stamens and polka-dotted petals. The building positively gleamed in the muted sunlight of the February morning. A crisp breeze whipped at the eucalyptus trees circling the gravel parking lot in a silvery-green windbreak. Tilting my head back, I took deep breaths of the spicy air, reveling in the unaccustomed warmth of the sun on my face. It was the first morning in over a week that the Central Coast hadn't been startled awake by one of the violent rain and wind storms that had ended California's drought this winter with a fervor not usually seen on the West Coast.

I'd grown to love the museum and co-op almost as much as the ranches I'd lived on all my life. After Jack died and I moved off the Harper Ranch, which he'd owned with his brother, this job had been my lifesaver. I threw myself into the daily rhythms of the museum and co-op, and with time, forged a new life. Though not one I would have necessarily chosen, I'd come to the point where waking up every morning was something I actually anticipated. Losing Jack taught me one important lesson. You had to enjoy each day given you, because it just might be your last. Something so simple to know, so hard to do.

Within a half hour, I was in the bedroom of my rented Spanish-style bungalow, jeans and pink flannel shirt on the floor, balanced on a makeshift dressmaker's platform of three old San Celina telephone books, doing what comes naturally to me when I'm around Dove—whining.

"I can't believe I'm going to wear this." Frowning at my image in the long brass mirror in the corner of my bedroom, I tugged at the tight bodice of the banana-yellow, hoop-skirted formal that was squeezing my midsection into jelly. From the waist down, I resembled a dime-store boudoir lamp shade.

"Quit wiggling," Dove said. "You're worse than a two-year-old." She gave my butt a whack with the back of her hand. I barely felt it under the layers of netting and filmy chiffon.

When I acquired the job as curator, I'd anticipated, between eccentric artists, rich patrons and the dependably crazy public, having to deal with a variety of unusual circumstances. Nothing in my imagination ever included hoop skirts. Except when Constance brought around the occasional dignitary in hopes of finagling a donation and I wore my calf-length black skirt with a silk cowboy shirt and my good Tony Lama deerskin boots, my work attire consisted of the same uniform I've worn most of my life—brown Justin Ropers and Wrangler jeans laundered soft enough to sleep in.

"Turn around so I can get the other side done up," Dove said. With tiny steps, I shifted position, trying not to topple off the slick phone books.

"Do I look as ridiculous as I feel?" I asked my best friend, Elvia Aragon. She lounged across my brass bed in a three-hundred-dollar Tabasco-red silk jogging suit, looking beautiful enough to grace a cover of *Elle* magazine.

"I don't know," Elvia answered. "How ridiculous do you feel?"

"On a scale of one to ten, I'd say nine and a half."

"Oh, no. Eight, tops." She laughed and crossed her dainty size five feet. They were clad in sparkling white Nikes that no doubt cost half my weekly salary at the museum and probably had only jogged the distance from the front door of her new lakefront condo to her perfectly restored 1959 British Racing Green Austin-Healy. That she was wearing American-made tennis shoes was a reluctant concession to the rabid second-generation patriotic sensibilities of her six younger brothers. As proud as she was of her Mexican heritage, in her heart, Elvia was a European, preferably French. She eyed me critically. "It is a sort of a Glinda the Good Witch look, isn't it? Being from Kansas, that should light Gabe's pilot, so to speak."

"Thank you, Ms. Blackwell, for that insightful fashion review." I hiked up the low-cut, sweetheart neckline and adjusted one tiny puffed sleeve. "What was your sister-in-law thinking when she picked out these bridesmaid dresses?"

"I have no idea. *Menudo* had more taste than Gilberto's wife. She's from Mississippi."

"Watch it, girlie," Dove mumbled, her mouth full of pins.

"I said Mississippi, not Arkansas," Elvia said. "Big difference." Her smooth milk-chocolate cheeks dimpled with a held-back smile.

"And don't you forget it," Dove said.

I ran my hands up and down my bare arms. "Are you positive you don't have something else in your closet? I feel so . . . exposed."

"That dress was made for a July wedding, not the end of February," Elvia answered. "And we dug through every piece of clothing I own. This is the closest thing I have to anything that remotely suggests the Civil War. Why in the world didn't you pick an easier theme for this Senior Citizen Prom than *Gone With the Wind?*"

"That was *your* little brother's doing. Ramon and his Adult Recreation 101 Class at the university. I'd have chosen a shuffleboard tournament."

"I think it's real sweet of those kids to go to all that trouble for a bunch of old folks," Dove said.

"Well," I countered, "they do get out of writing a twenty-page term paper for it. That's pretty strong motivation."

Elvia picked up her cup of Raspberry Delight herbal tea sitting on my nightstand and took a sip. "I'm still vague on how you became involved. I thought your teacher assistant days were over."

"Two of the ladies in my quilting class at Oak Terrace are on the Residents' Board there. When Ramon and his class presented their project to the retirement home's board but couldn't find an adult sponsor, Thelma Rook volunteered me. I think she did it just to force me into wearing a dress."

"Makes her a stronger woman than me," Dove said.

"You're one to throw stones," I said, reaching down and pulling at the strap on her faded denim overalls. "Are you anywhere close to being through? My toes are waving the white flag here in these pumps."

"Keep your britches on, I still got one little part left to do." Dove stood up with a groan, tossed her waist-length white braid over her shoulder and turned sharp blue eyes on Elvia. "What did you do, dance with a gorilla in this thing?"

"Gilberto's brother-in-law, Dwayne, from Tupelo," Elvia said. "A reasonable facsimile."

"I think I'll rest my knees and have a piece of that peach cobbler I brought you." Dove reached over and pinched my forearm. "Word to the wise, honeybun. If you want that man of yours to stay sniffing around, you best start keeping something more to eat in your icebox than Coca-Cola and Hostess Cup Cakes."

"If he wants food, let him date a chef," I said to her retreating back. She snorted in reply.

I kicked off my half-size-too-small satin pumps and sat on the bed, carefully avoiding the pins still holding part of the hem in place. "How's the Mardi Gras festival coming along?"

Blind Harry's, the combination bookstore and coffee house Elvia managed in downtown San Celina, had been chosen by the Chamber of Commerce as this year's official Mardi Gras headquarters. She was in charge of the Mardi Gras Street Festival and Parade to be held a week from today. It was, according to our own *San Celina Tribune*, the most authentic Mardi Gras celebration in the United States outside the state of Louisiana itself. It was started fifteen years ago by a bunch of Louisiana natives transferred to the Central Coast by the various oil companies to work on the offshore drilling rigs. When the drilling stopped, many of the workers stayed, along with their festive and sometimes rowdy customs. They fit right in here in festival-loving San Celina County, where any excuse to "let the good times roll" was welcome.

"Everything's on schedule so far," she said. Elvia was in her element with a project like this. Nothing made her happier than being in charge. "It's been more work than I anticipated, but the money we've taken in selling Carnival beads, trinkets and Mardi Gras masks has already made the books look better than the last five Februaries. That should upset Cameron a bit." Her delicate red lips relaxed in a tiny satisfied smile. Cameron McGarry, the mysterious Scottish owner of Blind Harry's, had originally intended the bookstore as a tax write-off to defray some of the profits of his three casinos in Reno. When Elvia took over the store five years ago, amidst all predictions to the contrary, she built the business into the most popular and profitable book-store in three counties by adding a basement coffee house, special sections for mysteries, romance and science fiction and acquiring the largest commercial inventory of ranching and animal husbandry books in the state.

The phone on the nightstand rang. Elvia handed the receiver across the bed to me and stood up, pointing toward the kitchen.

"Save me some," I said, my hand over the receiver.

"Benni?" The caller was female and distinctly aged.

"Yes?" I searched my brain trying to place a name to the semi-familiar voice. All fifteen women in my quilting class at Oak Terrace Retirement Home, a class sponsored by the Artists' Co-op and a small city grant, had my phone numbers at home and at work. While working on the projects for the coming Spring Has Sprung boutique two months from now, they'd taken to using them indiscriminately.

"Miss Violet," she said, her shaky voice sounding exasperated.

"Oh, yes, Miss Violet." I made a face at myself in the mirror. "How are you?"

All the ladies in my group had asked me to call them by their first names, except Miss Rose Ann Violet, who wasn't about to allow that sort of informality at this late date in her life.

"She said she was going to kill him."

"What?"

"She used the 'A' word, the 'B' word and the 'D' word. Twice."

I shifted the phone to my other ear, wondering if senility had finally become brave enough to move in on the indomitable Miss Violet. "What are you talking about?"

"Oralee Reid," she said. "And Brady O'Hara. Of course, I'm not surprised it has come to this. Poker is the devil's own game. After Hattie told us everything, he turned mean as a snake and never could be trusted. We had to watch him every minute. Nickels or M&M's. Doesn't matter to them."

"Excuse me?" It wasn't the first time one of my ladies had strung together a group of sentences that didn't quite fit with each other. Many of them were at Oak Terrace because of slight strokes, not just old age.

"Haven't you been listening, Benni Harper? My goodness, you haven't changed much, have you?"

She reprimanded me like my fourth-grade teacher, which was entirely natural, because she had been. Besides me, there were forty-two years of San Celina's most upstanding citizens who had felt the sting of her tart voice and the humiliation of having their name scrawled in chalk on the corner of her clean blackboard. She didn't teach everyone in San Celina the intricacies of fractions and the history of California missions, but there were enough of her alumnae around to swing a vote if they were so inclined.

"I am too listening," I said, my tone reverting to a childish grumble. I cleared my throat and attempted a more adult tone. "I'm sure Oralee was kidding."

"I think not. She swore on King Enoch's head."

"Really?" That shed an entirely different light on the matter. Oralee did not toss King Enoch's name about frivolously. He'd been her prize Black Angus bull, the core of her herd for years. About six months ago, he broke out of his pasture and was trotting across the highway, equipment waving in the breeze, heading toward a bunch of unsuspecting heifers, when he was struck and killed by a one-ton Ford pickup hauling five-strand barbed-wire fencing. The rancher driving the truck came through without a scratch, but a lot of people believe the shock of King Enoch's untimely death brought on Oralee's stroke and her subsequent stay at Oak Terrace.

"I think we should inform the authorities," Miss Violet said. "Isn't your new beau connected with the police department in some way?"

"In some way," I said vaguely, hoping she wouldn't remember how. "What exactly is the problem between her and Mr. O'Hara?"

Miss Violet sighed. "Oralee said that he's been cheating

at poker for the last two months. They play for nickels. Or M&M's.''

Well, that explained the earlier comment. The temptation was too great for me. "Plain or peanut?"

She sighed again. Louder this time. "Albenia Louise Harper, are you taking me seriously?"

"Yes, ma'am," I said. When Miss Violet used your full given name, it was time to stop joking. "I'm sorry. Can't you speak to Mr. Montrose about it? As manager of Oak Terrace, it seems to me he should be the one to straighten this out."

"That man!" Her voice grew as shrill as a parakeet's. "All he's concerned about is how many sugar packets we're using in our cereal every morning. He's absolutely no help whatsoever. He thinks he's going to save himself watching those horses. Why, we told him he was going to have to pay. Did he really think he would get off scot-free? You know, he never was dependable. Oralee should have known that, but a body can't tell her anything."

I didn't even attempt to figure that whole story out. "What exactly would you like me to do?" I asked with as patient and pleasant a tone as I could manage.

"Speak to Oralee," she said. "For some incomprehensible reason, she listens to you. Some control must be gained over that temper of hers or I shall be forced to officially place a request for a more agreeable room companion." Her voice lowered. "She smokes cigars, you know. In the bathroom at night. She thinks I don't know, but I do. Papa always said I had the nose of a bloodhound."

Miss Violet and Oralee shared a room in one of Oak Terrace's ambulatory wings, where the criteria for matching roommates was, at best, hit or miss. In their case, it was as unlikely a pairing as Minnie Pearl and Ma Barker. Miss Violet's frantic whispered voice interrupted an amusing picture of Oralee puffing away on an old stogie.

"Oh, my goodness. Guess who just walked into the room?"

I heard a muted grappling for the phone. Oralee's coarse, burnt-grass voice bellowed through the telephone line.

"Who is this?" It was a voice used to pinballing orders across hills dotted with thick-trunked oaks to men reluctant to oblige the instructions of a woman, even if she did own the ranch.

"Hi, Oralee. It's Benni Harper. Miss Violet has just been telling me—"

"I heard what Little Miss Rosy-Posy-Pudd'n 'n'-Pie was tellin' you. Did she mention that O'Hara is a scum-bellied, cactus-mouthed, card-cheatin' son-of-a-biscuit?" Only the slight slur at the end of her words gave away that she'd suffered a stroke to her left side.

For a moment, I sympathized with Miss Violet. I'd been on the thrashing end of this voice myself more than once. Eighteen years ago, when I was sixteen, to earn the down payment for my first car, I worked weekends for Oralee as a nightrider checking pregnant cows. She made it clear from the beginning she thought I was a snot-nosed kid with a smartass attitude she was only hiring out of respect for my daddy. She watched me like a savage old prairie falcon from underneath her stained and battered Resistol cowboy hat until I proved to her I knew the proper way to search for cows isolating themselves in preparation for birth, how to monitor their breathing and use my flashlight to check their sad, dark eyes for signs of trouble. She helped me pull more than one calf, her tanned, sun-leathered lips turning up in a rare smile while we watched the cow lick and lick its calf until the spindly legged baby stumbled up for its first milk. Twice when I pulled with her, we lost calves. Once, both the cow and calf. Each time, after a prolonged cussing fit, she didn't speak for the rest of the night. Then she fixed me warm almond milk and cinnamon toast in her old kitchen before I rode my paint horse, Zelda, home. I loved Oralee like she was one of my own relatives, but I didn't envy Miss Violet her roommate.

"Yes, ma'am, she did mention Mr. O'Hara once or twice in her conversation," I said. "Look, I'll talk to him myself about it tonight. I'm sure it's all just a misunderstanding."

"Bull paducah," Oralee replied. "Brady O'Hara is evil and a crook besides, plain and simple. Always has been, always will be. Thinks that store-bought-oleo tongue and devil smile of his can get him out of anything. You just better call the cops and have him hauled off to the clinker before I kick that Irish butt of his all the way to Tucson.''

"C'mon, Oralee, the police?''

"Bet you know that number by heart.'' A harsh noise came over the line—somewhere between a cough and a squawk. If I didn't know better, I'd have sworn it was a laugh. "We'll make that young crossbred stud of yours earn his keep by doing something besides sitting there on his sweet little ass''—I heard a noisy struggle through the phone—"Ouch! Don't you pinch me, old woman. Oh, for pity's sake—fanny—looking pretty.''

"I'll talk to Gabe about it as soon as I see him,'' I said, stifling my laugh. It would only spur her on. "I'll see what he can do. Are you ready for the prom?''

"Waste of time. I'm eighty-two. Don't got much to waste.''

"You have to go. It's the quilting class's project. And you *are* the president.''

"Only because Mittie Barntower bit the big one and you all elected the only other person who has half her marbles around here.''

"Oralee,'' I said with mock sternness. That comment probably earned her another black mark on Miss Violet's mental blackboard. "Look, I have to go. Dove needs to finish fixing the hem on my dress. I'll see you tonight.''

"Okay,'' she said, reluctantly. "You tell Dove 'hey' for me and thank her for that deer jerky she sent by Mac. It sure hit the spot. And don't you be forgetting to talk to that cop of yours, hear me?''

"I won't. I'm sure he can work something out with you two.''

"Well, I expect results or there'll be you-know-what-hot-spot to pay.'' Her voice became muffled when she turned away from the phone. "That make you happy, Miss Priss?''

"Oralee,'' I said in a loud voice. "Try and behave.''

"'Bout as much chance of that as a coyote at a jackrabbit convention.''

"Spare me the Western homilies. And wear a dress tonight. If I have to, so do you."

"When a bull fills a milk bucket," she said cheerfully and hung up.

I was standing in front of the mirror, studying the ridiculous-looking dress, envying the freedom from vanity people Oralee's age had, when Dove and Elvia walked back into the room. Elvia settled back down on the bed, a china-blue bowl of peach cobbler in her hands.

"Who were you yelling at?" Dove asked.

"Oralee Reid. And I wasn't yelling. I was just trying to get her attention."

"What'd that cranky old biddy want?" Dove asked, an indulgent smile on her face. Dove was one of the few people who never let Oralee get under her skin, probably because she gave as good as she got.

I gave a *Reader's Digest* version of the incident.

"Well, it's a real shame she's having a hard time adjusting to Oak Terrace, but poor Mac didn't have any choice. Even though her stroke was a small one, she was getting to where she couldn't run that ranch. And she refused to move in with him. One time he came to visit her and all the burners on the stove was going full blast while she was out in the barn repairing a hay crib. About scared him to death." Dove picked up the apple-shaped pincushion from the dresser, her face pensive. "I really feel for her. Leaving your home is hard."

"I know," I said, remembering the slow, satisfying tempo of ranch life—how Jack and I would lie in bed and laugh at the scratching of the squirrels playing tag on our wood-shingled roof, the new-fabric smell of fresh hay, the clump of his heavy work boots hitting the wooden service porch floor at the end of the day.

"Still having trouble sleeping?" Dove asked, reaching over and brushing my curly bangs out of my eyes.

I turned my head and didn't answer. Jack's death wasn't something I felt the need to talk about anymore. You get to the point where it seems as if everything that could be said, has been. What no one ever told you, and maybe couldn't, was how much grief was like one of those long, slow illnesses where bad and good days were as unpredictable as a pull on a slot machine. Just when you thought you had it licked, when you weren't paying attention, some memory hit you right between the eyes and your senses throbbed with the loss, leaving you trembling with an emotion not unlike fear.

But the good days were finally beginning to outnumber the bad. Having Gabe in my life helped. He had an arrogantly zany twist to his personality that could make me laugh sometimes when nothing else could. On good days, I could almost forget how Jack died, lying in a ditch, killed by alcohol and stupidity. Instead, I liked imagining him with my mother, who died when I was six, both of them sitting together on a long white front porch somewhere, shelling peas and watching over me. Oh, I had sleepless nights, but it was the still-unaccustomed city noises as well as getting used to sleeping alone that kept me punching channels into the early morning, cruising the cable stations from *The Donna Reed Show* to old Gary Cooper movies. I understood what Oralee was feeling. Losing a way of life is a lot like losing someone you love.

"Change isn't ever easy," Dove said softly. "Human beings are surely fond of what they already know. But the good Lord helps us adjust." She gave me a gentle push between the shoulder blades. "Now, you hop back up on those phone books and let's get this done. I got to get back to the ranch and cook your daddy's dinner. And don't you worry none about Oralee Reid. She'll be just fine. That woman is pure seasoned oak."

"Speaking of Oralee, how's the church liking Mac?" I asked. Oralee's grandson, MacKenzie Reid, had just been called as minister a month ago to the First Baptist Church over by Cal Poly University. It was a radical move for the conservative four-hundred-member church where I'd been baptized and married, then cried at both my mother's and husband's funerals. They were hoping, I'd heard through the grapevine, since I hadn't been the most regular attender lately, to attract a younger crowd into the aging congregation. Mac Reid was a hometown boy, just turned forty, and widowed five years ago when his young wife died of a brain tumor. He was a big man, ruggedly handsome and too charismatic for his own good. He and my Uncle Arnie, both six years my senior, had been best friends in high school. They used to tease me until I screamed, causing Dove to march them out to the barn to shovel manure. In the seventies, Mac played a pretty mean defensive tackle for Baylor University, and right before graduating, shocked everyone when he received and accepted a higher calling than even the NFL. Definitely not your typical Baptist minister.

"He's good," Dove said, bending down and going to work on the rest of the hem. "Which you'd know if you darkened the church's door more than once every three months." I didn't answer. "Talks real loud," she continued. "Keeps most folks awake, even that lazy back-row bunch."

"I always thought it was funny that Oralee's grandson became a minister," Elvia said, setting the blue bowl down on my nightstand.

"Probably a reverse kind of rebellion. You know kids," I said in a pointed tone. "When you push them one way, they tend to go the other." Dove just grunted.

"Is he living out at the ranch?" Elvia asked.

"Nope," Dove said. "Oralee doesn't know it yet, but he's put the place up for sale. He's got power of attorney since his dad died."

"Does he have to sell out?" I asked, feeling sad because I already knew the answer.

"He can't run the ranch and the church too. Besides, that place hasn't turned a profit for a long time. I heard he's been sending Oralee money for years. Even used up the money from his wife's insurance. You know most of the Reid land is leased from the oil companies and they're starting to sell it off now to developers. A plain old cattleman can't live off the land anymore." She looked up at me. "But then, I don't have to tell you that."

"That's for sure." I was still in the midst of helping my

brother-in-law, Wade, dissolve the holdings of the fore-closed Harper Ranch. Wade and his family had gone ahead and moved back to Texas to live with relatives, and we were transacting most of the business through the mail or over the phone.

"Are you really going to tell Gabe about Oralee and that card game business?" Elvia broke in. I smiled at her grate-fully. She knew how much thinking about losing the ranch bothered me.

"I guess I'll be forced to, since he'll see them tonight and he hates walking into situations cold. You know, since he and I have been seeing each other, I've had more people stop me in the street and tell me their problems. Mr. Treton next door grabbed me yesterday and told me he thinks the electric company is increasing voltage to the homes of sen-ior citizens in an effort to cause more static electricity, which short-circuits their hearing aids. He says the electric company owns all the hearing-aid manufacturers, and he wants Gabe to set up a task force to investigate. Offered to go undercover himself."

"That crazy old fool," Dove said. "He couldn't find a cowbell in his own bed."

"Then I find it hard to believe you'd find *anything* he has to say worthwhile. . . ." I gently tapped the top of her pillowy white hair with the back of my fingers. She didn't raise her head.

"He has something of interest to say every now and then. I just like being there when it happens."

The fact that she bribes Mr. Treton with home-baked bread and jars of her clover honey for information on my daily activities still tends to rattle my cage once in a while. Not that it stops her.

"All done," she said, standing up. "All I have to do now is whipstitch it real quick." I turned and studied my-self in the mirror.

"Well, look at me. All Scarletted up and ready to face whatever." I pulled at a strand of my curly reddish-blond hair. A little over two months ago, in a mindless, emotional moment, I'd cut my waist-length hair up to my neck and now had no idea what to do with it except poke at it once in a while. "Maybe I shouldn't have cut my hair."

"It looks fine," Elvia assured me, inspecting a strand of her own shoulder-length mink-black hair. "You look very contemporary. Very . . . cute."

I cringed inwardly the minute the word popped out of her mouth. Though I didn't usually spend much time thinking about my looks, at thirty-four and seeing a man eight years my senior, cute wasn't exactly the look I was striving for. Wirehaired terriers were cute. Opie Taylor was cute.

"Besides," she added, "anything is better than that boring old braid you used to wear everywhere."

"You're really pushing it today, Suzie Q," Dove said, shaking the tip of her own white braid at Elvia.

We were laughing at Elvia holding up her hands in playful surrender when a triple rap on the front door interrupted us. I looked over at the clock-radio on my nightstand. Eleven o'clock on a Saturday morning. Some things were getting as predictable as spring onions.

"Dove, will you answer it?" I picked up my full skirt and dashed into the bathroom, just off my bedroom.

"Benni, watch that hem," Dove complained.

"Please," I called. "I'm unarmed."

"You're what?" Elvia asked.

A minute later, I stood in the doorway of the bathroom and watched Gabe follow Dove into my bedroom. He looked especially attractive and unprofessional this morning in his tight black running shorts and a faded gray sweatshirt displaying a peeling picture of Albert Einstein.

"Hey, Chief Ortiz." I walked sedately toward him, hands behind my back, hoop skirt bobbing around my ankles like a bell around a clapper. We locked eyes and exchanged big smiles.

"Hey, Benni Harper." His eyes scanned me from head to toe. "You look like . . ." Words appeared to have failed him.

"Scarlett O'Hara?" I offered. "Vivien Leigh?"

He laughed. "Actually, I was thinking more along the lines of Little Miss Muffet."

"Well, there goes *my* donation to the Police Benevolence Fund."

"It is kind of cute." He reached over and ran a finger along my exposed collarbone, causing me to give an involuntary shiver.

"Hands off, mister," Dove said. "Until you're paying the bills."

"Yes, ma'am," he said, pulling his hand back and winking at me.

"Dove!" I said. "Do you mind?"

"Yes, I do," she answered. "That's what I was just saying."

"Look," Gabe said, "I was supposed to pick up my gray suit at the cleaners by three o'clock, but I have a special meeting with the city council. Could you get it for me and drop it by the station?" He pulled up his shirt to wipe the sweat off his face, revealing a hard, brown stomach.

"Sure," I said, trying not to stare at the line of coarse black hair trailing down and disappearing into his damp shorts.

"Thanks." He let his sweatshirt drop and grinned when he caught where I'd been looking.

Physically, our relationship had limped along with the speed of a hobbled horse, mostly due to my hesitancy to get involved. That didn't stop me from thinking about it. A lot.

"Eyes to yourself, young lady," Dove said.

My face tingled with warmth. "Gee, Dove, I don't think I'm embarrassed enough here. Maybe you could try a little harder and go for total humiliation."

"You were the one whose eyes were grazing where they weren't supposed to," she said, lifting her white eyebrows.

Before I could shoot a smart remark back, Gabe diplomatically broke in. "I need to finish my five miles and shower. Do you want me to pick you up tonight?"

"No," I said. "I have to be at Oak Terrace early to supervise things. I guess I'll see you there. Try not to be late."

"I'll try." He leaned over to kiss me, reaching for something from the back waistband of his shorts.

He was fast, but not fast enough.

When his lips touched mine, I pulled a small green water pistol from behind my back and shot him right in the temple.

"Head wound!" I yelled. "Fifty points. I win!"

"Okay, pipsqueak, prepare to eat worms and die." He sprayed me in the face.

"No fair. Head wounds mean you're out of commission. That's cheating." I fired back with short, rapid bursts.

"I'm going to whip the both of you," Dove said, scurrying out of range, but not before getting hit with a stream of water.

After some artful dodging on his part and some juvenile shrieking on mine, he gave one last pull on his trigger, then shook his empty red pistol.

"Ha," I said, waving my still half-full gun in front of his face. "Looks like you're out of ammunition."

"That's okay." He stuck his gun in the waistband of his shorts and wiggled his dark eyebrows. "I'm an extremely fast reloader."

"You are one cocky son-of-a-sodbuster." I stepped closer and squirted him between the eyes.

"Grandson," he corrected. "And no farmer jokes this early in the day or I will be forced to arrest you. I'll invoke executive privilege and conduct the strip search myself."

"In your dreams, pal."

Over on the bed, Elvia cleared her throat. "Considering his means of employment, that is an incredibly sick game. You two need some serious counseling."

"What they need to do is decide what they want to do with each other and get on with it," Dove said. "In my day we didn't make such a big darn deal of things. You tied the knot, did your business, then got up and fed the chickens."

Gabe turned and looked at me, his face solemn. "The deal's off, sweetheart," he said. "You never said anything about chickens." He turned to walk out of the room.

"Smart aleck," Dove said, picking up the yardstick leaning against the wall and giving him a sharp smack on the backside. I have to give him credit; he only gave a fraction of a flinch. Without breaking stride, he raised a large hand in good-bye, the back of his neck slightly red.

Dove turned and shook the yardstick at me. "Trouble with young people these days is y'all make a joke about everything. And you think too much. Discuss everything to death." She fanned herself and headed for the kitchen. "My heavens, I think I need a cup of coffee. And wipe that water off your dress before it stains."

Elvia gave a deep chuckle. "My brother would have paid fifty bucks for a picture of that. Can you imagine Miguel passing a snapshot around the police department of his boss getting a swat on the butt from your grandmother? Priceless."

"Dove has four sons, nine grandsons and two great-grandsons," I said. "Believe me, she is no respecter of men's butts." I went into the bathroom and grabbed a towel.

"So, what is the status between you and Gabe these days?" Elvia asked casually.

"Quo."

"As in *nada?*"

"You got it." I dabbed at the water that was causing the yellow chiffon to glue itself to my skin.

"I take it that means you don't want to talk about it." She stood up and brushed imaginary lint off the front of her thighs. "I'm deeply hurt. We've been friends since second grade. We've always told each other everything."

I ignored her and reached back to unzip the lamp-shade dress. My relationship with Gabe was something I wasn't ready to discuss in depth with anyone yet, not even my best friend. I was confused and nervous about going into another relationship, and when I get that way I tend to turtle into myself while trying to figure things out. It wasn't just the physical part that was intimidating, though after being married all my adult life to my high-school sweetheart, the thought of even taking my clothes off in front of another man was terrifying. It was really the emotional part that frightened me. I wasn't sure I ever wanted to love anyone again the way I had loved Jack. It was too hard when they left you. Fortunately, Gabe hadn't pushed it except in jest. He'd been happily divorced for seven years and wasn't even sure if he was staying in San Celina. His friend Aaron Davidson, San Celina's official police chief, had been diagnosed with liver cancer a month or so ago. Talking about the future was something Gabe and I both had reason to avoid. I stepped out of the dress and reached for my flannel shirt.

"Well, speaking of your love life, guess who's back in town?" Elvia's black eyes glittered with mischief.

"Forget my love life, and who?"

"Clay O'Hara."

"You're kidding." I sat on the bed and pulled on my jeans. Clay O'Hara. He hadn't crossed my mind in years, even though I knew he was Brady O'Hara's great-nephew. He had been the love of my life one whole summer when I was seventeen and mad at Jack for some reason I can't even remember now. Clay O'Hara, with the thick-lashed, wounded brown eyes, long, sandy sideburns and insolent pirate smile. "I wonder what he's doing here."

"Apparently seeing to his uncle's financial business. He came into the bookstore yesterday. When he saw me, he walked right up and the first question out of his mouth was about you."

I buttoned my shirt and tried to sound casual. "What did he ask?"

She inspected her long red acrylic nails. "Just wondered where you were living now. What you were doing. All I told him was where you worked. He knew about Jack."

I couldn't resist the obvious question. "How does he look?"

"Actually, pretty good. He still has his hair. And that killer smile. Remember the night he crashed the Senior Farewell Dance and cut in on you and Jack? If Jack had been wearing his buck knife that night, Clay O'Hara would be singing soprano now." We grinned at each other. That night they both ended up with bruised knuckles and swollen mouths and I didn't get a goodnight kiss from either one of them.

"That was a long time ago," I said, tucking my shirt into my jeans. "He's probably married with six kids."

"He didn't walk like a married man."

"What's that supposed to mean?" I laughed and threw a patchwork pillow at her. "You're a real troublemaker, Elvia Aragon." I checked my watch. "Shoot, I gotta go. I have to get Gabe's suit and drop by Oak Terrace and make sure those kids are actually getting the decorating done. And since I forgot to tell Gabe about Oralee and Mr. O'Hara, I better leave him a note."

"Picking up suits," Elvia said, tsking under her breath. "Sounds pretty domestic to me."

"I've picked up *your* dry cleaning a time or two," I pointed out. "I'm thoughtful to all my friends."

"Well, don't forget, a certain chief of police is a pretty hot commodity on the singles block in this town. In between refereeing senior-citizen fights and pouring punch, you might try to fit in a dance or two with him. You might also consider making this a night to remember."

"Pretty corny, Elvia. Wasn't that the theme for the Senior Farewell Dance? Wonder how long it took them to come up with that gem."

"Watch it, I was chairman of the dance committee. Besides, it was a night to remember for you."

"No kidding." Besides the fight between Clay and Jack, it was the first time Jack told me he loved me. He spoke the words from behind lips so swollen they could barely move, but got out "I love you" nonetheless. Then we broke up two days later for the rest of the summer. "I can't believe it was seventeen years ago."

"You know, something feels vaguely familiar about this prom business. I have an eerie feeling this is going to be another night you'll never forget."

"Maybe. But probably not in the way you think."

And, as so often happened in our friendship, we were both right.

2

OAK TERRACE RETIREMENT Home was located a mile outside downtown San Celina on a twisting two-lane highway
leading to Morro Bay. Its five salmon-colored mission-style
buildings were perched on a small rise, flanked by alfalfa
fields on one side and scrubby range land dotted with
white-faced yearlings on the other. It offered a top-of-the-
stagecoach view to anyone sitting in the English rose
garden in front of the administration building, a popular
spot for pipe smokers and marathon talkers.

By the time I arrived at two o'clock, Ramon and his
classmates had been decorating for a little over an hour.
They were in the process of transforming the normally staid
decor of the retirement home's combination recreation hall/
dining room into a party setting with kelly-green and
screaming-pink streamers and matching helium-filled
balloons. The decorations' connection to the Civil War was
tenuous at best, but the bright colors certainly gave the
room a more cheerful and festive look. I handed the bags
of McDonald's apple pies and french fries I'd bought for
the students to the nearest warm body and grabbed the
work-assignment clipboard. In a far corner, Ramon grap-
pled with two white and gold papier-mâché columns
borrowed from Cal Poly's drama department.

"The leaning tower of Tara," he joked when I walked

up. I tugged at the long, thick ponytail bisecting the back of his moth-eaten green and black Pendleton wool shirt. The hair and the thrift-shop clothing he prefers drives his five conservatively bent older brothers and his native Mexican father insane, which, of course, is why he does it.

Every time he let go of the left-hand column, it leaned precariously forward, as if pushed by the north wind. One bump from an out-of-control wheelchair and it would fall like a redwood tree marked for picnic benches.

We were attempting to re-create the porch of Scarlett's beloved mansion in the corner of the brown-tiled room next to the white brick fireplace. The two columns, left over from the drama department's somewhat ill-received adaptation of *I, Claudius,* along with two white wicker chairs, a painted backdrop of a fancy front door and a dubious likeness of Rhett and Scarlett, made up our souvenir photograph spot.

"Maybe we could attach it to the wall from behind with some fishing line and thumbtacks?" I suggested.

"Fresh idea. Hang on to it." He released the column and I grabbed the teetering pillar. "I'll go find the janitor. Maybe he has some." He bounded off toward the exit before a protest could squeak past my lips. Standing there with a clipboard in one hand and Tara in the other, I fervently hoped he wouldn't be waylaid by one of the many chattering female students twisting crepe-paper streamers and setting out napkins and paper cups. Ramon, the youngest of Elvia's six brothers, was the most easygoing of the Aragon boys, which made him fun, but not always dependable.

"Hey, Miz H., smile," a crackly, tenor voice called from my left. A bright flash temporarily blinded me.

"Todd Simmons, you'd better not be wasting film." I blinked and gave my head a small shake, trying to clear away the exploding stars. When my vision cleared, Todd stood in front of me, his normally serious pale blue eyes half closed in amusement.

"Just testing the flash." He aimed the camera again, but only shot me a wry smile. I couldn't help smiling back. It was hard to get mad at Ramon's best friend. He was a quiet, good-natured young man with a slim, sturdy surfer's build and skin the exact shade of Dove's homemade toffee. He'd inherited all the best features from both his Asian and Caucasian background. His shoulder-length, dark brown hair, perfect features and surprising eyes made it difficult for the girls to concentrate on their assigned tasks. He was also as smart as an old cutting horse. Seventeen and a freshman at Cal Poly, he was the pride and joy of his grandfather, Mr. Morita, who owned a fish store that Gabe frequented down in Old Town San Celina, our newest tourist trap. It was good seeing him smile. From what I'd heard, he'd had a rough time of it lately. His mother had died of cancer a few months ago, leaving only he and his grandfather in the family.

"Remember we have a lot of pictures to take tonight." I felt obligated to play the adult authority figure. "And find Ramon, will you? Tell him to get his fool self back here."

"Yes sir—I mean, ma'am." He slapped the heels of his black, high-topped combat boots together, saluted me, executed a semblance of a military turn and marched toward the exit. One of the girls decorating the tables giggled. I gave a dramatic sigh, suspecting it would be some time before I saw either Todd or Ramon again.

I started to call for help from one of the girls, when a hand the size of a grizzly paw and sprinkled with reddish-brown hair took hold of the column.

"I've always told my congregations it's women who prop up the home," a deep voice said. "Now I see I wasn't exaggerating."

"Mac," I said, twisting around and looking up into the smiling, full-bearded face of San Celina's most famous high-school athlete. At six foot four with eyes the color of worn pewter, he still looked like he could bench press three hundred pounds and whistle while doing it. "You're just the person I need to talk to."

"Whatever it is she's done, I'm sorry—I'll talk to her, but it won't help—and yes, I pray for her all the time."

I laughed at the mock look of despair on his craggy face.

With his chestnut beard and ruddy cheeks, he looked more like a Hollywood version of a Montana mountain man than a minister. "Well, I guess that pretty much answers anything I had to tell you about your grandmother."

"Believe me, Benni, there is nothing you can tell me about Grandma Oralee that I haven't already heard. She's incorrigible, I know, but she'd also give the shirt off her back to a stranger who even thought about shivering." He rubbed the back of his free hand up and down his neatly trimmed beard. When I'd first seen him a month ago, I'd teased him about it, telling him he looked like a *GQ* version of John the Baptist. According to Dove, the beard had been quite a controversial subject when the congregation hired him. Some people at First Baptist apparently still believed there was a direct connection between facial hair and liberal thinking.

"Actually," I said, "it's not that big a deal about Oralee. She and Mr. O'Hara are just having a slight disagreement about their weekly card game."

"Now, young woman," a loud, guttural voice declared. Brady O'Hara limped up and pointed the tip of his cherry-wood cane in my direction. "A disagreement is something that happens between civilized people. Oralee Reid wants to turn this into a barroom brawl, as she has most things all her life." His precise little brush of a white mustache quivered like a rabbit's nose while his still clear aquamarine eyes flashed in anger.

"Mr. O'Hara," I said, chagrined at being caught discussing him. "How are you?"

"That is a stupid question. My reputation is being maligned, my peace of mind interfered with and my money being stolen. How do you think I am? And just for the record, Reverend, I was most certainly not cheating. I merely bested your grandmother and she is not enough of a lady to admit it."

"Well," I said, looking up at Mac, who was still propping up Tara's porch like Big John did to mine. His eyes had grown dark with some undecipherable emotion. When he offered no help, I turned back to Mr. O'Hara. "Maybe you should try a different card game."

Mr. O'Hara brushed at the sleeves of his expensive tweed jacket. "Maybe she should try to learn some manners."

"You can jump in any time," I said to Mac out of the side of my mouth.

"You're doing just fine," he whispered back.

"I'll get you for this."

"When you two finish gossiping among yourselves, perhaps we can get back to the problem at hand," Mr. O'Hara snapped. "I understand she is threatening to call the authorities. I'll have you know I am not without influence myself in this town." He pulled a white linen handkerchief from inside his jacket and started hacking into it. It was a smoker's cough, ear-piercing and full of phlegm. In less than a minute, it became a full-blown choking attack.

I stepped over and patted him gently on the back. "Now, Mr. O'Hara, we can get this all straightened out without anyone calling the police on anyone else."

He jerked at my touch, turned and hit me across the shins with his wooden cane.

"Hey!" I yelped and jumped back.

"Young woman," he said, still sputtering from his attack, "I'll thank you to keep your hands to yourself and not use that condescending tone to me. I'll decide when and if the authorities need to be informed. I was dealing with unpleasant people like Oralee forty years before you were in diapers." He gave me a fierce look and hobbled away, his back as unyielding as a steel fence post.

"Did you see what he just did? And I let him. I should have kicked that cane out from under him."

"Nice Christian attitude," Mac remarked mildly, his arm still wrapped around the papier-mâché pillar.

"Easy for you to say, preacher. I didn't see you jumping in and trying to calm things down. What's the problem? You looked kinda mad."

"You were doing just fine," he said, ignoring my question.

"You may as well put that down. It appears Ramon was ambushed in his quest for the elusive fish line."

He leaned the column against the wall and sat on the floor, grunting as he stretched his legs out in front of him. He massaged his knees with both hands. "Forty years old and the arthritis of a seventy-year-old." He patted the floor next to him. "I try to let people work out their own problems before jumping in with my so-called professional opinion. You work here, right?"

I sat cross-legged next to him and nodded.

"Then this probably won't be the last time you encounter Mr. O'Hara or deal with the problem between him and my grandmother. I can't be here every time. And just remember, the peacemakers will be called the sons of God."

"Still a smart aleck, I see. That's probably why Dove is so impressed with you. She said it was about time the church got some fresh blood."

"Dove has always been a very special lady . . ." he said, a slight hesitancy in his voice.

"But?" I prompted. I knew that tone, especially when it pertained to my grandmother.

"Well, frankly"—he lowered his voice even though no one was close enough to overhear us—"she scares the heck out of me."

"Dove? You're kidding. With a grandmother like Oralee?"

"Grandma Oralee's a kick in the pants, all right, but she never interferes with anything unless it directly involves her. You know, she gave me the money for college and never once asked me about my grades or my social life." He leaned back on his elbows and regarded me with calm gray eyes. "Your grandmother is more . . ." He stopped, obviously not quite sure how to word his feelings.

"Nosy?" I offered. "Devious? Meddling? Opinionated? Stop me if any of these ring a bell."

His eyes glinted with amusement. "Well, she *is* extraordinarily concerned about other people's lives."

I laughed and pointed my finger at him. "Mac, there's not a person in your congregation who could find fault with that statement."

"Do you know that she gives me a written critique of

my sermon every week? I hate to admit it, but they're pretty good.''

''That sounds like Dove. The words 'mind your own business' do not exist in her vocabulary.''

''Well, I've only been here four weeks. Maybe I'll get good enough after a few months she won't need to do it anymore.''

''Don't count on it. I've been waiting thirty-four years. So, I haven't talked with you much since you've been back. How are you liking old San Celina these days?''

''Beats the heck out of L.A.''

''I have a friend who might not agree with you.''

''Oh, yes, the police chief.''

''Now, what makes you think my friend is the police chief?''

He just smiled.

''Okay, what did Dove tell you? And I want the truth.''

''Only that he's the acting chief of police and . . . that she likes him.''

''Liar.''

He rubbed his knees again and gave a low chuckle. ''Well, her exact words were that you'd actually found a man who might be able to stand that smart mouth of yours.''

''Now that sounds more like Dove. He's a nice man. A bit on the macho side at times, but I do like him. I think you would too.''

He glanced meaningfully at me. ''She also said he may not stay in San Celina. That has her a bit worried. She's afraid you'll get hurt.''

I held his gaze. ''I'm not a kid, Mac. I don't expect fairy tale endings.''

He smiled again, a slow smile that seemed partly sad, partly sympathetic. ''It's a sorry thing when we get to that point, isn't it?'' He stood up and held out his hand to me.

''Are you coming tonight?'' I asked, grasping it and pulling myself up.

''I volunteered to supervise refreshments, so I'll be sequestered in the kitchen all night.''

"Got out of wearing a neck choker, did you?"

"That agony is reserved for Sundays only. Sneak into the kitchen if you get time. I'll set aside some of the best goodies for you."

"You've got a deal. I guess it does pay to know people in high places."

He laid a huge hand on my shoulder and squeezed it gently. "Now that, Benni Harper, is a comment I should have made."

By five o'clock, Tara's columns had achieved semi-straightness, and the room, swathed in green and pink crepe paper, looked a bit like how a New Orleans jazz funeral sounds. And I was more than willing to call it a night already. My head felt thick and achy from the smell of the donated magnolia and carnation centerpieces. Balloons teasingly popped behind me no longer caused me to crack a smile. The endless chatter and bathroom noises of the post-adolescents gave me visions of firing a shotgun in the air and yelling for quiet. There was no doubt I needed some time in a warm bubble bath to readjust my attitude, but there was only enough time for me to dash home, take a quick shower, pull on that atrocious dress and hustle back to Oak Terrace. Less than two hours later, the prom was in full swing with the volunteer disc jockey alternating between Glenn Miller, Whitney Houston and an occasional Vince Gill song. The university students, faces tight with concentration trying to recall the fox trot and waltz steps learned in high-school gym class, danced the beaming residents of the retirement home carefully across the glossy tile floor.

"Ramon, everything looks great," I said, surveying the refreshment table while trying to unobtrusively hike up the front of my dress with my forearms. If I managed to make it through the night without flashing everyone like a drunken Mardi Gras reveler, it would be a miracle. "For a while there, I didn't think we'd pull it off, but it looks like we did."

"Yeah, it kinda does," he agreed. "Boy, this is a heck

of a lot better than doing a term paper." He grinned at me, his young face still as silky as a child's except for a few lovingly cultivated chin hairs.

The sparkle globe hung in the center of the dimly lit room shot diamonds of light across the dancers' faces and bounced off the shiny chrome of the dozens of wheelchairs parked along the sidelines like covered wagons pulled close for the night. A piccolo-voiced young woman in a skintight, red metallic dress organized a conga line. The enthusiastic leader was a lady with hair the same pale blue of this morning's sky driving a motor-driven wheelchair with a Dodgers baseball pennant taped to the back. Snaking past us, she tossed her head back, showed a mouthful of dentures and screeched a loud *arriba*.

Ramon and I looked at each other in surprise, then burst out laughing.

"Maybe somebody better check the alcohol content of that punch," I said. "Things are starting to get wild. And speaking of wild, where in the world did you get that tie?" I squinted in the shadowy light at his wide necktie.

"You like it?" He held it up for my closer inspection. On a pale brown background, a wavy-haired Veronica Lake-twin cocked her hips in a frozen hula. A dark brown fringe around her impossibly narrow waist jiggled when he shook the tie. "Three old dudes offered to buy it off me. I got it at the Woman's Shelter Thrift Store down by the bus station. Everyone grunge-shops there."

"It looks perfect with your suit," I said. He wore a dark brown double-breasted jacket that almost reached his knees, and baggy, cuffed pants. "Where's your machine gun, Mr. Capone?"

"Step up to reality, Benni. What do you expect, a gray wool job like some old lawyer dude? Only a loser would dress like that."

I looked around at the other kids his age. He was right. Except for the colors, which ranged from Todd's pure black suit complete with matching black shirt and tie to one kid's jacket and pants in a particularly stomach-turning shade of pea green, all his classmates were dressed identically.

"Well, don't mention that to Gabe when he gets here. You're sort of describing his favorite suit."

"That's different. He's an old guy. What's he got to look good for?"

"Remind me to repeat that remark to you when *you're* forty-two. Now, you get out there and start asking some of these ladies to dance. They've been looking forward to it for weeks."

"I hate to dance," he complained. "I think I should get extra credit for that."

"Just get out there and make someone's grandma happy." Before he could protest further, a voice as smooth as a soap opera villain's interrupted us.

"Everything looks quite marvelous, Benni."

I grimaced at Ramon and turned to face Edwin Montrose, manager of Oak Terrace Retirement Home and general mosquito in the ear for the last month as we planned the prom. "Thank you, Edwin."

"Gotta dance," Ramon said. I shot him an evil look. He rolled his eyes and eased away, leaving me in the slithery man's clutches. Edwin's strained enthusiasm and uppity manner had not made him a favorite with the Cal Poly students, so I'd been running interference during the whole project.

He wasn't extremely popular with the senior citizens either. The women in my quilting class referred to him behind his back as "Mr. Ed" because of his long-limbed spare frame and a perpetually tanned face with the sunken-cheeked look of a horse. Somewhere between the age of forty and fifty with protruding too-blue eyes and black, vinyl-looking hair, he was the type of man who would ask you to dance even if you had your head practically lying in your lap avoiding eye contact, then argue with you when you said no.

"Our guests seem to be enjoying themselves," he said, laying a damp hand on my shoulder. I moved back slightly, but it remained glued to me, stubborn as a horsefly. He had, unfortunately, bought into the fallacy that lonely widows were always in the market for the attentions of any available man, and nothing I could say or do would convince him otherwise. His behavior this last month had bordered on sexual harassment. I considered twisting my head and giving his hand a good, hard bite. The only thing stopping me was the suspicion he'd probably enjoy it.

"The kids did a great job," I replied. "I really should check the punch." I moved back, abruptly disengaging his hand and put the refreshment table between us, thankful that after tonight I wouldn't have to work closely with him again. Thelma Rook, who once owned the largest feed store in San Celina, and her roommate, Martha Pickering, tottered up. Martha, a former waitress, inspected with a jaundiced eye the selection of cinnamon-sprinkled butter cookies, bright strawberry tarts and chocolate-dipped macaroons.

"My dear Benni," Thelma said. "This is so much fun. I feel sixteen again." She touched long, large-knuckled fingers to the hand-beaded bodice of her silver and gray dress. I smiled at the woman who used to slip me sugar cubes from her husband's stash to take home to my Appaloosa mare, Bacon Bits. Sometimes the treats made it home, sometimes they didn't. Martha nodded her basketball bouffant of snowy curls in agreement and bit into a miniature chocolate eclair.

"I'm terribly glad you ladies are enjoying yourselves," Edwin said, coming around the table and standing close enough for me to gag from the smell of his Brut cologne. "We do try to provide here at Oak Terrace a rounded social environment specifically geared toward the discriminating senior. Isn't that right, Benni?" He smiled with long beige teeth and punctuated his sentence by reaching over and giving my shoulder a squeeze, leaving his hand in place.

"I suppose so," I said, jerking my shoulder and giving him a deep frown. He gave me his best patent-leather smile and dropped his hand.

"We know you do, Mr. Ed . . . um . . . Edwin," Thelma said, giving me a wink. "And we certainly appreciate it." Behind her, Martha gave an extravagant snort and picked up a strawberry tart.

The disc jockey put on an old sixties song—"Put Your Head On My Shoulder." Edwin turned to me, an eager, somewhat hungry look on his face. "Benni, I think they're playing our—" But before he could finish, Thelma interrupted.

"Well, look at what's coming your way, Benni," she said. "If only I were a few years younger."

I followed the direction of her eyes across the room and felt my heart give a little jump. Clay O'Hara walked toward us wearing a squinty cowboy grin under his sandy handlebar mustache and a dark Stetson on his head. His Wranglers, faded just enough to show confidence, were snug enough to show the outline of his pocketknife.

"Benni Ramsey." He parked his thick-chested figure in front of me, one hip slightly cocked. "The last time I saw you, you were on your knees in cow shit holding a red-hot branding iron."

"You always had a way with words, Clay O'Hara," I said. "And it's been Benni Harper for almost fifteen years."

"That's right," he said, pushing his hat back slightly and running his mahogany eyes the length of me. Subtlety was never his strong suit. "You went and married that kid, didn't you? Jack Harper and I didn't take to one another much, but I was real sorry when Brady sent us the news clipping back in Colorado."

"Thank you," I said. "So, I suppose that's why you're here, to visit your uncle?"

"Among other things." He pulled at his mustache with one rope-scarred finger and smiled.

Next to me, Thelma cleared her throat.

"Oh, I'm sorry," I said. "This is Thelma Rook. She's a resident here at Oak Terrace. And her friend, Martha Pickering."

"Ma'am," he said, touching two fingers to the roper brim of his fudge-colored cowboy hat, nodding first to Thelma, then Martha.

"And I'm assuming you and Edwin have met," I said.

"Of course we have," Edwin said, sticking a long-fingered hand out to Clay. Clay contemplated it for a moment before giving it a quick shake. "We had the pleasure a few days ago when Mr. O'Hara and his uncle were going over his uncle's will. He is seriously considering leaving a tidy little endowment to the retirement home." Edwin's narrow face grew complacent, thoughts of regular trustee checks probably dancing in his horsy head. "Not," he added hastily, "that we expect or even desire Mr. O'Hara's departure for a long, long time."

"Edwin," Thelma said. "You make it sound like we're waiting for a train here."

The song ended and the disc jockey's buttery voice came over the microphone. "Here's a waltz for you country fans. Grab your favorite cowgirl and give the little lady your best."

Edwin opened his mouth and I was on the verge of bolting, when Clay held out his hand.

"I believe you owe me this one," Clay said.

"I believe you're right," I answered.

We circled the floor in a country waltz as Anne Murray wondered if she could have this dance for the rest of her life. I didn't speak as we danced, trying not to think about how Jack used to sing along to this song whenever it came on the radio. By this time the floor was filled almost entirely with young people dancing with each other, performing for the weary senior citizens, who sat and smiled at them with the pleased expressions of new grandparents. We still had the crowning of the king and queen, helping the guests back to their rooms and cleanup. With a bit of hustling, I'd be home and under warm flannel sheets by midnight. I scanned the room looking for Gabe and wondering who I could ask to crown the king and queen if he didn't show up, when I realized Clay was speaking to me.

"Excuse me?" I said.

"I was saying you dance pretty good for someone who isn't even paying attention. And here I've waited seventeen years for this dance."

"Oh, Clay, I'm sorry. My mind's just scrambled with thoughts about what I need to do to get this dance wrapped up." I looked up into his brown eyes and marveled at how kind the aging process is to men. Do they really look better with a few pounds and some wrinkles, or is it just a cultural thing we're raised to believe? Whatever the case, Clay O'Hara had been a good-looking boy and he'd grown into a downright attractive man.

"Maybe thinking about Jack a little?" he asked softly, giving my hand a squeeze. The familiar rancher's calluses on his hand caused me to inhale sharply, and for a moment I longed for that hand to touch my cheek.

"Maybe."

"Then I'll shut up and let you think."

Working our way through the crowded dance floor, we swung by the refreshment table, where Brady O'Hara stood jabbing an angry finger at an arm-crossed Oralee. My heart dropped in dismay. All we needed now was Miss Violet to make it a knockdown dragout. I looked around, but couldn't spot her in the crowd.

"Oh, dear," I said, straining to peer over Clay's shoulder.

"Looks like they're at it again," Clay remarked.

"You know about the argument?"

"Haven't heard about anything else since I arrived three days ago."

We watched his uncle and Oralee each give one last retort, then storm off in separate directions. Oralee limped determinedly toward the kitchen, where she was probably going to chew on Mac's ear for a while, and Mr. O'Hara lurched toward the door leading through the side gardens to the bedroom wing.

"Well, I tried my best to bring about a truce this afternoon and your uncle gave me a knock in the shins with his cane for my efforts." Heat rose up my neck the minute the words popped out. What did I expect him to do, punish his uncle?

Clay's laugh was strong and clear, the laugh of someone used to open spaces. "That sounds like Brady. Am I going to have to worry about a personal injury lawsuit on top of all his other legal problems?"

"No," I said, laughing with him. "I can't believe I even mentioned it to you."

"He's an ornery old cougar, that's for sure. I humbly apologize on behalf of the entire O'Hara clan and promise to buy you a steak dinner in the best restaurant in town in compensation."

"That's okay. My pride was injured more than anything else."

"Old Brady's good at that." His voice seemed to take on a bite. Then he grinned again. "You know, when Dad sent me out here to get Brady's affairs settled, I don't know what I expected, but it certainly wasn't sharing a dance with a pretty lady in a hoop skirt. Especially one I remember so fondly."

"Expect nothing and be ready for everything. That's what my daddy always says."

"Smart man, your daddy."

When the song was over, we walked back over to where Thelma and Martha sat on metal folding chairs cradling cups of cranberry-colored punch.

Clay nodded at the two women. "Guess I'd better go see if Brady's all right before heading back to my hotel."

"Where are you staying?" Thelma asked, giving me a scheming smile.

"Down near the mission at the San Celina Inn."

"That's a lovely old hotel," she said. "I spent my fiftieth anniversary in a room there. It had a canopied four-poster bed and a beautiful Wedding Ring quilt. If I remember right, a bottle of wine came with the room."

"How romantic," Martha said.

"Is your wife enjoying our lovely Central Coast, Mr. O'Hara?" Thelma asked.

"Call me Clay, ma'am. And I'm **not** married at this particular time of my life."

"Girlfriend?"

"Not at the moment."

She raised her sparse white eyebrows at me and nudged Martha with her elbow. "That's a real shame, nice-looking boy like you, *all alone.*"

"Yes, ma'am, it is." One side of his long mustache twitched.

I tried to catch her eye and tell her silently to cut it out. The ladies in my quilting class, some of them without families of their own or grandchildren too far away or too busy to be more than a once-a-year birthday card, had taken an exaggerated and opinionated interest in my life, particularly the romantic part. They said it beat the heck out of *General Hospital* which, they claimed, was far too predictable for women of their advanced experiences. They adored Gabe, but were obviously not above encouraging another rooster to jump into the stew pot.

"Well, it was certainly good seeing you again, Clay," I said. "Maybe we'll run into each other again around town."

"Maybe," he said, his face thoughtful. "I'll be around for a couple of weeks or so, anyway."

After he left, I turned to Thelma and Martha. "And what was that all about, ladies?"

They looked at each other and gave high, tittering laughs.

"You two are worse than teenagers," I said.

We sat through three more songs and watched the few energetic dancers left improvise new dance steps. The grandfather clock next to the fireplace chimed ten o'clock—much later than most of these senior citizens were accustomed to. I'd come to the conclusion that Gabe was never going to make it, and decided since it looked better for the newspaper photographs to have an official type crown the king and queen, I would ask Edwin to do the honors. Predictably, just because I needed him, he was nowhere to be found. As a last resort, I thought of Mac, hiding out in the kitchen.

"Cute apron," I said, walking into the chrome and white commercial-sized kitchen. He stood in front of a large glass-front refrigerator wearing a red-and-white-striped baker's apron. It stated in bold black letters "I don't repeat gossip, so listen carefully."

"Like it?" He picked up a white-wrapped package from a pasteboard box at his feet and placed it on one of the refrigerator shelves. "I wore it to a church barbecue last Saturday. Made some of the less humorous members of the deacons board just a tad nervous."

I laughed. "I guess you do have some of Oralee in you after all."

He smiled mischievously. "Well, as she would say, I didn't lick it off the sidewalk."

I peered into the empty box at his feet. "What have you got there?"

"Fresh fish. Some old guy dropped it off. Guess they're having a fish fry tomorrow. Hey, there's some refreshments left here. Try the chocolate cupcakes. They've got butter-pecan filling."

"Sound great, but I don't have time. I was just trying to find someone to crown the king and queen, since it appears that Gabe got tied up somewhere. I can't even find Edwin, so can I count on you in a pinch?"

"Sure, can I keep the apron on?"

"You know, I'm beginning to suspect you're even more of a rabble-rouser than your grandmother."

"Conflict is good for a body. Keeps the blood moving."

"That doesn't sound very ministerial," I said. "Besides, I remember when your method of dealing with conflict involved a bottle of Coke shaken up and pointed at someone."

He winked at me. "Let's just keep that little secret between you and me."

"Speaking of conflict, I saw Oralee head in here about half an hour back. She and Mr. O'Hara were at it again. Is she okay?"

"Fine." His voice grew short.

"Mac, what is it?"

"It's . . ." He hesitated. His broad, normally jovial face became somber. "It's just this thing between her and Mr. O'Hara is starting to get annoying. I talked her into going back to her room so she could lie down for a while. He upset her so badly I was afraid she'd have another stroke." He picked up a section of newspaper sitting on the counter and started folding it into smaller and smaller squares.

"She's eighty-two years old, Benni. Another stroke could kill her. I wish that O'Hara character would just—" He stopped, took the compressed square, and with a flick of his wrist, tossed it across the room, hitting a large commercial mixer. The look of raw anger on his face surprised me.

"Mac, it's just a card game."

He took a deep breath, then exhaled slowly. "Sorry. I guess I'm a bit overprotective."

"I wouldn't let Oralee hear you say that. She'd make you shovel stalls for a week if you dared suggest she couldn't take care of herself."

"Well," Mac said, untying his apron. "Where do I go to crown the royal couple?"

"I'll let you know if I need you. I'm still hoping Gabe will make it. Besides, the king himself seems to be missing. We can't have the ceremony without him."

"Who are the king and queen?"

"Martha Pickering is the queen and I won't mention the king's name for fear of incurring your wrath."

"Not Brady O'Hara?"

"The one and only. You know, except for Oralee, he's actually pretty popular around Oak Terrace."

"Isn't it funny how money has a way of doing that?"

"C'mon, Mac, at these people's ages? How in the world could the size of his bank account possibly make a difference to any of the people who live at Oak Terrace?"

He looked at me soberly. "You are too naive, Benni Harper. Lust doesn't end when the Social Security checks start coming in."

I laughed nervously. "This is getting way too serious for me. I think I'll leave the worry of human vices to you. I just want to get this dance wrapped up. The only thing I'm lusting for right now is my nice, warm bed."

"You know where I'll be if you need me."

I walked back out into the recreation hall and peered around the crowded room, looking for Gabe, when Edwin rushed up, slightly out of breath, his long face shiny with perspiration. "Chief Ortiz just left a message at the front

40

desk. He'll be here in ten minutes.''

"Okay," I said. "I'll tell the band to play a few more songs and we'll start wrapping this up."

"Good, good," he replied. "The sooner the better." Then he hurried off, no groping, no wandering eyes. I wondered briefly what had got his dander up, then decided maybe I didn't want to know. I joined Thelma and Martha over on the sidelines and listened to them unabashedly gossip about who of the young adults was cheating on who and what two of the more adventurous agriculture students really cultivated in their experimental gardens.

"You two are a real couple of snoophounds," I said. "I guess I'm going to have to watch myself in your presence."

Thelma patted my arm with her cool, dry hand. "My dear child, your life isn't interesting enough for us to get really excited about."

"Well, pardon me. Maybe I should add a little vice to my life. Just for your sakes, of course."

She smiled with small even teeth faded the color of old piano keys. "We're working on it, dear heart."

Fifteen minutes later, in the middle of a rather lame recording of "Stardust," I was bending down and running a finger through the back of my pumps which felt two sizes smaller now, when Martha cleared her throat noisily.

"Your sweetie's here," she said.

Gabe stood at the entrance to the hall, eyes scanning the crowded room, looking both dignified and extremely sexy in his perfectly tailored gray suit. Sexy enough for me to almost forgive him for being late. *Almost*. Walking toward him, my legs wobbled slightly as the shoes bit into my feet.

"What's wrong, sweetheart," he asked in a sympathetic voice. "Got a rock in your hoof?"

"With the way I'm feeling right now, you're risking your very life with that remark. *Where* have you been?"

"Sorry, got tied up with the sheriff on that new intercounty cooperative program we're trying to hammer out. And he has *muy grande* marriage problems. He was on his third Coors when I pried myself away."

"Well, at least you made it. We need to get the king and

queen crowned and get everyone back to their rooms before they collapse.''

''How'd it go?''

''No major problems.'' I turned and looked over the crowd. ''Only thing I have to do is find the king now.''

''What about the queen?''

''That's Martha Pickering, the chubby lady over by the refreshment table. Believe me, she'll be there until the last tart is history. No, it's just the king who's my problem. In more ways than one.''

''What?''

''Brady O'Hara. I wrote about him in the note.'' By the look on his face, I realized he either hadn't read it or had forgotten what was in it. ''Never mind.'' I waved my hand impatiently. ''I'll tell you about it later. Right now, I just want to get this over with and peel this dress off.''

''That sounds intriguing. Need any help?''

''Oh, grow up.''

''Now, Scarlett,'' he said. ''Let's show a little of that famous Southern hospitality.'' I glared at him and he held up his hands in defense. ''Whoa, girl, just show me where I stand and I'll get out of your hair.''

I considered showing him the back of my hand, but pointed instead at Tara's porch.

He bent down and gave me a quick kiss on the lips. ''Cheer up, *gringuita*. It's not even ten-thirty yet. The night is young. Think of the possibilities.'' He touched a finger to my cheek.

''Easy for you to say,'' I muttered, limping toward the back of the room. ''You don't have a blister on your heel the size of a cantaloupe.''

I surveyed the crowd one last time hoping to spot Mr. O'Hara so I wouldn't have to hunt any further, when Todd Simmons rushed past me.

''Hey!'' I grabbed his arm. ''Don't get too far away. We're crowning the king and queen soon and the *Tribune* said they particularly wanted a picture of that.''

''Yeah, sure,'' he said, shifting his weight from one foot

to the other. He clutched his Nikon to his chest and kept glancing over my shoulder.

"Have you seen Mr. O'Hara?" I asked.

"Uh, what does he look like?" Something behind me continued to hold his interest. I turned to look and saw the girl in the tight red dress who'd started the conga line.

"He's wearing a greenish tweed coat and has a white mustache. He carries a highly dangerous cherry-wood cane." Todd looked at me blankly, flipping the lens cover on the Nikon open and closed. "Never mind, I'll find him. But don't you even think about leaving this room until I get him here."

"Sure," he said. "I'll be right here."

I looked back at the girl in red. I bet he would.

I took the shortcut through the kitchen to Mr. O'Hara's wing, thinking it was a good thing Gabe had finally arrived, because now even Mac was nowhere to be found. To speed things up, I slipped off my heels and started through the garden. Though I couldn't see anything but shadowy outlines in the partial moonlight, the sweet, earthy scents of the roses, early lilies, ferns and wisteria made such a soothing potpourri that I couldn't help but stop and inhale deeply, letting the coolness of the bricks soak into my tired feet. Maybe it was just my imagination, but it seemed suddenly as if people were jumping around like checkers on a giant checkerboard. Or maybe more accurately, like one of those high-speed five-minute chess games played for money that had recently become popular with the college students.

When I watched Ramon and Todd play one this afternoon, kitchen timer ticking away the minutes, Ramon remarked, "There's no fancy footwork in these games. The object is to capture the king as quickly as possible."

And at this particular moment, that certainly sounded good to me.

CLUTCHING MY SHOES to my chest, I hurried through the garden. Halfway across, a faint noise echoed through the cool darkness. It came from the small white ivy-stitched gazebo to my left. A giggle, then a muted *shush*. A young male voice murmured a laughing admonishment. A familiar young male voice.

"Ramon?" I called, moving closer and peering into the shadows. "Is that you? Ramon?"

He stepped down from the gazebo, rubbing the back of his neck. "Geeze, Benni, like why don't you use a bullhorn or something? I think someone in Santa Barbara might have missed it."

"You should be helping at the dance," I accused.

"I needed some fresh air."

Standing on tiptoe, I peered over his shoulder. "Who's in there with you?" Red sequins flashed in the moonlight. "She was just with— For Pete's sake, does she have a twin?"

"Huh?"

"Never mind. Help me find Mr. O'Hara so we can crown the royal couple and get this dance over with. Then you and the lady in red can exchange saliva to your heart's content."

He scowled at me. "Why don't you just be blunt or something?"

"I mean it. I'm not signing any of you kids off this project until everything is completely cleaned up. What happened to that wonderful altruism you all started out with?" I was tired and hungry and it was beginning to show.

"Altrue-what?"

"Forget it. Let's just find Mr. O'Hara, then we're all outta here."

After a short, intense conversation with his girlfriend, Ramon ambled up beside me.

"Well, where do we look?" he asked in a grumpy voice.

Ignoring his tone, I said, "We might as well try the obvious and check his room."

With its green tartan plaid bedspread and framed photographs of his travels in Ireland, Brady O'Hara's large private room was as neat and precise as his natty toothbrush mustache. It was also empty. He was one of the few residents at Oak Terrace who could afford such posh accommodations, having owned O'Hara's Department Store downtown for fifty years, and from what I'd heard, invested the money from its sale wisely. I'd spent many late August afternoons in the Smart Young Miss department of his store arguing with Dove about the real and imagined dangers of skintight jeans and whether bras were or weren't a necessary clothing option for a liberated sixteen-year-old. In the late seventies, when the Central Coast Fashion Plaza opened up on the edge of town, he closed the store and retired to his huge Victorian house where he cultivated an English flower garden and worked on long, rambling articles for obscure historical journals.

"Now what?" Ramon asked, jiggling one leg impatiently while I slipped my shoes back on my icy feet. The hallway, usually crowded with wheelchairs, walkers, nurses' aides and various visitors, was empty, all the guests living in this wing apparently enjoying the dance.

"Let's try the nurses' station."

We walked toward the center of the building, the heels

of my pumps clicking across the shiny tile floor like tiny gunshots. A lone attendant sat at the central station, hunched over a Spanish comic book. The front cover pictured a buxom blond woman and a Latino-looking Dick Tracy.

"Excuse me," I said to the attendant, a middle-aged man with a stiff black pompadour and a silver religious medallion around his neck. "Have you seen an elderly man go by here recently?"

"Yes?" His voice rose in question.

"Which way did he go?"

"Yes?" He surveyed me with friendly black eyes. "*No habla inglés.*"

I turned and looked at Ramon expectantly. He fired off a rapid question ending in "Señor O'Hara." The attendant's brown face remained blank. Ramon tried again. I understood the words *gringo* and *viejo*. Old white man. The man answered with a few words and a crooked smile, spreading his arms widely to encompass both hallways.

"What did he say?" I asked.

"Basically that the place is chock full of them," Ramon said. "Geeze, Benni, can't we just crown someone else? They all look alike. Who's going to know the difference?"

I shook my head and turned to the attendant.

"*Gracias,*" I said, then faced Ramon. "Let's split up. You check the rooms down the west and east wings. I'll take the north and south."

He heaved a dramatic sigh. "You're the boss." He started down the green-tiled hall, sticking his head unabashedly into the first room he came to and yelled, "Yo, Mr. O."

"Ramon," I hissed. "Try and show some respect. Knock before you go into a room. Someone might be in there. And check the east garden too."

Without turning around, he flapped his hand behind him mimicking a quacking duck.

"Smart ass," I muttered and headed left to check the north wing first. I walked down the corridor peeking discreetly into the open doors, knocking loudly and waiting a few seconds before opening the closed ones. Most of the white doors, in preparation for tomorrow, sported Valentine's Day decorations made in the weekly crafts class. Some enthusiastic residents had already gotten an early start and pasted green and orange shamrocks next to the hearts. The retirement home's obsession with holidays reminded me of elementary school. Though most of the guests enjoyed it, some, like Oralee, found it condescending. The battle to keep the door to their room bare or decorated was a tug of war between her and Miss Violet who, as a former grade-school teacher, felt right at home with holiday-fixation.

The last room in the north corridor was the crafts room, where I'd spent many hours in the last few weeks. It was a long shot, but I checked anyway. The cramped, window-less room held only the Steps to the Altar quilt the ladies started piecing a month ago, and our quilting supplies. Our next meeting would be this coming week at the co-op studios to stretch it out and start the actual quilting.

I closed the door and walked back toward the south side of the building, thinking about the blue and pink quilt.

"So, Benni," Thelma had said at our last meeting. "Just how many steps does it take to get to the altar these days?"

"I have no idea," I'd answered, trying to concentrate on what had become my main job with these expert quilters, threading a ready supply of needles.

"Just like in our time, no doubt," Martha said, stabbing her needle as aggressively through the fabric as she gave her opinions to the world. "It probably depends on who's doing the stepping."

Thelma reached over, grabbed a new needle and patted me on the shoulder. "You take your time, honey. And don't you forget, the smartest thing a woman can do is stick her feet in a milk bottle and wait for a wedding ring." Relaxed, time-softened laughter rippled through the room.

I passed the nurses' desk again, empty now, and couldn't help but wonder about the security at Oak Terrace. What if someone suddenly became ill? It was a subject I should discuss with Mac, since his grandmother lived here. It

47

seemed to me they should have someone around at all times, especially someone who could summon help in English. The community room revealed only one elderly lady with a Peter Pan haircut and two bulky hearing aids attached to her ears like small tan animals. "Never heard of 'em," she yelled to my question about Mr. O'Hara. Her eyes never left the green-tinted television turned to the show *Love Connection*.

The last room at the end of the south corridor made me smile. The masking tape down the middle of the door told the whole sordid story. Hearts made of red and pink construction paper and white paper doilies covered half of it; the other side was as bare as a newborn baby. I knocked on the closed door. Asking Oralee about Mr. O'Hara was probably taking my life in my hands, but maybe she had seen him wander by.

When there was no answer, I pushed it open.

"Oralee, have you . . . ?"

I felt like someone had punched me in the stomach.

The stench hit me first. Gamy, raw, suffocating. A body's last attempt to clean itself out. The creature lay on the floor at the foot of the two beds, face swollen and suffused almost past recognition—a disgusting purplish color Crayola would never vote to include in their palette. Bulging eyes. As if someone was angry enough to squeeze them right out of his head. I recognized the tweed jacket and the gray wool slacks. Mr. O'Hara wouldn't be wearing a crown tonight.

I froze, staring at his strangled body. Covering my nose and mouth with my hand, I swallowed convulsively and started backing out of the room. My shoulders hit something solid. I squealed in terror and swung around.

"Oh man, oh man," Ramon said, his dark skin mottled reddish-brown with emotion. He grabbed my arm and pulled me back.

"Go get Gabe," I said, giving him a shove. "Hurry."

"I can't leave you . . ."

"Someone has to get help. I'll be fine. Now go! Quick!"

"Wait," he said. "Benni, look." My eyes followed his finger to where it was pointing. There was something on one of the beds. The one with the red and brown postage stamp quilt that had at first glance appeared lumpy, unmade. Something else.

Someone else.

"Stay back," I commanded, then lifted the hem of my skirt and stepped over Mr. O'Hara's legs to reach the side of the bed, kicking a pillow that had fallen on the floor. Miss Violet stared up at me, her eyes as flat as the glass beads she always wore. The sour, greasy taste of the french fries I'd eaten that afternoon crawled up the back of my throat.

"Miss Violet," I said, trying to stave off the hysteria I felt bubbling up along with the french fries. I shook her gently. No response. I shook harder. "Please, Miss Violet." Her arm fell out from under the bedspread. Knowing I should check for a pulse, that she might still be alive, I reached down and took her cool delicate wrist in my fingers, praying for a fluttering, a movement. Feeling nothing, I jerked back and stumbled over Mr. O'Hara's legs in my haste to get out into the hall. Ramon stood dumbly waiting for me to speak.

"I told you to go get Gabe. Now go!"

He gave me a hesitant look, then sprinted down the hallway toward the exit.

I leaned against the doorjamb and sucked in deep breaths, wondering if it was smart to stay there. But common sense told me that most likely whoever did this had long gone, and I didn't want any of Oak Terrace's residents to wander by and accidentally look in. I eased out into the hallway and braced myself against the wall. Gold stars sparkled in front of my eyes, and fear caused my mouth to dry up as surely as if I'd eaten a mouthful of sand. It seemed an eternity since I'd sent Ramon for Gabe. Unbidden, Mr. O'Hara's purple face loomed up in my mind, and I felt myself start to quiver and give in to the urge to slide down. Firm hands caught my shoulders and stopped my descent.

"Are you all right?" Mac asked. His grim face gradually came into focus.

"How did you . . . I didn't even hear you come up."

"I passed Ramon in the garden. He said someone had died."

"In there. I told him to get Gabe. He'll know what to do." When he started through the door, I suddenly remembered whose room it was. "Oh, Mac, don't worry. It's not Oralee."

"What are you talking about? She's in the kitchen. I was coming to get her a sweater." He stepped past me into the room. After a few seconds, I heard a sharp intake of breath and a soft prayer, "Oh, Lord, no."

I leaned back against the wall, my heart still pounding, feeling relieved that Mac, with his substantial physical presence and experienced spiritual calm, was handling the situation. I took deep breaths in an attempt to keep my lunch down while questions chased around my mind like a blue heeler after sheep.

Who would kill Mr. O'Hara? And Miss Violet? They were two of San Celina's blandest residents. I'd known both of them all my life. Law-abiding, proper, boring. Who could want them dead?

Then something occurred to me. Was Miss Violet actually murdered? It was obvious, even to an amateur like me, that Mr. O'Hara was strangled. But Miss Violet, as far as I could see, didn't have a mark on her. Did she see something, the murderer perhaps, and die of fright? Of course, I hadn't pulled back the bedspread. I shuddered at the images conjured up in my mind and stuck my head through the door to ask Mac what he thought about it.

He was kneeling next to Miss Violet's bed, seemingly praying. I started to turn my head, embarrassed for intruding on such a private moment, when I saw him open her nightstand drawer, quickly search it and stick something in his pocket, his large body blocking my view of what it was. With only the slightest movement, he closed the drawer with his elbow.

"Mac, what are you . . ."

Steps echoing down the hallway distracted me. I turned to see Gabe approaching with a determined stride, Ramon double-stepping to keep up. Gabe already wore his Sergeant

Friday look. Dead calm. No emotion. Just the facts, ma'am. Every last one of them. *Right now.*

When he reached me, his mask slipped for a moment. He gently lifted my chin and searched my face with worried eyes.

"I'm okay," I said, blinking rapidly to keep the tears from flowing. "Really. Go ahead."

Satisfied, his cop look came back. "Where?"

I pointed to the open door. "Mac's in there."

"Who?" he snapped.

"I know it's a crime scene, but he's a minister and . . ."

A muscle jumped like a small fish in his clenched jaw. Crime scenes bordered on the sacred to Gabe. I knew that. But I would have no more kept Mac from going in there than I would have stopped a charging bull. There was a remote chance that Miss Violet might have still been alive and there are still some things more important than evidence. I tried not to think about seeing Mac remove something from the scene. Maybe it was my imagination. That was certainly what I wanted to believe.

Gabe started through the doorway, wearing a look that said whoever was in the room, religious affiliation or not, was in big trouble. I followed him in, watching his face apprehensively.

In an instant, his expression changed. Surprise, then incredulity covered his face. I moved closer to him, confused at his reaction. He had been a cop almost twenty years. I couldn't imagine anything shocking him. Besides, he wasn't even looking down at the body. I looked over at Mac. A similar look of amazement froze his broad features.

"Pancho?" Mac asked.

"Lefty?" Gabe replied.

"A cop?"

"A minister?"

"You two know each other?" I said.

GABE'S FACE SWITCHED from surprise back to his blank, impenetrable cop look. "Nice to see you again. Please step out of the room." His voice was pleasant but inflexible. "I hope you didn't touch anything."

"Good seeing you too," Mac said evenly, looking Gabe straight in the eye.

"How do you two know each other?" I asked. They both ignored me.

"Wait in the hall," Gabe said. "I'll need to speak with you both in a minute." He slipped on his round, wire-rimmed glasses, clasped his hands behind his back and stepped closer to Mr. O'Hara.

After Gabe's phone call to the station, it didn't take long before the hallway was full of police officers, uniformed and plainclothes, each jostling for room to perform their various crime-scene tasks.

Once Edwin had been informed of the incident, he pushed himself into the thick of things, strutting around importantly, telling the crime-scene personnel how to do their jobs and trying to get in and see the room and the bodies. When a detective threatened to slip one of the extra-large plastic evidence bags over Edwin's head and secure it with a rubber band, Gabe pulled Edwin aside. I watched with amusement as he sternly told him to take care of his own responsibilities and arrange for the elderly residents to return to their rooms with as little fuss as possible. Everyone at the dance who didn't live at Oak Terrace was briefly interviewed by one of San Celina's five detectives, had their photos taken and were asked to leave their names and addresses before departing.

Over the next few hours, Mac and I helped the staff accompany the frightened residents back to their rooms, saw to it that all the kids made it to their cars and helped Oralee get settled in her new room in another building. Knowing his grandmother wouldn't stand for anything less, Mac didn't mince words when he told her what happened to Mr. O'Hara and Miss Violet.

"Mac?" She gave him a sharp, inquiring look.

"Everything's fine, Grandma." He took her rawboned hand in his. "Don't worry."

"You're a good boy," she said, lying back on her bed and closing her eyes. The skin on her face looked as fragile as an egg shell and she lay so motionless, her thin-veined eyelids so still, it seemed for a moment that she'd died too. A lump lodged deep in my throat. We'd been so busy in the last few hours, I'd almost managed to push the reality of the two deaths to a dark, back corner of my mind. Miss Violet's round, animated face as she read *Charlotte's Web* aloud to my fourth-grade class flooded back to me in a painful Technicolor memory.

"I'm going to see Gabe," I said, suddenly wanting to look into his calm face, feel the security I associated with being in his presence.

"I'll come with you," Mac said. He turned to Oralee. "I'll be back before I go home. Don't worry. Everything's going to be okay." She nodded mutely and turned her head. A tear trickled down into a seam of her tanned cheek. She swiped it away impatiently. I squeezed her hand before leaving, biting the inside of my cheek to keep from bursting into tears. It frightened me to see Oralee so vulnerable, and it frightened me even more that Mac had essentially lied to Gabe.

We found Gabe in a small room off the nurses' station

where they were interrogating the comic-reading attendant. He had finally returned from an unauthorized break at a neighborhood bar and looked scared to death. Lieutenant Cleary, San Celina's chief of detectives, towered over the nervous man, questioning him in a rapid flow of Spanish. The dark-eyed attendant gave staccato replies, appearing somewhat confused that a black man wearing a corduroy jacket and looking like a college professor was speaking to him in fluent street Spanish. Jim Cleary's mild-looking exterior hid a cop who was a ten-year veteran of some of East L.A.'s toughest Latino neighborhoods. Jim took my statement next, then Mac's, then Ramon's. Mac and I lingered around the crowded nurses' desk, listening to the retirement home employees carp about who was going to get stuck cleaning up the murder scene, when Gabe walked over to us.

"You can both go home now," he said. "Come down to the station sometime tomorrow and sign your statements."

"Did he see anything?" I asked, pointing at the scared attendant.

He ignored my question and laid a hand on my shoulder, squeezing it gently. "Be careful driving home. Lock your doors."

"I have to stay and clean up," I said. "The recreation room is also the dining room. They're going to need it for breakfast tomorrow."

He narrowed his eyes and frowned, trying to decide if my reason for staying around was legitimate or just an excuse to hang around the crime scene. Though how we met was due to an unfortunate set of murders at the crafts museum, he'd attempted to keep the more gruesome aspects of his job separate from our relationship. I fought it, partly because of curiosity about his work and partly because if we were going to have any sort of a relationship at all, I didn't want it to contain any secrets. Besides, I found his attitude somewhat condescending.

I crossed my arms over my chest. "You sent all my helpers home."

"Let the staff do it. That's what they're paid for."

"It's my responsibility to see that everything is put back in place. You can't make me leave." Actually, I wasn't sure about the legal accuracy of that point, but I was betting he wouldn't fight me.

"I want you to go home."

I gave him a frustrated look which he returned with a stubborn one.

"I'll help her," Mac broke in. "It won't take long with both of us working."

Gabe glanced at him, an unreadable expression in his slate-blue eyes. "All right," he finally said. He turned back to me, his voice quiet and tense. "*Then* I want you to go straight home."

"I'm too restless," I said. "Besides, I never ate dinner. How about meeting me at Liddie's for something to eat?" The last thing I felt like doing at that moment was walking into a cold, lonely house and thinking about what happened to Mr. O'Hara and Miss Violet.

"I don't know when I can get there," Gabe said.

"I'll wait."

"You know I hate you being out alone this late at night."

I opened my mouth, ready to argue that I'd managed to stumble through a good part of my life without his some-times overpowering protection, when Mac spoke up again.

"I haven't been to Liddie's in years," he said. "Mind if I join you two?"

"Sure," I said. "And Chief Ortiz, I'll make sure and walk with him through that dangerous parking lot so he doesn't get mugged."

Gabe's lips compressed into a thin line under his black mustache. I knew he wouldn't flat-out fight with me in front of Mac, but this issue would be something we'd tangle over later. "As I said, I don't know how long I'll be." He whipped around and strode back toward the crime scene and a group of reporters who were waiting behind the yel-low crime-scene tape. At his side, one hand curled in a fist.

"Good old Pancho," Mac said, walking with me through

the garden to the recreation hall. "Still likes to be in control. Never was much of a team player. One heck of a quarterback, though."

"Okay, that's it," I said. "Tell me how you two know each other and what's with the nicknames?"

He smiled good-naturedly. "Nothing special about the story. Gosh, it must have been back about ten years ago, when I lived in L.A. Just a bunch of guys in Griffith Park playing pickup football every Saturday afternoon. All of us getting rid of one sort of tension or another. I quit after about a year, when it got too hard on my knees. Believe me, I almost didn't recognize him. Last time I saw him he had hair past his shoulders and a scraggly goatee."

"He was probably working undercover narcotics," I said.

I groaned when we walked into the recreation hall. It looked like it had been hit by a bomb containing green and pink crepe paper. "I've got jeans and a sweater in the car," I said. "I think I'll duck into a rest room and change clothes before tackling this."

"I'll go ahead and get started," he said.

I handed him a box of plastic bags I'd stashed in the kitchen and left him stuffing them with paper cups and plates.

"So, getting back to you and Pancho," I said a few minutes later. I'd pushed up the sleeves to my red cotton turtleneck, grabbed a broom and started sweeping up cookie crumbs.

"We all had nicknames back then." His eyes grew melancholy, and I knew his memories included more than the football games in L.A.

"And you expect me to believe you two never knew each other's real names or occupations?"

"You know guys, Benni. We probably could have gone five years and never discovered more about each other than what kind of drinks we brought in our coolers. That was what was so great about it. We didn't have to live up to any expectations."

I was admittedly mystified. No female I'd ever known

was capable of meeting with a group of women every week like that and not discussing everything from the graphic details of their first kiss to the length of their last menstrual cycle to their opinions on socialized medicine. "How in the world did you two manage to be in the same town for over a month and not run into each other?"

"What is there, forty-some thousand people in this area? I've never seen him in my church and I personally try not to antagonize the law. We don't exactly hang out in the same circles. Not so hard to figure."

"If you say so." We continued working in silence. Trying to keep my mind off the murders, I concentrated on the physical task of cleaning the room, but my thoughts kept drifting back to the gruesome picture of Mr. O'Hara and Miss Violet. I wondered briefly if Gabe knew that Mr. O'Hara had a nephew. After his sharp rebuke about getting involved, I decided to let Edwin inform him of Clay's existence and whereabouts. In less than an hour, the recreation room was back to normal. I twist-tied the last plastic sack, placed it next to the kitchen door and walked over to where Mac was setting chairs around the tables. "Well, I suppose we've done all we can do tonight. The kids will pick up the rest of the stuff tomorrow with Ramon's truck. I guess I'll meet you at Liddie's."

"Sounds like a plan to me. But first I think I'll check on Grandma one more time."

I walked out to the almost empty parking lot and it occurred to me while passing his Ford Bronco, I hadn't even thought to ask him about what he'd taken from Miss Violet's nightstand. Was it fear? Subconscious denial? Whatever it was, I knew I couldn't just let it go. I had to either confront Mac or tell Gabe. But, I decided as I started the truck and drove down the steep driveway of Oak Terrace, I wasn't about to do either on an empty stomach.

I STOPPED OFF at my house to drop off the dress and turn on the porch light. By the time I arrived at Liddie's Cafe, it was packed. Half the students at Cal Poly University must have had a test or term paper due the next day because, even though it was past one A.M., almost every six-person crimson vinyl booth was packed. I squeezed past a group waiting in the dusty red and brown entryway. Their ragged flannel shirts, gauzy dresses, black high-topped combat boots, pierced noses and three-tiered rice-paddy haircuts gave them a sort of Jack Kerouac-meets-MTV look. I would have laughed, except for the disconcerting memories of a certain pink paisley miniskirt and long hair singed crisp on the ends from being ironed.

Nadine, head waitress at Liddie's since before I could sit a horse, presided behind the cash register counting one-dollar bills. It surprised me to see her. Though the cafe was open twenty-five hours a day, as the yellow neon coffee-cup sign out front bragged, Nadine usually worked the morning shift. She preferred serving the early-rising ranchers and oil-field workers rather than the students, who she claimed gave her hives. Cops, who frequented the cafe because it was cheap and only two blocks from the police station, apparently fell somewhere in between. I studied the wall behind her while she finished counting. The owner of

Liddie's always displayed some kind of weird crafts on the greasy walls, trying to make a buck off tourists traveling north to the Napa Valley wineries or San Francisco. This latest bunch actually wasn't too bad. It was a collection of saws, all shapes and sizes, with carved wooden handles, each blade painted with a scene depicting some aspect of idyllic ranch or farm life. One long wide-blade showing a herd of white-faced baldies wearing droll, bovine smiles looked like a possible birthday present for Daddy. It would look perfect on the wall of the tack room that doubled as his office.

"What are you doing here so late?" I asked. Nadine double-wrapped a thin red rubber band around the last set of ones.

"One of my night waitresses flaked out on me. Said she was coming down with the flu, but she's more'n likely out whooping it up with that jug-eared boyfriend of hers." She picked up the eyeglasses hanging from a glittery chain around her neck and slipped them over her bony nose. Her flat tobacco-brown eyes ballooned. "I heard about the murders." Her thin shoulders allowed the incident one tiny shudder. "It's a terrible thing when you're not even safe in a place like Oak Terrace. Rose Ann Violet and Brady O'Hara were good, decent people. Don't seem right, them dying like that."

"I know it's scary," I said, touching her hand. "How in the world did you hear about it so fast?"

"I have my ways. Do you think it's a serial killer? Was there really red swastikas painted all over the room? I swear, it's all these L.A. people moving in. We never had stuff like this happen in the old days." She patted her pinkish curls indignantly.

"Who have you been talking to? There wasn't anything on the walls except pictures of Miss Violet's prize begonias and Oralee's photographs of Mac in his football uniform and cap and gown."

"My daughter Valerie's brother-in-law's cousin works as a nurse's aide at Oak Terrace. She said the room was ankle-deep in blood. That part's true, isn't it?"

"Nadine, you know I can't talk about it. Gabe would skin me alive."

"Where is the chief, anyway? We got some fresh papaya in for him today. Lord knows, he's the only one in this place who'll eat it."

"He'll get here eventually. You know how long all that scientific stuff takes."

"I know. Me and Ed's watched *American Detective* before. Now, tell me everything." She leaned forward eagerly.

"Cut me some slack, Nadine. You know I can't."

She pulled back, her lips pursed in aggravation. "It was a lot more fun talking with you before you started dating the chief of police." She jerked her long yellow pencil toward the back. "Mac just got here. He's got a booth in back." She handed me a plastic-coated menu.

"Breakfast or dinner?" she asked irritably.

I looked at my watch. "Uh, breakfast."

She grabbed the menu back. "No use bothering with this, then. I already know what you want. Chicken-fried steak and buttermilk pancakes, extra syrup, gravy on the side."

"Don't get too comfortable," I said, laughing. "You just might be surprised one of these days."

"I doubt that's possible." She tapered a skeptical eye at the artistic group of students filling the large corner booth in her section. Their bushy rust and purple hairstyles brought to mind a vegetable patch irrigated with radioactive water.

Walking across the speckled gold commercial carpet toward the back of the cafe, I tried to decide how to tell Mac that I'd seen him remove something from the crime scene. Studying the back of his chestnut-colored head bent over the menu, a part of me rejected the thought that he could do something so obviously against the law. But if he did, I was certain it was for a good reason. It had to be.

"Hey, preacher," I said, sliding in across from him. "Anything look tempting there?"

He laid the menu aside and smiled at me. "It's been

years since I've been in here, but everything's exactly the same."

"Not exactly." I pulled off my sheepskin jacket and stuffed it in the corner of the bench seat. "Check the prices. How's Oralee?"

"Better. The doctor came by and gave her something to help her sleep. When I think about her being in that room just before . . ." His full lips closed tightly over white teeth and his features grew flinty. He picked up a miniature packet of Knott's Berry Farm jelly and started flipping it over and over.

"She's okay, Mac." I reached over and touched his hand. "Gabe's real good at what he does. He'll catch the person who did this."

"I talked to him again after you left."

"You did?" An electric surge of relief raced through me. Now I wouldn't have to make the decision about telling Gabe what I saw.

"He said he's pretty sure Miss Violet was smothered. Probably by her own pillow."

"Oh, no." Nadine slipped my breakfast in front of me and my stomach rolled at the scent of the sweet pancakes and fried meat. I stared at it until it became a pale, blurry blob.

"What'll it be, Mac?" Nadine pulled a thick order pad from her calico apron pocket. She licked the tip of her pencil and waited.

"Just coffee," he said. "I have to save a hearty appetite for the six o'clock prayer breakfast the Ladies Missionary Union is putting on"—he glanced at his watch—"in approximately four hours." He sighed. "We certainly have plenty to pray about now."

"So, what else did Gabe say?" I asked after Nadine poured his coffee and left. I poured gravy over the steak and sprinkled it with Tabasco sauce, more for something to do than anything else. Mac shook his head and chuckled.

"I see the National Heart Association will never vote you their poster child."

"You're as bad as Gabe. Don't tell me you've gone the rabbit food route, too."

"I'm six years older than you, Benni. That wonderful time of life called middle age. Cholesterol, HDL's and all that jazz. I haven't eaten red meat in three years."

"It must be L.A. That town is like a cult. Daddy's going to go broke if people like you keep converting from being good, honest beef eaters."

"He could raise chickens. Or emus. I hear their meat is very low in cholesterol."

"Unless you have a craving for a butt full of buckshot, I wouldn't mention that to him or any of the other old-timers around here. Now, what else did Gabe say?"

"Not much. He was pretty close-mouthed. Seems like I remember him being a little less uptight, but it has been a while. And I really didn't know him that well."

"That's his Chief Ortiz persona. Don't you know cops are like schizophrenics? It's weird, the switching back and forth, but you get used to it after a while. I guess it's probably the only way a person could stay sane in that type of work."

"I can understand to a certain extent. It's not unlike what I do."

We sat in silence for a moment. I pushed the food around on my plate, taking a bite now and again, trying to ignore the sickly yellow cast the overhead lighting gave it. Just as I worked up the nerve to broach the subject of what he'd taken from the crime scene, Gabe entered the restaurant. He glanced around the room then strode toward us, impatiently pulling his tie loose and unbuttoning his collar button. Fatigue purpled the skin beneath his eyes. His chin was dark with late-night stubble.

"Hi." He kissed the top of my head before sliding in next to me. He gave Mac a tired smile. "Hey, Lefty, can't stay long, but whatever she's told you about me, don't you believe it." They reached across the table and exchanged a home-boy handshake.

"I've known Benni longer than you, Pancho. Why shouldn't I believe her?" They laughed in that way men do when they're pretending you're not there.

"Hate to interrupt the class reunion, boys," I said, "but what's going on at Oak Terrace?"

"Everything's under control," Gabe said.

"Any leads?"

He gave Mac a what-do-you-do-with-them look and said, "Don't worry about it, sweetheart."

If I had a shedding blade in my hand, that warm thigh pressing next to mine would have been minus one layer of expensive wool fabric and skin. "Gabe . . ."

"Drop it, Benni," Gabe said in a low voice. He shook his head No when Nadine walked up with the coffeepot and turned his attention to Mac. "So, Mac." He laughed. "It's hard calling you that. Have you stayed in contact with any of the old gang?"

I picked at my meal in angry silence as they relived old football triumphs and defeats. Fine, I thought, when they moved on to marathons, racquet ball and higher education. You won't tell me anything, I won't tell you anything. I drew pictures with my fork in the congealing white gravy, finally pushing it aside in irritation.

"That garbage is going to kill you," Gabe said, giving my half-eaten breakfast a look of disapproval. My habitual diet of beef-based fast food was something we argued about on a regular basis, sometimes in fun, sometimes not.

"Mind your own business," I said.

He and Mac laughed and started comparing HDL and LDL levels and miles jogged a day. I contemplated what a plateful of gravy-covered steak and syrup-swollen pancakes would look like spread across the front of a pale gray Brooks Brothers suit.

Their conversation on the ratios of muscle to fat was so intense, they didn't notice the man striding purposefully toward us. When he reached the twenty-foot mark, Gabe's radar kicked in and he glanced up.

"Benni," Clay said, ignoring Gabe and Mac and looking at me. The low brim of his chocolate-brown Stetson partially obscured his eyes. "I was driving by and saw your truck. I don't know anyone else in town. My uncle . . ."

"I heard," I said. "I'm so sorry."

"Thanks." The edges of his mouth turned downward. "And now some asshole police chief is looking for me. He left five messages at my hotel. That's all I need right now, some idiotic small-town cop with a junior college degree in police science trying to hang this shit on me. You live here. What do you know about this Ortiz character?"

I tried to send him a silent message with my eyes. I should have remembered that nothing halted Clay's mouth once it got started.

"I'm Ortiz." Gabe's voice could have cut diamonds.

Clay slowly turned his head and studied Gabe, as if he'd just noticed he was there. The barest hint of a smile lurked under his tawny blond mustache. "Of course you are," he said.

He certainly deserved points for quick recovery.

Gabe froze for a split second, then relaxed. "We've had some trouble locating you," he said.

"I was out."

"Apparently."

Have you ever seen two rams eye each other right before they lower their heads and charge? Did you know that rams are about the stupidest animals in the world, that they'll charge anything, even a brick wall, if they think it is threatening them?

"I have some questions for you," Gabe said.

"And since we've found each other now, I have one for you. Besides playing phone tag with the receptionist at my hotel, what are you doing about finding out who killed my uncle?" Clay pushed his hat back and rested his hands casually on his hips. His silver and gold oval belt buckle caught the overhead light and flashed. The only part I could make out from where I was sitting was "Roping 1989."

"We're investigating." Gabe leaned back and draped his arm across the back of the booth, his fingers lightly touching my shoulder.

Clay looked at me and winked, his mustache twitching. "Yes, sir, I can see you are."

Maybe it was just my imagination, but it suddenly felt

like Nadine turned up the thermostat twenty degrees.

There was another moment of silence.

Gabe's face was granite, Clay's amused, Mac's mild and expressionless. I waited for the fireworks.

Finally, Gabe broke the stand-off.

"My office, O'Hara. Eight A.M."

Clay smiled slowly. "Wouldn't miss it." He turned languid, thick-lashed brown eyes on me. "Honey, I still owe you that steak dinner."

"Don't worry about it," I said quickly. "With all that's going on . . ."

"No, ma'am. I always pay my debts. I'll be calling you." He adjusted his hat, turned around and walked out.

Gabe turned to me, his dark eyebrows furrowed. "What was that all about?"

"Nothing," I said, toying with my water glass. The air vibrated while a silent but significant battle commenced between us.

"So, Pancho." Mac broke into the skirmish with a light, bantering tone. "What do you say we saddle up the ponies and ambush him at dawn? We could head him off at the pass."

I tried to catch Mac's eye, shake my head No, but he kept his easygoing gaze on Gabe's still face. The one thing I'd learned early about Gabe is you don't joke around about his work. Clay implying Gabe wasn't doing his job properly was something Gabe would obsess about for weeks. He wouldn't say anything, but it would be there under the surface, turbulent as a volcano, and he would put in even longer hours than his already extensive ones, to prove he wasn't slacking off.

Gabe brought his hand up to his mouth, as if he had to forcibly keep himself from saying something he might regret. Oh, Mac, I thought. You've really done it now. After a minute or so, Gabe's hand dropped and a smile softened the hard angles of his face.

"You had my number from the first time we met, didn't you, Lefty?" He tossed a sugar packet at him.

Mac grinned, caught it and pretended to read the writing

on the back. "Says here that if your enemy is hungry, you should feed him, if he is thirsty, give him drink, and that way you heap burning coals upon his head. I think somebody is telling you to take the good Mr. O'Hara out to dinner."

"Let me see that." Gabe grabbed at the packet. Mac stuck it in his shirt pocket.

"Trust me, Gabe. Would I lie to you?"

For a moment, I thought I saw a hint of emotion flicker across Mac's face, as if he realized the irony of what he'd just said.

Gabe slid out of the booth and stood up. "I've got to get back to the scene. You two going home?"

"I'm going to sit here for a while," Mac said. "You two go ahead. I've some thinking to do."

Gabe contemplated Mac thoughtfully. "We should get together again. Soon."

"See you later," I said, reluctantly pulling on my sheepskin jacket. What I really wanted was to stay and attempt to pry out of Mac what it was he picked up in Miss Violet's room. But I didn't know how to accomplish that with Gabe standing there waiting to walk me to my truck.

"I'll look forward to it," he said to Gabe, then looked at me. "Come by my office down at the church. I'll dig out some of my old albums and we'll make fun of our pictures." I searched his face for some sign of guilt or fear, but only saw the reddened eyes of a slightly weary man.

"How's the new carburetor doing?" Gabe asked when we reached my truck. His father, Rogelio, had owned a garage in Derby and Gabe spent every Saturday of his life hanging out there until his dad died of a heart attack when Gabe was sixteen. In the almost three months we'd been seeing each other, my battered Chevy pickup had received as much attention from him as I had. He was a gifted mechanic, and the truck was running better than it had the whole fifteen years Jack and I had owned it.

I didn't answer. I was still irritated by his attitude in the restaurant. It's not that I wasn't used to chauvinistic behavior. Jack was raised by a Texan to whom the word "redneck'' was considered a compliment, and some of it had naturally rubbed off. It's just that I'd always shared in all areas of Jack's life. That's how ranch life worked. He had considered me an equal partner, so the part of the ranch that was his responsibility was discussed between us in great detail. It seemed inequitable for Gabe to know so much about my job and me, but keep so much of himself hidden.

"You still mad?" He leaned against the side of the truck and pulled me to him. I shifted uncomfortably, avoiding the bulk of the pistol at his hip.

I laid my head against his warm chest and kept silent. For me, that was more effective than a speech. I listened to the slow beating of his heart, knowing the kindest thing would be to give in, send him away with a smile and a kiss. But, as Dove would say, pure Ramsey orneriness runs through my veins.

He rested his cheek on the top of my head and sighed. "Benni, we've talked about this before. There are aspects of my job I can't share with you, that I *won't* share with you. They're too ugly. I want to protect you from that."

I pulled away and stepped back, sticking my hands in my coat pockets. "And what if I don't want to be protected?"

"I'm sorry, but you don't have a choice in this. I wish you'd never found the bodies, that you weren't involved. But since you are, I intend on keeping it to a minimum. You'll sign your statement tomorrow and that'll be it."

"You didn't have to act like such a chauvinist in front of Mac."

"I wouldn't act like that if you'd leave things alone. I wasn't about to discuss the case with you in front of Mac."

"Gabe, you don't suspect him? He's a *minister*."

"I have to suspect everyone, sweetheart. I can't afford not to. And just for the record, he wouldn't be the first man of God to break a commandment."

"And what about me? After all, I'm the most logical suspect."

He smiled, reached over and stroked my cheek with the

back of his hand. "I guess I'll just trust my instincts and make an exception in your case. Now, what's all this about dinner with Hopalong Cassidy?"

"Nothing. It was just a joke. His uncle whacked me in the shins this afternoon with his cane and I told him about it at the dance when we were . . . talking."

"So I've heard." The ironic tone in his voice was unmistakable.

I growled under my breath. Throttling was too good for Thelma and Martha. "That's right, I forgot, you know everything that goes on in this town. We danced. So sue me."

"Watch yourself with him, Benni."

"For Pete's sake, it was just a dance with an old friend."

"You know him?"

"It was a long time ago. I was seventeen. He visited his uncle for the summer and we had a few dates. That's it." That wasn't just it, but it was certainly all I was going to tell him.

"Well, old friend or not, I know his type and they're never anything but trouble. Stay away from him." His voice carried the same drill-sergeant authoritative tone I'd heard him use with his patrol officers when they got too rowdy.

"Excuse me, but I do believe the last time I checked, I didn't have Gabriel Thomas Ortiz branded on my butt."

His laugh was low and intimate when he pulled me back to him. "Not yet anyway." He trailed his warm lips down the side of my neck.

I slapped his shoulder with my palm. "Webster needs to invent a new word for you. 'Arrogant' doesn't even begin to cover it."

He nuzzled my neck, his day-old growth of beard as scratchy as a new grooming brush. "What *is* that perfume you're wearing? It's driving me crazy."

"You know I don't wear perfume."

He nibbled my ear lobe. A sharp current shot up my spine.

"You jerk," I said, trying not to give in.

He lifted my chin and kissed me, deep and lingering, his big hands cupping my face. "*Como te quiero, mi corazon,*" he murmured. His thumbs stroked my cheeks as he kissed each corner of my mouth. The rough feel of his fingers caused my insides to swell and ache. I leaned into him, tantalized by his strength, the sureness of his touch, his gentleness. I wanted to stay mad. Nothing had been resolved. He'd danced around the issue with the finesse of a man experienced in avoiding touchy subjects.

"I'll follow you home," he said a short time later. He slipped his arms inside my jacket, fitting his hands around the small of my back, pulling me flush against him. Resting my head in the crook of his neck, I inhaled deeply, drawn to his warm, nighttime scent.

"I only live three blocks away. No bad guys between here and there."

His hands tightened, drawing me closer. "I really think I should follow you home. Check the place out. Maybe tuck you in."

I pulled out of his arms, shaky with desire. "Thanks, Chief, but right now, I think I'd be safer taking my chances with the bad guys."

He reached over and traced the shape of my lips with his finger. "*Algún dia, querida.* Soon."

"Yes," I promised and meant it.

When I reached my front porch, I wished I'd let him follow me home, if only to borrow the six-cell, police-issue flashlight he always carried in his old sky-blue Corvette. The new porch light installed by the landlord had some kind of an electrical malfunction that was costing me a fortune in light bulbs and had left me more than once fumbling in the night attempting to unlock my front door. In the chilly darkness, my keys dropped, jangling unnaturally loud, startling into silence the Great Horned Owl nesting in my oak tree. A branch creaked, and up high, foliage rustled as he took silent flight. The tree frog who had taken up residence underneath my bedroom window wasn't so particular. Even when I dropped the keys a third time, muttering irritably to myself, his cheerful song continued to ring through the night. Then another sound caught my attention. One that wasn't a part of the natural early morning symphony. The rumble of a car engine.

I moved back in the shadows of my porch and watched the white car creep slowly past my house. It was a standard issue rental car—the kind of Ford or Chevy stamped out by the millions wherever it is they build them these days. Nothing particularly sinister, but then again, not normal for after two A.M. on my little tree-lined side street. The car sped up once it passed my house. I stepped out from my hiding place in time to see it turn the corner, illuminated for a moment by the flickering street light at the end of the block. Distance kept me from seeing much, but one thing stood out. I pulled my jacket close around me as some emotion gripped my heart—curiosity, anticipation, fear?

It was the outline of a dark cowboy hat.

6

"WHAT IS THE good of you living in town when I have to hear everything third-hand from Gladys Flickner?" Somehow, over the phone lines, Dove's voice managed to rattle my bedroom windows. Holding the receiver away from my ear, I slit open an eye and peered at the gray light of early morning seeping in around the window shade. A bright light flashed. Deep rumbling followed seconds later. Rain rapids flowed through the metal gutters. Mother Nature, not Gramma Dove. This time, anyway.

"Are you awake?" Dove asked.

"Debatable," I muttered, sitting up. "I got in after two A.M. Did you really want me to call you then?"

"Do you have to ask? So, what happened? And while you're talking, tell me who that cowboy was you danced with. You two looked quite fetching, I hear."

"How did you hear about that? Mr. Treton wasn't anywhere near the dance." I closed my eyes and pictured surveillance cameras with a satellite hookup to Dove's new wide-screen TV.

"He's not my only source. You'd best remember that. So, who was he and what about the murders? Poor Rose Ann and Brady. I swear, I'm taking my shotgun with me if you ever put me in one of those places."

"Dove, what I know about those murders will fit in the

proverbial thimble and Gabe is not spilling so much as a bean my way." I groaned and pulled my blue plaid comforter closer around me. "Listen to me, two platitudes in one sentence. This exhibit of cross-stitch samplers is like a muzak version of 'It's a Small World'—it leeches onto your brain and won't let go."

"Honeybun, I see I'm going to have to teach you a thing or two about getting information out of a man. In the meantime, what about that other boy? And how are you doing on those interviews for the Historical Society? Have you written anything yet? They need those chapters yesterday so we can get them to the printers."

The San Celina Historical Society, where Dove currently held the position of president, was publishing an oral history book on San Celina during World War II. Due to my somewhat questionable qualification of a twelve-year-old history degree from Cal Poly, they decided I would be the perfect person to research and write the last third of the book—the section on the treatment of the Japanese community during the forties. Also, since I was doing it for nothing, my salary fit right in their price range. I suspected it was also a ploy on Dove's part to finally wrest some value out of what she considered a useless education.

"Dove," I said, not even trying to sort out her questions. "I've been awake exactly three minutes and I haven't had any coffee yet. Can I get back to you on all this? Besides, aren't you going to be late for church?"

"It's seven o'clock. I've got plenty of time."

"In the morning?" I moaned.

"I've been up for three hours. Heavens, it's almost lunch time. City life has turned you mushy, child."

"Dove, I repeat, I haven't had my coffee yet. Do you think you can call me back in, say, two hours? Or better yet, two days?"

"Well, who licked the red off your candy, Miss Grumpy Pants? And just for the record, how are you going to spend your day? I know it won't be in church, so I hope you're at least doing something God wouldn't be ashamed of."

I sighed and ran up the white flag. It would be quicker

and easier to give her a rundown of my day than to make any attempt to convince her I was a mature, responsible adult perfectly capable of supervising my own physical and spiritual life. "I'm going to the museum and catch up on some paperwork and then I've got twelve or so samplers to mat and frame. I have the list of people I need to interview and I'll be calling them as soon as I can get to it. I still need to go to the library and do some research. The *Tribune* is on microfilm there back to the twenties. You'll get a rough draft as soon as humanly possible. Don't forget I have another job. You remember, the one that pays my rent?"

"I talked to Constance yesterday. She said you had plenty of time to do this project."

I bit back the first response that came to my lips, since Dove was still physically capable of washing my mouth out with soap. "Look, she doesn't really know what it takes to keep the museum and co-op going. The cross-stitch exhibit is scheduled to open next week and a reporter for the L.A. *Times* is considering doing a small article for the travel section. That will look real good on grant applications and I don't have much time to finish."

"Then I guess you'd better quit laying around like the Queen of Sheba and get to work. And you watch your step with that O'Hara boy. He might have settled down some, but I wouldn't bet a yearling on it. There are plenty of us who remember that summer he lived in San Celina. We all breathed a sigh of relief when Brady sent him back to Colorado. He's got a pretty face, but you know you can't tell the quality of the wood by the color of its paint."

"If you knew who he was, Sherlock, why did you ask?"

"Just wanted to see if you'd lie." She gave a crafty chortle. "You just behave yourself. Don't disgrace the family name. *Khodahafez.*"

"Ho-da-ha what?" I repeated to the buzzing receiver. Ever since Daddy and his five siblings banded together last Christmas and bought Dove a satellite dish, strange things had started popping out of her mouth. At least stranger than usual. Not to mention her kitchen. Nadine confided in me that Daddy had been sneaking down to Liddie's two or three times a week for his typical dinner of beef and potatoes because Dove had served up a dish she'd copied from some foreign cooking show. He swore, Nadine said, that even the barn dogs wouldn't touch the leftovers.

After a quick phone call to Elvia to inform her of what happened at Oak Terrace so she couldn't complain that she always heard everything last, I made myself a cup of extra-strength coffee softened to a pale brown with canned milk. I took it and two Oreo cookies scrounged from the bottom of the cookie jar and settled down on the sofa, pulling over my legs the autumn-hued Dresden Plate quilt Aunt Garnet sent me for my last birthday. Sunday was supposed to be a day of rest, so that was just what I intended on doing, for a few hours anyway. I traced my finger over the small stitches of the quilt thinking about Miss Violet and Mr. O'Hara and how their lives were a lot like this quilt—finished, purpose accomplished. I guess that made the rest of us still works-in-progress, the final design a mystery, not knowing until our lives were over whether our pattern was pleasing or jarring, brought comfort and warmth to others or just lay on the bed and looked pretty. What patterns, what circumstances led up to Miss Violet and Mr. O'Hara's lives being ended in such a cruel way? It was a question I knew was plaguing Gabe right now. And I'd known him long enough to be certain he wouldn't rest until he found the answer.

I pulled the quilt up to my chin and studied Jack's brown leather recliner. Next to it, on my great-grandmother's antique mahogany table, books were piled haphazardly, books Gabe was studying in preparation for writing his master's thesis in philosophy—Kierkegaard, Pascal, Gabriel Marcel, C.S. Lewis, St. Augustine. I picked up the yellow legal tablet and glanced over the notes he was making. Most of it didn't make sense, as personal notes usually don't: *Order of Precedence in Ethics; The Collision in Human Existence—a man who can bear being alone during a whole lifetime is farthest removed from the infant; Lying is a science, Truth is a paradox—if a person does not become what he understands, then he does not really understand it; Death is irreversible because Time is irreversible.* He had drawn a square around one thought, as if by framing it in the heavy lead of his pencil, it would be engraved in his being: *The only person who can do my real self harm is me.* I wondered which philosopher that came from. Once or twice, I'd flipped through the books he read, hunting in the highlighted passages for clues to his thoughts. So many of them seemed to dwell on death, apparently a popular subject with philosophers, and because of what he did for a living, I suppose I could see why it was a subject that fascinated him. He was such an enigma—an odd, unpredictable mixture of the physical and cerebral that both excited and troubled me at times.

I reached over and grabbed the extra large navy LAPD sweatshirt hanging casually over the chair arm. Holding it up to my face, I inhaled the heady resonance of his herbal aftershave and a strong, almost gingery scent uniquely his own. Living all my life except for the last eleven months on ranches, smells were important to me—they told you things, like whether rain was coming, how sick a cow was, if there was mold in the hay, how hard a person really worked that day. But, somewhat reluctantly, my long-held beliefs were changing. Gabe sometimes worked long hours and never broke a sweat. And what he did had just as much, if not more, value than saving a sick calf. At thirty-four, I was learning that your senses can't always discern the truth.

By ten o'clock, I'd had my third cup of coffee and was ready to face the day. I pulled on old boots, my most comfortable pair of Wranglers, a thick, off-white fisherman's sweater that Dove had knitted for me last Christmas, and headed for the museum.

When I pulled into the gravel parking lot of the museum, a clap of thunder reverberated like a kettledrum, and hailstones the size of Grape Nuts pelted the Chevy's cab. Since it was Sunday, fewer cars than usual were in the small parking lot, though it might have been the weather keeping the artists home next to their cozy fireplaces. Californians, even the semirural variety, didn't possess the mental constitution to fight the elements that people further north and back East acquire as a matter of necessity. It was not something any of us cared to admit. I'd never pulled a calf in 20°-below weather, though I knew men and women who had. I always felt a bit diminished around those hearty Wyoming and Montana ranchers—some of them my own uncles and aunts—as if I never really belonged to the club, though I'd spent more than my fair share of time with an aching arm dripping long strands of mucus and afterbirth from a cow's difficult calving.

Belonging somewhere. And with someone. What we search for our whole lives. What I had and lost. What Oralee was trying to reconcile at such a late date in her life. I sat in the truck and stared at the black steering wheel, touching the small groove on the right side where Jack used to nervously run a thumb back and forth as he drove. I couldn't help but wonder if the anniversary of his death this coming week would change something in me. All the "firsts" were over now—first Christmas without him, first birthday, first wedding anniversary, first . . . everything. Would the second year be any easier, or just different?

Pulling out the museum keys, I unlocked the thick carved door. Whichever co-op member's turn it was this month to open the studios, he or she had been thoughtful enough to turn on the heat. Saturday's mail lay on the glass counter of the small lobby gift shop. Strolling through the main hall, I scanned the return addresses, bills mostly, one grant application, one letter of refusal for a grant from a civic foundation in San Francisco. It was getting harder and harder for the museum to acquire donations, what with the recession and all. I spent a good half of my working hours filling out grant requests and drafting letters of beggary to foundations and individuals who publicly professed, even in a small way, a love for the arts. We had operating expenses to last us three months, but after that, who knew? Luckily, my salary as well as basic expenses like electricity and water were funded personally by Constance Sinclair herself, bless her noblesse-obliging little heart.

A few remaining rolled quilts from our last exhibit of

antique quilts by San Celina women were stacked in the corner for their owners to pick up, and stacks of cross-stitch samplers, framed and unframed, patiently waited my attention. The hailstones slowed to a light rain, so I took that opportunity to dash across the red-tiled patio between the museum and the studios. Honeysuckle vines canopied the wooden trellis connecting the buildings and dripped sweet-smelling drops of water on my head. Through the mist, the tiny windows of the old stables shined amber with warmth and welcome. Paperwork first, I decided, then the fun part of cutting mats, framing the samplers and deciding their arrangement on the adobe walls.

Both pottery wheels were churning away when I walked into the spacious main workroom. Sweet-eyed Roberto sat at one. He was one of our newest members, a talented young artist who specialized in brilliantly colored Brazilian pottery. Malcolm, our most experienced ceramicist and one of the original members of the co-op, sat at the other. As I walked past, heading toward the back rooms and my office, Malcolm gave me a pained look.

"Help," he said, his arms gray and shiny elbow-high with wet clay.

I gave him a suspicious look. He was known for being a great practical joker. "How?"

He grinned under his granite-colored goatee, long and straggly enough to give him a rather devilish aura. "My back. Scratch. Please."

I reached over and scratched the middle of his blue flannel shirt.

"To the left. Lower. Harder. Oh, yeah." A deep moan of pleasure erupted from the middle of his chest.

"I don't recall this being in my job description."

"Thanks, don't tell my girlfriend, but that was the best I've had all week."

I slapped his back good-naturedly. "I am going to tell her."

"Hey, heard there was a little excitement at that old folks' dance last night."

"You heard already?"

"Haven't you seen the newspaper? There's a special insert on the murders. Buddy of mine works there. Said they called everyone up at home and had them haul their asses down there early to get it out. They're hunting bear for breakfast going after your boyfriend. The article said violent crime has done nothing but climb since he took over as chief."

"I think that's a bit of an exaggeration."

"It's those new owners. Ever since those sleaze buckets took over the *Tribune,* it's sounded like one of those tabloids. Haven't missed an issue yet. I left a copy on your desk." He turned off the wheel, picked up a stained towel and started wiping his hands. "They happened to mention you found the bodies. And that it wasn't your first time." He smirked at me. "Finding bodies, that is." Roberto's dark eyes widened in alarm.

"Great," I said. "I was hoping all that was in the past."

"Benni, you know most of the people in this town are part pachyderm," he said. Roberto's smooth face looked confused. He was still new to this country and to English.

"Quit showing off that worthless college degree of yours. Elephants," I said to Roberto. The confused look deepened. "You started this, Malcolm. Explain it to him. I have to get to work."

Warming my hands with a cup of microwaved *café au lait,* I sat down in my chair and read the headline of the *Tribune* spread across my old wooden desk.

HOW SAFE IS SAN CELINA? INTERIM POLICE CHIEF HAS NO ANSWERS. The picture of the body bags being loaded into the county coroner's black van did have a tabloidish look to it. In the background, the photographer caught Gabe holding a paper cup of coffee, standing with military erectness, wearing that severe, somewhat unsympathetic expression he always assumes whenever he is really upset. Mac was in the picture also, standing to Gabe's right, his face more visually acceptable, tense and somewhat worried. The article did cast a negative light on Gabe's administering of the police department. His only comment had been "No comment," obviously the reason for the headline. It went on to give the basic information the police were releasing to the media. The chief investigating officer and media liaison would be Lieutenant James Cleary, Chief of Detectives. And in true tabloid fashion it was noted that the person who found the bodies, one Albenia Harper, unavailable for comment at this time, was said to have a "relationship" with a certain high official in the police department. The reporter questioned whether this would hamper the investigation of the well-loved teacher and the prominent San Celina businessman.

I couldn't help but feel a little irrational guilt, though it certainly wasn't my fault I found Mr. O'Hara and Miss Violet. There was no doubt in my mind that Gabe was going to be in a bad mood today. He hated having his picture in the newspaper, almost as much as having aspersions cast upon his abilities.

I threw the article aside, propped my feet up on my desk and decided to concentrate on the more important issues of the day, namely Calvin and Hobbes' latest dinosaur adventure. A few minutes later, Malcolm sauntered in.

"So, think the chief will sue?" he asked, plopping down on the old chrome-and-vinyl office chair in front of my desk.

"He's going to be in one foul mood today," I said, peering over the top of the newspaper at Malcolm. "And on Valentine's Day too. Guess there's no romance in my future tonight."

"Valentine's Day! Oh, no, I completely forgot. Judy's going to kill me."

"You still have time. I'm sure Sav-on Drugstore has a few Whitman's Samplers left."

"If it were only that easy. Since she went down to Orange County to visit her sister and got hooked on Godiva chocolates and South Coast Plaza, she hasn't been the same. Drugstore candy would guarantee I'd be scratching my own back for a month."

I folded up the comics and swung my legs down. "What's that old saying? Can't keep them down on the farm once they've seen the city or something like that.

Guess it's going to be a lonely Valentine's Day all around.''

"Did you have big plans?"

"Not gigantic, but I did make reservations at The Rusty Spur. You know how hard it is to get those on holidays. We'll probably go there at least. He does have to eat."

"Well, hope your night goes better than mine," he said morosely.

I glanced at my watch. "It's only eleven-thirty. The mall is open until six. You have plenty of time to buy a present."

"You're right, but time isn't my only problem." He grabbed the comics, tucked them under his arm and headed for the door. "This calls for some serious concentration. I wonder how much credit she has left on her Master Card?"

After he left, I picked up the phone and dialed Gabe's private line at the station. Lieutenant Cleary's mild tenor voice answered.

"Jim? Is Gabe there?"

"He's talking to the mayor on the other line. Want to hold?"

"Sure." While waiting, I opened envelopes and sorted my mail. Five long minutes later, when I was almost ready to hang up, Gabe's voice, terse and distracted, came on the phone.

"Yes, Benni, what is it?"

"Just wanted to say Hi." I could hear him breathing, waiting. "And I wanted to see if we're still on."

"On? For what?"

"Dinner. You're finally going to experience a true San Celina tradition. The Rusty Spur. My treat. We have reservations for seven o'clock."

I swore I could hear gears grinding in his head. "Oh, sweetheart, I totally forgot. I don't know, we're up to our necks here."

"But . . ."

"Just a minute." I heard him put his hand over the receiver and a sharp, muffled conversation take place. In less than thirty seconds, he came back on the line. "Is that it?"

"You have to eat. Besides, reservations at the Spur aren't that easy to get on . . ." I paused, feeling a bit embarrassed reminding him about what day it was.

"I'll see what I can do. You know the first forty-eight hours after a homicide are—" He stopped while someone spoke to him. His voice came back on the line, apologetic, but unwavering. "I'll get right back to you, I promise."

"Okay," I said with a sigh.

I spent the next three hours at the word processor working on the brochure for the cross-stitch exhibit so I could drop it off at the printers the next day. After three refusals, I finally agreed to speak to a *Tribune* reporter. He wasn't happy with my short, irritable answers to his questions. To recover, I retreated to our small kitchen where I was heating some milk for hot chocolate when Mac appeared in the doorway. He carried a brown package in his hands.

"That smells good," he said. "Got enough for two?"

"Sure," I said, walking over to the old refrigerator for more milk. "Have a seat." I pointed to the pink Formica-and-chrome dinette table in the corner. "Gosh, you look gorgeous." He wore an immaculate pin-striped navy suit, a stiff-collared white shirt and a burgundy and royal blue paisley tie. With his thick, longish hair and shiny beard, I could see what a powerful and appealing figure he could be standing behind First Baptist's wooden pulpit. "This is the first time I've seen you in your Sunday-going-to-meeting clothes."

He set the package on the table, and loosened his tie, giving a slight groan of relief. "Maybe you should come to church more often."

I laughed. "I definitely walked into that one. I'll start coming again, really. I've just been lazy." I poured more milk into the beat-up aluminum pan, then added more cocoa. "Well, church attendance will probably be the least of your problems once it hits the singles grapevine that you're up for grabs."

His pale gray eyes squinted with attractive laugh lines. "It's so refreshing talking to you, Benni. You always make me feel like a regular human being."

"As compared to what?" I asked, stirring the milk.

"As compared to being a minister—as in 'Watch what you say, he's a *minister*.' "

"Gabe says the same thing about being a cop."

I poured both of us a mug, then joined him at the table. "So, what brings you around on a Sunday afternoon?"

"Well, I was just visiting Mrs. Blakeman. She's down with the gout again, but she had some samplers she wanted you to consider for this new exhibit, so I volunteered my delivery services."

"Great, let's take a look at them." I carefully unwrapped the package and held the samplers out at arm's length. "These are wonderful." I read them out loud: "East, West, Home is Best—Myra Blakeman 1943" and "The kiss of the sun for pardon, The song of the bird for mirth, One is nearer to God's heart in a garden, Than anywhere else on earth—M.B. 1946."

"Amy used to do this kind of stuff," Mac said softly. He reached over and touched the tiny cross-stitches.

"It must be hard coming back here," I said. He and his late wife, Amy, met in San Celina his second year of seminary when she was taking summer classes at Cal Poly and he was visiting Oralee. He married the bubbly, raven-eyed nursing student three months after they met, breaking quite a few female hearts when he did.

"It's not too bad," he said, sipping his drink. "It's been five years. I know this might be hard for you to see now, but it does get easier."

"I never really thanked you for all the phone calls last year. Your phone bill from L.A. must have been astronomical. Sometimes they were the only thing that saved my sanity."

"I knew what you were going through and I've come to the conclusion, though some might argue with me, that's one of the reasons we suffer."

"Why's that?"

"So we can truly empathize with others." He picked up one of the samplers. "These are good, aren't they?" He pointed to the date on one of them—1943. "Did you know Mrs. Blakeman's youngest son was killed at Pearl Harbor?''

"Believe it or not, I do," I said. "I thought her name sounded familiar. I've been doing a lot of reading about San Celina County right around that time. We lost quite a few guys from this area."

"Working on a thesis?"

"Nothing that official. I'm writing the last section of the Historical Society's book, *San Celina—The War Years*."

"How did you get involved with that?"

"Dove, how else? She's president, or maybe potentate would be a more accurate title." I set the sampler down and picked up my cocoa. Talking about the Historical Society made me think of Miss Violet, who had been one of its oldest and most ardent members. The memory of Mac removing something from her room last night still pricked at my conscience. It was either confront him now or talk to Gabe. Mac was such an old friend, I really felt as if there was no choice.

"Mac, what did you pick up in Miss Violet's room last night?"

His face froze for a moment, the corners of his mouth tightening. Then just as quickly, his face relaxed. "What are you talking about?"

I wanted to say, You're a minister, don't lie, but I didn't because he hadn't actually lied. Yet. So I did what Gabe always did when he wanted someone to talk. I kept quiet and waited.

He tugged at his ear lobe and studied me. After what seemed like ten minutes, but was probably less than two, he answered.

"Benni, I'm not going to lie to you—"

"Good."

"And I'm not going to ask you to keep it from Gabe—"

"Even better."

"But there's more to this than it appears. People could get hurt."

"Mac, people have already been hurt. They've been killed."

His cheeks flushed red. "I know that. But I'm pretty sure what I took doesn't have anything to do with Miss Violet's or Mr. O'Hara's murders."

"How do you know?"

"I don't, but I also didn't have any choice. I can't tell you what to do, but I also can't tell you what I took."

"Mac, that's withholding evidence."

"I'm sorry, Benni." He carried his mug over to the sink, where he washed and rinsed it with the ease of someone who had taken care of himself for a long time. Shaking it dry, and setting it in the plastic dish drainer, he turned to me, his face a mixture of sorrow and inflexibility. "You have to do what you feel is right. And so do I." Without another word, he turned and walked out the door.

I stared at the empty doorway for a long time after he was gone. Of all people, I should have understood how sometimes doing what was "legal" and what was "moral" was not always the same thing. I'd found myself in that same confusing position not long ago. But, since being around Gabe, I'd been trying to look at things from a different perspective. Like how the law is the only thing we have keeping our society, or any other, from complete anarchy; that if you believe taking the law in your own hands is right, it gives people who might not be as moral or intelligent as you the same right. As Gabe once said, that was just one small step away from lynch mobs.

Gabe. I looked at the black and pink Felix the Cat clock on the wall over the stove. Five o'clock and he hadn't called yet. This was the part of relationships I found so hard after all the years of being married. If it were Jack, I wouldn't even hesitate picking up the phone and telling him to haul himself over here, it's Valentine's Day and we're going to dinner. But I couldn't do that with Gabe. I walked back to my office and stared at the phone for fifteen minutes, sending unsuccessful mental signals for him to call me. So, telling myself that women had been liberated since the sixties, and ignoring my great-aunt Garnet's Arkansas drawl inside me scolding "Men don't respect women who chase them,'' I picked up the phone. Lieutenant Cleary answered again.

"Just a minute, Benni, he's right here." In seconds, Gabe came on the line.

"I'm sorry," he said before I could speak. "I was going to call you in the next ten minutes, I swear. It's right here on my things-to-do list."

"Right," I said, trying not to sound grumpy or childish, though I felt a little of both. And I couldn't help but wonder what number I was on the list. "So, do you want me to come by the station or do you want to meet me at my house?"

"Well . . ." His voice was hesitant.

"Gabe," I whined, telling Aunt Garnet's voice to go pick pokeberries. "I made reservations."

"I'm sorry, I really can't."

"But—"

"Benni, you know the first—"

"Forty-eight hours after a homicide is the most important," I finished. "I know, I know. You don't even get a meal break?"

"We'll send out for something."

"But—"

"I'm sorry, but I warned you police work would be like this. We'll go out another time. I promise I'll make it up to you."

"How about if I bring something there?"

"Sweetheart, I can't. I don't have time for any distractions. Look, some lab results just came in and I have to go. I'll call you later. Be good." Before I could say another word, he hung up.

I growled at the receiver. Distractions? Be good? Hanging up when I still wanted to argue? Sometimes his attitude went way beyond condescending into downright parental. "Fine!" I snapped at the phone. "That's just fine." I leaned back in my chair, one foot propped on the desk, so deeply engrossed in my irritable mood I didn't even notice Clay standing in the doorway until he spoke.

"Ma'am, if I had a bottle of Black Velvet in my hand,

I'd offer you a drink," his low voice drawled.

It sounded so much like something Jack would have said, I laughed and answered, "Sir, if you had a bottle of Black Velvet, I'd take it."

His weathered face smiled broadly as he covered the distance from the door with two steps of his expensive black cowboy boots. Dropping down into the chair in front of my desk, he propped one foot up on the top in imitation of me.

"Hard day at the quilting rack?" he asked. The wet spots on the shoulders of his green, crisply pressed Western shirt told me it was still raining. He slipped off his hat and gave it a couple of shakes.

"Just a hard day in general." I tilted my head and stared at the writing on the bottom of his boot. Lucchese. The Cadillac of boots. Each pair handmade and rarely under five hundred bucks. It appeared at least someone's ranch wasn't in receivership these days.

I took a deep breath, trying to cover my sigh. Clay O'Hara could be amusing, I knew that better than anyone, but right then, another man was the last thing I felt like dealing with.

"Well, how about that drink, then?" he asked.

I propped my other leg up on the desk and studied the scuffed toes of my brown Justins. I really needed to buy a new pair. "I was just kidding. I don't drink."

"Nothing more challenging than a sober woman."

"What?" I said incredulously, shaking my head. "Clay O'Hara, you haven't changed one bit in seventeen years."

"Hey, it's my dad's line, not mine."

"Sure fell off your lips easy."

"You sound like a woman who needs a good meal. Or a .22 and some tin cans."

I crossed my ankles, considering his suggestions. Both sounded pretty good at the moment.

"When a lady has to think that hard, I'd recommend the meal first," he said firmly, standing up and adjusting his silver belt buckle. "So, where was it they had those incredible steaks the last time I was here? They were almost as good as Colorado beef."

I hesitated before answering, knowing where this was traveling and not entirely sure I wanted to take that trip.

"The Rusty Spur," I finally said.

"That's right." He slipped his hat back on and held out a hand. "Well, then, let's go." I stared at it, trying to decide what to do.

"I'm lonely, Widow Harper." He grabbed the toe of my boot and gave it a shake. "And you're probably the only person in this old town who'll spear a bean with me."

"Spear a bean? What's that supposed to be, your Louis L'Amour impression?"

"Now, Mrs. Harper, I'll not stand by and listen to one of the greatest Western authors of all times maligned. Why, my grandpappy would turn over in his grave if he heard you making fun of his idol." He rested his rough hands on his tooled leather belt and gave me the smartass grin that had earned him a citation for more than one moving violation from the San Celina Police Department seventeen years ago.

"Oh, what the hay," I said, swinging my legs down. "I am hungry and yours is the best offer I've had all day."

"Of course it is."

"*Only* offer I've had all day," I amended.

His grin gained a half inch. "I'm not proud."

"But you are persistent."

"You should know."

After asking Malcolm to lock up, I picked up my sheepskin jacket and walked out to the parking lot, where Clay waited leaning against my truck. The rain and wind had taken a breather and dusk was falling clear and calf-killing cold.

"I'll drive," I said, pulling my keys out of my leather purse.

"Mind if I do?" He opened the passenger door as if I had no choice.

I jingled the keys in my hand, uncertain whether I should be irritated or not. "You have something against women in the driver's seat?"

He feigned a horrified expression. "Why, no, ma'am.

My mom would cut my ears off and feed them to me in a sandwich if I even contemplated a thought like that. She's sixty-eight years old and still breaking ill-behaved horses and uppity grandsons. It's just that I've been driving that little putt-putt around for almost a week.'' He pointed at the white Ford Taurus I'd seen drive by my house last night. "And I'm itching to feel a real engine underneath these jeans. On the other hand, I consider myself a liberated man and I'd be proud to be your passenger.'' He gave me an amused look that made me suspect there was no way I was going to maneuver out of this without appearing petty.

I thought for a moment, then tossed him the keys. "Be careful. The clutch sticks.''

"Yes, ma'am.''

"And quit talking like a character on *Gunsmoke*.''

"Yes, ma'am.''

It was dark by the time we reached the Pinos Canyon Road turnoff from U.S. 101. Driving on the murky two-lane highway toward the small foothills separating parts of the county from the Pacific Ocean, Clay kept the Chevy's headlights on bright, adjusting them lower whenever another vehicle passed. He punched on the tape player, and one of Gabe's Southern jazz tapes came on—Mulgrew Miller and his wild, bluesy piano.

"Yours?'' he asked. I shook my head no.

"Didn't think so.'' He popped it out with a sarcastic snort and turned on the radio where KCOW was playing Eddie Rabbitt who was driving his life away. Traveling up the lonely highway west toward the restaurant, darkness wrapped around the rolling hills and occasional empty farmhouse, isolating us from everything except the drawling sound of the deejay's voice, the growl of the truck's engine and our own breathing. I was so accustomed to going to The Rusty Spur with friends and family, I'd forgotten its desolate location. Thinking about Miss Violet and Mr. O'Hara, what had always been familiar was now taking on an ominous cast and I began to wonder if dinner with Clay was such a good idea. What did I really know about him except that he was Brady O'Hara's nephew and gave me one of the wildest summers of my life when I was too young to know better? The memory of his car driving slowly past my house last night caused an inward shudder. Staring out the window of the truck, it suddenly occurred to me that he could have easily killed his uncle last night. The question, of course, remained, why. I slipped my hand through the handle of the truck door, gripping it tightly while trying to talk some sense into myself. I was seeing goblins in the shadows and that probably had a lot to do with the paranoid words of a certain police chief. What reason could Clay possibly have to kill his own uncle? Now, that was a good question. One I didn't have a single answer to because I knew exactly zilch about this good-looking, smooth-talking cowboy in tight jeans and oil baron boots driving my truck like he'd been doing it all his life.

"Awful quiet over there," Clay said. "What're you thinking about?"

"Nothing. Turn right at the San Celina Landfill sign."

He let out a deep breath and flipped on the turn signal. "Makes me nervous when a woman says she's thinking about nothing. In my experience that usually means she's thinking about a real big something."

"There it is," I said and unbuckled my seat belt.

The Rusty Spur is one of those three-generation-owned restaurants the locals like to take out-of-town friends and relatives to, but keep secret from tourist guides and newspaper reporters. It only opens for dinner and only serves one thing, the most mouth-watering, corn-fed-tender, artery-clogging beef in San Celina County. Some say in the whole state of California. With only the San Celina Landfill a distant neighbor, the faded, russct-colored clapboard building that was once a bunkhouse squatted among a thick grove of oak trees twice as old as most of the residents at Oak Terrace. The only other building was a large shed in the back that housed Bill the owner's colorful collection of pre-World War II license plates and antique farm equipment. On slow nights Bill left the cooking of the steaks to his two sons-in-law and gave impromptu tours of his personal museum to whoever was waiting for a table.

"Shoot, this place hasn't changed since the last time we ate here," Clay said. We walked through the crowded parking lot to the front of the restaurant where patrons, clutching long-necked bottles of beer, milled around waiting for their names to be called. Valentine's Day as well as most other holidays was a San Celina County tradition at The Rusty Spur. When you brought your date here, people suspected things were getting serious.

We were seated right away at the table I'd reserved for Gabe and me near the smoke-smudged brick fireplace. The packed room radiated with body heat; the smoky, molasses smell of beef broiled over oakwood permeated the wooden walls. Snatches of conversations flew over our heads, beer-vibrant voices, loud and competitive as tree frogs, carped about water rights, oil wells being shut down, the price of a bunch of Santa Gertrudis calves down at the Templeton Stock Auction last Friday afternoon. From the crackly speakers above our heads, the Judds sang brightly, assuring all the girls present that it's okay to have a night out once in a while.

"That's not the chief," our waitress blurted out when she came to take our order. She wrinkled her freckled nose and swung her long blond ponytail. Suzy was the younger sister of a girl I went to high school with and someone I'd taught the rudiments of barrel-racing to when I was twenty and she was ten. She leaned over and whispered to me, "What do I do with the halibut?"

Clay looked at me curiously.

"Have you got a cat?" I asked.

"No, but my boyfriend's mother does."

"Tell it 'Happy Valentine's Day.' "

She raised her thin eyebrows and took our drink orders—Coke for me, Lone Star beer for Clay—and walked away with a bouncy step.

Clay took a sip of his water. "What was that all about?"

"Just some plans that fell through."

"With the cop?"

I dug through the cracker basket in front of us and didn't answer. I chose a package of Ritz Crackers and fumbled with the cellophane for a few seconds before tossing it aside. Gabe was the last thing I wanted to discuss with Clay. "So, were you and your uncle close?"

He looked at me steadily; his dark eyes held a hint of wariness. "Not really."

"Was your dad upset when you told him?"

"None of us knew Uncle Brady very well."

"Then why are you—"

"What's their specialty cut here?" He leaned back in the pine-wood captain's chair and held the plastic menu in front of his face.

"Tri-tip," I said. "When is your uncle's funeral?"

He lowered the menu and closed it slowly, never taking his eyes off my face. "So, what's the deal with the fish? Señor Ortiz have something against good old American beef?"

"Look, I don't want to talk about him. I was wondering when your uncle's—"

"Good," he interrupted. "Neither do I. Tell me, are you getting the same *déjà vu* feeling I'm getting? It feels like the last seventeen years never happened."

"Hard to believe, isn't it?" I picked up a carrot stick from the relish dish Suzy had placed between us. "Now, about your uncle—"

"Forget him. Remember that old red and white Chevy I had? We had some good times in her, didn't we?"

"Clay," I said, frustrated. "Why don't you want me to know when your uncle's funeral is?"

"Why's it so important we talk about it right this minute?"

I dropped my eyes and studied the paper place mat in front of me, tracing the caricature of the frowning Angus bull with my finger. Maybe he was more upset about his uncle's death than he wanted to admit and here I was, pushing at him to talk about it. "I'm sorry, I was just wondering when his funeral was going to be, that's all."

"Honey." His voice held just the slightest clip of irritation.

I looked up. He leaned forward and rested his elbows on the brown Formica table. "Since you seem to be so concerned about Brady's final resting place, I'll tell you what I know. According to his lawyer, he had requested there be no service and that he be cremated. He'd already bought a crypt down in Santa Barbara. Soon as the county's done with him, off he goes. Good enough?''

"So I guess none of your family is coming out then."

"No."

"That's it?'' It seemed such a sad, lonely end to a life spent living in the same county for almost sixty years. "What about his friends?''

Clay's laugh was low and bitter. "I don't think we have to worry about that.''

"What do you mean?''

"Just what I said. Now let's forget the old fart. We have better things to talk about. You know, I never could remember whether your eyes were brown or green. I can see why now. What do they call that, hazel?''

"Forget my eyes, Clay. What about your uncle? Don't you care—''

"Remember the Mid-State fair? Nineteen seventy-six, wasn't it? You wore the most incredible miniskirt. Some kind of blue jean material if I remember right. That long hair of yours just touched the end of it. I couldn't keep my eyes off the bottom of that skirt. Sometimes when I'm out feeding cattle on a cold winter morning, when the wind chill factor's about twenty below, I think of that skirt and I warm right up. What happened to all that gorgeous hair anyway?''

"I cut it,'' I said sharply. No matter what kind of a man Brady O'Hara was, it seemed to me that his death deserved a little more respect than Clay was showing it. "You sound as if you didn't like your uncle very much. Why not?''

Before he could answer, Suzy appeared, perky smile and order pad all ready.

"You know what's good,'' Clay said to me, tapping a finger on the menu. "I'll leave myself in your hands.''

I ordered two tri-tip dinners, medium rare—one regular cut, one cattleman's cut—with all the trimmings, fresh green salads with ranch dressing, corn on the cob and huge

Idaho potatoes, heavy on the sour cream and butter, and of course, an order of San Celina's famous salsa. I had a feeling Clay was one of those guys who had no idea what his cholesterol count was and didn't give a pig's snout.

Through the rest of the meal, whenever I tried to steer the conversation back around to his uncle, Clay wriggled out of it by replaying some incident of that short, hot summer we shared seventeen years ago. More than once he had me laughing at some crazy thing we did that I'd completely forgotten about. But something in me couldn't let up about his uncle. I don't know what I was searching for, maybe assurance that Clay had nothing to do with the murder, that Mr. O'Hara had other enemies who might want him dead. Or, as Gabe would more than likely say, maybe I was being just plain nosy.

"What do you think of that new Lorrie Morgan song?" he said at one point, after I asked him another question about his uncle. He speared a large chunk of salsa-covered beef and chewed thoughtfully.

"Which song is that?" Though I listened to KCOW on a regular basis, I never was one to pay attention to who was singing what.

"I think the title is 'What Part of No Don't You Understand?' "

A flush of embarrassment crept up my neck. I finished the rest of the meal in relative silence, only uttering the occasional polite response as he rambled on about his ranch in Colorado, the Triple O, where they were experimenting with a particularly hearty crossbred mix of Brahma and Red Angus. On the drive back, he didn't press me for conversation, but instead sang along softly with the radio in a decent baritone. Through the filmy truck window, I watched the dark shapes of fences and oil wells move swiftly past us in the opaque darkness and wondered just where this Colorado cowboy fit into the whole business.

The museum was locked up tight and the parking lot empty when we pulled up next to his white rental car.

"Thanks for the steak," he said. "But I owed you dinner. My debt's not paid."

"Don't worry about it. It was paid for ahead of time."

"So I guess I stole someone else's Valentine present." By the smirk on his face, it obviously didn't bother him much.

I ignored his remark and stared out the windshield, not knowing exactly what to do at this point.

"Hey, I did appreciate your company." He reached across the distance between us and touched my cheek. His hand felt just like I thought it would and my heart took a low hurdle. "It's the first meal I haven't eaten alone since I came to California."

"No problem," I said. "It was fun talking about old times." I stiffened slightly when his hand moved down and started stroking my neck. I turned my head and looked at him. His brown eyes looked almost black in the semidarkness of the truck's cab.

"Well now, Happy Valentine's Day," he said in a husky voice, sliding across the bench seat. His hand slipped to the back of my neck and the next thing I knew, he kissed me. His lips were cool and slightly chapped, mimicking his rough hands. I felt surprised and excited and seventeen again. As quickly as it happened, it was over and he glided back across the seat and opened the door.

I slipped behind the steering wheel and started the truck, my face on fire, my heartbeat roaring in my ears as loud as the truck's eight-cylinder engine. He tapped on the glass. I took a deep breath and rolled it down.

He leaned through the window, resting his sandy blond forearms on the door frame. He loomed close enough for me to smell the sharp tang of salsa and beer on his breath and notice that one side of his mustache was slightly shorter than the other. "What is it?" I said, attempting to keep my voice cool and level.

"I had one fine time tonight, Widow Harper," he said. "Even if you do think I had something to do with my dear uncle's unfortunate departure from this earth."

What could I say to that? He had a heck of a way of phrasing things so that whatever I answered would appear awkward. I decided to go for flippant. "Did you?" My laugh came out shakier than I intended.

"Well, now," he said, his voice dropping an octave. "If I did, you must be one brave woman, being alone here with me like this."

I felt my mouth turn to cotton. *Or a stupid one,* I thought.

"See you around?" he asked.

"Maybe."

"You know, the best way to find out if I did or didn't is to keep a sharp eye on me." He pulled at his mustache and winked.

"Be careful," I said with more boldness than I felt. "I just might."

"I'll look forward to it."

I rolled up the window and watched him walk over to the Ford. He took his time, knowing my eyes were on him, his sharp-toed boots pointing slightly inward, his hips moving with that arrogant rhythm that always seems a natural companion to expensive boots.

He was, as Daddy had so severely lectured me seventeen years ago, one slick-oiled piece of machinery. That was in the lobby of the old police station, where Daddy was picking me up because Clay, then nineteen, was being held for speeding, resisting arrest, and for having an open container of beer in the car. I realize now how scared Daddy must have been, but at the time all I could think about was Clay's smoldering brown eyes and the way his lips made me forget about everything practical and sane.

One slick-oiled piece of machinery. Slick enough that I didn't find out one real piece of information about him or why he was here taking care of his uncle's business in San Celina. Slick enough that I almost didn't care. Slick enough, maybe, to have gotten away with murder.

"Clay O'Hara," I said out loud, following his white car out of the parking lot. "You'd better not have. You just better not have."

I could have sworn I heard him laugh.

IT WAS TEN o'clock when I arrived home. Three messages blinked a cheerful Morse code on my answering machine, making me feel, if not popular, at least not friendless. The first two didn't require an answer—Dove reminding me again of the meeting with the Historical Society tomorrow morning; Elvia informing me the books I'd ordered about compiling oral histories were in. The third was short, to the point, and demanded acknowledgment.

"Are you there? Pick up." A long pause. "Call me at home." Click. Sergeant Friday strikes again. He must not be making any headway on the murders; his cop voice was still intact. I'd complained about it before—him using that autocratic tone on me. Always apologetic, he would improve for a while, then fall back into it. Dialing his number, I thought about his eighteen-year-old son, Sam, whom I'd never met, and wondered if Gabe talked to him like that when he was growing up. Though it was over twenty years since Gabe had served in the Marines, there was still something of the military about him at times, especially when he was under stress.

"Hello?" His voice was sharp, stringent. In the background, I heard saxophone music. Bobby Watson, I'd be willing to bet. Brain-clearing music, he called Watson's wild modern jazz.

"Officer Harper reporting in as commanded, sir." I put a Marine grunt's emphasis on the "sir."

"I'm sorry," he said automatically, his voice softening. "It's been a long day. I was worried about you."

"You're always worried about me," I said flippantly. "I'm fine. What's new on the case?"

"Benni." His voice held a warning.

"Can't I even ask you about your day?"

"Try 'Hi, honey, how was your day?' "

"Hi, honey, how was your day? Anything new on the case?"

Silence.

"Okay," I conceded. "Did you ever eat dinner?"

"Yes, we sent out for Chinese. Did you?"

I hesitated for a moment. Why had I brought up dinner? Was it subconscious revenge? "Yes," I said.

"What did you have?" What a considerate guy, always so concerned about my dietary habits.

"Steak." Did he know already? San Celina's grapevine usually burned swift as a grass fire, but I didn't think even it was this fast. He was getting as bad as Dove. Then again, maybe it was just my guilty conscience. Only what did I have to feel guilty about? We weren't married, engaged, or anything. In irritation at myself and at him, I blurted it out.

"I went to dinner with Clay O'Hara."

Another stony silence, then: "Why?"

"Because he asked me. And because I wanted to."

"What I had to say about him didn't even cross your mind?"

"It crossed."

"And was this personal, or are you just sticking your nose in where it doesn't belong?"

He and Clay certainly had one thing in common. There was no way I could answer that question without hanging myself, so I kept quiet.

"Look," he said. "I'm dead on my feet. I really don't have it in me to get into this right now."

"That's certainly fine with me. I'm tired too. Any other orders before I hit the sack?"

"As a matter of fact, yes. You still need to come down and sign your statement."

"I'll do it tomorrow. Is that all?" I tried hard to keep the snap out of my voice. I don't think I succeeded.

"Sweetheart, Clay O'Hara is a suspect. I can't tell you to quit seeing him, but I can ask you. We don't know yet where he fits into this." He spoke each word slowly and distinctly, straining to keep his voice pleasant.

I'm not sure why, but I found myself in the uncomfortable position of defending Clay, even though I suspected him myself. "He hasn't been charged with anything yet, has he?"

"Not yet."

"And he's not your only suspect, is he?"

A reluctant "No."

"Gabe, don't you think that because of the way they were killed it was someone who did it on the spur of the moment? I mean, if the killer had been planning this ahead of time, don't you think—"

"That does it," Gabe interrupted in a cold, fed-up voice. "This is the way it plays, Benni. I am not asking you now, I'm telling you. Stay out of this. This is not a game or a movie or a novel. This is real. People have been killed and the person who did it would probably not hesitate to kill you or anyone else if they felt threatened. Am I making myself clear?"

"Yes, sir," I said coolly. "Anything else?" I had just about had it with being talked to like a junior-high student caught smoking in the bathroom.

"Yes. You're a babe in the woods when it comes to men like Clay O'Hara. Trust me, his prurient interest is only going to hurt you."

"You know, contrary to what your overinflated male ego would like to believe, I am not a naive teenager. I'm thirty-four years old and have been around a few men in my life—some even rougher than Clay O'Hara. I was watching out for myself long before you came into my life, Ortiz, and I'm certain I'll be doing it long after you're gone."

The silence was as thick as pecan pie filling.

"Anything else?" I asked.

"No." His voice could have been the ice cream on top of that pie.

"Then I guess I'll see you around." I hung up before he could answer. When the phone rang ten seconds later, I ignored it. And whoever called hung up in the middle of my answering machine message.

The next morning I woke up in an appropriately foul Monday mood after tossing and turning all night, first replaying Mac's conversation with me, then Clay's, then Gabe's. By the time I poured enough caffeine into me to jumpstart a Clydesdale and smooth out the grainy feeling behind my eyes, I had less than forty-five minutes to make the Historical Society meeting in the old library building downtown. I stood in front of my closet for ten of those forty-five minutes trying to decide what to wear that was both comfortable and somewhat professional-looking. I settled on my new black Wrangler jeans, a pumpkin-colored linen shirt, a black wool jacket interwoven with a rust-colored Southwestern pattern, and my black boots. I gave the pale lavender circles under my eyes a second glance, then decided that I'd known these ladies all my life—they'd seen me plenty of times without makeup; one more time wouldn't kill them.

According to Hereford Hank, KCOW's new morning deejay, San Celina had no rain ahead at least until Sunday. He predictably followed that pronouncement with Willie Nelson singing "Blue skies, nothing but blue skies do I see." I hoped my own day would be as balmy. Elvia would be ecstatic. The Mardi Gras festival and parade were going to be held this Saturday rain or shine, but she'd get a better turnout if things were dry. I knew Gabe would be glad, too. Trying to maintain peace and order at a street festival and a parade in the rain would have been a nightmare.

You are not going to think about him today, I told myself sternly. Him or Clay or Mac or any other man. You have your own work to do. I picked up my notes for the Historical Society and headed for the door.

The San Celina Historical Society was located on Santa Rosa, two blocks north of Lopez Street, the city's main drag, where Blind Harry's bookstore and all the best parking spots were. I pulled my truck into the municipal parking lot nearest Blind Harry's, my destination after the meeting. I paid the city its two-dollar ransom with the quarters I always kept handy now that Gabe made me keep current on my parking tickets, and even though I was five minutes late, strolled leisurely down Lopez, enjoying the Mardi Gras window displays. Since it was Monday, dirt-splattered trucks and mid-size American cars crowded the streets. Ranchers, as well as many of the county's senior citizens, preferred to do their shopping on the first day of the week when the downtown area was less congested by sidewalk-hugging groups of college students. In front of Blind Harry's, a lone street musician perched on an overturned plastic trash can and strummed a small acoustic guitar with Bruce Springsteen's face painted on the front. I dug through my purse and dropped a handful of change into his overturned Giants baseball cap.

"May your husband always desire you and your children be accepted at Harvard," he sang.

I smiled my thanks and turned to study Blind Harry's window display, which without a doubt, outshined everyone else's with its gaudiness. One of Elvia's clerks was a Commercial Art major at Cal Poly and it showed. Feathered and sequined Mardi Gras masks in the shapes of birds, mimes, and eerie-looking humanoids were hung among curly strands of metallic ribbons in the official Mardi Gras colors of royal purple, bright yellow and grass-green. A giant red crawfish with evil, crustacean eyes stood stirring a huge black cauldron filled with mannequins dressed in blue gingham shirts and straw cowboy hats. A poster advertising the rules of the Greatest Gumbo in the West Contest was posted in the window.

I passed a corner bakery, tempted for a moment by the warm almond and cinnamon smells wafting from its open door, but continued toward the old library. For years the Historical Society had met in a cold damp basement storage room of the city hall. When San Celina constructed the new library on a bluff overlooking Central Park last year, Dove and all her cronies used every bit of political influence they'd acquired in their years of volunteering and snatched up the old brick Carnegie library for the official San Celina Historical Museum. Walking up the natural stone steps through the arched entrance of the museum brought back fond memories of Saturday afternoon story-hour with Miss Delilah Seems, the children's librarian for almost thirty years, of the sticky vinyl sofa next to the checkout desk where I first read *My Friend Flicka* while waiting for Dove to finish her shopping in town, and of Jack and me kissing on the marble bench under the willow tree off the magazine room.

As I suspected, no one at the Historical Society even noticed I was late. I'd spent my whole life attending these things with Dove and I knew the first thirty minutes was always spent eating and indiscreetly criticizing the refreshments provided by some hapless member. The victim today was Sissy Brownmiller. I was glad I hadn't stopped for a croissant at that bakery. Sissy's pastries have won first place at the Mid-State Fair ten years in a row.

"About time you got here. Have some of this corny coffee," Dove said, pointing to the coffee maker.

"That's *Kona* coffee, Dove," Sissy said with a sniff of her sloped, pump-handle nose. She'd run against Dove three times for Historical Society President and never won. It was a bee the size of a 757 in her bonnet. "It's a special Hawaiian blend. I acquired it on my last trip to the Islands."

"Tastes like that diesel sludge they serve up at Hogie's Truckstop on the interstate," Dove whispered to me. "It's got a lovely aroma, Sissy," she said in her normal booming voice, then clapped her hands sharply. "Ladies, let's get seated, we have a full agenda today."

I grabbed a coconut eclair and a cup of the disputed coffee, which was actually quite good, and sat in the back row of metal folding chairs in what was once the reception area of the library.

The first half hour was taken up discussing Rose Ann Violet's thirty-nine-year membership with the Society, the shock of how she died and just how much should be spent on flowers. The next half hour was spent deciding what type of floral spray should be sent; there was a short, heated debate between Sissy Brownmiller and Edna Steinburg about what color roses represented what sentiment. Dove presided behind the fold-out table in front, gavel clutched in her plump hand, looking like she'd dearly love to bop both Sissy and Edna a good one over the head. I caught her eye and pointed at my watch. This was the highlight of the day for most of these thirty retired ladies, but it was only the beginning of mine. Dove pounded the table and glared at the squabbling ladies.

"White roses with pink carnations," she decreed and they knew better than to argue. "Now, Benni has a report on her progress with the history book."

I gave a quick summation of my intentions, then asked if there were any questions.

"Seems like it's taking you an awful long time," Sissy said. "The rest of the chapters are done. We need these books out before summer. That's our busiest time in the museum."

"I'm working as fast as I can," I said, trying to keep my voice from sounding too crabby. "I'm only one person."

"Maybe you should get some help," a voice down in front suggested.

"Great," I replied. "I'll gladly accept help from anyone." You could have heard an eclair drop. I wasn't surprised to find that everyone wanted to tell me how to do it, but to actually get out there and sit for hours listening to people ramble on about old memories, then organize those thoughts into a readable account, was quite another story.

"I'll do the best I can," I said, from behind gritted teeth. "I'll enlist help *somewhere*."

"Good," Dove declared. "Meeting adjourned." She slammed the gavel down and the flock of old ladies crowded back around the refreshment table like parking-lot pigeons fighting for McDonald's french fries.

"See you later." I patted Dove's arm and started for the door.

"Just a minute, young lady," she said, grabbing my sleeve. I recognized the tone of voice and my first instinct was to deny it and run. My mind moved swiftly over the last few days, searching for what I could have done to get myself in trouble.

She pulled me aside and looked me straight in the eye, her face serious. "I talked to Gabriel this morning," she said.

"How nice for you both," I said. "Is he well?"

"Don't get smart with me. He says you're getting too involved in Brady and Rose Ann's murders."

"No, I'm just—"

She held up her hand. "No back talk. This time I think he's right. They don't know nothing about why they were killed and that crazy person is still out there."

"But—"

"I trust him, Benni. He knows what's best for you."

"You know, I already have a father, and since I haven't heard from him, he is apparently the only one who thinks I am capable of deciding what's best for my life.".

"You are without a doubt the orneriest piece of business in town. I don't know who raised you, but they are going to have to answer to the good Lord for their sins."

I laughed and hugged her. "Don't worry about me, Dove. I'm really not as involved as he's leading you to believe. It's just hard not to be curious, me finding them and all. Tell me, can you think of any reason why someone would kill Miss Violet and Mr. O'Hara?"

"Honeybun, there's at least a hundred people who'd want to kill Brady and no one I know who'd want to kill Rose Ann, irritating as she could sometimes be. Like I said, you'd better leave all that to Gabriel. It's what we pay him for." She turned and started back toward the refreshment table.

"Who called who?" I said to her back.

She turned around, her expression guarded. "What?"

"Did you call Gabe or did he call you?"

She hesitated a split second too long.

"Don't lie to me," I warned.

"Depends." Dove's face looked as guilty as an egg-sucking dog's.

"On what?"

"On which would make you madder."

"Spill it," I said.

"He called me."

"Thanks, that's all I need to know." I started for the door, my temper gauge well on its way to boiling. Who did he think he was? Dove was genetically entitled to her constant interference in my life, but Gabe was quite another matter.

"Now, Benni . . ." Dove's voice trailed after me. I lifted my hand in good-bye and kept going. It was clear that Chief Ortiz was going to have to be set straight on where the authority granted him by the good city of San Celina ended.

When I reached the bottom step, another voice called out to me. Sissy Brownmiller looked both ways, as if checking for traffic, before carefully picking her way down the five stone steps. I waited on the sidewalk, wondering what she could possibly have to say to me.

"I heard you and Dove," she said, moving close enough for me to smell her White Shoulders perfume and see the damp pockets of beige powder settling in the filigreed lines of her face.

"Yes?" I said warily. She and Dove had carried on a feud of sorts ever since I could remember. There were times when Dove about drove me to drink, but I'd be whipped with barbed wire and dragged through a cactus patch before I'd be disloyal to her.

"I know something about Rose Ann Violet that no one else does." She puckered her lips and sniffed daintily. Gossip was Sissy's main source of entertainment and one of her few talents. And she wasn't one to hide her talents under a bushel basket.

My first inclination was to walk away. I wouldn't put it

past Sissy to make something up just to cause trouble. On the other hand, I couldn't take a chance. I'd learned from experience the information you need sometimes comes from the most unexpected places.

"Well, what is it?" I asked impatiently, a bit ashamed at myself for even listening to her.

"Not here," she whispered, though she and I were the only ones on the sidewalk. "Come by the store later this afternoon." Sissy and her son, Mel, owned a stationery and gift shop downtown. She was apparently going to draw this out as long as she could.

"Sissy, I'm real busy. If you have something to say, just say it."

She gave me a sour look, then turned and peered furtively over her shoulder. "All right, I just don't want anyone to see us talking."

"Then I suggest you tell me what you know and we can both get on with our day." I agreed with her on one thing. I didn't want anyone, especially Dove, catching us talking. She would pry out of me in ten seconds whatever Sissy told me. I had never been able to successfully lie to Dove and I doubted that at this late stage in my life I'd be able to start.

"It happened when I was ten," she said, then paused.

"What did?" Cross-stitch homilies being on my mind, I was reminded of the one about the curious cat. I hoped I wouldn't regret hearing anything she had to say.

"You know, of course, that my father was a doctor." She raised her bony nose and gave me a challenging look.

"Yes." Until he died ten years ago, Dr. Brownmiller was the only doctor that Dove, as well as half the town, would consent to see even though at seventy-nine he could barely curve his arthritic hand around a stethoscope. Everyone in San Celina had loved Dr. Brownmiller almost as much as they detested Sissy.

"Well . . ." Her voice went down so low, I had to step closer to hear her words. "When I was ten, he got a house call in the middle of the night to go to Miss Violet's house." She paused dramatically.

"So?" I said.

"I went with him because Mother was out of town. Aunt Anissa—I was named for her, you know—was sick down in Oceanside, and Mother went to take care of her baby, my cousin Stevie, who was a lawyer in Burbank before they disbarred him in '63 because of some shady real estate dealings. I don't really know the whole story, but apparently he bought into some time shares in Hawaii . . ."

"Sissy," I said irritably. "Miss Violet. Let's get back to Miss Violet."

"Don't rush me. You know, you always were an impatient little girl, Albenia Harper. And such a trial to dear, dear Dove. I suppose it comes from losing your mother so early. Why, if you'd been my daughter I'd—"

"Sissy!" I snapped. It occurred to me that I could strangle her here on the street and there wasn't a person in San Celina who wouldn't be a convincing defense witness for my temporary insanity plea.

"Okay," she said, a smug look on her face. The only thing she enjoyed more than gossip was getting someone's goat. "This is what happened. Because it was so late, Father had to take me with him. I was curled up in the back seat of our old Plymouth with my pillow and blanket while he went inside to Miss Violet's. I was asleep for the longest time until voices woke me up. I stuck my head up just barely enough to see where we were. That's when I realized we were at Miss Violet's."

"How did you know that?"

"I saw her. She was standing on the front porch talking to Father."

"Was she okay?"

"She was standing there, wasn't she? I heard Father's voice get mad and start yelling and that frightened me because Father *never* raised his voice, so I ducked down and put my head under the blanket."

"Could you hear anything he was saying?"

"No, but when he got into the car, I pretended to be asleep in the back and he was talking to himself to beat the band."

"What did he say?" I wasn't sure how, or if, any of this had to do with Miss Violet's murder, but she had me hooked now and I wanted to hear the rest of the story.

"Something about the law is the law. You got to trust the law."

"When was all of this?"

"Well, I was ten years old and I remember seeing Christmas decorations. It must have been just after the war started. That would be 1941."

I stood there for a moment and looked at a complacent Sissy. I don't know what she thought she'd accomplished by telling me this about Miss Violet. A house call over fifty years ago. How could that have anything to do with why Miss Violet and Mr. O'Hara were killed?

"Was there any record of this call?" I asked. "What was it for?" If I knew Sissy, I'd bet she was nosy enough to have read all her father's records, a fact that would have ruined Doc Brownmiller's career had anyone known it.

"Yes," she said. "My father *always* kept very accurate records."

"Well," I prompted. "What did it say?"

"Cuts, lacerations, a broken hand, a prescription for pain pills."

Then I asked the obvious question. "Who was it?"

"The name on the chart was Rose Ann Violet."

"So something happened to Miss Violet."

She tilted her head and looked at me oddly. "I don't think so. She was my teacher that year and she was in school the next day, fit as a fiddle."

"Is that it?" I asked, hitching my purse over my shoulder and starting to turn away. The information was interesting, but I still couldn't see how it had anything to do with the murders. Sissy just liked having someone pay attention to her and I'd given her enough of my time.

"No." The superior tone in her voice caused me to turn and look back at her expectantly. The shadows from the trees next to the old library stained the hollows of her face, giving it a feral look. "There was someone else there on the porch and they could probably tell you a lot more about what went on that night than me.''

''Who?'' I asked, just wanting to get away from her before she stretched this revelation into another windy tale that led nowhere.

She gave a small nasty smile. ''Why, Oralee Reid, of course,'' she said, as if it could be no one else.

8

"I DON'T KNOW," Elvia said, after I'd told her everything I'd learned so far, leaving out the part about Mac. I still wasn't sure what I wanted to do about that and didn't want to be confused by someone else's moral convictions. "Maybe this time Gabe and Dove are right."

We were sitting downstairs at one of the round oak tables in the book-lined coffee house, testing her cook's latest Drink of the Month, a concoction honoring Mardi Gras. It was made with the Café Du Monde chicory coffee Elvia bought directly from the original cafe in New Orleans, half-and-half, pecan extract and chocolate syrup. Drinking my second one, I couldn't decide if it was good or just irresistibly bizarre.

I almost agreed with her, but I wasn't ready to admit it. "But seriously, do you think that Sissy Brownmiller would have ever gone to the police with this information?"

"Probably not," Elvia said, her voice doubtful. "But the story she told you doesn't seem to have anything to do with Miss Violet and Mr. O'Hara's murders."

"Maybe not, but I'm going to have to talk to Oralee about it, if only to satisfy my curiosity. Then I'll tell Gabe everything and forget it."

"I'll believe that when I see it," she said dryly. She took a tiny sip from the foamy drink in front of her and grimaced. "I think I'm going to tell Jose to pass on this one."

"Gee, I kind of liked it." I peered down into my empty glass mug.

"There's certainly no accounting for *some* people's taste."

"Who has taste?" Ramon clumped down the scuffed wooden stairs in unlaced black combat boots, baggy jeans and a flannel shirt washed almost plaidless. Todd, Nikon in hand, dogged his heels in clothes so similar they could have come from the same derelict. Ramon slipped an arm around his sister's shoulders and gave her an exuberant hug.

"Not you, that's for sure, *m'hijo*," Elvia said fondly, reaching back and tickling his stomach lightly. "What are you two *muchachos* up to?"

He perched on the wooden arm of her oak chair and grabbed her drink, making a face after taking a gulp. "Don't tell Mama—"

She drummed her long peach-colored nails on the table. "Famous last words."

"We're cutting class," Todd finished for him.

She twisted around and gave Ramon an irritated look. "You little flake. What class are you cutting?"

"Nothing important, *madrastra*," Ramon said. "Just history. Who cares about what happened a hundred years ago? Live for today, that's my motto."

"You'd better live it up then, because there'll be no tomorrow for you if Mama finds out you aren't going to class." Elvia folded her arms across the front of her peach and cream Donna Karan suit.

"She won't if everyone keeps their mouths shut," he said, ignoring her scowl and flashing me the captivating white smile that earned him the nickname of "Ramoneo" from his five older brothers. "Help," he mouthed.

I held up my hands. "Don't get me involved in this family squabble. I have enough problems of my own, thank you very much."

"Have any reporters talked to you yet about finding the bodies?" Ramon asked eagerly. "One interviewed me, you know. It was so cool."

"One called me at the museum. I gave him the facts, then told him I'd bite anyone who tracked me down for any more interviews."

"Whoa, harsh lady," Todd said.

"Not harsh, just too busy for yellow journalism." The antique mantel clock sitting on one of the bookshelves chimed softly. "Speaking of busy, I need to get to work. Got a ton of things to do today."

"What things?" Ramon asked. Having known him since he was born, I was wise to his ploy. The longer he kept me talking, the longer he avoided Elvia's lecture on the importance of a college education.

"Some interviews, some work at the museum. Just stuff."

"Interviews? Like for what?" He arranged a wonderfully fake look of interest on his face. I couldn't remember what his major was, but he wouldn't go wrong considering a change to Theater Arts.

"For the Historical Society. They're putting together a book about San Celina during the war years."

"You mean, like the sixties?" Todd asked.

I rolled my eyes at Elvia and we both laughed. Another reminder of our advancing age. It was hard to believe there was a whole generation of kids who when they heard the word "war" instantly thought of Vietnam. "No, World War Two. I'm doing the section on how the Japanese-Americans were treated in San Celina during that time."

"Wow, are you going to talk to Todd's grandfather?" Ramon asked. "He's Japanese."

"Did he live on the Central Coast during the forties?" I said, turning to look at Todd.

He shifted the camera from one hand to the other, looking uncomfortable. "I guess. He's owned the fish store a long time. Since before I was born."

"It's that one in Old Town, right? I forget the name."

"Morita's."

"That's right. Gabe shops there once in a while. Do you think your grandfather would talk to me?"

He shrugged noncommittally. "Grandfather doesn't talk

much about the old days. . . .''

"Well, maybe I'll drop by sometime and ask him. Don't worry, it won't offend me if he doesn't want to. There's lots of people who don't like talking about that time."

Looking relieved, Todd nodded at Ramon. "Ready to split?"

"Just a minute," Elvia said. She stood up and pointed an elegant finger at her brother. "I want to know just how bad you're doing in history."

Ramon jumped up and started backing toward the stairs. "Gotta go."

"Ramon." Her stern older-sister voice stopped him in his tracks.

"I'm not flunking or anything," he said. "It's just that today we were supposed to give a progress report on our history projects . . ."

"We're partners," Todd put in.

"And we're sort of, well, kind of . . ." Ramon threw everything he had into his smile. She didn't fall for it.

"You haven't done a thing on it," Elvia finished.

He laughed and blew her a kiss. "Smart women are so sexy."

"Ramon, Ramon," she scolded. "Don't you realize how important a college education is?"

He moved behind her and flapped his hand in a quacking motion, like he did the other night. Since it wasn't directed at me this time, I couldn't help laughing.

Elvia frowned. "You're not helping things, Benni." She turned back to Ramon. "What exactly is your project?"

"Well, that's sort of a problem," he said, looking like a puppy who'd missed the newspaper. "We . . ."

"Don't have one," Todd finished. "And it's due in two weeks."

Elvia's black eyes flashed with anger. I knew Ramon was in for a real tongue-lashing unless someone intervened. Like so many times when he was growing up, I jumped in to save him.

"What kind of project do you have to do?" I asked, an idea forming in my head.

Ramon scrunched his face in consternation. "It can be anything to do with local history. Some people are tracing their roots. Some are just doing a report on one of the missions. One guy is researching ghost legends of San Celina County."

"Radical idea, huh?" Todd said. "I wish we would have thought of it." He raised his camera to the ceiling and peered through the viewfinder. "Super high-speed film. Pictures of protoplasmic gases."

"I have an idea," I said.

"What?" Ramon's face pleaded, *Get me out of this, please.*

"I've got the Historical Society on my back about getting this section on the Japanese written for their book. My problem isn't doing the writing, but taking the time to do the interviews. I absolutely have to get back to the museum and work on the new exhibit and I need to start compiling the information I've already collected into something readable. If I gave you and Todd a tape recorder, a list of questions and some film, you could do some of the interviews and help me write up the histories. Do you think your teacher would consider that an adequate project?"

"I don't know," Ramon said. "Could you talk to her?"

"Why don't you talk to her?" I asked.

"She and I . . . Well, she doesn't exactly . . . It's like this, I . . ."

"He put a dead mouse in her desk last week," Todd explained. "Wearing a little Napoleon hat."

"I couldn't make a small enough coonskin," Ramon said.

"Ramon!" Elvia cried. "This isn't high school. When are you going to grow up?"

Ramon grinned and wiggled his eyebrows. "Could you talk to her, Benni? Tell her Todd and I are serious about this. It'll seem more official coming from you, you having such an important job now and everything."

"Cut the bull, Ramon." I ran my fingers through my hair and wondered what I'd let myself in for. I could certainly use the help, but Ramon and Todd weren't the most mature teenagers I'd ever known. "Okay, I'll talk to her, but you two have to promise me, no practical jokes or goofing off on this project. These interviews have to get done so I can start writing them up. And this subject is very serious. You'll need to show respect to these people."

Ramon stood up and held up three fingers. "I do solemnly swear to be a good scout and do my best for you and this project."

"Since you were thrown out of the Boy Scouts the same month you joined, that doesn't set my mind at ease," I said. "But I guess I have to trust you. I know you guys will do a good job." I said the words with more conviction than I felt. "If your teacher okays it, then I'll call you tomorrow and we'll set up some interviews for this week. What's her name?"

"Mrs. Thompson. Thanks, Benni, you're a real pal. Peace, love and all that baloney." Ramon held up two fingers in a V before running up the stairs, Todd close behind him.

"Are you *loco?*" Elvia said, walking back up the stairs with me to find the oral history books she'd ordered. "You're going to get those two jokers to do some real work? Are you serious?"

"Yes, yes and yes," I said, though my voice wasn't convincing even to me.

I called Mrs. Thompson from Elvia's office. She agreed to meet with me in half an hour, though she was a bit confused as to why I'd be concerned with the history projects of two of her students when I wasn't related to either of them. A tense edge crept into her voice when I mentioned Ramon's name. I wondered how much of a sales job it would take to bail him out.

You *are* crazy, I told myself, driving toward the campus. You have enough to do without supervising two teenagers on a history project. But if I could organize them right, and they did what they were told, it would actually save me time. On that optimistic note, I bought a two-hour parking pass from the machine at the tree-lined entrance to Cal Poly and pulled in across from the student store, aptly named the Cougar's Lair. Besides textbooks, it sold everything from backpacks imprinted with the snarling mascot's picture to milk and ice cream from the agriculture department's Guernsey cows. I was ten minutes early for my appointment, so I took a seat on a paint-chipped wooden bench under a budding decorative plum tree. The red brick History and Cultural Arts building, where Mrs. Thompson's office was located, didn't look any different than when I attended classes there fifteen years ago.

A wind had sprung up from the south, blowing away any lingering clouds, leaving a bold, brilliant blue sky and air smelling of wild mustard, salty earth and springtime. Around me, the raucous, noontime chatter of students brought back memories as clear and sharp as the air. I'd spent more days than I could remember sitting here with Jack and Elvia and other friends, complaining about teachers and parents and trying to decide what to do that Saturday night. Everything seemed so certain then. We knew exactly how we felt about things, where we were going, how we would get there. Our concrete plans reminded me of the mosaics created by one of our artists at the co-op—bits and pieces of stone and glass laid out just so—the scene becoming clearer as you stood further and further back. Except our lives weren't really like those mosaics, whose pieces, once the artist placed them, could be cemented permanently into place. Looking back, I realize now we were more like kaleidoscopes—our designs twisting this way and that, unpredictable as clouds, changing sometimes for the better, sometimes not, but always open to that unexpected color combination we'd never think of on our own.

Mrs. Thompson's office was the typical tiny cubicle awarded to tenured professors at Cal Poly. I knocked on the tan metal door and a crisp voice commanded me to enter.

"Ms. Harper?" The fiftyish, Japanese woman in tortoise-shell eyeglasses and a nubby, honey-gold suit, stood up to greet me. Her office was small, but deceptively spacious. Pastel-framed Japanese watercolors depicting slender cherry trees and faceless women in kimonos decorated the wheat-colored walls. A pink-and-white-etched teapot with matching cups sat on a bamboo tray on the scarred credenza behind her. The top of her standard-issue steel desk held only a pale green blotter, a porcelain pencil cup painted with a red-legged crane, and her black telephone. She had achieved the roomy feel by eliminating everything but the necessities.

"Yes, are you Mrs. Thompson?"

"Mariko, please." She shook my hand firmly, then gestured to the inexpensive metal office chair next to her desk. I hung my purse over the back and sat down.

"I'm Benni Harper," I said. "A friend of Ramon and Todd's."

"Ah yes, Ramon." A pained look glided across her face as she sat down in her high-back chair. "He is something, our Ramon."

"He's a good kid," I said, somewhat defensively. He was like a brother to me and I couldn't help feeling protective.

"Yes, he is." She smiled ruefully. "I just hope you never have to teach a class with him in it. He's one of those students who drives a teacher insane while at the same time making great conversational fodder for the teachers' lounge. He's actually quite bright, just not very focused."

"He's the youngest of seven children," I said, though I wasn't sure why I felt compelled to give her that information. "His mother's favorite."

"I'm not surprised." She leaned back in her chair and folded her hands across her lap. "So, tell me about this project."

She watched me intently with intelligent black eyes while I explained what the Historical Society was doing, why I was involved and how I thought Ramon and Todd could help.

"I heard through the grapevine here that a section of the book was going to be on how the Japanese-Americans were treated during the war," she commented. Her eyes continued to study me.

"What do you think about it?" I wondered if she were upset because I, a Caucasian, was asked to write that section.

"It's a wonderful project for Ramon and Todd to be involved with and I say it's about time someone told that story. As a matter of fact, I wouldn't mind being interviewed myself."

"That would be great!" Then I hesitated, doing a quick calculation in my head. "No offense, but were you old enough to even remember anything about that time?"

She gave a laugh as light and airy as one of her Japanese prints. "No offense taken. Thank you for the compliment. Actually, I'm fifty-nine years old. I was seven when they sent us—my mother, my brother and me—to a relocation camp in Arizona. I remember it quite vividly."

This was too good to pass up. I reached into my purse and pulled out the hand-held tape recorder the Historical Society had purchased for me. "Do you mind being recorded?"

"Not at all." She glanced at her delicate gold watch. "I only have about fifteen minutes, though. Faculty meeting." She wrinkled her nose.

"No fun, huh?"

"Have you ever been to one?"

"No."

"Let me put it this way: I'd rather have root canal."

"Well, hopefully my questions won't be that painful." I turned the tape recorder on, then pushed it across the desk toward her. "First, what do you remember about the day Pearl Harbor was bombed?"

She sat forward in the chair, her eyes focused on the machine. "It was Sunday morning. I was getting ready to go to the movies. I had been very good all week and my mother promised to take me. I can't remember what we were going to see, but I remember being very excited." She touched her silver-streaked pageboy and stared at the top of her desk as if she were seeing the words there. "My hair. I remember I couldn't get my hair to go how I wanted. I was very upset about that."

"How did you hear what happened? Did your mother tell you?"

"El Toro told us."

"Who?"

She gave a crooked half-smile. "That was what everyone called the siren on top of the firehouse because it sounded like a cranky old bull. The minute it bellowed, my mother turned on the radio to see where the fire was and we heard the report about Pearl Harbor."

"Then what did you do?"

"Well, we didn't get to go to the movies. I was angry and acted quite bratty about it if I remember correctly. But I was only seven and the word 'war' had no real meaning for me. I only remember my mother sitting in her maple rocking chair, silently rocking back and forth, tears running down her face. When my father and brother came home from the grocery store my family owned, they sat up until late that night talking in Japanese about what would happen to us. A few times they sent me out of the room, when my mother got very upset and started crying out for her mother and father." Mariko's mouth sagged at the corners and her face seemed to age as she talked. I reached over and started to turn off the tape recorder.

"We can do this another time, if you like," I said.

She waved my hand away. "No, I'd like to finish. The meeting can start without me." She was silent for a moment, as if she'd lost her place in her memories.

"What happened the day after Pearl Harbor?" I prompted.

"My parents were Issei. Do you know what that means?"

"They were born in Japan."

"Right. But my older brother, Kazuo, and I were Nisei— American-born—so therefore citizens. We were lucky. My father was a very shrewd businessman. He'd put all his bank accounts in our names. Two days after Pearl Harbor, they froze all the bank accounts of the Issei. Many farmers couldn't pay their workers and so their crops went unharvested. They couldn't even draw out money to buy food."

"Your father must have been a very smart man."

She tilted her head; her dark eyes held a hint of anger. "Too smart, maybe."

"Why do you say that?"

"He was very active in the Japanese community. Many times when I was a girl we had delegations from Japan stay with us to learn from my father how he ran his store, Yamaoka's Groceries. My father, Yoshimi Yamaoka was very important in San Celina County. He knew all the big farmers in the area and he would take these men from Japan out to the farms to see how they worked. The men used to bring me beautiful dolls in glass cases dressed in hand-stitched kimonos made of real silk in the most amazing yellows and reds and blues."

"He must have been very respected in the community."

"He was," she said softly. "They arrested him the day after Pearl Harbor was bombed."

"Who did?"

She stood up and straightened her nubby skirt, signaling that the interview was coming to a close. "An old friend of my father's, the county sheriff, came with three deputies. They all had guns. By order of the FBI, my father was arrested by men he'd eaten breakfast with." She looked at her hands. "Because of his involvement in the community and because of his contacts in Japan, he was considered a so-called risk to national security. They took him to North Dakota to a camp. Of course, we didn't know that at the time. We didn't know where they'd taken him until the end of the war. A couple of months later, in February, my mother and I were sent to an assembly camp at a racetrack in Southern California. Then later to a camp in Poston, Arizona. When we boarded the bus, there were soldiers standing guard with rifles. In Japanese, I kept asking my mother what did we do, why were we being sent to jail. She just cried, jerked my shoulder and told me to speak English."

"I'm sorry," I said, not knowing what else to say.

"Don't get me wrong," she said. "Some people were good to the Japanese and we were especially fortunate. My mother sold our store to a Caucasian friend. After the war, he sold it back to us for the same price he paid. Not everyone was that lucky, though. Many, especially those who leased their land or their stores, lost everything." She smiled at me. "Now, I really must go before I am drawn and quartered by my department head."

I turned off the tape recorder and put it back into my purse. "Thank you for your time. When I write this up, I'll drop it by for your approval. If there's anything else you'd like to add, we can do it then. Also, if you wouldn't mind, are there any pictures of your family that you'd consider letting us use in the book?"

"I'll look through my mother's albums," she said, locking the door behind us.

As she started to walk away, I thought of something. "Do you think any of the other members of your family would talk to me? I mean, if any of them are still living around here."

"My mother might. She's lived with me since my father died ten years ago. And my brother . . ." She paused and swallowed hard. "My brother was ten years older than me. He came with us to the camp and later that year the Army came and asked for volunteers. He became a part of the 442nd Regimental Combat Team. Most people don't know this, but they were the most honored combat unit in the war. He was killed in Italy in 1944."

"I'm sorry," I said again.

"My father was never the same," she said quietly. "When the war was over and we reclaimed our store, he worked just as hard, but it wasn't the same. For a Japanese man to lose his only son . . ." Her face drew in with sadness. "My father loved me very much, but I wasn't a son. You understand?"

I nodded, thinking maybe I did, a little. Though the Ramsey name was carried on through my father's nephews, his line stopped with me. Even if Jack and I would have had a son, he wouldn't have been a Ramsey. I often wondered if that bothered my father. "Can I ask you one last thing?"

"Certainly."

"The person who bought your store and then sold it back to you. I'd like to interview him or his relatives. It would make a nice sidebar to your story. Would you mind telling me his name?"

She shook her head slightly, a quizzical look on her face. "I guess there's no reason why you would know."

"Know what?"

"Mr. O'Hara. Brady O'Hara, poor old soul. He was the man who saved my family's store."

9

ON THE WAY back to my truck, Mariko Thompson's words rang through my mind in a jumbled cacophony. I'd done some reading on what had happened to Japanese-Americans during World War II, but this was the first time I'd heard a personal story. I tried to imagine the confusion Mariko must have felt as a little girl, the fear of her parents, the unspoken anger at a country so willing to use the youth and patriotism of their son while at the same time tearing their family apart. And all simply because of the color of their skin, the shape of their eyes. Why weren't we taught this in school? Even my American History classes in college seemed to have skipped over the story of the Japanese-Americans. Then there was the revelation about Mr. O'Hara. To say I was surprised at his kindness and generosity would be an understatement. It certainly didn't fit the cranky old man I'd encountered at Oak Terrace. But then again, people weren't always what they seemed. I'd lived long enough to know that.

As I walked past the Snak Shak, the toasty scent of corn dogs and fried tacos ruffled my taste buds. According to Daffy's brazen little fingers, it was a little past one o'clock. Guilt about the way I didn't answer the phone when Gabe tried to call back last night started to prick at my conscience. Mahi's Fish Taco, one of his favorite restaurants, was on the way back to town, so I decided a conciliatory lunch was the mature, grownup thing to do. Someone had to be adult in this relationship, I told myself, deliberately ignoring the memory of my juvenile refusal to answer the phone last night.

Old Woody station wagons, topless Jeeps and rust-eaten Toyota Land Cruisers equipped with an imaginative array of homemade surfboard carriers crowded the parking lot of the bright aqua and white wood-frame building. Mahi's was a popular eatery with most of the Central Coast's surfers, body builders and health food fanatics. As always, I looked a bit out of place in my jeans and boots among the baggy jams, salt-crusted topsiders and Pirate Surf tee shirts of the regular customers, but this was Gabe's favorite food, and I knew he wouldn't turn it down no matter how mad he was at me.

A blond guy wearing a crew cut and a lime-green "Surf the World" tee shirt packed two orders of char-broiled fish tacos, Peruvian rice and spicy black beans to go while I talked with the owner, Joe Miyamoto. Part Hispanic and part Japanese, he was a short, thick-chested man with a laugh you felt down to your heels. Every time we ate here, he had another half-breed joke for Gabe, each one more outrageous than the last.

"Chief Big Shot too busy to leave the office, huh?" He threw in extra containers of their extra-hot jalapeno chile salsa.

"You know how it is. Crime never sleeps."

"Well, tell him I caught that wahoo just for him 'cause I knew it was his favorite." Joe spent half his time on his family's fishing boat catching the *pescado de hoy* listed on the blackboard every morning.

"Joe, you know as well as I do that he doesn't let *anyone* slide on their parking tickets."

He laughed. "Hey, it doesn't hurt to butter up the law when you can. Why do you think I keep this around?" He handed me a can of Welch's Grape soda. "What does he see in that stuff?"

"Beats me," I said, handing him my money. "I think

it's all those electrical storms they have in the Midwest. Short-circuited his brain.''

I couldn't decide if my luck was good or bad when I drove into the police department's parking lot and his Corvette was in its space. I looked at his personalized license plate—68 VET. It had a triple meaning—the year of the car, the year he graduated high school midterm, the year he went to Vietnam. Layers of meaning. Seemingly straightforward on top, more complex as you delved into it. A lot like its owner.

"What are you doing up here?" I asked Miguel, another of Elvia's six younger brothers. He sat behind the front counter filling an old gray stapler. Gabe had recently instituted a new policy under which none of the patrol officers worked the front desk unless they were injured. A waste of good training, he'd said.

Miguel slammed the stapler shut and shoved it aside. "Hurt my knee last week trying to handcuff some stupid-ass drunk college twerp. I'll be back out in a few days."

"Head honcho around?" I asked.

His broad chest inflated and he let out a sharp breath, narrowing his dark-chocolate eyes at me. "Oh, he's around all right. What I want to know is what you did to him and whatever it is, cut it out before the whole force goes on strike."

"Bad mood, huh?"

"The worst." He buzzed the swinging door to unlock it and let me into the office area. "Do something, Benni. Before there's a mutiny."

"You know, I am not the only thing in his life that could cause a bad mood."

Miguel gave a mocking snort. "I have a girlfriend. Nothin' messes with our minds like you women."

"Turn blue," I said cheerfully, reverting to one of our childhood insults.

"I mean it," he called after me. "They're cutting the plank out in Maintenance right now."

It took me a few minutes to dig up the nerve to knock on the heavy wood door bearing the brass nameplate

AARON DAVIDSON, CHIEF OF POLICE. Another reminder of the tenuousness of my relationship with Gabe. Would they offer him a permanent job now that it was practically certain Aaron would resign? Would he take it? Did I really want him to?

When silence answered my second knock, I opened the door. The room was cool and empty and so quiet the sound of the city's maintenance yard filtered through the large picture window on the north wall. I walked across the plush brown carpet and set the two white lunch sacks on the corner of his desk. The papers spread across the polished oak executive desk told me he'd only stepped away for a moment; otherwise they'd be neatly filed away. Studying someone's workspace when they aren't around reveals a lot about a person, though this office didn't tell me anything about Gabe I didn't already know—organized, quiet, calm, but with an electric undercurrent of activity, of things getting done quickly, properly. It still looked as if he were visiting though, something that vaguely troubled me. The decor in this room had become familiar to me in the last few months: the surrealistic cactus painting behind his desk, the brass Star of David paperweight, the picture of Aaron's wife, Rachel, and their daughter, Esther, on the oak credenza behind the tall black leather executive chair. But nothing said "Gabriel Ortiz," even though he'd worked here almost six months. After a minute or so of honest resistance to temptation, I riffled through the papers on his desk, my heart a pulsating drumbeat in my ears. Most of them were scientific jargon that didn't mean squat to me, but one page was as clear as a mama cow's bawl on branding day. It was a faxed copy of a Delta County, Colorado, Sheriff's criminal record on Clayton O'Hara. He'd been arrested three times in 1988 for DUI, twice in 1990 for simple assault, and twice in 1992, both times for aggravated assault, battery and resisting arrest. In each case the charges were dropped or reduced with sentence suspended. It didn't take a dummy to see he'd apparently never learned to control that temper of his and that someone, probably his father, had quite a bit of influence in Delta County.

I carefully slipped the fax back where I found it and was standing by the window observing the workers in the maintenance yard when the door opened.

We contemplated each other warily for a moment, neither of us knowing exactly what to say. I broke the silence.

"I brought you lunch."

"So I see." He sat down in his chair, his face blank, his eyes steely and unwavering and lobbed the ball back into my court.

I walked over and stood next to his desk. "Look, I'm sorry I hung up on you last night. That was rude."

"Yes, it was."

"But I don't like you calling my grandmother when you don't like something I do."

"I wouldn't if you'd listen to me and stay out of this investigation." He leaned back in his chair, a critical, cool look on his face. "I'm only thinking of your safety."

I crossed my arms and stared back. In my opinion, my safety wasn't the only topic of debate here. Anger flickered between us like static electricity, but this time I wasn't going to be the one to give in.

"Look," he finally said. "I'm having a real bad day and I'd rather not get into this now. Why don't we just deal with it later?"

"We're going to have to deal with it someday," I pointed out. "One way or another."

"I'm starved," he said, opening one of the bags. The smoky aroma of broiled fish and warm corn tortillas filled the room. "This looks great." He opened the other bag, pulled out the sweating can of grape soda, and grinned.

"I don't see how you can stand that stuff," I said, annoyed but secretly relieved. Deep down, I wanted to avoid the conflict as much as he did.

"Well, it's not as good as Nehi, but it'll do." He stripped off his navy suit coat, loosened his tie and rolled up the sleeves of his white shirt.

We talked about inconsequential things as we ate—how he was going to fix the clutch on my truck, my interviews for the Historical Society, our plans to visit Aaron and Rachel the day after tomorrow.

"I'd better get back to the museum," I said, stuffing empty wrappers in the white bags. "I don't have much time left to finish this exhibit."

"Just a minute, I want you to see something." He shuffled through the papers he'd stacked to the side while we ate. He held out the fax containing Clay's criminal record. "I thought you'd like to take a look at this one more time."

"What do you mean?" I hoped my face didn't look as guilty as my voice sounded.

The edges of his mouth turned down in a jaded look. I grabbed the fax, skimmed it and shoved it back across the desk. "So?"

"Since you insist on seeing him, I just want you to know who you're dealing with."

"So he has a bit of a temper. I knew that. That doesn't mean he would kill a couple of harmless old people. These were probably barroom brawls. Big difference between that and murdering senior citizens."

Gabe propped his elbow on his chair arm, rested his chin in his hand, and regarded me with unblinking eyes. The question in them was the same one in my mind, though I wasn't about to say it out loud. Why was I defending Clay? What possible difference could it make to me one way or another? For an uncomfortable moment, I felt seventeen again. Maybe the answer lay there somewhere. Of course, the scenario was a bit different this time. I was a grown woman and Gabe definitely wasn't my father.

"I gotta go," I said, tossing the bags in the trash and heading for the door.

"Benni—" His serious tone stopped me, my hand frozen on the doorknob. Reluctantly, I turned my head around.

He sat forward in his chair and picked up a pencil, moving it back and forth through his fingers. "There's no reason for me to tell you this."

I let go of the door and faced him. He continued playing with the pencil. "Well?" I said impatiently.

"Our source in Colorado says Clay and his father might

inherit a substantial part of Mr. O'Hara's estate."

"You don't know what's in Mr. O'Hara's will? I thought the police had access to that sort of information."

"Unfortunately, we don't until it's probated and made public record. And that could take months or years depending on how long his attorney chooses to hold things up."

"What does Clay say?"

"Obviously, he's not talking."

I thought about that for a moment. "Even if he does inherit, that's just circumstantial evidence."

"True." He pulled at his mustache and frowned. "But we're waiting for more information about how badly they could use that money and how quickly they need it. As you well know, cattle ranches aren't the best way to make a living these days. Circumstances may have compelled your Mr. O'Hara into deciding he couldn't wait for his uncle's natural death."

"But why would he kill Miss Violet? That doesn't make sense. There were plenty of opportunities for him to kill his uncle without making it a double murder. Why would he risk that?"

"Good questions. And ones *I* will find the answers to, not you."

"I'll ask you one more time. Is Clay the only suspect?"

"No." He lifted his chin slightly.

"Who are the others?"

He laughed sarcastically and stood up. "I'm not that crazy. I'm having a hard enough time keeping you away from Clay O'Hara. You think I want to make my job even more difficult? Now be a *muchacha buena* and go back to the museum."

I cocked an eyebrow. "Be a good girl? Really, Gabe, let's not try for the sexist Hall of Fame here."

"Sweetheart, I was just kidding," he said, coming around the desk and putting his arms around me. I pulled out of his embrace and reached for the door. He held it closed with the palm of his hand. I briefly contemplated a wrestling match, but he outweighed me by over eighty pounds. Resting my hand on the doorknob, I stared at the corded muscle under the dark hair on his forearm and tried to ignore the urge to touch my lips to it.

"Benni," he said. "Have a heart. Let's not argue anymore."

I opened my mouth, ready to give another smart retort, when a peppery knock rattled the door.

"Just a minute," he called out, his hand still flat on the door.

I twisted the knob and pulled lightly. "Okay, Tarzan, you can cut the chest-beating routine any time now."

"Not until we've hammered this out or you're at least smiling."

I glared up at him. "Isn't that just like a man? Now that *you're* ready to talk, I'm supposed to snap to it. Well, guess again, pal."

"I don't have any appointments. I can stand here all day."

The phone on his desk buzzed.

"Looks like your adoring public is calling," I said smugly. "You'd better let me go before your employees get the idea you're ravishing me in here or something."

He bent his head, brushed his lips across the soft, vulnerable spot just under my ear and whispered, *"Querida,* you don't know ravishing yet."

The rasp of his mustache against my neck caused my stomach to lurch and a nervous laugh gurgled from my throat.

"That's better," he said, releasing his hand.

"Friday, your chauvinism is beyond compare," I said, irritated at my body's swift response to him. "And don't overestimate your abilities."

"Just the facts, ma'am, just the facts."

I groaned. "Give me a break."

"I'll call Rachel tonight and see what would be a good time to go and see Aaron," he said, walking back to the buzzing phone, a confident grin under his thick mustache. "I'll let you know."

"Pardon me," I said, pushing past the patrol officer

standing outside the door, his face pink with embarrassment. Then I slammed it loudly behind me. Gabe's laugh sounded through the thick oak.

Miguel's sour look hadn't changed in the last hour. "Did you kiss and make up?" he asked. "Can I call Maintenance and stop construction?"

"You know, you're being awfully cocky to someone who could tell stories to your macho buddies about your rabid fear of lizards, when you really stopped wetting the bed, what your father's favorite nickname for you is—*mi pollo chiquito. . . .*"

"Ah, Benni," he said, glancing around to see if anyone heard, his cheeks a rosy nutmeg. "I was just kidding."

"That seems to be the operative word around here today," I said.

As I walked back out to the truck, needles of guilt still pricked at my conscience because of the information I was keeping from Gabe. But as much as he was beginning to mean to me, I couldn't imagine a permanent relationship with someone who insisted on keeping me out of a whole section of his life. It was simply a matter of trust. Was I in love with him? Who could tell? The last time I fell in love I was sixteen years old. My emotional feelings for Gabe felt entirely different from those I remember experiencing when I first met Jack as an adolescent, though my physical reactions were embarrassingly similar. All I knew was that at thirty-four, relationships were certainly more complex. Of course, I don't know why that should surprise me, everything else was too.

Since, as usual, I couldn't figure out my personal life, I decided to get back to the museum and catch up on some work. I'd had three new assistants in the last two months, none of whom lasted longer than two weeks. We could only afford to pay minimum wage for the twenty-hour-a-week position and the students who had tried the job came to the astute conclusion that McDonald's or Taco Bell was easier and less responsibility. My preferred method of supervision was to give my assistant a job list for the week and have the work completed without any further prompting from me. That proved to be too complicated for most college students. I was almost done with the cross-stitch exhibit, but there were piles of paperwork to catch up on, a maintenance check on all the equipment, more beggary letters to compose and send and a stack of forms that needed to be filled out for the city concerning the earthquake safety of the museum. That didn't even include keeping everything clean and supplies ordered. Desperation for an assistant was rapidly overtaking me.

While driving past the museum's nearest neighbor, the monolithic silver building of the Coastal Valley Farm Supply, I automatically searched the crowded parking lot for familiar ranch trucks. At the San Celina Feed and Grain Co-op across the street, I spotted the white GMC pickup of Daddy's best friend, Mr. Allison. He was probably sitting on one of the hay bales in back, spitting from his cheekful of Copenhagen into an empty Coke can and complaining about the low price his Angus calves were fetching this year. It seemed a lifetime ago when my weekly trip to one or both of those places was as much a part of my life as the daily flossing of my teeth.

The museum's gravel parking lot was packed with cars. Most of the artists were over the post-Christmas doldrums and gearing up for the Mardi Gras Street Festival where the co-op would set up a large crafts booth. The festival-loving Central Coast was a lifeline for most of the artisans, bringing in throngs of tourists and locals to purchase their work. In the co-op studios, every corner bustled with some sort of activity—the buzz of conversation and machines sounded almost as comforting to me as the sound of lowing cattle.

"You've got a visitor," Malcolm said. He switched off the spinning pottery wheel and twisted around to face me. "Actually, I think he's an applicant."

"Oh, that's . . . great," I said, trying to sound enthusiastic and wondering what Cal Poly's job placement office had sent over this time.

"Your excitement is overwhelming," he said with a

chuckle. He picked up a stained rag and started wiping the slick clay from his hands.

"Well, you have to admit, things have been a bit erratic for me in that department lately."

"Cheer up, this may be your lucky day."

"Yeah, right." I headed toward the long hallway that leads past the woodshop and storage rooms, humming "I Feel Lucky" by Mary Chapin Carpenter, hoping my positive attitude would influence fate. Passing by the open door of the woodshop, I waved to the three men cutting out animal-shaped clock faces for the tole painters. The saws and sanders buzzed in a high-pitched symphony that smelled as sweet and full of possibilities as the first day of summer.

Ahead of me, my office door loomed. Behind it could be a prize or a dud. I was beginning to wonder if the lady at the placement office had a grudge against me. Of course, the less than enthusiastic response to the job might have something to do with the fact that my last assistant was killed on the premises. I opened the door and looked at the young man sitting in the visitor's chair in front of my desk, cradling a camera in his lap.

"Todd," I said, surprised. "I . . . Can I help you?" I looked around my small office. "There was supposed to be someone here from the college for the assistant's job. Did they leave?"

"It's me," he said, looking down at the floor, his fingers caressing the Nikon. "I want it."

"Oh." I sat down in my chair, a bit taken aback. "I thought Ramon said you worked with your grandfather. We need someone who can work at least twenty hours a week. Sometimes on the weekends. Can you manage two jobs and your classes too?"

"Yes," he said, studying his heavy black boots. One foot moved up and down in a nervous hammering.

I waited for him to elaborate. I liked Todd, but I didn't need someone who'd overfilled his plate just because he needed money for some new lens or something.

His bottom lip jutted out in that half-defiant, half-ashamed look adolescent boys get when forced to ask an adult for a favor. "My grandfather's store, it's . . . it's not doing so good. He can't really afford to pay me."

There was a moment of uncomfortable silence. "That's too bad," I said. "I guess a lot of businesses are having trouble these days."

He exhaled sharply and tossed his long silky hair. "It's not that he's stupid or a bad businessman or anything. It's just that . . ." He paused, his Adam's apple moving convulsively. "My mom's and grandmother's funerals cost a lot of money. We . . . uh . . . didn't have insurance and stuff." He looked down and started picking at the red, raw cuticles on his brown chemical-stained fingers.

"Your grandmother?" I said, confused. "I'm sorry. I didn't realize . . ."

He didn't look up. "She had a heart attack a couple of months before my mom . . . well, you know." He brought a forefinger up to his mouth and chewed at a piece of skin.

I studied the doodles on my desk blotter, in a quandary about what to do. My heart said, Give him the job and pick up any slack he can't handle; my head said, He's a nice kid, but you can't save the world and you don't have time for this.

While I argued with myself, he avoided my eyes and played with the zoom lens on his Nikon. I knew it was hard for a boy his age to tell anyone his personal problems or to ask for help. I also knew I was taking a chance hiring him. But how could I say no? Maybe he would be a better employee than any others I'd had simply because he needed the job so badly.

"Okay," I said, sitting forward. "We'll give it a try. Do you know how to use tools at all?"

"Sure," he said, his face brightening for the first time since I walked into the office. "I'm real good at fixing things."

I stood up and walked him to the door. "Come by tomorrow at ten o'clock and I'll give you your first week's assignments."

"Thanks. You won't regret it, I swear." He gave me a

grateful smile and loped off down the hallway.

"I sincerely hope not," I said under my breath. Getting in the middle of someone's family problems was the last thing I needed right now. With Mac and Clay and their complicated positions in the murders of Mr. O'Hara and Miss Violet and with the cross-stitch exhibit due to open in the next two weeks, not to mention those chapters for Dove I still needed to research and write, or my tennis-match relationship with Gabe, I didn't need an emotionally upset teenage assistant. I was seriously considering Elvia's suggestion to post the job in the senior citizen center next to the library. She'd gotten two of her most dependable employees that way. My only hesitation was that the heavy lifting required by the job might prove to be too much for a person in their sixties or seventies. But at this point, if Todd didn't work out, I might reconsider the seniors and work out something with the men in the co-op about the heavy lifting.

Cheer up, I told myself. At least he isn't having girlfriend problems. *Yet,* said a reproachful little voice inside me.

For the next hour I tried to concentrate on the cross-stitch exhibit, but I couldn't get Sissy's revelation out of my mind. The only person who could clear up what happened that night and whether it had anything to do with the murders, was Oralee. I also knew I couldn't ask her about it without talking to Mac first. He and I had been friends too long for me to be that deceitful. And I knew I'd want to horsewhip anyone who bothered Dove behind my back.

At First Baptist, his secretary, a sixtyish matron with a no-nonsense brown wool suit and a protective, motherly feeling for her employer, put me through the wringer before revealing Mac's whereabouts. Mondays were apparently his only day off and he'd driven out to the Reid Ranch to clear brush and chop some wood. Driving over Rosita Pass toward North County, I rehearsed my explanation about why I felt it important for me to question Oralee about a fifty-year-old incident. To be truthful, I couldn't come up with one good reason why I should be involved, something that made me increasingly apprehensive as I neared the turnoff for the Reid Ranch. I drove up the long gravel driveway resisting the thought that Gabe might be right and that I should stay out of it.

The long brown ranch house and peeling outbuildings appeared sad and neglected in the early afternoon sunlight. Mac's dark blue Ford Bronco crowded the narrow driveway in front of the empty house whose brick-lined flower beds sprouted a field of crispy flower stalks and green, healthy weeds. Oralee had been gone only three months, but it didn't take long for nature to start reasserting itself. The front lawn, once her pride and joy, was a tan, dry square with two fresh gopher hills marring its smooth expanse. When I stepped down from my truck, the sharp afternoon breeze hurled Emmy Lou Harris' stereophonic voice over the top of the house. "I was born to run," she wailed. In the backyard, I found Mac in a black tank top and tattered Levi's, swinging a long-handled axe as if his life depended on it. His biceps were large and tanned, his pale nickel-sized vaccination scar visible from where I stood. I watched for a few moments just for the sheer pleasure of observing a perfectly formed example of the male half of our species using his muscles as God intended.

"Hey," I called out. "Cut me a cord while you're at it."

He glanced up, startled. With an embarrassed grin, he wiped the shine off his forehead with the back of his hand and turned the radio down. "Hi," he said. "What are you doing here?" His face grew anxious. "There's nothing wrong with Grandma, is there? The phone here was disconnected a while back . . ."

"Nope," I said, walking toward him. "I just wanted to talk. I charmed your secretary into telling me where you were. It wasn't easy, either." I sat down in an old tulip-back metal patio chair. "Do you have a few minutes?"

"Sure," he said. He leaned the long axe against the chopping block and pulled up a matching rusty chair. "What can I help you with?"

His face appeared so genial, so eager to listen, I looked

down and studied my hands, unable to meet his gentle gray eyes.

"Benni," he said softly. "Is there something wrong between you and Gabe?"

"No," I said quickly. "I mean, yes, but that's not why I want to talk to you. I . . ."

He leaned back in his seat, his bulk causing the metal chair to give out a painful screech. "It's about what happened at the murder scene, isn't it?" His voice sounded weary, as if the subject were a problem he'd spent years contemplating with no hope of an answer.

"Sort of," I admitted. "Actually, someone's told me something that I think only Oralee can shed some light on and I wanted to ask you if it was okay if I talked to her."

He stroked his beard, his eyes uncertain. "I guess it depends on what it is."

Watching his face, I repeated Sissy's story. The retelling made it seem even more improbable and dramatic. He seemed to absorb my words, his face expressionless as a sponge. When I finished, he nodded but didn't comment. Waiting for his response, I watched a mockingbird dart from an elm tree to an oak to a dying pine, marking its territory with a concert of borrowed chirps and trills. I wished I could tell it not to worry, soon it would have the whole place to itself, at least until the land is divided up into two-acre ranchettes or planted with rows of wine grapes.

"I'm not going to forbid you to see my grandmother," Mac finally said. "She's lived life on her own terms for too many years for me to step in and tell her what to do. She trusts you and I trust her, so whatever she decides you should know is fine with me." He paused, adjusted himself in the squeaky chair and continued. "I want you to know I'm going to talk to Gabe tomorrow. Putting you in the position I did wasn't fair."

"You're going to tell him what you took from Miss Violet's room," I said, relieved, though just slightly. I wasn't entirely off the hook. I still had to tell Gabe I had known about it all along and try and make him understand why I didn't tell him right away.

"I'm going to tell him I took something," Mac said evenly. "What I took has been destroyed, so it has no power over anyone anymore."

"That's not going to satisfy him," I said. "He'll want to know what it was."

"I can't tell him."

"Why not?"

"I can't tell you that. It's not my story to tell."

"Is it Oralee's?"

He shrugged and stood up, rubbing his hands on the sides of his jeans. "I do have one question for you, though."

"What's that?"

"Why are *you* so interested in all this?"

Good question. It had been a good question since the beginning of this whole business, and I wasn't going to tell him he was way down on the list of people who wanted to know the answer. I gave him the only one I'd been able to come up with.

"I don't know. I just can't seem to let it go. Or it can't seem to let me go."

"Maybe it's easier."

"Than what?" I looked at him, confused.

"Dealing with the real issues in your life."

"Such as?" I said, annoyed at what sounded like a superior tone in his voice.

"You and Gabe."

Now he was getting too personal. My throat constricted in anger. "Maybe you shouldn't be looking for ticks on someone else's dog, Mac. How do you justify what you've done with the sermons you preach on Sunday?" The minute the words were out of my mouth, I regretted them. The pain that swept across his face told me he'd spent some troubled hours wondering just that very thing.

"I can't," he said, picking up a large piece of oakwood and setting it in the middle of the chopping block. The muscles of his arms flexed when he picked up the axe. His face was cool, his eyes flat as primer paint. "Is that all?"

I inhaled deeply, then let it out. "Yes," I said, still angry, but also hurt over this rift between us. "I would never do anything to hurt Oralee, Mac. You know that, don't you?"

He lifted the axe high over his head and slammed it down, splitting the oak log in half. I jumped back when one piece landed inches from my left foot.

"I sincerely hope not" was all he said.

10

WHEN I STARTED for home, it was close to six o'clock and getting dark. Driving back over Rosita Pass in the lavender twilight, I rolled down my window and let the sweet, intoxicating smell of early spring wash over me. The hills, brown and fuzzy as a terrier's coat, were already splattered green in spots as if some environmental artist had thrown sporadic buckets of brilliant emerald paint over them. I rested my eyes and mind on the black, turned-over fields and the sturdy young cows bunched together near water troughs, guarding their calves. In a sky that seemed too blue and heavy to hold them, hawks swept and dived for gray ground life among the uniform rows of plastic-covered berry plants. I felt a soft comfort settle inside me. Despite the human confusion that rumbled beneath us all like a separating of the earth's plates, the cycle of seasons, like a dependable worker bee, droned on.

Mac's dilemma was not one I envied. Whatever evidence he took, it was obvious he did it to protect his grandmother. I'm sure I would have done the same thing, but I also knew, that being a minister, he would be judged by a harsher standard than I would have been. Hating myself for even considering it, I couldn't help but wonder how far he would go to protect his grandmother.

I swung by Baskin-Robbins for my dinner of a chocolate

fudge brownie sundae, drove home and parked myself on the sofa, trying to figure the whole mess out. A part of me wanted to run to Gabe and confess everything, place it all in his competent hands and return to my artists and my samplers and my Historical Society interviews. But Mac and Oralee were like family to me. I had to talk to her before my mind could lay it to rest.

I was lying back on the sofa, attempting to push my boots off with my toes without actually sitting up, when the phone rang. In no mood to talk to anyone, I did something I despise in other people—screened the call. After hearing the message, I was glad I did.

"Benni, this is your daddy." Daddy's voice was stiff and he enunciated each word slowly, as if talking to a toddler or a very stupid adult. I tried to tell him when I bought the machine to just talk normal when he left a message. "What do you mean?" he'd asked indignantly. "I am talking normal."

"Your daddy," he repeated, in case I didn't quite get it the first time. "You can tell that gramma of yours I will not eat that pig slop she's been cooking *one more night*. A hardworking man deserves his meat and potatoes. Tell her." The sound of his angry hang-up cracked across the room like a bullwhip.

I ate three more spoonfuls of my dinner, telling myself if I was a truly good daughter I would call him back and find out what was really going on. Five minutes later, I was still thinking about it when the phone rang again.

"Benni." Dove's sharp voice waited for my response. Knowing her, she probably already knew I was here. Just out of spite, I kept listening.

"Benni, answer me." Her voice rose an octave.

"Yes, ma'am," I called from where I was sitting. She probably had my house bugged, so why bother picking up the phone?

"Wherever you are, when you get back, you can tell that daddy of yours if he don't like what I cook, he knows where the pots and pans are. I refuse to fry potatoes *one more time*. Seventy-five years is long enough. Ahmad says

Persian food is very healthy. I hear they live to be a hundred and twenty there in—well, wherever his people live."

Beep.

Just like old times. When I was growing up, Dove and Daddy would get mad at each other and communicate through me for days. The answering machine added a whole new dimension to it, though. I'd never had one when I lived with Jack at the Harper Ranch. Dove would just come stay with me until Daddy finally came to his senses, agreed with her and apologized. With the help of modern technology, this feud could last months. I wondered what would happen if I mailed them the tape. And who the heck was Ahmad?

Past experience helped me decide to leave them to their own devices, at least for tonight. I spent the rest of the evening catching up on laundry, dirty dishes and scanning the books on writing oral histories. At eleven o'clock, just before I turned out my light to go to sleep, Gabe called to say good night. He'd fallen into the habit about a month ago and it had gradually become part of my bedtime ritual, one that made me a little nervous because I'd grown to look forward to it, even depend upon it. The loneliness of falling asleep alone had been one of the hardest adjustments to make since Jack died. That and waking up to a silent house. With all its problems, I had liked being married. As irritating as men could sometimes be, I enjoyed their unpredictability and the way, without you noticing, their strong musky scent gradually permeated the hidden corners of your possessions and your life.

"I missed you today," he said. "I wish you were here beside me right now. I swear I'd—"

"Don't say anything you might have to arrest yourself for, Friday." I broke into his words with a laugh. "Besides, this time of night, I might not be able to resist."

"That's what I'm counting on."

Then we laid in our separate beds, comforted only by goosedown and the sound of each other's voices. On the same wavelength for once, we stayed away from anything about the murders. I thought about telling him what I'd learned from Sissy and Mac, then decided against it. I'd have to tell him sooner or later, but I didn't want to ruin this peaceful truce we'd finally achieved.

"Dream sweet, *querida*," he said, before hanging up. "That's an order." His voice was mild and sleepy. Its low, late-night sound wrapped around me with the warmth and security of an old wool blanket.

"Yes, sir, Chief," I answered, contemplating for a split second just how long it would take for me to drive my truck the three miles to his house.

The next morning, in penance for my dinner, I fixed myself some oatmeal, telling myself I could truthfully inform Gabe I'd started eating healthier. I stirred butter, brown sugar and half-and-half into my cereal, attempting to make it taste a little less like pasty water and thought about Oralee. The ladies from the Oak Terrace quilting class were being bused to the museum to start quilting on the Steps to the Altar quilt today. The quilt was king-sized and the small crafts room at Oak Terrace couldn't comfortably accommodate a quilt rack of any size. Maybe I could pull Oralee aside and casually ask her about Sissy's story concerning her father's late-night house call.

I pulled on jeans, a red and blue plaid flannel shirt, then walked out on the front porch to check the temperature and decide what sort of jacket I'd need.

"Hey, Mr. Treton," I called to my neighbor. He looked up from the hedge that separated our two yards. It had been trimmed with precision that befitted his thirty-year stint in the Army. "What's new?"

"Have you talked to your young man yet?" He pointed his wooden-handled clippers at me. "About the electric company?"

"Yes, sir," I said. "It's on his list of things to do but maybe, just to jog his memory, you should give him a call." I laughed to myself, picturing the conversation between them. "I've got to go now. Have to get down to the museum and turn on the heat for my quilting class."

He grunted and went back to his pruning.

On the way to the museum I stopped at The Donut Corral

to pick up a few dozen doughnuts to serve with coffee and tea during our mid-morning break. The sky was thick with clouds, some white cotton, others mottled a foreboding coyote gray that blatantly disregarded the forecast earlier in the week for clear skies. Apparently the weather today would be a toss of the coin. Even Angus Al's weather report on KCOW this morning straddled the fence—"Maybe rain, maybe not. Your goose is as good as mine." He honked his squawky blooper horn. They were inordinately fond of barnyard humor on KCOW.

It felt peaceful being alone in the museum and inspecting the almost finished sampler exhibit. The adobe walls and free-standing cork-covered display boards the woodworkers had designed and built were crammed corner to corner with samplers. There was enough reading material here to rival the new library over by Central Park. After fiddling with the thermostat back in the studios, I returned to the museum and strolled through the exhibit, straightening a frame here and there and rereading some of my favorite verses.

"A house is made of brick and stone, A home is made of love alone—To my daughter, Sarah, on the day of her wedding—M.E. Worley 1926''; "Let me live in the house by the side of the road and be a friend to man—Jan Anagoni, Taos, N.M. 1962''; "To cultivate a garden is to walk with God—Hendricka Bas 1943''; "A Merry Heart doeth good like a Medicine—Suzanne Matthews 1931''; "A sorrow shared is but half a trouble, A joy that's shared is a joy made double—Retha Smith to Birdie Baker, Kingman, Kansas 1954''; "Remembering is the sweetest flower, Of all this world's perfuming, Memory guards it sun or shower, Friendship keeps it blooming—Kathleen Webb 1919.''

I'd even contributed one of my own samplers. I'd saved a corner spot in the back of the room and when it was hung, I would feel the exhibit was finished. I pulled it from under the counter in the gift shop and studied the familiar colors and patterns—the blue border of hollyhocks, the deep brown, contented-looking cattle, the peach-colored house with a man and woman in overalls standing in front. The words were as well known to me as the feel of Dove's hands.

"Grow old along with me! The best is yet to be, The last of life, for which the first was made, Our times are in His hand—ALR to JWH, San Celina, California, February 1, 1978."

My wedding present to Jack. It had taken me three months to stitch. Long, warm evenings in front of the fire with Dove, planning my future, a future that looked as certain and optimistic as Browning's words. I'd packed it away at the bottom of my cedar chest when I moved from the ranch, unable to bring myself to even look at it. But when this exhibit came about, something compelled me to dig it out. I sat in front of the chest at the foot of my bed, wondering if seeing it would upset me. But only happy memories surfaced when I unwrapped it from its tissue paper cocoon. I'd discovered in the last year, somewhat to my surprise, that the things I thought would tear my heart out, sometimes gave me the most comfort. Displaying this symbol of Jack and me in the exhibit seemed right somehow. I unrolled some paper towels and started cleaning the film from the glass, when a knock sounded on the locked front door. The round oak-framed clock above the door said seven. I opened it with some hesitation. There wasn't an artist in the co-op who would be up this early, no matter how far behind in their work.

Todd stood there, his rangy arms dangling at his side, looking naked without his usual camera.

"Sorry," he said, holding up his hands. "I thought I'd come early to start work. When I saw your truck, I thought . . ." He stuck his hands into the pockets of his baggy black jeans and ducked his head, hair flopping in his face. "I can come back at ten like you said." He looked back up at me helplessly.

"No, come on in," I said. "I was just putting a few finishing touches on the exhibit. I'm glad you decided to come early. It was going to be almost impossible for me to get that quilt rack set up by myself."

His face relaxed slightly from its uneasy expression. It

took all I had not to hug him like he was one of my young cousins and tell him everything was going to be okay.

Even with two of us, it was difficult getting the frame set straight on the sawhorses. Thanks to four of the co-op's quilters, the quilt itself had already been stretched and squared-off evenly on the rack, and the three layers of backing, batting and top had been basted together. After setting a dozen or so metal folding chairs around the quilt, I put Todd to work washing long-neglected windows and vacuuming the museum.

The minibus from Oak Terrace arrived at nine sharp, and within half an hour everyone was situated around the quilt rack, mouths and fingers moving a mile a minute. I'd prudently spent part of the night before filling all the pincushions I could find with threaded #10 Between needles—a favorite size with the ladies. I picked up a needle and sat next to Thelma. I listened with amusement to the women's high, silvery voices as they compared the successes and foibles of their children and grandchildren. The sound of their voices relaxed me, bringing back childhood memories of long summer visits down South to Dove's only sister, my great-aunt Garnet. In Sugar Tree, Arkansas, quilting bees were a twice-a-week habit with the Women's Missionary Union of her church. A good deal of my sex education was acquired by faking sleep on Aunt Garnet's scratchy Victorian sofa and listening to the quilting ladies refer obliquely to the trouble the new wives of the Darcy brothers had due to the rather oversized proportions of their "maleness" or how "that" was never satisfied, no matter how often it happened. Always, just as it started to get detailed and my seven-year-old imagination went wild trying to picture exactly how it all fit with what my obnoxious thirteen-year-old Uncle Arnie told me one of Daddy's Black Angus bulls would do to my sweet-faced little heifer, Dossie, Aunt Garnet reprimanded them in her tight, hard-shell Baptist voice. "Little pitchers have big ears, ladies." She knew I never could sleep in the daytime. Dove would give a big laugh, slap her sister playfully on the shoulder and tell her it was better than me learning it behind the barn.

"So, Benni," Thelma said after a while. Her eyes never left the small diamond she was rocking her needle through. "Have you seen that nice boy, Clay, lately?" On the other side of her, Martha chuckled.

"Just how bad is this flu you said Oralee has?" I asked, sidestepping her question. I had been disappointed when Oralee didn't show up, and wondered just how I could go about approaching her at Oak Terrace.

"Flu, my eye," rabbit-faced Vynelle Williams said. "She's just too lazy to quilt."

"Now, Vynelle," Thelma scolded good-naturedly. "She really wasn't feeling good. Heavens, who can blame her? What happened to Rose Ann and Brady scared all of us more than a tad."

The other ladies in the group murmured agreement. It was exactly the opening I was looking for.

"How's everyone taking the murders there?" I asked.

"Most everyone's doing okay," Thelma said. "Edwin's been running around like a chicken with his head cut off, but then he's always like that."

"Have the police talked to any of you individually?"

"Yes, indeedy," Vynelle said. She snipped a thread, stuck her empty needle in the pincushion sitting on the quilt and picked out another threaded needle. "The next day. We all had appointments to see them in the dining hall."

"What kind of questions did they ask?"

Vynelle looked back down at the quilt and snorted. "The obvious. Who liked Brady, who didn't. Same with Rose Ann. They seemed a bit incompetent to me. Matlock would have had this solved and the murderer in prison by now." She gave me an apologetic look. "No offense to your beau or nothing."

I smiled. "Well, Gabe is certainly no Matlock. What did you tell the detectives?"

"The truth, of course. That the only person that hated Brady that much was Oralee, but then that hasn't been a secret for fifty years."

"You mean their feud is that old? Why did they hate each other so much?" I stopped my stitching and looked around at the ladies.

They eyed each other and remained silent.

I turned to Thelma. "C'mon, what are you all holding back? What about Oralee and Mr. O'Hara?"

Thelma patted my hand. "My dear, some things are best left in the past. Believe me, it was so long ago it couldn't possibly have anything to do with Rose Ann and Brady now. They're in a better place. We should just let them be."

"Well, Rose Ann might be, but I wouldn't be taking bets on Brady," Vynelle said.

"Vynelle Williams!" Thelma admonished. "Now you hush." She turned to me. "We've been at this for an hour. Don't you think it's time for a little coffee break?" She stood up and stretched her thin body. The rest of the women followed her lead and I pointed them toward the coffee, tea and doughnuts Todd and I had set up in the co-op's small kitchen.

"Thelma, could you wait a minute?" I asked as the women moved slowly down the hallway. When everyone was out of the room, I looked her straight in the eye. "Would you just tell me what the deal is between Oralee and Mr. O'Hara? Did you tell the police about it?"

Thelma inspected me with her shrewd brown eyes. "Why do you want to know?"

"The truth?"

"Young lady, seeing as I was your Sunday School teacher for three years, I think I'll ignore that question."

I looked down at my boots, kicked at the floor, then glanced back up. "Gabe has zeroed in on Clay O'Hara because he's the most obvious suspect, but I think he's wrong. I think there's more to it than that."

She looked at me a long time before she spoke. "He is a fine-looking boy." Her lips curled into a small smile. "And very personable."

"Who?"

"Both of them. But I was referring to the O'Hara boy."

"That's not the reason," I protested, trying not to smile back.

"He reminds you a bit of Jack, doesn't he? Or at least that time of your life."

"I just don't think Gabe is being fair," I said weakly. I shifted uncomfortably from one foot to the other. I thought I'd done a good job keeping those thoughts hidden, even from myself. Apparently, my mixed feelings were about as secret as the recipe for Tollhouse cookies.

"Besides all that, you're Dove's granddaughter and you can't stand it when there's a secret you aren't privy to."

I grinned. "That's probably closer to the truth than anything."

She shook her head doubtfully. "I'm not sure what I know about Brady and Oralee has much bearing."

"Why don't you let me decide?"

"I suppose it can't do any harm." She sat down in one of the folding chairs. I sat next to her. "This is actually quite common knowledge. To anyone in our group, anyway."

"What's that?"

She laced her fingers primly in her lap. "Oralee and Brady were quite an item in our younger days."

"An item? You mean they were . . ." I didn't quite know how to put it, good friends, dating, lovers? That last one was too incredible to imagine.

"I mean they were going to be married."

"What?" I leaned toward her, my voice coming out in something resembling a squawk. "They were engaged? Mr. O'Hara and Oralee? When? What happened? You've got to be kidding."

"Now, Benni, don't act so shocked. Hard as it is to believe, all us old folks were as young as you and your beaus at one time. Some of us were known to really cut a rug."

"But Oralee and Mr. O'Hara?" I couldn't in my wildest stretch of imagination picture *that*.

"Brady O'Hara was considered quite the catch back in those days, you know. And Oralee was a pretty attractive woman herself."

"But they're as different as fried chicken and sushi. How in the world could two people so different be attracted to each other?"

She tilted her head and smiled. "Well, dear heart, that's something you'd probably understand better than me."

I rolled my eyes. "Forget my love life. So, what happened to their romance?"

"No one really knows. It was around the time the war started. Everything was crazy those first few months." She touched her pearly gray hair tentatively. "All I know is one day they were engaged, the next they weren't speaking to each other on the street. San Celina was a lot smaller back then. The town itself, that is. With Camp Johnson full of Army boys, there were thousands of military people living in the county, but the hometown folks knew everything that was happening with each other. But, you know, no one ever found out who really broke the engagement. We all talked about it for weeks. We wondered if maybe it had to do with his younger brother being killed at Pearl Harbor, but no one ever found out. Brady O'Hara was not one to share his feelings with anyone."

"His brother was killed at Pearl Harbor?"

"We lost a lot of boys that horrible day. Those few hours changed all our lives forever."

I chewed on my bottom lip and considered what she'd told me. Intriguing gossip though it was, I couldn't see how it would have anything to do with his death, or Miss Violet's, fifty years later.

"Did he and Miss Violet ever have anything going on?" A crime of passion maybe? Right, I chided myself. Fifty years later Oralee smothers Miss Violet and chokes Mr. O'Hara because of spurned love.

Thelma shook her head No. "Not that I ever heard. I told you I didn't see how any of this would help you. Besides, I think there may be other reasons why Brady would be more valuable dead than alive."

My ears perked up. "Like what?"

Her voice went down into a whisper even though there was no one else in the room. "You know Oak Terrace will get a large endowment now that Brady's dead.''

"I remember Edwin mentioning something about it. Are you suggesting that Edwin knocked him off to get money for the retirement home? I know jobs are tight these days, but if Oak Terrace went under, I'm sure Edwin could find a job somewhere.''

"Maybe after he got out of prison.''

"What?'' My small shriek brought a satisfied smile to her face. I shook a finger at her. "Okay, Thelma Rook, you old gossip. You've known something all along. Now come clean, or I'll be forced to bring out the truth serum.''

She gave a merry little laugh. "Oh, Benni, the look on your face was worth it. I'm being a bit facetious, really. What I'm about to tell you is pure gossip, so I hope the good Lord will forgive me.''

"C'mon, don't torture me,'' I said.

"You know, most people, even the ones who work at Oak Terrace, think that once we senior citizens check into a retirement home we've completely lost all our faculties. They act like we can't see, think or hear.'' Her lips grew tight in irritation. I knew what she meant. "Invisible'' was the word. It had happened often since I'd started teaching the quilting class at Oak Terrace. Many of the retirement-home workers, and even some family members, would discuss the residents as if they weren't present.

"So,'' she continued, "we hear a lot of things they don't think we hear.''

"Like what?''

"I was sitting on that sofa in the front lobby. You know, that hideous green vinyl one? These two nurses were talking with the receptionist about how they were thinking of looking for new jobs because a girl in Accounting said the books at Oak Terrace were looking a little shaky these days.''

"Shaky?''

"Money being shifted around and such. They started whispering, not thinking I could hear, but believe me, that's one part of me that's still working just fine. They said''— she paused for emphasis—"that *someone* in charge of a certain retirement home has a bit of a gambling problem."

"Edwin? A gambler?"

"That's what I heard."

"And he's getting the money from the retirement home," I reasoned.

"Apparently so." She looked at me smugly. "So you see, a nice bit of money like that endowment could come in real handy right now for our Mr. Ed."

"No kidding," I said, sitting back in my chair. "But murder?"

"Well, he and Brady did get along pretty well. Heaven knows, Edwin made up to him enough, but I think once Clay arrived and started helping his uncle with his finances, that endowment business was on shaky ground. I wouldn't be a bit surprised if that was why Clay's daddy sent him down here. He must have got wind of Brady's intentions."

Before I could react, the ladies started wandering back into the room and took their places around the quilt. As I stitched, I thought about what Thelma had just told me. Granted, if Edwin was embezzling money from Oak Terrace and Mr. O'Hara was leaving the home money in his will, Edwin might have found a way to work it so that the money he'd embezzled was covered. I wasn't sure how all that complex accounting worked; the books I'd kept at the Harper Ranch the fifteen years I'd lived there were fairly uncomplicated. My college accounting classes and the books that came with the word processing program we'd purchased had more than sufficed. But these days miraculous things could be done with computers. A person with the necessary know-how could make numbers do the ten-step in triple time. And I'd happened to find out, during the course of working with Edwin on the Senior Citizen Prom, that his major in college had been accounting with a minor in computer science. If anyone could pull off a little piece of technical hocus-pocus, Edwin probably could.

Then again, a little voice inside me said, Clay might have decided he wanted his uncle out of the way *before* he could change his will and leave anything to the retirement home.

Maybe Mr. O'Hara had decided to leave it all to Oak Terrace or to someone else.

I worried the new information like a dog digging for marrow in a fresh bone. What exactly was in that will? A lot seemed to hinge on that.

We ended the quilting session about noon with plans for the ladies to return next week. Thelma boarded the minibus last. As I helped her up the steps, she whispered, "I'll keep my eyes and ears open and call you if I hear anything."

"No," I said, remembering the cool, lifeless feel of Miss Violet's hand. "Thanks for your help, but I should never have gotten you involved. It could be dangerous. I think you should forget about it."

With surprising strength, she pulled her arm out of my grasp and looked me square in the eye. "Now, Benni Harper, do you really think I'm going to sit around and let you have all the fun?" She turned to the bus driver. "Home, James," she said in a regal tone. "And make it snappy. I've things to do."

"Be careful," I called after her and the bus driver gave a good-natured wave, thinking I was talking to him.

The bus pulled out of the parking lot just as Clay's rented white car turned in. The fluttering in my stomach could have been either excitement or dread. Lately, those two sensations were beginning to feel like identical twins. I was confused about my feelings for Clay. I'd dreamed about both him and Gabe last night, a wisp of a dream I could barely remember, but it brought me awake in a trembling sweat and left me feeling vaguely aroused and vulnerable. I felt trapped somehow, as if they both had some sort of power over me.

"Hope you're not thinking about me," Clay said, stepping out of his car.

"What do you mean by that?" I snapped, irritated that genetics had given me the sort of face that couldn't win a poker hand if my life depended on it.

"Just what I said. With the frown you're wearing on that

pretty face of yours, I hope it's not me you're thinking about.''

"It's not. I'm just real busy. Is there something I can do for you?'' The quicker I got rid of him, the quicker I could put all those discomforting thoughts out of my mind.

He leaned against the fender of the car and crossed his arms. I looked up at him, my eyes lingering momentarily on his mouth, remembering the other night, remembering seventeen years ago. ''Well?''

"I do believe there is. As a matter of fact, it could be mutually satisfying for both of us.'' He gave me a sleepy-lidded smile, daring me to react to his innuendo.

I pushed my bangs back impatiently and said, ''Clay, what do you want?''

Unruffled, he said, ''Sounds like the red in your hair is winning today, so I'll just have my say and let you get back to work. The attic at Brady's place has got three trunks full of old stuff—papers, books, things about San Celina County. I hear you're affiliated with the Historical Society.''

"Yes, so?'' I wondered where he'd found that out and what else he knew about me.

"So, I need to get someone to take a look at it. It doesn't mean anything to my family and I was thinking the Historical Society might find some use for it.''

"Maybe,'' I said, knowing that Dove and the other ladies in the group would cut off a finger for something like this. Mr. O'Hara had been a resident of San Celina County for almost sixty years. There had to be tons of documents and photographs that would add to the body of knowledge about the county. Normally, the idea of going through the old trunks of someone like Brady O'Hara would have fascinated me, but I suspected Clay had more on his mind than adding to the annals of San Celina history.

"Why don't you give the Historical Society a call and see if one of the members would like to go through it with you?'' I asked.

"I went by the museum and the lady at the reception desk gave me Dove's phone number, and well . . .'' He looked at me with an exaggerated hangdog expression. "I never was one of her favorite people." He balanced one heel of his elegant boots on the toe of the other, his face pensive.

Unable to resist, I softened. "No, you weren't," I agreed. For a moment, he was nineteen-year-old Clay O'Hara again—the boy with the long dangerous sideburns and cocky attitude who buried his head in my lap and sobbed when his dad sent a letter telling him his brown Labrador, Galveston, had been caught under a tractor's tires and killed. "When do you want to go through them?"

He stood up, straightened his hat and grinned and I knew I'd been had. But somehow, right then, it didn't matter. "Whenever's the most convenient time for you." He lowered his voice to an intimate rumble. "Maybe, if you work real hard, I'll even buy you dinner afterwards."

"Let's just worry about the trunks right now," I said. I wasn't sure if I was ready for another dinner with him, or another of his kisses. I took a deep breath. Tomorrow was too soon. I ran through the day after's schedule in my mind—morning with Gabe to visit Aaron and Rachel, one o'clock, Miss Violet's funeral. I couldn't miss that. "How about four o'clock day after tomorrow?" I said.

"Fine. Where do you want me to pick you up?"

"I'll meet you there." There was no way I was going to be stuck in the boonies with Clay O'Hara and no means of escape. I hadn't lost *all* my senses. "It's out past the airport, near the Wheeler Ranch, right?"

"Right." He opened the car door, then turned, a teasing squint to his warm brown eyes. "Tell me something, Widow Harper."

"What's that?"

"Are you really irritated at me coming to see you or just at yourself for being glad I did?" Before I could answer, he climbed in the car and started the engine.

I watched him drive out of the parking lot and wondered what I'd let myself in for. You can handle Clay O'Hara, I told myself firmly. There is nothing he can make you feel or do that isn't totally under your control. You call the shots in this game.

That irritating little echo of Dove's voice came back to me, as it does whenever I start feeling too arrogant:

Only if you hold the winning hand, honeybun. Only if you hold the winning hand.

THE NEXT MORNING, my conscience got the better of me, and when I arrived at the museum, I called Gabe.

Dialing his number, I debated with myself about how much I should tell him. I was beginning to lose track of what I knew and what I was keeping from him. Doodling question marks, triangles and hearts on my notepad, I waited for him to answer.

"Ortiz," he answered in his dominant, chief-of-police voice.

"Hi, it's me."

His voice relaxed. "Finally, a voice that doesn't want something." A full-throated laugh rumbled pleasantly in my ear. "You don't, do you?"

"Actually, I'm going to give you something. That is, if you promise not to get mad at me or ask me questions about my source." I didn't want the police questioning Thelma again and bringing attention to the fact that she knew something.

"What is it?" His voice turned stiff.

"I mean it. Promise me."

"Benni . . ."

"I mean it."

Something resembling a growl came over the phone lines.

"Okay," he snapped. He'd known me long enough now to know how stubborn I could be.

"It's rumored that Edwin Montrose has a slight gambling problem."

When he didn't react, I continued. "Apparently it's being said that he could have embezzled some money from the retirement home, and the endowment that I heard Mr. O'Hara was thinking about leaving to Oak Terrace could help hide Edwin's little predicament."

He still didn't react and I wondered how much of this he already knew.

"Is that it?" he asked.

"Pretty much."

"I guess it's basically a waste of breath for me to ask who told you this."

"Yes, basically." I waited for him to lecture me. As usual, he surprised me.

He gave a sigh into the receiver so heavy I could almost feel his warm minty breath. "What am I going to do with you, Benni Harper?"

"I guess I'm probably the last person who knows the answer to that one. Maybe you should ask Dove."

"She told me she gave up on you when you turned thirteen."

"See," I said cheerfully. "You're in good company."

"Just be careful. This is serious business. You aren't—"

"A trained professional, I know, I know," I finished. "I am being careful. I told you what I found out about Edwin. Doesn't that count for anything?"

"Look," he said, his voice weary. "Will you promise me that you'll tell me *everything* you find out? Will you at least do that?"

I was silent, not wanting to lie, but knowing there was no way I could make that promise. Not yet. I wanted to ask if Mac had talked to him yet, but I didn't. If he hadn't, then I'd have to explain to Gabe why I'd even asked.

"If I think it's relevant," I hedged.

He blew out an angry breath and I tensed, waiting for his tongue-lashing. He fooled me again. His voice shifted into neutral. "I talked to Rachel and Aaron today."

"How's he feeling? The chemo's done now, isn't it?" I was more than happy to change the subject. "What time do we go over there tomorrow?"

"Nine o'clock. She says Aaron's had a good couple of days. We can stay for an hour or so."

"I wish there were more we could do to help."

"I know." He cleared his throat. "There's something I need to tell you."

"What's that?"

"Aaron officially resigned last week."

"Oh." I didn't know what to say. Or rather, I knew, but didn't want to ask. "Well, that's no surprise, is it?"

"The city council offered me the job."

"That's great." I hesitated, wondering why he hadn't told me before now. "I guess."

"You guess?"

"I mean, if it's what you want."

He sighed again. "I don't know what I want. Right now, I think I want to get in my Corvette and play Route 66."

"Well, send me a postcard." If he expected me to beg him to stay, he was talking to the wrong lady.

In the background, I heard a buzz.

"I have another call," he said. "I'll pick you up tomorrow morning about eight-thirty."

"That's fine. Talk to you later."

"Right," he said, his voice distracted and distant.

At least your conscience is clear, I told myself as I hung up the phone and glanced over the list of people I needed to call for the Historical Society interviews. Well, another little voice said, semi-clear. You didn't tell him everything.

And why should I? I argued back. He might not even be police chief next month. And who cared anyway? What did we really have? A few kisses, a few meals, some fun times. That's what dating was all about, right? I was free, adult and single. I could do anything I wanted. I could.

And so could he.

As I studied the list of interviewees, I got that funny feeling you get when you feel someone watching you. I looked up and Todd was standing in the doorway, staring.

"Hi," I said. "When did you get here?"

"About a half hour ago. I finished everything on the list you gave me. Is there anything else you want me to do?"

I sat back in my chair, pleasantly surprised. "Gee, I have to think . . ." This deal with Todd just might work out, I thought optimistically. He was quick, quiet and hardworking. An assistant from heaven. Don't get too used to it, a voice inside me warned. Remember the unpredictability of teenagers. I looked at my watch. Ten o'clock. "Well, you're so efficient that I'm going to have to make up another list. Don't you have any classes?"

"Not today." He stood quietly watching me, waiting, it seemed, for something.

I looked at him curiously. "I guess you can come back tomorrow. I'll figure out something for you to do then."

"Okay," he said, nervously flipping his shiny brown hair out of his eyes. "See ya."

I spent the rest of the day setting up interviews and making up a general question sheet that I'd use with each subject. At four o'clock, as I was walking out the door, a group of quilters were setting up in the main studio, ready for an evening of stitching.

"A Quadruple Irish Chain," I said. "That must have been fun to piece. How big are those squares, anyway?" The stair step squares' striking color combination of sea-green, antique white and black and gray would make this quilt an easy sale.

"One inch," one of the quilters said. "And it's going to take a lifetime to quilt. Not that it matters now."

"Why is that?"

"We did it on order for Mr. O'Hara, that man who was killed. And he already paid for it. We were going to ask you what we should do with it now."

"I guess legally it should go to his heirs. I'm going to talk to his great-nephew tomorrow. I'll ask him." And, I thought, it'll give me a legitimate reason to ask him if he knows who inherits in Mr. O'Hara's will.

"Well, let us know," the woman said and bent over the quilt.

My alarm didn't go off the next morning, so when Gabe knocked on my door I was still pulling a brush through hair knots only people with very curly hair understand. He was dressed in casual yuppie clothes—khaki chinos, a pale yellow Izod polo shirt, beat-up leather topsiders with no socks and, his only concession to the sharp Central Coast winter breezes, a brown distressed-leather bomber jacket.

"You look like you need this worse than me." He handed me his commuter mug of coffee before climbing into the Corvette. "We need to stop by the fish store downtown before we go to Aaron's."

"Why?" I sipped at the coffee while reaching over and turning the heater to high. The one thing I don't like about convertibles is, even with the top up, they never feel warm.

"Pick up some of their smoked salmon for Aaron. Rachel says for some reason it's one of the few things his stomach is able to tolerate."

We fought through the senior citizen breakfast-crowd traffic downtown and found a parking space three blocks from Morita's Fish Market and Deli in the Old Town section of San Celina. Gabe grabbed my hand and tucked it inside the pocket of his jacket. We walked down the street past the restored brick and adobe buildings that once held the city's major commercial businesses, but now housed funky shoe boutiques featuring Doc Martens and Birkenstocks, French-style bakeries and gourmet pizza restaurants. Right at that moment, strolling down the already busy street, taking in the mixed scents of yeasty bread, the sharp, metallic smell of just-washed sidewalks, the sage and oregano from cooking pizza sauce, feeling the warmth of Gabe's large hand enveloping mine, contentment filled my heart, all the more sweet for the fact that I knew, like most good things, it would last for only the briefest of time. But I was learning to savor moments like this, store them up in my mind for the future, to withdraw on days when it didn't seem possible that there was one beautiful thing left in the world.

Mr. Morita, Todd's grandfather, was wiping off the red-checked plastic tablecloths on the three round tables sitting in front of his combination fish store/deli. A matching awning of red-striped canvas shaded him from the unusually bright February sunlight. He looked up when he heard us approach, his oval face, the color of orange pekoe tea and as softly creased as an old boot, breaking into a welcoming smile when he saw Gabe, one of his best customers. I guessed him to be somewhere in his middle to late sixties.

"Chief Ortiz," he said. "So good to see you." He ran a sturdy hand over the thin hair just barely covering his head. "What can I get you today? Nice red snapper? Fresh-caught today. Halibut maybe?"

"Just a pound of your smoked salmon," Gabe said.

We followed him into the small, clean store and watched him wrap up the order. After he handed the white paper package to Gabe, he turned to me. "Is there something you like?"

I shook my head. "Not today, thank you." Then it dawned on me that there *was* something I wanted from him.

"Mr. Morita," I said. "Were you living in San Celina before 1941?"

He looked at me oddly. "Since 1936."

"That's great." I explained to him quickly about the Historical Society book and how his grandson would be involved in it. Maybe that would soften him up about talking to me. "Would you talk to me about that time of your life?" I watched him carefully. About a third of the people I'd called yesterday had refused to be interviewed for the book, though no one had actually been rude about it. Some people apparently had no desire to relive that difficult time of their life and who could really blame them?

He wiped his hands on his spotless apron, his face soft and blank. "I am very busy. There is much work here these next few days with the festival, but maybe next week." He gave me a practiced, public smile and turned to a chubby woman in hot-pink bicycle shorts who wanted some crawfish for a Mardi Gras party she was throwing that weekend. I mentally put him on my "maybe" list.

* * *

Aaron and Rachel lived in a small blue and gray saltbox house in Morro Bay on a bluff overlooking Morro Rock and the Embarcadero. The flower boxes under the front windows were bare, a graphic reminder of the seriousness of Aaron's condition. Rachel's needlework and her flowers were her two great passions, her refuge when the pressures of his illness became too much for her. Though I hadn't known her long, I admired her quiet strength and the dignified way she accepted this tragedy in her life. Aaron was the humorous one, a lover of silly jokes and nicknames; he teased Gabe, causing him to grin like a teenager and blush by telling him he should call me Peanut because I was so short and by the look in his eyes, he couldn't get enough of me. He made Gabe laugh in a way that gave me a glimpse of what he must have been like as a younger man. And Rachel, with the easy grace of a natural mother, waited on and nagged Gabe in her gentle, affectionate voice. He relaxed around the Davidsons in a way I'd never seen before. A part of me was jealous that they had known him since he was twenty-two, had such a long history with him. I tried to imagine him an eager rookie, riding with Aaron through the rough streets of East Los Angeles. But even with the photos Rachel showed me of a dark, lanky Gabe and a robust, auburn-haired Aaron, I couldn't picture it.

"I'm glad you came," Rachel said, leading us into the living room. She was a spare, delicate woman in her late fifties with short, silver-streaked brown hair and eyes the intense reddish-brown of port wine. Her navy wool skirt hung loosely on her hips; her pale blue cashmere sweater seemed a size too big. "Aaron's out on the patio. He's been so looking forward to seeing you both." She pushed back a stray strand of her neat hair and answered Gabe's worried look with calm eyes. "He had a rough night, Gabe, but he says the sunshine makes him ache less."

Gabe laid a hand on her narrow shoulder, kneading it absently. "Is there anything you need, Rachel?"

She sighed deeply, letting herself relax for a moment under his touch. "Nothing you can give me, dear." She reached up and patted his hand. "It's just enough that you're here. Why don't you go see Aaron while I fix us some tea?"

"Go ahead," I said to Gabe after Rachel went into the kitchen. "You need to visit with him alone for a little while. I'll come out when Rachel brings the tea."

"Okay," he said and walked toward the French doors off the dining room. Through the thin lace curtains I could make out the outline of Aaron sitting on a patio chair, facing the back yard garden.

I sat down on the gray leather sofa and looked around the room. It was decorated in a way that reflected Rachel's personality, in subtle, elegant grays and blues with touches of maroon and rose in the needlepoint pillows and framed Degas prints. A brightly polished brass menorah reigned alone on the cherry-wood mantel. Framed pictures of their daughter, Esther, a Hebrew translator for a small publishing house in New York, sat on the delicate curved-leg end tables. A piece of needlework lay folded neatly across the arm of a maroon wing-back chair. I picked it up and read the tiny words stitched in single-strand gold embroidery thread on antique white 18-count Aida cloth.

"Hear, O Israel: The Lord our God, The Lord is One."

"I started that during Aaron's last stay in the hospital," Rachel said, walking back in the room.

"It's beautiful," I said, holding it away from me and admiring the elaborate border of intertwined grape vines, deep golden roses and the palest of yellow honeysuckle. "What will go here?" I pointed to a blank area underneath the finished verse.

"The same verse in Hebrew. I can only work on it a bit at a time these days. I think I regret choosing so small a fabric, it tires my eyes so, but it's too late to change now." She smiled ruefully.

"It'll be worth it when it's done," I said. "It has a delicacy that would be lost with a larger count. I wish it were finished. I'd love to exhibit it down at the museum."

"Since I seem to only work on it at the hospital, I suppose I hope it's never finished. Shall we join them on the patio?"

"Benni Harper!" Aaron's voice strained with the physical effort of his greeting. His gaunt, sallow face lit up in a smile. "My favorite *shiksa* cowgirl. Come give me a hug. Turned any bulls to sopranos lately?"

He was wearing a navy blue sweat suit and a blue and red Kansas JayHawkers cap, a gift from Gabe. When I bent to hug him, his back felt as frail as fish bones underneath my fingers. I closed my eyes and inhaled his musty, dying scent, trying to imagine the bulk of the man who could once pin Gabe to the ground.

"How're you doing, Aaron?" I chose a patio chair next to him.

"Still got the forked end down," he said, gesturing at his thin legs. "Though just barely these days."

Gabe walked over to the edge of the backyard, peering over the back fence at the Embarcadero below, where tourists took pictures of the crusty commercial fishing boats, bought sea shell wind chimes and Styrofoam bowls of oniony clam chowder. Morro Rock gleamed obsidian-black in the bright sunlight. Rachel handed me a fragile china cup of tea and fussed about, rearranging Aaron's tea and cakes until he told her to quit being a Jewish mother and go show Gabe the impatiens that were blooming across the back fence.

"She's always trying to feed me," he said to me, as we sipped the strong, minty herbal tea. "And she never lets me have caffeine anymore."

"She feels helpless," I said. "She probably feels like if she can control your diet, she can control everything else." I picked up an iced ginger cake and took a bite. Though Aaron and I had visited less than a dozen times since we first met two months ago, from the beginning we'd established an easy, open rapport. We knew the cancer gave us no time for the indulgence of social artificiality, and also knew the one thing we had in common was we cared about Gabe.

"I worry about her." His dark eyes seemed to sink further into their hollows. I couldn't help but notice how the yellow in his skin seemed deeper than the last time we'd visited, as if some unknown artist's hand had painted on another thin layer of color. "She needs to do something besides take care of me. It's going to be harder for her when . . ." His voice trailed off.

I reached over and took his hand. It felt shriveled and dry and scratchy, an old man's hand, even though Aaron had just turned fifty-nine two weeks ago. "She'll be okay. It'll be hard, but she'll be okay."

"I know she will. No doubt she'll be at the synagogue every day, trying to mother whoever will let her. It's not only her I worry about." When he looked over at Gabe, his breath came out in a loud shudder. He pulled the black velour robe that was draped across the back of his chair over his shoulders. "I never can seem to get warm these days," he said with a small laugh. Gabe laughed at the same time. The sound echoed across the lawn and we watched him dip his head close to Rachel's ear, point at something down on the Embarcadero, and then her high, thin laughter joined his.

"It's good to see her happy for a change," Aaron said. "I can't seem to make her laugh anymore." His face grew liquid with sadness. "Sometimes, she almost seems angry with me."

"She's not angry with you," I said. "She's just angry with . . . life. I still get that way sometimes. Trying to figure out why things happen. Being grateful for what you've had, but angry because you don't have more, don't have it all. Then ashamed at your greediness when there are people in the world who've never had one tenth of what you've had."

He shook his head and stared out at the silvery ocean. "I feel like I've failed her. A real man sticks around, takes care of his family."

"Excuse me, Aaron, but that's about the biggest piece of cow crap I've ever heard from you. You didn't choose for this to happen."

He gave me a small, close-mouthed smile. "I can always depend on you to tell it like it is. You're right, but I'm still afraid, Benni. Not so much for me, but for her. She's going to have to grow old without me and that tears me up. I want to tell her that, but when I look into her beautiful eyes, I can't. We've been married thirty-three years and I've known you two months. Why can I tell you and not her?''

"Because you have nothing to lose with me. Because you're still her husband and want to protect her. That isn't a bad thing, you know. Deep down inside, I think it's what everyone craves."

"What's that?"

"Someone who loves them enough to take care of them."

He reached up and adjusted his cap. "Smart words from such a pretty little package. No wonder Gabe is in love with you."

I laughed and smacked his hand gently. "Says who?"

"You mean that boy hasn't spoken up yet? What's the matter with him? I guess he and I are going to have to have a little talk."

I pointed a finger at him. "Don't you dare say a thing, you wily old matchmaker. We're working on our relationship, but things are kind of . . . complicated. You know how different we are. It's going to take a little time."

He grabbed my hand, squeezing it with amazing strength, his voice intense and full of more than just physical pain.

"Time is something that can't be wasted, Benni. You and I know that. Forget the differences. No matter what, promise me you two won't throw one single minute away. Not one single minute."

Before I could answer, Gabe and Rachel walked back within hearing range.

"You'll never believe what we just saw," Gabe said, still laughing. Rachel tucked her arm in the crook of his, an indulgent, relaxed smile smoothing out the worried lines of her face.

"What's that?" Aaron asked.

"Gabe's in danger of losing his status as a Los Angeles refugee," Rachel said. The cool air caused her pale cheeks to blush a delicate rose. "He now makes fun of the tourists almost as wickedly as we do."

"Bermuda shorts and cowboy boots on a guy that had to weigh two-sixty, at least. We don't even allow that in Southern California." Gabe reached over and gave Aaron a gentle slug on the arm. "He had about as much taste in clothes as you, *amigo.*"

Aaron lifted his nose and sniffed with feigned hurt. "Mr. Button-down-collar-Midwest-yuppie here was always jealous of my droll and unique sense of style."

We all laughed, and Rachel walked over and placed a hand on Aaron's shoulder, giving us the subtlest of looks. The physical strain of our short visit was already showing on Aaron's face, though he tried to mask it with a trembling smile. I laid a hand on Gabe's arm and said, "I think we'd better go."

"Not already," Aaron said. "You just got here."

"Benni's right, *compa,*" Gabe said. "You need your rest. We'll come again soon."

"If you have time," Aaron said. "I don't want you goofing off on that job and make me look bad." His face grew pensive. "Sometimes I miss that place like fire. Give me a quick rundown on the O'Hara-Violet murders."

Gabe turned his back to me and gave Aaron a brief summary of what they'd found out so far, not revealing anything I didn't already know.

"Dig deeper on the nephew," Aaron said, his face thoughtful. "In most cases, as you well know, it's a family member and usually the most obvious suspect." Gabe glanced quickly over at me, and it took everything I had not to stick my tongue out at him.

"Yes, I know," Gabe said. "But we're looking into other possibilities. I'll tell you more the next time I come to visit."

Right, I thought, when I'm not with you.

Aaron's eyes moved from Gabe's face to mine, an astute look on his face. Then he said to Rachel, "Did you ask Gabe about that noise?"

She touched her throat with a delicate hand. "I almost

forgot. It's the car," she explained. "It's making an odd noise, and Aaron wants you to look at it."

"No problem," Gabe said. He went over to Aaron and stooped next to the chair, laying a hand on his friend's arm. For a moment, they stared at each other, silent. "You behave yourself," Gabe finally said, squeezing Aaron's arm. "Do what Rachel tells you."

Aaron reached over and grabbed Gabe's hand. "Always have, little buddy, always have."

Rachel walked us out front where a dark blue Cadillac Seville was parked. After some fiddling around under the hood, Gabe turned to Rachel. "It's just a cracked spark plug. I'll pick one up at the parts store and bring it out tomorrow." He closed the hood with a bang and turned to me. "Ready to go?"

He was unusually quiet on the drive back to San Celina, but I chalked it up to worry about Aaron. From my own experience, I knew there wasn't anything anyone could say or do to make this any easier for him, so I didn't even try.

"Are you going to Miss Violet's funeral?" I asked when he pulled up into my driveway.

"No," he said. "But I'll have men there, though I doubt they'll find out much. I expect there will be quite a crowd."

"Probably."

I unbuckled my seat belt and reached for the door handle.

"Benni, we have to talk about something." The serious tone of his voice caused me to freeze.

"What about?"

He rested his hands on the steering wheel and stared straight ahead. "Mac came to see me yesterday."

My pounding heart seemed so loud, I was certain it would burst my eardrums. "Oh, really? Why?"

"I think you know."

I studied the hands clenched in my lap. "Maybe you should just tell me."

He hit the steering wheel so hard it sang, and a barrage of Spanish burst from him. It sounded, in the enclosed area of his car, more menacing than I knew it actually was, but that didn't mean I had to listen to it, so I opened the car door and stepped out. He sprang out of the driver's seat and was standing next to me before I closed the door.

"Benni, did you know he removed evidence from the scene?" At that moment, the eleven inches his six-foot frame had on me felt more like eleven feet.

"Yes, but . . ."

He hit the hood of the Corvette with his palm. "Do you know how much I wish you hadn't said that? I was hoping, praying, that it wasn't what I suspected. What am I supposed to do now? You want to tell me that?"

"Did Mac tell you?" I asked, trying to buy time because I had no explanation that would satisfy him.

"He didn't have to. When I asked him if anyone else knew about this, he asked if he could be excused from answering that question. It didn't take a genius to add up that equation."

"Did he tell you what he took?"

His lips thinned underneath his mustache. "No, that's why I'm asking you about it. I want to know exactly what you saw, and"—his voice dripped with sarcasm—"if it's not any trouble, just why you didn't tell me about it five days ago?"

"All I saw was him taking something out of the nightstand. That's it. And I was going to tell you."

"When?"

"I don't know. I was trying to find out if it had any bearing on the murders before I did."

He made a disgusted sound deep in his throat. "You just don't get it, do you? What you did makes a mockery out of everything I stand for, everything I am. Do you understand what it will look like, what I'll look like, when this comes out? Has it penetrated that thick, stubborn skull of yours that you broke the law?"

I was perilously close to breaking down and sobbing, but I wasn't about to do it here in broad daylight in front of Gabe. I swallowed hard and took a deep breath. "He's my friend, Gabe. What else could I do? And by the way, just out of curiosity, which bothers you more, me breaking the law or your precious public image?"

"I am not even going to dignify that asinine remark with an answer." He walked around the car and got in. I followed, past the point of regretful tears and into the angry kind.

"What are you going to do to him?" I asked, standing next to his open window.

"What can I do? I don't even know what he took and he won't tell me. Frankly, I don't even know why he bothered to come in." He started the engine and shifted into reverse.

"Okay, tell me this, Gabe. Tell me what *you*, the great upholder of law and order, would have done if it had been Aaron. Or Rachel. Or your son. Tell me you would have turned them right in without a second thought. You tell me that and maybe I'll consider your point of view."

He was silent for a moment, then answered in a flat, cold voice. "It's obvious we are never going to see eye-to-eye on this subject, and since who I am appears to be so reprehensible to you, I suggest we end whatever it is we have right now before someone really gets hurt."

"Fine with me," I said.

As I watched him drive away it hit me, like a fist in the stomach, how little we actually knew about each other, how whole parts of our lives were lived before we'd even met and how different those lives had been. "Forget the differences," Aaron had said. Simple, wise advice from a good friend. But, it appeared to me, at this moment, impossible to take.

FIFTEEN MINUTES LATER I was changing into a navy silk dress for Miss Violet's funeral and saying all the things to my reflection in the mirror that I hadn't thought to say to Gabe. I was furious and hurt and feeling so crazy, I wanted to scream. I would have too, if I could be certain Mr. Treton was out of hearing range. It would only take the slightest peep out of me and he'd immediately call Dove, and trying to explain the situation to her when I didn't even understand it myself was beyond my present emotional capability. It seemed impossible to put into perspective what my true feelings were when my hormones had an entirely different agenda. Gabe drove me nuts, but the thought of never seeing him again terrified me. If old age is a return to your childhood, as so many of the staff at the retirement home enjoyed pointing out, then middle age must be adolescence again. The confused and angry feelings I was having were so similar to what I experienced at fourteen, I wouldn't have been surprised to find acne sprouting on my chin.

First Baptist Church's new parking lot thronged with cars parked somewhat haphazardly because the contractor still hadn't painted in the lines for parking yet. Attendance at Miss Violet's service was predictably heavy, with both legitimate mourners who'd had her as a teacher or friend and with curious gossips hoping for a tidbit to take home.

After signing my name in the guest book, I slipped into a back pew, feeling both at home and alien in the comforting cyanic blue of the sanctuary. I concentrated on the large olive wood cross suspended over the crystal water of the baptismal and let the familiar gospel songs and Mac's deep, liquid voice wash over me. I didn't listen too closely, fearing the memories it would stir. Though in the last year I'd come to church sporadically, this was the first funeral I'd attended in this building since Jack's. I looked down at the faint indentation where my wedding ring once was, and wondered where I'd be a year from now. Feeling tears gather at the back of my eyes, I turned my mind to the distraction of the murder investigation. It seemed a safe thing to dwell on, a puzzle to be solved, if you didn't think too deeply about the people who died.

Looking around, I had to admit Gabe was right about one thing. It would be almost impossible for his detectives to pick out the murderer in this crowd. One of his detectives, a skinny, bespectacled Hispanic man who'd just been promoted to plainclothes, stood at the back of the church and slowly scanned the crowd. The searching manner cops have, the lingering looks they give certain faces, was becoming familiar to me now. I'd teased Gabe about it, telling him he scrutinized everyone as if they were a wanted fugitive. A wounded expression crossed his face at my comment. "You're not far off," he'd said. "I hate it, but I've gotten to the point where I label everyone I meet 'victim' or 'suspect.' It makes me sick and sometimes"—he paused for a moment, hunting for the right word—"angry, I guess, like something's been stolen from me."

When the service was over and the procession past her coffin started, I slipped out, knowing the dry eyes I'd maintained during the service would fail me then. Besides, I'd spotted Dove on the other side of the church and I was determined to avoid her. All she'd have to do was take one look at my face and she would know something was wrong, and at this point, I didn't feel up to talking about it to anyone.

Next to my truck, Mr. Morita fumbled with the keys to

his small blue Honda. He wore a fuzzy brown sports coat and a dark fedora.

"Hello, Mr. Morita," I said.

He looked up, startled, and I was surprised to see tears streaming down his round face. I paused uncertainly, then asked, "Is there anything I can do?" I dug through my purse and handed him a clean tissue.

"Thank you," he said, taking the tissue and quickly wiping his eyes. "She and my Hatsumi . . ." he said in a tremulous voice. "Good friends. Rose Ann was her teacher. Our daughter, Keiko, her name Keiko Rose for . . ." He turned his head and held the tissue up to his mouth.

"I'm sorry," I said, touching his shoulder. I couldn't imagine what he was going through losing his daughter, his wife, and now, apparently, a good friend of the family. "Is there anything I can do? Would you like me to find Todd or drive you home? We can arrange for someone to pick up your car."

"No, no," he said, shaking his head vehemently. "Todd is a good boy. I take too much his time already. He needs studying to keep up grades. I'm okay, okay. I go back to work now."

I watched him climb into his little car and pull slowly out of the parking lot. Driving back to my house, an intense weariness overtook me that I recognized as grief. Only unlike when I grieved for Jack, this feeling had no center, no one thing to focus on. All I knew was after visiting Aaron this morning, fighting with Gabe, attending Miss Violet's funeral and seeing Mr. Morita's sorrow, I felt as if there wasn't one single thing in the world to feel happy about. I thought about giving Clay a call at his hotel and telling him to just ship the trunks to the Historical Society and call me sometime, like in a year or so. All I wanted to do was crawl into bed and stay there forever. While changing back into jeans and a long-sleeved white tee shirt, I called the museum to see how things were going and whether Constance had left any messages for me. Since the exhibit was done, but wouldn't open until next week, and I was caught up on my paperwork, I didn't feel a need to go in. Vegetating

seemed a good alternative. I picked up a grape Tootsie Pop
that had somehow appeared on my messy coffee table and
turned on the television to CMT, the twenty-four-hour
country music video station. They were taking call-in requests for ''cryin', lovin' or leavin' '' songs. After my fifth
''leavin' '' song, I decided anything was better than sitting
there crying in my chili, even wrangling with Clay O'Hara.
At least it would take my mind off things. But first, since
I hadn't seen her at the funeral, I would go by Oak Terrace
and check on how Oralee was getting along. You're not
being nosy, I told myself. She's your friend, you would do
this even if she didn't have something you wanted to know.

The afternoon air had the crisp smell and refreshing
translucence that always seemed to precede a rain storm on
the Central Coast. Off to the north, smoky gray storm
clouds seemed to boil over the horizon, bubbling our way.
The thought of stormy weather cheered me. Though we'd
had plenty of rain this year, my psychic rain barrel wasn't
full yet. A stormy night next to a cozy fire was just what
I needed. My heart sank as the picture blossomed in my
mind. I didn't have a fireplace, but Gabe did. Suddenly, I
wished for sunny weather.

Oak Terrace's hallways were as busy and crowded as
usual, the murders of six days ago already old news. The
unending job of feeding and caring for the aged and infirm
was like tending a newborn child or ailing animal; in the
midst of tragedy, life must go on. I was turning down the
west wing of the Magnolia building, heading toward Oralee's new room, when I literally rammed into Edwin's chest
bone. His hands enveloped my shoulders, holding them a
little too long after realizing they were female.

''Benni!'' he said in an overly delighted voice.

''Edwin.'' I pulled back and started to move around him.
''Can't talk. I'm on my way to visit . . .''

''You're just the person I wanted to see,'' he said, his
voice as smooth and appealing as a glob of Vaseline. ''I
have something for you.'' He flashed an intimate smile. If
he'd had a handlebar mustache, I swear he would have
twirled it.

"What?" I asked suspiciously.

"Oh, no," he said, his tone playful. "You'll just have to come to my office and see for yourself."

Where do men like Edwin come from? And who trains them? I gave him an irritated look. "Look, Edwin, I've got someplace to be at four o'clock. I don't have much time. Is this something that absolutely has to be taken care of today?"

"Only if the museum wants its money." His expression turned smug. He knew he had me. I took my job with the museum and co-op seriously and would even brave his slimy little lair if I thought it contained something that belonged to us, especially a monetary something.

"Okay, I'll be there in a little while," I said reluctantly. "Whatever it is better be quick though. My appointment is very important."

The door to Oralee's room was closed, but George Jones's cajoling voice seeped through the thin wood veneer. Oralee's curt voice granted permission to enter. The room's decor was as plain as Oralee herself, with pictureless walls covered in a tan flame-stitch wallpaper and rust-colored curtains on the one window. The bed closest to the door was empty, neatly covered with one of the institution's dark brown bedspreads. Its matching metal nightstand, bare of any personal items, established the fact that currently Oralee was the sole occupant of the room. She sat in a cushioned maple rocking chair next to her bed, which was covered with a calico Log Cabin quilt; a crocheted afghan rested neatly at the foot. She wore a rose velour jogging suit and white quilted house slippers. A red photo album rested in her lap, and next to the chair her stained Acme work boots waited for one last trip to the barn. She slowly raised her head from studying the album when she saw me.

"I knew you'd be comin'." Her hands gripped the album so tightly, they strained against the skin of her large knuckles, like hard seeds threatening to burst from old fruit.

Since there were no other chairs in the room, I sat on her bed and faced her. "Have you talked to Mac?"

"Yes." She averted her eyes when I looked directly at

her. "He's a good boy. I never meant for him to get involved."

"You realize what he did was against the law. He could go to jail. At the very least, it could cost him his job and his reputation."

"Couldn't be helped," she said, in a voice as sharp as a snapped wishbone. "I told him he didn't have to. Was his choice. We all got to live with our choices."

I took a deep breath, not wanting to get angry, but feeling it start to smolder inside me. "Do you realize what kind of a position this puts me in? Or Mac for that matter?"

"Can't be helped," she stubbornly repeated.

"Oralee, what was it that Mac took and destroyed? I have to know. It's not fair that I don't know."

Her eyes bore straight into mine, and I thought I saw a glint of fear there. "No." Her voice was a hoarse whisper. "It stops here. Even Mac doesn't know."

"He doesn't?" I leaned back, surprised.

"No."

"But he told me . . ."

"He was trying to protect me. He brought what it was to me, and I got rid of it. He didn't do nothing wrong. It was me all along, and I'll tell that to that policeman of yours if I have to."

"Oralee, just tell me it doesn't have anything to do with Mr. O'Hara's and Miss Violet's murders and I swear I'll let it go. Just tell me that."

Oralee lowered her head and studied the photograph album in her lap intently. "Justice was done" was all she said.

"What's that supposed to mean?"

She raised her head, her face remote. "Just let it be, Benni."

"One thing, Oralee, I just want to ask one more thing." Sissy's story. I had to find out what really happened that night.

"No!" Her voice barked with the same vigor and command I'd remembered as a teenager. She looked back down at the album, turning a page slowly. "Now, go on with you.'' I'd known her long enough to know when there was no arguing with her.

I turned when I reached the doorway. "I hope it's worth it, Oralee. Whatever it is you're hiding. I hope it's worth all the people it's hurting."

She never raised her head.

"This better be good," I muttered, walking toward the administrative offices and Edwin. They were located at the front of the building, just off the newly decorated lobby. It was the one place in Oak Terrace where the throat-narrowing smell of ammonia and alcohol was not present. Various shades of kelly-green and peach decorated the outer offices. The pseudo-adobe walls displayed "original" oil paintings of crashing waves and neat, Disney-like fishing boats, the type of art you'd find at swap meets for $29.95. No one sat behind the metal secretary's desk. Next to the dark green blotter, peach silk fuchsias in a cheap white vase danced gently from the air conditioning. I started to knock on the partially opened door of Edwin's office, when his voice, frantic and with a touch of desperation, stopped my hand in midair.

"Don't worry," he said. "I'll get it." There was a long silence. "Just give me . . ." Another long silence, punctuated by his voice growing high with anger. "I told you it was . . ." Then, "Yes, I remember." His voice lowered. "Yes, I know. I'll take care of it." He hung up.

I stood quietly for a minute, letting some time pass, so he wouldn't think I'd overheard his conversation. I was studying one of the ocean scenes, trying to fit the words I'd just heard to anything connected with gambling, when his door flew open.

"Edwin!" I said, jumping back.

"Benni!" he said, just as surprised. "How long have you been there?"

"I just walked up," I said quickly. "What do you have for me?"

"For you?" He jerked his head back, eyebrows bunched together in question.

"The museum," I clarified. "You said you had something for the museum."

"Oh yes, in here." I followed him into his large, mostly bare office. It was decorated in the same shades of peach and green as his secretary's, but the pictures had a Santa Fe K-Mart look to them. A personal computer sat on one side of his desk and piles of papers were spread all over the desktop. Was somewhere among them proof that he really was embezzling funds? He rummaged through the papers on his desk, pulled out a long pink check and handed it to me.

"What's this?" I asked.

"Residents' council decided the leftover money from the prom should be donated to the co-op. It's not much but . . ." His voice trailed off as he turned away from me. I watched his long fingers comb feverishly through the papers, realizing anything he had done would probably be so deeply buried within the bowels of that computer it would be entirely outside the realm of my amateur-sleuthing abilities. After a minute or so, he looked up, perplexed. "Is there something else?" he asked.

"No," I said. "I guess this about wraps up the prom business." I paused for a moment, then decided to take a chance. "Edwin, is everything okay?"

"Yes," he said, his voice going suddenly sharp and high. "Why do you ask?"

"No reason," I said, backing up, sorry I'd asked. "You just seemed a bit preoccupied."

"Running a retirement home isn't easy," he said, jutting his chin out belligerently. "Everyone thinks there's all the money in the world—we need new chairs for the TV lounge, we need a filtering system for the drinking water, we want more variety in the meals. We want, we want, we need. Where do they think that money comes from? This is not a charity. The owners expect the place to make a profit every month and when we don't . . . How am I supposed to make the dollars stretch? These people's Social Security checks don't even begin to cover it all. Everyone thinks we have all the money—" He stopped. "Sorry," he said abruptly, his cheeks turning ruddy. "Bad day. I shouldn't be boring you with my problems."

"It's all right," I said, for the first time feeling a little sympathy for him. But, I thought, that doesn't begin to answer the questions I still have about you. Edwin seemed too wimpy to actually kill anyone, no matter how desperate his situation, but then again, the manner which both Mr. O'Hara and Miss Violet were killed was pretty cowardly. Edwin probably would never attack a man his own age, but an elderly man who had something he needed and an old woman who was a witness? People had certainly been killed for less.

"Well, I have that appointment," I said. "Thanks for the check, Edwin. Hope the rest of your day goes better."

He waved at me distractedly and went back to pawing through the papers on his desk.

I drove through town toward my meeting with Clay, engaging in the same mental debate that had plagued me from the beginning of the murders: What should I tell Gabe? though right now it seemed like a moot point. And what was there to tell really? An ambiguous story about a doctor's mysterious house call fifty years ago, an equally ambiguous overheard conversation between Edwin and an unknown person, Oralee's cryptic statement about justice being done. What was any of that, anyway? A bigger mystery than any of it was whether what I did to protect Mac and Oralee was right. Would I do it again, knowing the outcome? I had never felt so divided in my loyalties or so confused about the matter of right and wrong. Pulling out on the open highway, heading south of San Celina toward Mr. O'Hara's house, the argument about trust Gabe and I had this morning on the ride to Aaron's floated back to me.

"There's no such thing as partial trust," he'd said, shifting into fourth gear and driving twenty miles over the speed limit as he always did.

"I agree," I answered, gripping the door handle.

"So, why don't you trust me?"

"The same reason you don't trust me."

He punched the accelerator. The throttle opened and the

car jumped forward. We passed a Camaro doing at least seventy-five miles an hour. "I do trust you."

"Right," I said. "That's why we have all those wonderfully intimate conversations about your work. Have you ever gotten a speeding ticket?"

"I trust you with things that are your concern. And no."

"That's exactly how I feel," I said. "And you should."

He glanced over at me, his face grim. "You seem to forget, Benni, that anything to do with these murders is my concern. Just because we're . . . friends, doesn't mean charges can't be brought against you."

"For what?" I said indignantly.

"Obstructing justice, for one thing. Interfering in an official police investigation, for another."

I chewed the inside of my cheek, wondering how much he knew. "I'm not obstructing anything, and even if I were, you're telling me you'd bring charges against me? Some . . . friend."

He tightened his fingers around the steering wheel, probably wishing it was my neck. He answered with the low, dispassionate voice he uses whenever he's right on the edge of losing his temper. "*I* don't bring charges, Benni, the DA does. Why are you fighting me on this? What could possibly be that important?"

I played with the catch to my seat belt and didn't answer.

"Why can't you trust me?"

"I do trust you," I protested one last time before we stopped in front of Aaron and Rachel's house.

But I didn't. Not entirely. Not in the way I had trusted Jack. I had to admit that to myself when I pulled off the highway and drove up the circle driveway in front of Mr. O'Hara's Victorian house. Trust was something that took a willingness to risk, to open yourself to hurt, something Gabe and I both had problems with. What was it I wanted from him? More enthusiasm about staying in San Celina, I suppose. More of a role in his life than just someone he ate with occasionally, teased and kissed. More than just a quick tumble in the old symbolic hay loft. I couldn't help but compare our relationship to what Jack and I had, though I knew that was unfair and not unlike Gabe comparing me to every woman he'd ever made love to, a troubling thought that had crossed my mind more than once. Not that it mattered anymore. We were officially broken up, though I wasn't sure if we were ever officially together. Was this what dating was all about? Though I would hesitate admitting it to anyone, I couldn't see the point. You get to know someone's favorite foods, the things they like to watch on TV, what their tongue feels like, for cryin' out loud, just to wave good-bye, tell them to have a nice life, at the end of six or seven months? And then you do it again, over and over, until what? You found the man of your dreams or you were too old for men to want anymore? It seemed like such a waste of time. There had to be a more efficient, less emotionally exhausting way for people to get together. Then something Jack once said came back to me just as clearly as if he were sitting across the seat from me. "Benni, honey, for someone who jokes around as much as you do, you sure take life seriously." Maybe he was right. Maybe I should just relax, and as Dove says, put my quarter on the table and play the cards dealt me. Then again, this was the advice of a woman who has been known to hold an extra ace or two in her overall pocket.

I pulled up directly behind Clay's white rental car and stared up at Mr. O'Hara's house. A Victorian architectural masterpiece, it stood three stories high, with two turrets, a front porch bigger than my living room and enough windows to make you want to buy stock in the company that manufactures Windex. Painted three shades of green ranging from an olive-drab for the basic structure to shades of pine and apple green for the gaudy gingerbread trim, I sympathized with whoever had to maintain all that glossy wood. It was hard to believe that one man had lived alone in this monstrosity. From my years of working on county history with Dove, I knew it was once the mansion of Ryder Kauffman, one of the original land barons of San Celina County back when Constance Sinclair's relatives actually lived at the hacienda that was now the folk art museum.

I walked across the wide front porch up to the gargoyle-carved front door and reached for the brass door knocker. Before I could let it drop, the door opened and Clay stood before me in a tight black tee shirt, faded Wranglers and freshly shined boots.

"Wondered if you'd chickened out." He gave a mocking half-smile and held the door open. I stepped inside the entry hall and looked through the double doors to my left into the vast—and bare—oak-trimmed living room.

"What happened to all the furniture?" I'd seen this house furnished once, four or five years ago when the Historical Society had convinced Mr. O'Hara to open it for one of the holiday home tours of famous San Celina residences. He'd owned an amazing amount of authentic and very expensive Victorian furnishings. I remember thinking then that it felt like he'd bought and furnished the house for someone who had never lived in it. After hearing about him and Oralee, I wondered if it had been intended for her, though I could no more imagine her living here than I could picture Dove minding her own business.

"The people who bought the house didn't want the furniture. Before Brady moved to that retirement place a month ago, he arranged to have an antique dealer take the whole shebang. Probably got ripped off, but he said he just wanted to get rid of it." He touched my elbow and pointed across the living room to double swinging doors I remembered led to the kitchen. "Got some coffee and doughnuts in the kitchen if you're hungry."

"Coffee sounds good," I admitted. Our boots made a lonely, hollow sound on the shiny living room floor.

In the dark wood kitchen, three old black leather trunks were set out on the parquet floor. On the tile counter there was an obviously new thermos, a box of chocolate glazed doughnuts, some cubed sugar and a quart of milk. Clay poured some milk into one of the two thick blue mugs sitting next to the thermos, added two lumps of sugar and filled the remainder with hot coffee. "Sorry there's no microwave to heat the milk," he said, handing the mug to me. "But it wouldn't help anyway, 'cause there's also no electricity."

I laid my purse on the counter and took the mug with a smile. "I can't believe after all these years you remember how I take my coffee."

"I have a good memory for things that are important to me." He hopped up on the counter. "Besides"—he gave a big grin—"you had coffee at the restaurant the other night."

"That's right," I said, laughing. "I did. Well, at least you're honest."

"Trustworthy too." His voice was ironic. "A regular Rocky Mountain Roy Rogers. Just ask anyone. Except my ex-wife, that is."

We looked at each other for a minute; then I turned to look at the trunks, embarrassed by my obvious suspicion. "Have you gone through these yet?"

"Just enough to see that it's nothing but a bunch of junk about his store and some old cards and letters and crap. Like I said, he wasn't that close to our family, so none of it means much to us."

I opened one of the trunks and poked through the top layer of accumulated papers and mementos. A sweet, mysterious smell, redolent of old perfume, hardly worn fancy clothes and dried flowers wafted up and enticed me.

"There's a lot of stuff in here," I said, after looking quickly through all the trunks. "Can we load them in the back of my truck?"

"At your service, ma'am," he said, jumping down off the counter and reaching for the thick leather handles of one trunk.

"Here, let me get one side," I said. "These are pretty heavy."

"Now, Widow Harper," he said. "You get on back and just let me impress you with how macho I am. I've bucked bales twice as heavy as these puny little things."

"It's your chiropractic bill."

After all three trunks were loaded into my truck, I went back into the kitchen to get my purse, Clay following close behind me.

"Going already?" he said. "You didn't even have a

doughnut." He held the box out to me. "And I promised you dinner. Where do you want to go?"

"Thanks, but I have a dinner date," I lied.

"You mean the cop is actually taking some time off from trying to scrounge up evidence against me?" He raised his thick blond eyebrows and tossed the box of doughnuts on the counter.

I shrugged, not willing to lie that much. "I almost forgot," I said, remembering the Irish Chain quilt. "Your uncle ordered a quilt from the co-op and it's going to be done soon. Who owns it now?" I avoided his eyes and picked up a chocolate doughnut, tearing pieces off it and popping them in my mouth. When, after a minute or so, he didn't answer, I looked up.

He leaned against the counter, his jean-clad legs crossed, smiling with amusement.

"What's so funny?" I said, laying the doughnut down.

"Benni, I'm one of the primary heirs in Brady's will. If you wanted to know that, all you had to do was ask."

"All I wanted to know was who to give the quilt to," I said stiffly. "It *is* my job."

He shook his head, still smiling. "And yes, we can use the money. Name me a ranch today that can't. Does me telling you this make you trust me just a little or has Señor Ortiz totally poisoned your mind about me?"

"I have to go," I said, feeling that this whole exchange was rapidly getting into areas best left alone. He laid a hand on my arm. His hard calluses caught on my thin cotton sleeve.

"Before you go, I have someone I want you to meet."

"Who?"

"Trust me, you'll like her."

"Her?"

He grabbed my hand and pulled me through the glassed-in back porch, down the steps, into the sprawling back yard. The half-acre garden was slightly overgrown after a month's neglect, and the native flowers—long pale green horsetail rushes, baby blue-eyes and daisylike mule ears—were starting to take over what was once one of the most envied English flower gardens in the county.

"Where are we going?" I asked, knowing he was probably up to no good, but intrigued as a teenage girl by his enthusiasm. We picked our way through the tangled garden toward a green wooden gate. About two hundred feet beyond the gate lay the long white fences of the Wheeler Ranch. In the distance, about a half mile to the west, their sprawling ranch house and outbuildings nestled beneath a grove of dusky green oak trees. A windbreak of fifty-year-old blue gum eucalyptus lined both sides of the house. The Wheeler family bred a superior line of polled Herefords and, on a smaller scale, barrel-racing horses—in their case, a swift and agile cross between a quarter horse and a Thoroughbred.

He released my hand when we reached the fence, hopped over, giving out a sharp whistle as he cleared the top. About a hundred yards away, in the middle of a small herd of horses, a slender blood bay mare lifted her head from a watering trough. Her mane was black, with matching legs, and her coat a deep glossy red that flashed almost carmine in spots in the pale sunlight. She stood about seventeen hands high, with a lean head and a thick-muscled chest. I pulled myself up to the top of the fence and watched Clay walk lightly toward the herd.

"C'mon, you sweet thing," he cajoled in a low voice, pulling lumps of sugar from his pocket. "Look what I got for you here. Come here, sugarbaby." The mare and I both quivered at the soft sound of his voice. The cool late-afternoon breeze blew the gathering clouds closer. I hugged myself in my thin cotton shirt and relaxed, letting myself enjoy the gentle tone of his horse-breaking patter. It had been a long time since I'd watched a man seduce a nervous animal.

He pulled a large blue bandanna out of his pocket and walked toward her. Ridges of muscles in his back flexed under his tee shirt as he twirled the bandanna into a long rope. Clay and the mare had obviously shared this dance before, because although she was restless, her hooves pawing the ground with nervous energy, she didn't bolt when he approached her. He crooned in his tantalizing baritone, feeding her sugar, his right hand stroking her long, elegant neck. Before she realized what was happening, he'd slipped the bandanna rope under her neck, grabbed a handful of her mane and pulled himself up. She blew angry breaths, hating that she'd been tricked, but after a bit of wrangling for control, he managed to walk her over to where I was perched.

"Very impressive work, cowboy," I said. "The Wheelers will hang you by your ears if they see you, though."

"Have to catch me first," he said, reaching up to straighten his hat. A brisk gust of wind whipped through and snatched it from his hand, sending it flying into a muddy patch of pasture.

"Shoot, that's my good 20x," he said.

I laughed. "That's what you get for buying such a fancy hat. Better stick to K-Mart straw the next time." I jumped down off the fence and picked it up, brushing a smudge of mud off the velvety crown. He took it from me solemnly, then held out his hand. "Ride?"

"I don't think so," I said, looking with apprehension at the fidgety mare.

"C'mon, sugar, when was the last time you rode bareback with a cowboy?" He stroked the mare's neck to calm her, stuck his booted foot out and stiffened it to make a human stirrup. "Live a little."

Temptation overtook sense and I grabbed his hand, used his foot and pulled myself up behind him. The mare started and dropped her back legs slightly, not happy with the extra weight. I grabbed Clay's waist and pulled myself close against him.

"That's more like it," he said.

"Just ride," I said, loosening my grip, though not much. He clicked softly and the horse started walking. So familiar was the leathery, animal scent of his skin and the faint smell of detergent on his shirt, that I wanted to rub my face slowly across his broad back, recapturing a lost time, if only for a counterfeit minute. But I held myself away from the tempting scents, and concentrated on the warm strength of the mare's muscles rolling under my legs.

In the middle of the field, something—a sharp change of wind, a movement on the ground, or just the decision she'd had enough—caused the mare to startle, give a sharp twist and a small crowhop. Clay and I found ourselves, in the blink of an eye, lying on the ground. The mare shook her head in triumph and trotted back toward the water trough.

I rolled over and lay flat on my back trying not to groan out loud. The storm clouds rolling across the sky were darker now, steel-gray warrior clouds readying for battle. Maybe, I thought, feeling a small twinge in my back, I'll just lie here a while and watch them. Lifting my head, I tentatively moved each leg. A few feet away, Clay pulled himself up and scrambled over to where I was lying.

"Honey, are you okay?" He ran his hands over the length of me, searching for injuries as he would an animal, his hands lingering on certain areas longer than necessary.

"I'm fine," I said, pushing his hands away and sitting up. "Calm down, Clay. It's not the first time I've kissed grass."

He pulled his knees up and rested his arms on them. "I should have known better than to trust that old buzzard head. Sorry."

"No one held a gun on me." Behind us, a cold gust of wind threw the mare's nicker our way, making me shiver. "She's laughing at us."

"Yeah, well, I guess we deserve it." He licked his finger, reached over and scrubbed at a spot on my cheek. "Got some mud there."

"I've got some mud everywhere," I said, ducking my head and brushing at a stain on my knee. The feel of his saliva was cool on my cheek and seemed so intimate a gesture, I felt my heart tangle in my rib cage. I picked at a dandelion, embarrassed to look up. "Is it just me or is the ground harder than the last time I was thrown off a horse?"

He laughed and slapped at some mud on his boots. "I do believe it's a scientific fact that the earth is definitely getting harder. Has something to do with the greenhouse effect. Saw it on one of those magazine shows."

"Sounds more like the bullshit effect to me," I said, looking up and smiling.

"Can't fool you, Albenia Harper. Never could."

"And don't you forget it."

He reached over and rubbed his thumb on my cheek. "Got another smudge." The next thing I knew, tricked as surely as the mare a few minutes ago, he'd pushed me down and captured my lips with his. But then again, maybe not tricked. Maybe, unlike the mare, I'd wanted to be captured all along. Giving in, I savored the taste of him this time, like a glass of iced sun tea, spicy and sharp, the smell of the land clung to him, the warm, shadowy aroma of horse and earth. At this moment I didn't care whether it was real or not, I only wanted to taste him, hear the deep male sounds of his harsh breathing, feel the strength of familiar callused hands holding me. I wanted to forget all the hard, sad things that had happened this last horrible year. I wanted to be seventeen again.

He rolled over on top of me, kissing me deeply, his solid weight pinning me to the damp pasture. He slowly eased a rough hand under my shirt. When he touched lace, I stiffened, suddenly frightened by my vulnerability.

"I have to go," I said, squirming out from under him. I jumped up and started walking toward the fence, tucking in my shirt, blood rushing through my veins at such a speed, I thought I would die if it didn't slow down. In seconds he was next to me, one long easy stride to two of mine. I shook off his hand when he tried to help me over the fence.

"Honey," he said. "What's wrong?"

I didn't answer, but kept walking toward the house. What did he expect me to say? I certainly wasn't going to tell him the truth, that his kiss caused the same yearning in me that Gabe's did, or how much that feeling confused me. How could I feel the same with both of them? Having been with Jack from such a young age, I'd never separated sex from love; it had never even been a consideration. While everyone else our age was out learning how to play these games, Jack and I were carrying full loads in college after sitting up half the night calving heifers. Or spending frustrating afternoons rounding up stubborn yearlings and late nights at the computer trying to figure out how to stretch the credits to cover the debits or in the barn trying to patch together old machinery so it would last one more year. Seventeen years ago, Clay and I were closer to being equal in experience, but since then, the gulf between us in terms of relationships yawned wider than the Grand Canyon. So I just didn't answer.

When I reached the kitchen, I picked up my purse and headed for the front door. Before I got halfway across the living room, he grabbed my shoulder firmly and turned me around.

"Let me go." I struggled to pull away, dropping my purse on the floor. He grabbed my other shoulder and held fast.

"Not until we talk about this."

"There's nothing to talk about."

"I think there is."

"Well, I don't care what you think. We kissed. Men and women do it all the time. You're a good-looking guy and, as far as I can tell, a great kisser. Is that what your male ego needed to hear? Now, let me go."

His eyes narrowed in irritation while his fingers bit harder into my shoulders.

"Just let me go, Clay," I said in the firmest voice I could manage. A tiny knot of fear started in the pit of my stomach. What was I thinking coming out here like this? This man was virtually a stranger to me and we were miles away from anyone, in a house that didn't even have a phone. Don't panic, I told myself. I looked him straight in the eye and pulled against his hands one more time.

In an instant his face changed, the anger gone as quickly as it sparked and he wrapped his arms around me, gently rocking me back and forth. "I'm so sorry, honey," he said. "I lose this temper of mine too easy. It's like there's this part of me . . . I didn't mean to scare you." His hand came up and stroked my hair.

"You didn't," I lied. "Now really, I have to go." I pulled away, picked up my purse and started for the door. "Thanks for the trunks."

He followed me out onto the wide front porch and stood watching me, one tanned arm circling a post. When I started the truck's engine, he sprinted down the steps, two at a time, and rapped on the window. Hesitantly, I rolled it down.

"There's something you should know," he said, resting his forearms on the window edge. "Did Señor Ortiz tell you about me and my uncle?"

"Chief Ortiz doesn't confide in me," I said coldly, keeping my eyes straight ahead.

"Well, I'll tell you then. I hated my uncle. More than anyone in my life. He loaned my dad money ten years ago when the Triple Ought was in hard times, then called in his loan knowing we couldn't pay it. He owned the ranch with the stipulation that when he passed away, ownership would revert to us. Then a month ago he changed his mind and decided he wanted to liquidate all his assets and leave everything to some stinkin' historical magazine back East that promised they'd name it after him. He hadn't done it yet though, and I was sent here to try to keep him from it."

I had to ask. "Did you?"

"Yes. I kissed his wrinkled ass until he agreed to leave the will as it was." He gripped the edge of the truck's window. "I'll be truthful and tell you I'd do anything to keep the Triple Ought, even kill him. But I didn't have to." The truck sputtered, and I pushed the accelerator to bring it back to an even idle.

I didn't voice what was racing through my mind, that he could have killed his uncle to keep him from changing the will again.

"You have the wrong idea about me, Benni. Ortiz had your mind made up before I even had a chance."

"That's not true."

"Are you saying you trust me, then? We started something real nice seventeen years ago and I think you're just as interested as me in seeing what might have been.''

I flexed my fingers on the steering wheel, refusing to look at him. "I can see one thing hasn't changed in seventeen years, that colossal ego of yours.''

"You can't deny what happened out there in that field.''

I didn't answer.

"Look, I do agree with your boyfriend on one thing, you poking around asking questions can get you hurt. I don't want that, I really don't.''

"He's not my boyfriend. And I'm not poking around in anything. I really have to go.'' I shifted out of neutral into reverse and started inching the truck backward.

"One last thing.'' He walked along with the truck, his brown eyes narrowed into slits. "You and me, we've got unfinished business, and it *is* going to be taken care of, you have my word on that.'' He slapped the side of the moving truck as if it were an animal he was releasing out to pasture and walked back toward the house.

ON THE DRIVE back, I rolled down both windows in the truck, letting the damp wind from the coming storm whip through the cab and cool my burning cheeks. I couldn't stop thinking about how Clay's words seemed to be loaded with trapdoors and how possible it was that he had killed his uncle and how I still craved the taste and feel of his lips. Well, I said to myself, you wanted answers, you got them. The problem was, nothing seemed any clearer. I was still left with a bunch of questions and two men I'd gladly strangle if given half a chance. So when I got home, after paying the two hefty college students who lived next door five bucks to carry the trunks into my living room, I did what most women do when they can't figure out why men do what they do.

"We have to talk," I said into the phone to Elvia. "Now."

"This sounds serious," she said. "Come down to the store." In the background, Cajun music so upbeat it hurt my teeth, almost drowned out her words. "We can talk in my office. Thank goodness I had it soundproofed last year."

"What in the world is going on there?"

"I'm downstairs. They're gearing up for Saturday. Jose is trying out a new recipe for crawfish etouffee and needed musical inspiration. You'll have to try some. It actually looks quite good."

"Why don't we meet at Liddie's?" I said. "I'm hungry, but I don't feel like experimenting tonight."

"Things are pretty busy here. Is a half hour okay?"

"Take your time. I have a lot to think about anyway."

I sidestepped the trunks on my way out the door. If I experienced another sleepless night, and I was willing to bet I would, at least I'd have something to do now.

I smiled when I pulled into Liddie's parking lot and saw who was parked there. The blue Ramsey Ranch truck looked as if it hadn't been washed for five years. It must be one of the cooking-show nights and Daddy had "business" in town. Business that consisted of a blood-rare steak and a double order of country-fried potatoes. In the entry way a large group of senior citizens stood at the wooden "Hostess will seat you" sign, debating on whether Howard Johnson's was a better deal. They were having an all-you-can-eat fried chicken tenders night. Ignoring them, Nadine barreled straight for me.

"How are you . . ." I started. She clamped her thin fingers onto my wrist with a powerful grip that belied her sixty-five years.

"You've got to do something," she hissed. "They're driving me crazy as a June bug and I'm too old for this. Working nights is bad enough, but there's nothing that says I got to put up with this." Her tiny brown eyes bulged with agitation.

A couple of the senior citizens inched closer, their faces lit up with curiosity. "What is it, Nadine?" I asked, pulling her aside.

"That's what." She pointed toward the back of the restaurant. "You talk to them, Benni, and tell them they'd better shape up or I'm shipping them out." She jerked her glasses off and glared at me.

"What?" I said, following her finger, though not her reasoning. Across the room, my father sat in a booth wearing a sun-faded Western shirt, his silver head hunched over a large oval dinner plate. "Is Daddy bothering you?"

She trailed her finger across the room and the picture started getting clearer. Dove sat four booths away, a fried chicken leg poised in front of her mouth, her bright blue eyes boring a hole into the top of her son's head.

"What's going on?" I whispered.

"They aren't speaking, is what's going on. At least not to each other. Tell Ben this—" Nadine's voice went into a pretty fair imitation of Dove's gear-grinding voice. "Tell Dove that—" She imitated my father's grumpy bass. She pointed a knobby finger at me. "You can just tell *them* the next time they want to send a message, call Western Union!" She whipped around, grabbed a bunch of red menus and snapped at the nosy seniors, "Well, is it Howie's or us? Make up your mind 'cause I ain't got all night."

I walked slowly across the carpet trying to decide who I should approach first, thinking, I really don't need this right now. Both their heads popped up. A choice would have to be made. I looked at Dove's glowering face, then at Daddy's stoic one. My feet felt as heavy as hundred-year-old oak stump. After a few seconds, I gave Daddy an apologetic look and slid into the booth across from Dove. I knew he'd forgive me—he knew better than anyone the terror of Dove crossed.

"What's going on between you two?" I asked. "You're driving poor Nadine bananas."

Dove took a fierce bite off her chicken leg. "Nadine Brooks should have never stopped taking her hormone pills. I merely told her to inform my eldest son that I would be ready to leave in fifteen minutes and if that didn't suit him, I'd find another way home even if I had to hitchhike."

"You mean you two drove into town together?" I laughed and picked up one of her french fries, touching it to the ketchup in her plate before popping it into my mouth. "You didn't talk for a whole half hour? That I would have to see to believe." I reached for another french fry. She pushed my hand away.

"Get your own dinner and quit being a smart mouth. You can just inform your father I won't speak to him again until he apologizes. I mean it."

I snagged another french fry and slid out of the booth. "Dove, this is ridiculous. Why can't you and Daddy resolve your problems like adults?"

She gave me a crafty look. "You mean like you and Gabe?" she said, her voice dripping sorghum molasses.

I held up my hands. "Okay, okay, point taken. But at least *I* don't expect someone else to do my dirty work for me. I live and die by my own sword."

"I'm going to take a sword to your backside if you don't get over there and tell your daddy what I said."

"Yes, ma'am," I said good-naturedly. "By the way, just out of curiosity. Who is this Ahmad who is wreaking such havoc in the Ramsey household?"

She lifted her chin slightly, her bright eyes flashing. "He is a very nice man with a very nice family. His wife, Farideh, is a college professor and he has two beautiful children, Mitra and Mehran, who always get straight A's in school."

"That's interesting, Dove, but who are they? New members of your church?"

"Heavens, no, child. He lives in New York. He's the star of *Gourmet Cooking with Ahmad* and a brilliant Persian and French chef. He cooked for the President once. I reckon your daddy thinks his taste buds are more special than the President of the United States."

"Dove, you know Daddy just doesn't like to experiment with new foods. Can't you compromise and cook what he likes part of the week?"

"I've compromised for seventy-five years." She folded her arms across her chest. "He eats what I cook, or he starves. Tell him."

I slipped in across from Daddy. He continued dissecting his steak without looking up. "Got a load of hay coming in on Sunday," he said in his low drawl. "With this rain we're gettin', we shouldn't have to buy as much next year. Dang weekend ranchers and their horses drive up the price something terrible. Havin' to go further and further to buy it every year."

I ignored his normal carping about horse owners.

"Daddy, why don't you just apologize? You know you'll have to eventually. Why not just get it over with?"

"I'm sticking to my guns this time, squirt," he said, not stopping the flow of food to his mouth. "Is it too much to ask for a man who works hard all day to expect food he can eat? Food he can understand? You haven't tasted that crap she makes. Green stuff I've never seen nor heard of before. Sprinkles it with some kind of yellow powder we got to drive clean to Santa Barbara to buy. Stuff cost more an ounce than gold. You know, I'm thinking she goes out in the pasture and digs up weeds to cook. It's crossed my mind that she might be trying to poison me." He spit out a piece of gristle, then sawed off another large piece of steak. "I've put up with her for fifty-six years. I've done my time. I'm thinking of shipping her up to Kate's. It's high time one of her daughters took her." My aunt Kate, two years younger than Daddy and Dove's oldest daughter, lives in Wyoming on a small ranch outside of Rock Springs. Aunt Kate would love taking Dove on, she'd been itching to for years. Her husband, Rex, a part-time sales rep for John Deere, might not be as thrilled.

"Dove hates the winters up there. You know she'll never go."

"I'm doin' it, I swear I am. I'm buying the ticket tomorrow."

I sighed, not knowing exactly where to go with this now. Then I remembered a saying that Daddy always said *his* daddy used to say when things twisted out of a person's control. Grampa Ramsey called it the country cure for high blood pressure: "If it starts to rain, let it." Sounded like good advice to me.

"Well, Daddy," I said, "I guess there's nothing I can do for either of you and I've got a ton of work to do, so just let me know where Dove's staying so I can write." He grunted and speared a forkful of ketchup-covered fried potatoes.

"Have a nice trip," I said, walking past Dove and giving the top of her table a sharp tap with my fingers.

"What?" she squawked, but I double-stepped and

scooted out the front door before she could get another word out. Elvia was walking up the steps as I was coming down.

"What's wrong?" she asked. "Place full?"

"Too full for me," I said. "Look, I'm sorry to drag you all the way over here, but I've changed my mind and I think I just want to go home. Can we do this tomorrow?"

"It's man problems, isn't it?"

"Is it that obvious?"

"You might as well be wearing a sandwich sign."

Elvia and I walked back through the parking lot in the comfortable silence of old friends. During my conversations with Dove and Daddy, twilight had crept in, bringing with it tule fog like low, rolling smoke. The oak trees and Chinese elms cast odd shadows over the vehicles, making it look as if someone had splattered black paint over the hoods. The wind was higher now, whipping the upper branches of the pine and eucalyptus trees, causing the leaves to softly rustle. The air had a waiting feel that matched my mood, a faint rusty scent that promised another bout of rain. When we reached my truck, Elvia laid a warm hand on my arm and gave me a long, measured look.

"Okay," she said. "What's going on?"

I leaned against the truck and kicked at the gravel with the heel of my boot. "This is really embarrassing."

"Come on, Benni, we've been friends since knee socks. There isn't anything you can't tell me. Don't forget, I remember your first kiss."

"Alberto Cirrone, third grade," I said and we both laughed.

"So what's the problem and I want details."

"You know, they'd hate me for saying this, but in some ways Gabe and Clay are a lot alike."

"As in?"

"Moody, unpredictable, irritating to the point of obnoxious when they don't get their way."

She laughed. "We've already established the fact that they're *men*."

"You know, the last time I went through anything like

this I was seventeen years old. . . ."

"I remember. So, which one really curls your toes, *amiga?*"

"That's sort of the problem . . ."

"Why, you little pig. Most women would pull out their acrylic nails for one decent guy and you've gone and grabbed two. Not bad for someone whose idea of a beauty routine is splashing her face with cold water and polishing her boots."

"Very funny. I'm really confused here. Gabe is . . . well, you know. And Clay. There's just something about him. We have a lot in common and there's all these old memories but . . ."

"But what?"

"What if . . ." I didn't want to say it out loud. That gave it too much validity. But the question remained, What if Gabe was right about Clay?

She put her arm around me and gave me a little shake. "Look, take it from someone who has lived her entire life with more than her fair share of male hormones, it's not the end of the world. Somehow, things will all work out."

I snorted and gave the small hole I'd dug with my heel one last jab. "Yeah, good advice. Wish it was easier to take."

"Get back to work," she said. "That's the best cure I know. Let Gabe find his killer and Clay take care of whatever it is he's here to take care of and just get back to your own work. And don't worry about it. Believe me, they certainly aren't losing any sleep over it."

Her advice was sound and reasonable and I knew she was right, so when I got home, the first thing I did after changing into warm sweats was open the trunks. Armed with a notebook and a cup of cocoa, heavy on miniature marshmallows, I started separating the items into three piles—personal articles, things to do with San Celina history and items pertaining to Mr. O'Hara's store. I could see why Clay's family wouldn't want most of it. The letters and photographs were primarily of people and events that took place in the last sixty years in San Celina County.

During the forties through the sixties, Mr. O'Hara belonged to almost every civic club and organization in town, was even president of two of them—the San Celina Farm Bureau and the San Celina Association of Retail Distributors.

Three cups of cocoa and four hours later, I had everything separated. The rain finally arrived with the eleven o'clock news. With both chattering softly in the background, I started looking at the first pile, the one I'd designated "personal." Most of it was old photographs and postcards, a couple of old leather photo albums, a wooden book with two dogs carved on the front and the word "Scraps" that seemed to contain newspaper articles Mr. O'Hara found important. Most of the postcards were of his travels outside of San Celina—colorful photos of Irish castles and rolling green hills dotted with plump sheep, black and white photographs of men in long Western coats watching other men in stained, ragged chaps riding bulls at the 1915 Colorado-New Mexico Fair, one of a group of mariachis on "Ave Augustin Melger" in Mexicali, one of a bullfight, blood running down the bull's side in a black trickle as the matador held the cape out in what appeared to be a welcoming embrace.

Fortunately for the Historical Society, Mr. O'Hara was a fanatical historian. All the photographs, Christmas cards and postcards were labeled and dated. There were envelopes of money, colorful, foreign bills that reminded me of play money—long red bills 100 Cien Pesos from Chile, faded multicolored bills from France with a picture of a woman in a kerchief holding a baby and a hoe, a series 1944 Deutschland Eine Mark that he must have bought or been given during World War II. The photographs that appeared to be of family I set aside for Clay. Though he didn't think he'd want them, there might be someone in the next generation of O'Haras who might. Halfway through the personal pile, I grew tired of looking at photographs of people I didn't know standing in front of old Model A's or posed behind donkeys painted with zebra stripes in Tijuana, Mexico. I moved over to the San Celina pile. Here there were pictures and memorabilia I recognized, having seen many like them through the years of helping Dove catalog and store things for the Historical Society. There was a marvelous, clear picture of the old fire house which burned down shortly after World War II, showing the wooden bell tower that housed El Toro, the same siren that was such a big part of Mariko's memories.

There were pictures of places that still existed—the original San Celina train depot built back in the late 1870's, now a favorite restaurant of Gabe's serving healthy "California Cuisine" that couldn't stick to your ribs even if you drenched it in Krazy Glue, the old brick Safeway store with the block letters USO on the second floor, which was turned into an antique mall ten years ago, the mission-style San Celina Inn where Clay was currently staying.

Fatigue finally got the better of me about one A.M. The small, uneven print of the newspaper articles and faded old letters were becoming one big blur. I stood up and stretched, my eye catching a flat, unopened box at the bottom of the trunk. The heavy twine that was wound tightly around it was knotted and old. It took five minutes and a gold steak knife to free the box. It contained a small silky flag with tassels and a gold star in the middle. The kind that was displayed in the windows of homes where a member of the family was killed in combat. I studied it for a moment, thinking about what Thelma had told me about Mr. O'Hara's brother. Was it his brother's death that caused him to break up with Oralee? Grief did have a way of sometimes causing you to do things you later regret. I folded the flag back up and slipped it back into the box.

After a long, warm shower to loosen up my stiff neck, I picked up the wooden scrapbook and three ledgers from the "department store" pile, and went to bed. I flipped through the payroll ledger, mentally trying to convert the wages of fifty years ago to 1990's dollars. Another of the ledgers listed the cost of office supplies and employee expenses. I set it aside to show to Elvia. She'd get a real kick out of it. The last one appeared to be a record of personal loans made throughout the years he owned the department store. I trailed a finger down the names looking for any I recognized. I stopped at the name Yoshimi Yamaoka and wondered if that was Mariko's father. I continued to go through the ledger, and an odd pattern jumped out at me. Except for a scattered few Smiths, McGregors and Tripps, most of the names in the loan ledger were Japanese. I flipped through the ledger, trying to quickly calculate the amounts loaned. Beginning in late December 1941, Mr. O'Hara started loaning hundreds of thousands of dollars to the Japanese community, apparently, if I was reading the ledgers accurately, without any sort of interest at all. Many of the loans were paid back, which he meticulously noted, but many more of them weren't. I skipped to the end of the ledger. The last loan was made in the early seventies right before the store officially closed. I set the record book down on the nightstand and turned out the light. Though I was exhausted and the lighted dial of the clock-radio read 1:54 A.M., I tossed and turned and stared at the dark ceiling, the incongruity of Mr. O'Hara's hostile personality and his altruism as confusing to me as the two other men I was trying not to think about. I couldn't do anything about Gabe and Clay, but I could certainly look deeper into Mr. O'Hara, though there was no doubt I'd have to do it as unobtrusively as possible.

The next morning I woke with a lighter feeling in my heart than I'd felt for days. No reason why, except that the sun streaming through my kitchen window was warm and bright and, as I drank my coffee, an orange and black monarch butterfly performed its elaborate fan dance on the wooden ledge just for me. I mulled over the ledger books while eating my Lucky Charms cereal. No more oatmeal for me, I decided, except where it belonged, in chocolate no-bake cookies. A thought occurred to me while reading through the lists of names again.

In my bedroom, the San Celina telephone books were still piled in front of the mirror. I started looking up the names in the ledger. Out of over a hundred and fifty people to whom loans were made since 1941, twenty-five of them were still listed in the San Celina phone book. Many more of them had matching last names that could indicate a descendant of the original borrowers. I copied down the names and addresses of the twenty-five, not exactly sure why. I wouldn't have any trouble with having a reason to talk with them—the Historical Society interviews would help me there—but how in the world would I bring up something as personal as the money loaned to them by Mr. O'Hara? I suspected that the elderly Japanese, not being raised in the sometimes-too-open atmosphere of Western Culture, would probably be reticent about discussing such a private matter as a loan. Somehow I'd have to work it into the interview questions.

I drank my now lavender-colored milk straight out of the bowl and quickly changed into a pair of brown Levi's and an antique-white tailored shirt. Scrounging up my old leather backpack, I threw in the ledger, my tape recorder, a steno pad and a couple of mechanical pencils. Right before I left, I phoned Ramon. He'd promised to meet me at the museum and accompany me on these interviews so he could get an idea of what I wanted him and Todd to do. A little voice inside me warned me to call and remind him. Señora Aragon answered in her soothing, caramel voice.

"*Buenos días, señora,*" I said. "It's Benni."

"*Buenos días, chiquita,*" she said. "*Cómo esta?*"

"*Muy bien, gracias.* Is Ramon there?"

I heard her click her tongue. "*Perro flojo!* That lazy dog! He is not even out of his bed." Her tone was scolding, but affectionate. There wasn't much Ramon could do wrong in his mother's eyes.

"He's supposed to go with me today on the Historical Society interviews. Please tell him I'll be there in thirty minutes." Only by picking him up could I guarantee I wouldn't be sitting at the museum waiting for him to wander in whenever the mood struck him.

"I'll tell him, *chiquita,*" she said, her voice doubtful, giving me the ominous feeling I'd be doing the interviews alone today.

The sky was a bright, hard blue that caused me to hunt around in my backpack and slip on my sunglasses. The leaves on the trees shimmered from the rain last night and the breeze was downright cold. It seeped in around the rotting rubber weatherstripping of the truck windows, and by the time I drove across town to pick up Ramon, I was ready for a cup of Señora Aragon's strong hot coffee.

The cheerful yellow and white Aragon house sat on the corner lot of a neighborhood of older San Celina homes. Like many of its neighbors, it boasted a deep front yard, a couple of stark, towering walnut trees just starting to green, and a homemade swing set made of used truck tires and water-stained four-by-fours. The eclectically styled wood-frame house reflected the history and size of the Aragon family. They'd bought the house when Elvia was born and additional rooms had been tacked on as the family grew, the painted outside walls the same color, but the wood just dissimilar enough to give it an enthusiastic but slightly cockeyed look. Pulling up into the Aragons' narrow, flower-lined driveway always made me feel like a little girl again. I'd spent so much of my childhood staying "in town" with Elvia so I could participate in some after-school activity that this house was as much a part of my sense of "home" as the Ramsey Ranch.

When I walked into the kitchen, Ramon slumped bleary-eyed at the round maple table in a pair of his older brother's baggy green Army pants. He rested his head in his arms, his wavy hair tumbling around his bare, bony shoulders.

"You're not going like that, I hope," I said, helping myself to a cup of coffee and putting one of Señora Aragon's sweet Mexican pastries on a plate. Licking the pink frosting off my thumb, I opened the huge refrigerator and peered in.

"The milk's right here," he said in a grumpy tone. "And I'm not going at all. I think I have the flu."

"He has the lazy sickness," Señora Aragon said, walking into the room carrying a handful of colorful flowers in her brown, dimpled hand. She raised thick black eyebrows at me in a mocking manner that reminded me so much of Elvia, I laughed.

"Ah, Mama," he said, lifting his head. "I really am sick. I'm not even going to class today."

"He comes in at three o'clock in the *mañana* and complains he is *enfermo*." She slapped his smooth back. "I should tell your papa what time you get in and we'll see how sick you are."

"Mama," he whined. "You promised. I said I'd call next time."

She turned to me, shaking her head. "What do I do? He is *mocoso* but . . ." An indulgent look softened the heaviness around her deep brown eyes. She held out the bouquet of flowers to me. "You go see Jack today, *sí?* He always likes my flowers."

I glanced over at the Sav-on Drugstore calendar attached to the white refrigerator with two ladybug magnets made of pipecleaners and a grandchild's love. A warm flood of guilt washed over me. Today was the anniversary of the day Jack was killed, and it had begun without me even remembering. I took the flowers grown in Señora Aragon's small greenhouse and held them up to my face. The daisies, calla lilies, and pink roses gave off a clean, earthy scent that brought back a sharp memory of Jack. The first month we were married, to make the old Harper ranch house seem more like ours, we bought a hundred dollars worth of flowers to plant in the front window boxes and flower beds. As we removed them from the trays in the screened service porch of the house, we started a dirt fight that ended with us making love on the scratchy wooden floor, rolling among the empty plastic trays in a frenzied attempt to quench the fire that seemed to perpetually burn in our nineteen-year-old bodies.

"*Gracias, Mama Aragon,*" I said softly, taking the flowers and squeezing her hand. "He always said you grew the prettiest flowers in the county."

"*De nada, niña,*" she said, touching my cheek.

A sonorous groan filled the warm kitchen. Ramon pushed himself out of the chair with dramatic slowness, hugging his brown chest with smooth, hairless arms. "I'm going back to bed."

"Ramon," I said. "You were supposed to go with me today. How else will you . . ." His frantic eye action stopped me. I guess his mother didn't know about his problems in American History yet. I sighed. "Fine. I'll do it alone this time. But you promised—"

"I called Todd," he broke in. "He said we could switch places. He's supposed to meet you at the museum by nine o'clock."

"You had this planned all along," I said accusingly, looking up at the wall behind him. The red hen-shaped clock read ten minutes to nine.

"Yeah, right, Benni, like I can plan when I get the flu." His voice was sarcastic, but his soot-colored eyes smiled at me.

"Your mother's right, you are a brat." I turned to her. "Why do we put up with him?" She gave me a sympathetic smile and handed me some wet paper towels and tin foil to wrap around the ends of the flowers.

Todd sat in his little white Toyota waiting for me when I arrived at the museum fifteen minutes later.

"Well, looks like it's you and me, partner," I said. He looked up at me, his face expressionless.

"I guess," he said in a subdued voice. I wondered if he and Ramon had argued over who was going today. Ramon, as sweet and amusing as he could be sometimes, could also drive you crazy with his flakiness. This was probably not the first time Todd got stuck doing Ramon's work.

"Well, just observe what I say and do. Don't worry, I'll have a list of questions for you and Ramon to use when you go out by yourselves. Usually once you get older people talking, they do most of the work. Sometimes the hardest part is breaking away."

Our first interview was with a Mr. Kuroda who lived in a mobile home community not far from Oak Terrace. He waited for us on his front porch among an impressive array of blooming orchids. He was a wizened, balding man in his early seventies with clusters of dark brown age spots on both cheeks and a wide, ready smile. He wore a plaid sports shirt, gray slacks and a brown wool sports coat. He'd taught at the Japanese-language school in the Buddhist temple during the early forties. As I'd requested over the phone, he'd laid out piles of old black and white photographs. I set Todd to labeling Post-its with Mr. Kuroda's name and address to place on the backs of the photographs we'd take with us.

Mr. Kuroda held a small red silk pillow in his lap. As he talked, he turned it over and over, smoothing the fringe with his hand. His parents had owned a small farm out near the state prison on the road to Morro Bay. They grew celery, pole beans and winter peas and sold much of their produce to Chinese restaurants up and down the coast. Like Mariko's brother, he'd volunteered for the armed service, but had been stationed in North County at Camp Johnson teaching the Japanese language and customs to the officers of the 87th Infantry Training Battalion. It was what saved him from going to one of the relocation camps. As a teacher in the Japanese school, he would have been one of the first to go.

"The day after Pearl Harbor they started taking men," he said. "Anyone who owned a boat or had anything to do with fishing, those who had contributed to Japanese organizations, those who taught martial arts. Even the Buddhist monks. Anything that was too Japanesy. They were sent all over—South Dakota, Montana, New Mexico. Not the regular camps, but special ones, just for the high-risk people. Luckily, I was okayed by the draft board and I spent the whole war right here in the county."

"What happened to your family's farm?" I asked. His smiling face became pensive.

"Right after Pearl Harbor, many people were very kind, but so many others would have liked us to just go away. The San Celina Farm Bureau, the Grower-Shipper Fruit and Vegetable Co-op, the San Celina County Farmers, the San Celina County Association of Retail Distributors, some labor unions, some posts of the American Legion. These people were our friends and neighbors, but we could see what was coming. Those who owned stores sold off as much as they could for prices that would break your heart. Then there was an article in the newspaper—an editorial that was titled 'The Japanese Alien Menace.' It was in January, right after a Union Oil tanker was sunk off the coast a few miles from here. Oh, the article said it wasn't aimed at Japanese-Americans, but the distinction between the 'enemy' and us was already getting hazy. My father kept saying, 'They want our land, that is the whole thing, they want our land.' '' He gave an ironic laugh. ''And many times, he was right.''

''Did they get your family's farm?'' I asked.

''No,'' he said, hugging the silk pillow to his chest. ''We were luckier than most. We had someone who bought our farm, then sold it back to us when my parents returned from the camp. But not everyone was that lucky. Our patron had only so much money.''

''Was this patron Mr. Brady O'Hara?'' I asked, though I knew the answer. I'd checked the ledger before the interview. The Kurodas' name was one of the first on the list.

''Yes,'' he said, a bit surprised. ''How did you know?''

''Research,'' I said vaguely.

I continued with the rest of my questions, not mentioning Mr. O'Hara again until right before the end of the interview. ''Mr. Kuroda, I was just wondering one small thing about the loan from Mr. O'Hara. Why did he help you? Was he a personal friend of your parents or something?''

''Actually, no.'' Mr. Kuroda's face became puzzled. ''We didn't know him at all, though of course we traded in his store. It was the biggest department store within a hundred miles in those days. I was the one who told my parents he was buying up Japanese-owned properties with the written legal documents to sell them back to us when the war was over.''

''How did you know he was doing this?''

''Until the war, I worked with Rose Ann Violet as a teaching assistant,'' he said. ''Such a wonderful woman. So tragic what happened to her and Mr. O'Hara. She was helping me fill out applications and pass the tests to go to the university in San Francisco so I could become a teacher in the public school. She asked me about my parents' farm and then told me Mr. O'Hara could help me. That all I had to do was mention her name.''

"And he did it? Just like that?"

"Just like that," he said.

Driving on the interstate toward our next interview with the Sukami sisters, I contemplated Mr. Kuroda's story. Next to me, Todd sat quietly looking out the window, and after a while, I felt guilty for being so self-absorbed and tried to draw him into a conversation.

"So, what do you think about Mr. Kuroda's story?" I asked, turning on the road that led to the Sukami house.

"It's sad, I guess." He shrugged, apparently uninterested in anything that happened that long ago. "Can I change this?" He started flipping the stations on the truck's radio before I could answer, stopping at one that was playing one of those lovely, mind-numbing rap songs. He turned his head away from me, looking out the window, beating the rhythm of the obviously familiar song on the side of the door.

"Sure," I said, wondering for the second time today whether having Ramon and Todd help me on this project had been one of my wisest ideas. Neither seemed interested enough to be of any use to me.

The interview with the Sukami sisters, Haru and Yoshi-ko, was a bit more lighthearted than Mr. Kuroda's. They were in their early seventies and had lived in San Celina since the early thirties. They regaled us with hilarious stories about learning the English language and customs and how as teenagers they managed to sneak away from their strict father and attend the beach parties held by their school chums. Even Todd cracked a smile when they told the story about their father using a metal rake to chase away an amorous boy who came calling. By the time the boy's story made the rounds at school, the rake had become a samurai sword and their small but sturdy father had gained an impressive twelve inches and seventy-five pounds. I finally felt comfortable enough to steer the conversation around to Mr. O'Hara and his loans, and found, not to my surprise, their story was almost identical to Mr. Kuroda's. The only difference was their family had owned a small notions and gift store. Apparently Mr. O'Hara had not only bought up all their stock at full price, but kept the lease going on the building until they returned. Because of him, they were able to come back to San Celina County after spending the war years in Manzanar, the internment camp in the high plains of Inyo County. They were not at all reluctant to tell me about Mr. O'Hara's kindness and were understandably shocked at his murder.

"We were very sorry to hear of his death. I wonder why there was no service?" Yoshiko, the younger sister, said.

"He requested that there wouldn't be one," I said.

"You know, if Mr. O'Hara hadn't helped our family," Haru said, "we would have had to start over somewhere else like so many others did. Our father loved San Celina and wanted to return after the war. It was very kind of Mr. O'Hara, though we don't know why he did it. When our father went to the department store to thank him in person, he wouldn't see him."

"That's odd," I said. "I wonder why?"

She softly crumpled the delicate ecru doily she'd been tatting during our talk. "That always bothered our father, that he could never thank him face to face. But it was all done through Mr. O'Hara's accountant. My father sent Mr. O'Hara a beautiful blue and white china tea set, but it was sent back with no explanation. Why he helped us, people who were strangers to him and then refused our gratitude, remained a mystery that troubled our father until the day he died. But he must have been good-hearted, don't you think? Why else would he help us?"

"I have no idea," I said. Yet, I added silently.

14

"IT'S PAST NOON. You hungry?" I asked Todd when we
left the Sukami sisters and pulled onto Interstate 101. To
our left, a billboard advertising Hogie's Truckstop Cafe
flashed by. A pie-faced man wearing a red ten-gallon hat
and clutching an oversized knife and fork in his hands
promised "Good Vittles—Two miles ahead—Biscuits and
Gravy 24 hours a day."

"I guess," he said, turning his head to stare out the window.

"I'll treat you to lunch. Hogie's okay?"

He gave a noncommittal shrug. I assumed it meant that
as long as he didn't have to pay, it was fine with him.

Hogie's had retained all the scarred, fifties truckstop li-
noleum ambience that made it such an interesting place to
work fifteen years ago. The songs on the jukebox were by
country singers who hadn't had a hit in twenty years, there
was Brach's pick-a-mix candy in a huge green plastic bowl
next to the cash register, and as Dove would say, the coffee
wasn't just strong, it was downright stout. When Jack and
I were first married and our cut of the Ramsey Ranch profits
was too small to meet our needs, I worked graveyard shift
here three nights a week. I look back now and wonder how
in the world I survived going to school, working on the
ranch, sleeping in the early evening and working nights

slinging ham and cheese omelettes and pouring endless cups of coffee.

I peered over the sea of rainbow-colored feed caps and sweat-stained cowboy hats and steered Todd toward a torn leatherette booth over in the corner. Above us a clattering, dust-sticky fan ruffled the paper place mats. Our waitress, a chubby middle-aged blonde wearing a faded Stanford sweatshirt, asked us what our pleasure was in a smoky, Tanya Tucker voice. She served us water without asking and whisked our orders back to the cook before we could drop a quarter in the table-top jukebox. Her well-worn Etonic jogging shoes assured me that this woman took her job seriously.

"So, how's school?" I asked, settling somewhat crookedly into one side of the bench seat. A cotton volcano of stuffing erupted from the side nearest the wall.

"Okay, I guess," Todd answered. He picked at a cigarette burn on the pale green Formica table with his thumb and avoided my eyes.

"Do you like your classes?" I felt like someone's boring old aunt asking such unimaginative questions, but I couldn't think of how else to get a conversation started with him.

"Sure. I guess."

There was a long stretch of silence. Well, you tried, I thought, and decided that companionable quiet would suit me just fine. While we waited for our food to arrive, I flipped through the selections on the jukebox. Luckily, conversation was unnecessary when our strawberry malts, cheeseburgers and chili fries arrived. I turned my thoughts to what I'd learned about Mr. O'Hara, and was so deep in contemplation, Todd had to rap sharply on the table in front of me to get my attention.

"What?" I asked, surprised he was even talking. Maybe his problem had been calorie deficiency.

"Who are the flowers in the truck for?" he asked. By the slightly exasperated look on his face, it was apparently not the first time he'd asked.

"Sorry, just gathering a little wool." I picked up a chili-covered french fry. "I'm going to the cemetery later. They're for my husband's grave."

"Oh." He looked down at his empty white plate, running his thumbs around the edge. "When did he die?"

"Last year. On this date, as a matter of fact."

"Oh." He dug at the cigarette burn again, this time with the edge of his fork. "What did he die of?"

I looked at him curiously. "A car accident. Todd, you've been friends with Ramon for a while. You knew about Jack."

"Yeah, I know. I . . ." He set the fork down carefully next to his plate. A red flush crept up his smooth, tanned neck.

"Is there something wrong?"

"No." His voice gave a sharp squeak.

Remembering that his mother had died only a few months ago and suspecting that was where this was going, I prompted, "Is there something else you want to know?"

"I, uh . . ." His voice cracked and he picked up the pepper shaker, unscrewed the cap and poured a mound into his empty plate. I resisted the motherly urge to grab it out of his hand.

"Todd," I said softly, taking a chance. "Do you want to ask me a question about death?"

"Sort of." He stuck his finger in the mound of pepper and started making circles. "I was wondering if maybe you knew . . . I mean, if you could tell me . . ." He shoved the plate away irritably. "Never mind. It was stupid. Forget it."

"No, I won't forget it," I said. "And I'm sure it's not stupid. Look, just try me. Whatever you say is between you and me and that mountain of pepper there. Okay?"

Grave aqua eyes contemplated me for a moment. He gave a deep sigh. "Okay. I guess I was just wondering if you could tell me when it starts to . . . uh . . . feel . . . you know, better. I mean, after someone, after they . . . well, you know."

"Oh, Todd," I said. "I know losing your mom is a hard thing. And your grandmother too. I don't know what to tell you, except for what it's been like for me. Really, I guess it just depends on the person. It's taken me longer with Jack than it did with my mother, but I was only six when she died. Sometimes she seems more like a dream than a real person. Emotions are a funny thing. To tell you the truth, there are still times when it feels like it was yesterday that Jack died and I'll cry like it just happened. Then there are days when I don't think of him at all.''

"I do that." His face got that still, transparent look toddlers get right before they cry. "I go to bed at night and then I realize I haven't thought of Mom all day. I hate myself for that. Except for me, there's no one else to remember her, and like an asshole, even I forget." He slammed his fist on the table, his mouth turned down in disgust.

"What about your grandfather?" I asked "Don't you two ever talk about her?"

"Benni, I don't *get* him. He goes on like it never happened. Go to the store. Come home. Buy the fish, clean the fish, sell the fish. He's already put away all her pictures. I found them and asked him and he just said, it's over now, forget it. So I put them up in *my* room. I think all he cares about is his stupid fish and his stupid customers." He picked up his mustard-stained napkin and started tearing strips off it.

"Todd, everyone handles grief differently. Maybe your grandfather just couldn't bear to look at her picture, especially so soon after your grandmother died."

"He should sell that place." He pushed the shredded napkin aside. "He's too old and it doesn't make money and if he thinks I'm going to—"

"That going to be all for you folks?" Our waitress gave us a large, baking-soda white smile, ripped our ticket off her pad and slapped it down on the table.

"That should do it," I said. Todd slid out of the booth and headed for the door. I paid the bill and desperately tried to think of a way to continue our conversation. He obviously needed someone to talk to and I doubted that I'd be able to convince him to get counseling, so it looked like it would have to be me.

He sat in the truck waiting for me, his face blank as a cat's. I started toward the museum, trying to figure a way to restart our earlier conversation. Finally, I just blurted out, "Todd, would you like to go to the cemetery with me?" I suspected his mom and grandmother were buried there too. Maybe that would make him feel better.

"No," he answered, without turning his head. Then added, "Thanks, anyway."

"Sure," I said. Well, that's that, I said to myself. Better stick to your quilts and samplers and leave human emotions to the professionals. My heart ached for what he was going through.

We didn't say another word to each other the rest of the drive back. When I dropped him off, I told him since tomorrow was Saturday and I'd most likely be at the co-op's Mardi Gras booth all day, he was free until Monday morning.

"Maybe I'll see you at the festival or the parade?"

"Maybe," he answered. "Thanks for . . . uh, lunch."

"No problem," I said, watching him climb into his little car and drive out of the parking lot without a backward glance.

The sky was streaked with shades of mauve and red by the time I reached the cemetery. Surrounded by towering old Monterey pines and pale-barked Valley oaks, it was out past the county gun range on a road that eventually leads through the foothills to the ocean. Jack and I had passed this cemetery hundreds of times on the way to the beach, stopping occasionally so I could leave flowers on my mother's grave.

"Make sure I get a good northern view when I check in here," Jack always teased me while I arranged our grocery-store bouquets of odd-colored carnations and white daisies. "I don't want to spend eternity with the sun in my eyes."

He was buried in the newer section, where if you stood back and squinted your eyes, you could almost believe it was a park where children play Red Rover and a pickup baseball game could occur at any moment. It's only when you're actually walking on it that the little marble squares remind you that there are no games being played here. It had been almost a month since I'd last visited his grave. Even so, the grass around the stone was neatly trimmed.

"Hey, Dagwood," I said, arranging Señora Aragon's flowers in the in-ground vase in front of his black marble marker. "It's Blondie." I sat cross-legged on the damp lawn and faced the stone, brushing traces of grass off the letters of his name: *John William Harper II—Beloved Husband, Son and Brother—Born February 25, 1958—Died February 19, 1992—You Are Always in Our Hearts*. "Making some good sandwiches up there?"

Like his cartoon counterpart, his sandwiches were legend in the Harper family—odd combinations of ham, roast beef, bologna, peanut butter, pickles and pimento cheese spread. Weird mixtures that would turn most people's stomachs. He always declared in his teasing tenor voice there wasn't anything put between two pieces of bread that he wouldn't eat. That remark predictably inspired somewhat raunchy suggestions from his brother, Wade, and the ranch hands.

The first few months after he died, I came to his grave every day. Before it happened to me, I had always looked in a slightly condescending way at people who seemed to worship the ground where their loved ones were buried. I couldn't comprehend why they felt the need to decorate a piece of ground with flowers, flags, metallic balloons and Christmas trees. Their obsession was baffling to me.

"Nothing's there," I'd say to Jack. "Why do they keep coming back?"

"It's somewhere to go," he'd answered simply.

After he died, I realized how much better than me he understood human nature. I knew that the real Jack, the one I laughed with, fought with, made love with, wasn't underneath that carpet of grass. But I kept coming back to it, the way you compulsively examine a wound as it slowly turns into a scar, checking to assure yourself that, yes, it happened, it really happened.

Then I would skip a day, then two, then Dove and Daddy

needed my help at the ranch, or we had a busy day at the museum. Before I knew it, my daily life didn't include this place anymore. It was probably something Daddy could have told me; he and I visit my mother's grave together only once a year on Mother's Day and had as long as I could remember. But I suppose he realized I had to break away in my own time and, without realizing it was happening, I had. I felt ashamed sitting there looking at Jack's shiny headstone. It was almost as if he had died again, only this time it was me who pronounced his death. I closed my eyes and remembered the last time we made love, two days before he died. Nothing special about it, just the soft, comfortable lovemaking of two people who knew each other's bodies as well as their own. Would we have felt more passion, made it last longer, said all the things we didn't say anymore if we'd guessed it was the last time?

Thinking of last times, Todd came to mind. Ramon had told me Todd's mother had died of cancer. I wondered what the circumstances were the last time he saw her. I picked up half of Señora Aragon's flowers.

"You don't mind sharing, do you, honey?" I asked Jack. I walked over to the cemetery office to ask for directions to Keiko Simmons' grave. It was only a short distance from Jack's. I set the flowers down in front of the rose-colored marble and read the headstone.

Keiko Rose Watanabe Simmons—Born September 20, 1942—Died December 1, 1992. Delicate lilies-of-the valley were carved on the four corners of the shiny pink stone. I stared at the headstone for a moment, then looked to the left of it. A matching headstone read: *Anthony Simmons— Born March 31, 1943—Died September 12, 1985.* Todd had been nine years old when his father died. Old enough to feel the pain of loss, but not truly understand it. I wanted so badly to help him with his grief, but couldn't think of one single thing I could do.

Thunder sounded in the foothills to the south, where the wispy clouds had thickened. I walked back toward my truck, my feet sinking slightly into grass still spongy from last night's rain. Except for the cemetery's maintenance truck, mine was the only vehicle left on the grounds. I looked across the wide expanse of lawn and could just make out the outline of the flowers I'd placed on Jack's grave. The wind whipped the tops of the pines, releasing a clean, metallic smell into the air. A blue and gold Garfield balloon broke away from an arrangement and danced up into the swirling air.

I stood in front of the truck and watched the wind flatten the bouquets people had so carefully placed. A part of me didn't want to leave. Somehow I knew this visit was different, that I wouldn't return for a long time and that when I did, it wouldn't be the same.

"We'll be together forever," Jack said to me on the day we got married. We had crept away from the reception at the Harper Ranch, from the well-wishers and joke-tellers and hid in the hay loft, feet dangling over the side. We drank from the stolen bottle of champagne that Dove, because we were only nineteen, wouldn't let us drink toasts with and giggled at my uncle Arnie. He'd found Daddy's old guitar and was treating the guests to a rather pitiful rendition of a Carpenters' song—"Close to You."

"Right," I said, pushing him back in the loose hay. His chest was hard as iron from working cattle and bucking alfalfa bales. Touching it never failed to make me catch my breath. "Forever until I'm forty and you trade me in for two twenty-year-olds."

"I'd never do that," he said, reaching up and pulling me down to him. The sweet warmth of his kiss made me wish that moment would last forever. "I'll never leave you, Benni." He looked deeply into my eyes. "You do believe that, don't you?" Before I could answer, his brother, Wade, found us and forced us to come back to the reception, where we kissed for the photographer, threw the bouquet, ate wedding cake made by Dove and Aunt Garnet, and started our life.

I still wonder what I would have answered if Wade had come just thirty seconds later.

15

Before pulling on clean Wranglers the next morning, I received three phone calls from frantic artists. But even all the little emergencies of missing booth poles, broken pots and whose turn it was to get the front display area, didn't fracture my peaceful frame of mind. By all rights, I should have felt terrible. After seeing Jack's grave, I'd come home and curled up on the sofa, using Gabe's sweatshirt for a pillow. Gabe's comforting scent, memories of Jack and confused feelings about Clay muddled my brain most of the night, keeping me awake until almost dawn. But by the time the sun lit my window shades, for no logical reason, I felt strangely content, though a bit punchy from lack of sleep. Your goal, I told myself while pulling on my new pair of brown calfskin Nocona boots and soft chamois shirt, is to get through one whole day without going into emotional overload.

At the museum, I spent the first hour of my day putting the finishing touches on the cross-stitch exhibit: laying out the printed programs, rearranging a few samplers, choosing the cross-stitched items we'd sell in the gift shop. The L.A. *Times* reporter had called and we'd set up an appointment for the interview at eight o'clock Monday morning, right before the Oak Terrace group arrived at nine to continue work on the Steps to the Altar quilt. She'd liked the idea of incorporating the Oak Terrace quilting class into the article. Clay called twice. Luckily, both times someone else answered the phone and I didn't return his calls. To tell the truth, I had absolutely no idea what to say to him.

I was sitting in the kitchen enjoying my third cup of coffee, when Jan, one of our fabric artists, walked in. A willowy blonde with a musical laugh and a gentle nature, her generous Scandinavian mouth drooped in an uncustomary scowl.

"It's our turn, Benni," she said. "The mud-slingers had the front display area at the last festival." A conflict had been brewing all morning between the quilters and the potters, and though I felt guilty for avoiding what *was* part of my job, I'd been slipping around trying to stay away from both groups.

"Well," I said, thinking that was just about all the opinion I had about anything this morning.

"They are so arrogant," she continued. "Malcolm keeps calling it our potholder and blankie display. This from a Neanderthal who makes glorified ashtrays."

"Well," I said, more sympathetically this time and adding a concerned-looking tilt to my head.

"We'll share the space," she said firmly, pouring herself a cup of coffee and adding two heaping teaspoons of sugar. "That's the most I'll give in."

"Sounds fair," I said to her retreating back.

I volunteered to haul a load over to the booth, more to avoid the possibility of hearing the potters' side of the display issue than for any virtuous reason. After dropping the pots and quilts off at the blue-and-white-striped booth, I nabbed one of the last spots in the public parking lot on Lopez Street. According to the pealing of the mission's bell, it was nine o'clock. I walked down the already crowded sidewalk to Blind Harry's to watch Elvia panic and perhaps steal one of Jose's chocolate chip muffins. The bookstore wasn't open yet, but peering through the front window, it was obvious by the frenzied activity that Elvia, in her General Patton-style of management, was gearing them up for the long, hopefully profitable day.

A hermaphrodite answered my knock on the locked front door. The left side of "it" was dressed in jungle camouflage army fatigues and half a Dodgers baseball cap; the right side wore half a red skirt, white silk blouse, faux pearls and half a yellow curly wig.

"Brad, or maybe I should say Barbara. You look like something out of a Truman Capote novel," I said. "How do you know which restroom to use?"

"The ladies, of course," he said, green eyes twinkling. The female eye wore makeup resembling the pattern of a peacock feather. He was Elvia's assistant manager, an employee she trusted so completely he even knew the combination to the safe. This was going to be his last Mardi Gras in San Celina for some time. He graduated from Cal Poly in June and was heading north for veterinary school at UC Davis. Elvia had been whining about it for months. "The hardest part," he said next to my ear, locking the door behind me, "is when I have to smack myself for getting fresh."

"You're sick," I said.

He chuckled and straightened his half-mustache. "As is the whole world, Benni. Especially today. *La Padrona* is upstairs in her cave. Be careful, she's baring her canines this morning. You'd better grab a mask before all the good ones are gone." He pointed at the display of feathered and sequined masks near the door and loped off toward the children's section.

I dug through, picked out a deep brown and green feathered one with slanted cat's-eye slits outlined in emerald sequins, and headed upstairs. Elvia sat behind her antique mahogany executive desk, typing on her laptop computer. She wore a form-fitting black jersey dress accented with South American copper jewelry and trimmed around the neck with feathers in the multicolor browns and rusts of a hawk's tail. An elaborate matching mask made of satin and sequins with tall, perfect feathers rested on the corner of her desk.

"This thing must be three feet high," I said, picking it up and looking through the eye slits. "I stole one of your masks, by the way. Brad said I could.'' I held it up in front of my face.

She looked up from her computer, her black eyebrows knitted together in irritation. "What am I going to do when he leaves? Are you sure you don't want to quit that museum job of yours? You'd like the book business. No temperamental artists. Great benefits. I need someone I can trust.''

"I have done many foolish things in my life, especially lately, but there are some things even I am not crazy enough to do.''

Her frown deepened. "Are you implying I'm difficult to work for?''

I just smiled, picked up her coffee cup and took a sip.

"Get your own," she said, grabbing at the mug. "I hate drinking after people.''

I held the coffee out of her reach. "Be nice, I'm here to help. Got anything you need me to do?''

"As a matter of fact, yes. You can take the truck out back and go pick up our crawfish order from Morita's. Jose has both his assistants chopping vegetables or some such thing, and I think I'm going to open a half hour early, so I can't spare any of my clerks.''

"For you, dear friend, anything." I took another sip of her coffee and set it back down in front of her.

"Why are you so cheerful this morning?" She gave the cup a cross look, pushed it aside and waved at me to leave. "Never mind, I'm too busy to hear about your love life. The keys to the truck are in the register.''

"I've decided this whole love business is too complex. I think I'm going to buy a new horse. An auction's coming up in Paso Robles in two weeks. Maybe I'll get back into barrel-racing. That's what I need, a hobby. I have too much spare time on my hands. You know what they say about idle hands.''

Elvia gave a dainty snort.

"I'm serious. Who needs men? All their brains are in their front pockets anyway.''

"Take it from someone who has been there. Do not, I repeat, do not make any rash decisions about anything while you are in this state of sexual hysteria. Wait until you're rational again."

"I am perfectly rational," I said, with dignity. "And I am not in any state of hysteria whatsoever."

"Well, don't say I didn't warn you. Now go get my fish. And the mask is five ninety-five plus tax. You can add it to your account, which you are a week and a half late in paying this month, I might add."

And people wonder why the bookstore's such a success.

When I drove into Morita's back parking lot, a plain white refrigerated truck pulled out, leaving one of the three employee spaces free. Mr. Morita's Honda and Todd's white Toyota occupied the other two. I knocked on the back door and when no one answered, walked in. An old wooden desk sat in the corner of the room. Piled haphazardly on the pitted top were stacks of old invoices, dusty ledgers, and a handleless blue teacup and matching teapot. Next to the black phone sat one of those cheap gold multi-photo frames from K-Mart. I started to pick it up and look at the black-and-white and color snapshots, when angry voices interrupted me. They came from behind the swinging doors separating the storeroom from the market. I stood on tiptoe and peeked through one of the small glass windows. Mr. Morita jabbed a thick finger in the air in front of Todd's chest. Todd stared at the ground, his face tight and flushed with anger. Then Mr. Morita reached up and sharply slapped the side of his grandson's head. Todd raised a fist and held it in front of him for a split second, his body trembling as if grasped by a seizure. I held my breath, waiting. Todd let out a small whimper, dropped his hand, turned and barreled toward the swinging doors. He banged them open, just missing me.

"Wait," I said, as he ran past me, his long hair flying behind him. But he kept going, reaching an arm out and sweeping it across the desk, sending the picture frame and tea set crashing to the floor before slamming the back door. Mr. Morita walked in on me picking up pieces of broken glass and throwing them in the plastic trash can.

"So sorry," he said. "My grandson, he is . . ." He

picked up a broom and started sweeping up glass and china with brisk, definite strokes. His face was empty of emotion.

"It's okay." I smiled, trying to put him at ease. "He's a teenager. Hormones, you know." I shook the picture frame over the trash can, dumping the rest of the shattered glass. Most of the pictures were old. The largest, a black-and-white five-by-seven, was of a young Japanese couple dressed in forties-style clothing. She was a bit chubby and very pretty and looked to be about Todd's age. The man looked a year or two older. "Is this you and your wife?"

"Yes," he said, his voice so low I had to bend my head to hear him. "We were just married."

"When was it?"

"April in 1942." His dark eyes grew soft and liquid. "My Hatsumi was a good wife. A very good wife." He shook his head in disgust. "Not like grandson. He's like his mother, always fighting this, fighting that."

I peered closely at the fuzzy photograph. There appeared to be stables in the background, a chain-link fence, some children playing with a ball of some kind. Mr. Morita and his new wife squinted against the bright sun. "Where did you get married?" I asked. "Was this somewhere on your honeymoon?"

He set the broom aside and took the picture from me. "The guard was very kind. We were not allowed cameras, but he felt pity on us, just married and no marriage picture. He could have gotten in much trouble. His name was Joe. He gave us a beer to drink, to toast our marriage and made us laugh with stories of his little boy. He came from Nebraska and his father grew corn. He wanted to grow corn too, when the war was over. Just like his father. He felt bad about having to guard us. He said, 'I'm sorry, Mr. Morita, I'm sorry.' Over and over. Like *he* make the camp. I told him, it's okay, not his fault, think about corn he has to go back to."

"Oh," was all I could manage to say. I hadn't even put two and two together when he mentioned the date. "That's a wonderful story, Mr. Morita. Would you mind if I wrote it up and put it in the Historical Society book?"

He looked troubled for a moment. "I don't know . . ."

"I know it doesn't mean anything to Todd now, but maybe it will someday, when he gets older. When he can appreciate what you and your wife went through to give him what he has today."

"Maybe," he said. "Maybe not. Sometimes maybe just better to forget."

"Please," I said, thinking that perhaps when I wrote it up I could show it to Todd. Then he could see what his grandfather had gone through, why his store meant so much to him, even maybe why he found it easier to ignore reality, even a reality as terrible as the deaths of a wife and daughter.

"Okay," he said wearily.

I looked quickly over the rest of the pictures. They were the usual family snapshots and school portraits. I guessed that Hatsumi or perhaps Keiko, Todd's mother, put together this collage for Mr. Morita. One was obviously Keiko's first school picture and another was Todd's. Another was a family shot of Mr. Morita, Hatsumi, Keiko holding Todd, and another Japanese man in some sort of military uniform.

"Who is this?" I asked, wondering if Mr. Morita had another child.

He glanced over at where I was pointing. "Todd's father."

"Anthony Simmons?" I looked back in confusion at the photograph. He didn't appear to be part Caucasian.

"No, *real* father," Mr. Morita said. "Leo Watanabe. Died in Vietnam. Now, I must get back to work." He picked up a broom and started sweeping up the glass.

"Oh," I said, wondering where Todd's Caucasian genes came from, but knowing it would be rude to ask. Maybe I'd ask Ramon the next time I saw him—or maybe even Todd himself. I stood awkwardly watching him sweep, then suddenly remembered why I'd come to the fish store. "I'm supposed to pick up some crawfish for Blind Harry's."

"Of course, of course," he said, setting the broom down, nodding his head and smiling. "Right here."

I loaded the boxes of frozen fish in the back of the truck, and after dropping them off at Blind Harry's, I decided to take a walk down to Bonita Street, where the major part of the Mardi Gras Festival was taking place. Both entrances to the side street, which intersected Lopez, were blocked off with sawhorses and arched with gold, green and purple helium-filled balloons. Long yellow plastic tape resembling police-line tape, with the cheerful command "Have a Happy Mardi Gras" in purple print decorated the wooden booths. Plastic Mardi Gras beads in gaudy, brilliant blues, pinks and oranges, gold "King Baby" earrings, sparkly metallic wigs, and cheap plastic masks of Bill and Hillary Clinton, Ross Perot and Bozo the Clown seemed to be selling quicker than the street vendors could restock the plastic bins. Though it wasn't eleven o'clock yet, food booths featuring dirty rice, crawfish gumbo, sweet potato pie, red beans and rice, shrimp po-boys and muffelata sandwiches were already pushing their wares.

In front of Marshalls Jewelry Store—since 1889—a green and purple crepe paper skirt surrounded a long folding table where two elaborately decorated chairs were the thrones for this year's Mardi Gras King and Queen—Jeff and Marie Booker—twins who finished first in team roping at last year's Mid-State Fair Rodeo. A big yellow sign in front of the table stated "Judging area for the Greatest Gumbo in the West. Proceeds go to St. Mary's Shelter for Abused Children." A list tacked to the front named the volunteer participants. One of the entries was the San Celina Police Department, and before I could catch myself I thought, I'll have to ask Gabe who the Cajun cook was. I swallowed hard and walked away, trying to ignore the depression that gnawed at my heart. At the co-op's crowded booth, feelings between the warring creative factions seemed to have cooled down. Jan and Malcolm were laughing at a mime prancing behind a woman with a poodle dyed pale lavender and wearing a small black Mardi Gras mask attached to its tiny head with wide rubber bands. The front display area contained an equal amount of pottery and quilts.

I was waiting in line to get something to drink and trying to decide whether I really wanted to try some gumbo this early in the day, when a hand gently grabbed the back of my neck.

"Buy you a beer? Root beer, that is."

I looked up at Mac, my stomach lurching with anxiety, remembering the last time we talked at the Reid Ranch. The friendly smile on his face reassured me. "Sure, I'll always accept a free drink."

"Let's go over here," he said, carrying our frosty cans over to a vacant wooden bench across from the Old West façade of the San Celina Brewing Company. Crawfiche Pye, this year's official Mardi Gras band, was playing a Dixieland jazz version of "Bye Bye Blackbird." We sat silently watching the musicians—a pocked-faced Asian boy on electric guitar, a surfer with a blond ponytail and black math-teacher glasses on bass fiddle, a fat woman in an orange muumuu playing congo drums and two men dressed like the Blues Brothers blowing trumpets the color of stainless steel.

"You look tired," Mac said. The band struck up a calypso version of "Go Down Moses."

I took a sip of my root beer. "Bad night. The memory goblins came to visit. You know how that goes."

"Yes, I certainly do," he said, sitting back and stretching his arm across the back of the bench. "How's Gabe?"

"I guess you'll have to ask him."

"I was afraid of that. I'm sorry if what I did caused trouble between you two. I didn't tell him you saw me."

"I know you didn't, but he's a good cop. He figured it out on his own. Don't worry about it. Sometimes these things just aren't meant to be."

He slipped his massive arm down around my shoulders and hugged me. "I don't think that's the case here. I've seen the way he looks at you."

"You didn't see the way he looked at me when he found out I held something back from him. I don't think you realize how sacred crime-scene evidence is to him."

"I have my suspicions. He really read me the riot act

when I went in and confessed. And everything he said was absolutely right. I have no excuse, except that I don't want my grandmother involved.''

"Does he know what you picked up has to do with her?''

"I think he might, though he didn't press it. You're right, he's not a stupid man. He said he wouldn't bring charges against me, at least not right now. There's an officer on duty in my grandmother's wing at night. I have a feeling Gabe's just biding his time, waiting to see what might happen. Whatever he has up his sleeve, he's not telling me.''

"Or me.''

He drained the rest of his root beer. "I went to the board of deacons on Tuesday and told them what I did. I've kind of thrown them into a quandary. The church will have to take a vote. Looks like I may not be living in San Celina much longer." He stretched out his arms in front of him. "I don't know what to do about Grandma, though. She'd hate me leaving here, but if the church asks for my resignation, I'll have to go somewhere else.''

"I talked to her on Wednesday.''

He rested his ankle on his knee and gave a noncommittal sound.

"She wouldn't tell me a thing," I continued. "She said that you didn't know what this was all about, that you were lying to me when you said you did. Were you?''

He watched the musicians and tapped the empty can on his thigh in time to the Cajun rhythms. "I can't talk about that," he finally said.

"Is that a yes or a no?''

He gave a sigh worthy of his wide chest and crumpled the can with one hand. "You know, it seems like in less than a week, everything I've spent the last twenty years learning about morality has flown out the window. I found out something about myself I didn't like.''

"What's that?''

"The realization that, for certain people, I would do anything, even break the law, to protect them. And if I can break man's laws so easily, will God's laws be far behind?

What kind of minister, what kind of Christian does that make me?''

I looked at my hands, knowing my answer would be inadequate. But it was the only one I had. ''The human kind, I guess.''

He shook his head in disgust and tossed the crumpled can in the recycling bin next to the bench. ''I need to walk. See you later.'' He stood up and started to move into the crowd.

''Wait,'' I said, tossing my can after his and dodging people to catch up to him. ''What about Oralee? Are you just going to leave it like this?''

''What do you mean?''

''Maybe if you and I talked to her together, she'd tell us what this is all about and it'll help solve the murders and . . .''

''Benni, just let it be.'' His voice was low and sharp. ''Things are bad enough . . . I mean it. We burned that letter . . .'' He stopped abruptly. ''Just stay out of it,'' he said and pushed his way into the crowd.

''Okay,'' I said out loud. ''So it was a letter. Big deal. That doesn't tell me anything.''

I bought myself a shrimp po-boy sandwich more for something to do than hunger and walked over to Lopez Street to watch the city workers set up the bleachers and judging booths for the parade. I waved to Miguel, who was supervising the placing of the police barriers. He was dressed in the jeans, navy blue polo shirt and dark San Celina Police windbreaker that the officers wear when they're on crowd control at the more casual city functions. I perched on the brick wall in front of Currant's, a Danish-style bakery and coffee house, and took a bite of my French roll, gagging on the excess mayonnaise. I opened it up and started popping the fried shrimp into my mouth, trying to decide what to do about Oralee and Mac. With each shrimp, I counted off, ''get involved, don't get involved.'' That seemed to be as logical a way to make a decision as any. I was down to five shrimp and no closer to a conclusion, when the sound of knuckles on glass made me lose count.

I turned around and peered through the rippled window of Currant's. Over in the corner, next to the smoke-stained potbelly stove, a chubby hand beckoned me. I tossed my sandwich in the trash can and went into the coffeehouse.

"Russell," I said. "I haven't seen you in ages. How's retirement?"

Russell Hill, my former history professor and mentor from Cal Poly, was sitting at one of the round glass tables with Mariko Thompson and an elderly Japanese woman wearing thick horn-rimmed bifocals and a beautiful brick-red mohair sweater. He wore the same baggy blue sweater, faded corduroy slacks, brown-on-brown saddle oxfords and neat, peppered goatee he'd taught in every day of his thirty-year academic career.

"Benni Harper, that's entirely your fault, not mine." He stood up and with the old-fashioned manners that always endeared him to his students and colleagues, pulled out a Shaker-style chair. "Where have you been keeping yourself these days?" he asked in the low, rolling monotone that, much as they loved him, sometimes put his students to sleep on warm spring afternoons. He turned to his companions. "Forgive me, before we start reminiscing, this is Mariko Thompson, a colleague, and her mother, Mrs. Yamaoka. We are all out today to enjoy the festival and parade."

"Nice to meet you," I said to her mother, then turned to Mariko. "Hello again. I love your sweatshirt." It was a bright turquoise painted with a pale Santa Fe-style cow's skull. "Mariko and I met recently," I explained to Russell. "A student of hers . . . well, never mind, it's a long story. She was kind enough to let me interview her for the Historical Society book."

"I heard you were roped into working on that project," he said, leaning back in his chair. "I think it's great."

"You would. Really, I am enjoying it when I can get to it. It would be more fun if they weren't pressuring me to finish so quickly."

"Ah, deadlines," Mariko said, laughing. "Where would Mylanta be without them?"

"Did you look over the copy of your story I dropped off at your office?" I asked Mariko.

"Yes, I made a few additions if that's all right."

"That's great. I have fifty pages to fill and, as I told you, time is running short." I turned to her mother, remembering that Mariko said she might talk with me. "Mrs. Yamaoka, would you consider talking to me about your memories of San Celina during the war?"

"I would like that," Mrs. Yamaoka said in a clear, vigorous voice that didn't seem to fit her eighty-odd years.

"Great! When would be a good time for us to talk?"

"How about Monday afternoon? That gives me time to . . ." She paused. "How do you say it? Find my thoughts."

After agreeing on a time of two o'clock and getting directions to Mariko's house, where her mother lived, Mariko and Mrs. Yamaoka excused themselves to go to the festival.

"Alone at last," Russell said, pulling his chair closer and leaning toward me. "Now tell me the real story behind the retirement-home murders. Egad, if this keeps up, we could start having one of those sick Hollywood-type tours—famous murder spots in San Celina county. You, naturally, would serve as tour guide."

"I really am getting a rather gruesome reputation, aren't I?" I said, ruefully. "Sorry, but I don't have much to tell you. All I know is what I read in the newspaper."

"Cut a curious and bored old man some slack. I know you and the head gendarme have a slightly more than professional relationship. Brighten my day, Ms. Harper, with a tasty tidbit of tawdry doings among the elderly."

"Look, forget that. I swear I don't know anything, and Chief Ortiz and I are no longer a society-page item. You know, I've been meaning to call you. I was wondering if I could prevail upon you to read through my chicken scratches before I turn them into the Historical Society."

"I'd be happy to," he said. "How is it coming?"

"Okay, I guess. Between that and the job at the museum and all the other complications in my life, it seems like I don't have two minutes to call my own these days. That's why I haven't been in touch with you."

"Well, you must rectify that in the near future," he said, patting my hand. "I miss our conversations. How's the bovine business?"

"Up and down. It's not as bad as Daddy would lead you to believe, but it's certainly not what it used to be."

"Not much is, my dear, not much is."

"Speaking of how things used to be, can I pick your brain for a minute?"

"Whatever's left of it after thirty years of academia is yours."

"You lived in San Celina County during the war, didn't you? Were you old enough to remember much?"

"I was but a lad in short pants, but yes, I remember it vividly. Why do you ask?"

"I have a question for you. What do you remember about Brady O'Hara during that time?"

He looked at me shrewdly. "What exactly is it you want to know?"

"What was he like? Was he a nice man? Did people like him?"

He tilted his chair back and folded his hands across his small paunch. "Did you know my father was mayor of San Celina during the war years?"

"No, I didn't."

"That meant we had a lot of people come to dinner who were very powerful in city politics."

"Would one of them have been Mr. O'Hara?"

"Of course. Granted, I was thirteen at the time, so you have to take into consideration that any adult other than a man in uniform didn't interest me much, but he does tend to stick out in my mind."

"Why is that?"

"He was adamantly for the relocating of the Japanese. Right from the beginning, even before Pearl Harbor. Ranted and raved about it more than once at our dinner table. And he wrote a plethora of letters to the editor of the *Tribune* on just that subject in the months preceding December seventh." He took a sip of his coffee. "What does this all have to do with his murder?''

"I'm not sure, yet. Look, can you keep a secret?'' I was dying to tell someone what I'd found in the ledgers.

"Nasty old gossip that I am, I can usually keep myself from babbling out of turn if absolutely required. Out with it, young woman. I haven't heard a succulent piece of scuttlebutt in ages.''

I told him briefly about the loans in the ledgers, watching his face the whole time.

"Certainly odd,'' he said, rubbing his chin. "Not at all what you'd expect of Brady. But do you think it has anything to do with why he and poor, unfortunate Rose Ann were murdered, and more importantly, have you informed your inamorato of any of this?'' He pointed out the window.

Across the street, Gabe, wearing the same uniform of navy windbreaker and snug Levi's as his young officers, had his mouth pressed up to a compact walkie-talkie. I watched him check the patrol officers' work, loping through them in the loose-limbed walk he adopted whenever he wasn't wearing a suit. He wore the Timberland hiking boots I'd talked him into buying a month ago.

"You can't wear those old topsiders all winter,'' I'd said, on our first clothes shopping trip together. "Especially with no socks. How about these? They'd be very warm.'' I held up a pair of black Tony Lama bullhide boots.

He'd kissed the top of my head and laughed. "*Querida,* I'll put on a pair of cowboy boots the same day you wear a red leather miniskirt and four-inch heels.'' We compromised on the hiking boots.

I sucked on my bottom lip and turned back to Russell. "He's not my . . . whatever you called him. We're not seeing each other anymore.''

He raised his eyebrows and smiled serenely.

"Oh, keep quiet,'' I said irritably. "I think I'll go wander around the festival some more. If it's okay, I'll drop those pages off at your house sometime next week.''

"Fine.'' He gave me a measured look. "Benni, whatever it is you're doing, just be careful.''

"All I'm doing is what some very special teacher once told me, something about faithfulness to the truth of history involving more than research. Some nonsense about imbuing themselves with the life and spirit of the time, being a sharer of the action."

"Ah, yes, Francis Parkman. Virile old fellow. Lived with the Sioux Indians for a time. Was also known to be quite batty. Well, in all fairness, I must counterbalance those meanderings with words from the great G.K. Chesterton himself, "Don't ever take a fence down until you know the reason why it was put up." He reached over and patted my hand. "Your curious mind made you one of my best students, my dear, but sometimes the past is best left in the past."

"I'm sure it's nothing, Russell, but I can't help wanting to know why a man who distrusted the Japanese so, whose brother was killed by them, would turn around and for years after that be their biggest benefactor. Don't you find that odd?"

"In my advanced years and small accumulated store of wisdom, I have learned to not question the oddity of man's behavior, but to accept the good of it and mourn the bad."

I stood up. "Well, I'll let you know what I find out."

"I'll be anxiously awaiting your phone call."

Outside, I was alternately relieved and disappointed to find Gabe gone. I had nothing to say to him, yet I longed to hear his voice. I started walking listlessly back toward Bonita Street and the festival, when Miguel called to me.

He jogged toward me, his nightstick bouncing against his thigh. His jacket blew open revealing the leather shoulder holster hugging his chest. If someone had told me fifteen years ago that the eight-year-old boy I caught cheating at Old Maid would someday be keeping law and order in the streets of San Celina, I would have choked with laughter.

"What's up?" I asked.

"I thought you'd want to know."

"Know what?" The sober look on his young face frightened me. "Miguel, what is it?"

"Aaron. He's in the hospital. I guess he had some kind of attack."

"Oh no, when? Does . . ." I started to ask if Gabe knew, but caught myself. Of course he knew.

"A half hour or so ago. The chief just got word. He's on his way over there. Look, I have to get back. I just saw you and thought you'd want to know."

"Thanks." I turned and walked back down the street toward the festival. What I really wanted to do was go to the hospital and be with Gabe and Rachel, but I also knew how awkward it would be. It would be obvious to her something wasn't right between me and Gabe and she didn't need any other pressures right now. On the other hand, I didn't want her to think I didn't care. Debating what I should do, I took a short cut to Bonita Street through Gum Alley, a forty-some-year unofficial city landmark. The city council's annual vote to clean up the gum-ladened walls was always met with virulent protest from two generations of gum-chewing artisans. The two-story brick walls of the alley were decorated with a sticky collection of colorful flowers, hearts, initials, greetings, philosophical maxims and fraternity symbols. I glanced up, as always, to make sure the "JH lvs BR—1975" in traditional Bazooka-pink still held its spot. Perched on Jack's shoulders, it had taken me almost an hour to create.

For the rest of the afternoon, while helping sell pots, quilts and wooden toys, I worried about Aaron. The parade always started promptly at 6:31 P.M. when the Mystik Krewe of Mardi Gras blew the official Mardi Gras trumpet, so around five-thirty, people started claiming spots and setting up lawn chairs along Lopez Street. I decided that once the parade started, after seeing Elvia's float, "Harry's Blind Book Krewe," I'd stop by to the hospital. Surely Gabe and I could maintain an amicable manner long enough to visit Aaron.

I was folding up the unsold quilts when a voice with the same tonal quality of tin foil across the teeth whined, "I want one, Eddy. Please, pretty please."

Walking around the corner of the booth was a bubble-haired, tiny-waisted lady in her thirties with hair as red and shiny as a grocery store apple and probably just as natural. She unfolded a queen-sized maroon and black quilt, letting the edge of it scrape the pavement.

"Careful," I said irritably, lifting the edge and brushing it off.

"Eddy," she whined again. "I want it. It's only four hundred dollars. It'll match my bedroom and you won all that..."

"Sure, why not?" Her companion stepped out from behind the side of the booth. I looked up into a face I'd seen way too often in the last month.

"Enjoying the festival, Edwin?" I asked politely, trying not to show I'd heard his companion's comment about winning money.

"How much did you say the quilt was?" he asked, looking down at me, his voice cool. He pulled out a thick roll of bills.

"Four hundred dollars," I said.

He peeled off eight fifties and handed them to me.

"Oh, Eddy, thank you, thank you," the woman gushed, hugging the quilt to her chest as I wrote out a receipt. "He's such a generous man," she said to me. "You should have seen him today. It was like he was psychic. I took my manicure money and put..."

"Dodie, I don't think Ms. Harper is interested in what we did today." He grabbed her arm and pulled at her to leave.

"On the contrary," I said, holding out his receipt. "I could use a little extra money myself right about now. Who looks good in the fourth tomorrow?"

He frowned and pulled again at Dodie's arm. "Let's go. We want to get a good spot for the parade."

"Don't you want to know the pattern of the quilt you just bought?" I asked, knowing I shouldn't, but thinking some things are just too right not to have a divine hand in them somewhere.

"Oh, yes," his date crowed. "What is it?"

I looked Edwin straight in his protruding eyes and grinned.

"Spiderweb," I said, smiling sweetly. "The pattern's name is Spiderweb."

Edwin shot me a furious look before pulling Dodie into the crowd.

"What was that all about?" Malcolm asked.

"Nothing," I said. "I was just bored and teasing some twerp."

"Better be careful," he said. "You know how weird people get around Mardi Gras. Jon's on a double shift down at the emergency room tonight."

"Poor guy." I had met his sister's husband at the last co-op potluck. A tall, easygoing black man, his specialty was emergency medicine. He had worked at County-USC Medical Center in Los Angeles for ten years until burnout from gang warfare sent him home to San Celina.

"Yeah, well, they need the money. She's pregnant again and the ultrasound says it's twins."

By six o'clock, thirty-one minutes before the parade was due to start, it was already dark. We packed up all the unsold items and Malcolm loaded them in his pickup to take back to the studios.

"We can dismantle the booth after the parade," he said. "There's an hour before the Masked Ball, so we'll have plenty of time."

"I can do it," I said. "I'm not going to the dance anyway."

He looked at me in sympathy. "Chief stood you up, huh? Want me to see if I can scrounge you up a date? I think I saw some desperate-looking characters down in line at the Mission Food Bank."

"Look, pal, when I need help in the romance department, I'll put an ad in the Personals," I said, throwing a pot holder at him and laughing.

A light rain started ten minutes before the parade, but it only seemed to dampen the streets, not anyone's spirits. In the dark, the painted faces and feathered masks seemed to multiply, and in the misty shelter of the foggy night the crowd became louder, acted bolder. The various Krewes were lining up their floats; screams of liquor-induced laughter and carefree tossing of cheap plastic necklaces and the coveted Mardi Gras doubloons had already started. The police had replaced their dark windbreakers with yellow slickers and were strolling up and down the street, asking people to please stay on the sidewalk. I pushed through the throng, trying to maneuver a spot where I could catch a glimpse of Blind Harry's float, a contraption shaped like a huge sparkly book. A young man in a metallic brown wig, wearing a suede Daniel Boone outfit and a stiff cardboard canoe strapped around his waist, fell against me, pushed by the crowd.

"Sorry," he said, swinging his boat around and smiling. "Canoe forgive me?"

"It's okay," I said, smiling back. After I was elbowed in the ribs by a clown, accidentally tripped by Richard Nixon and had beer spilled across the front of me by a man in white face wearing a green top hat and tails, I decided that Elvia would just have to show me pictures of the float. I pushed my way to the back of the crowd and started walking toward my truck. Luckily, the municipal parking lot where I'd parked exited to a side street that completely avoided the parade route. I'd stop by the hospital and see how Aaron was doing, then head home. I cut through Gum Alley to avoid the crowds.

"Happy Mardi Gras!" A blond half-drunk Indian brave in a full feather headdress with red and yellow lightning bolts painted on his cheeks offered me a strand of shiny pink carnival beads.

"Thanks," I said, reaching out for them.

He pulled them back, staggered a little, and gave me a lascivious smirk. "You have to earn them, darlin'. What're you going to do to earn them?"

I leveled a cold look at him and showed him a fist.

"Good enough for me, lady." He tossed the beads at me and walked away muttering. "Criminy, some people just don't know how to have a good time."

I picked them up off the ground and slipped them around

my neck. If Aaron was feeling okay, I'd give him the beads and tell him the story. He'd get a big kick out of it.

I was almost to the end of the alley when I felt a hand on my shoulder. Thinking it was another Mardi Gras crazy, I started to turn around, a retort all prepared.

"Don't!" the low, disguised voice said. A cold damp hand grabbed the back of my neck. Something hard and metallic poked into my side. I froze, my heart a hard knot in my chest.

"All I have is ten dollars," I said. "You can have it. Just let me go."

The hand tightened. There was an overpowering smell of wet rubber as strong fingers dug into the side of my neck. I gagged low in my throat.

"No," the voice said. He pushed me through the alley, the hard object jabbing my side, toward the back of a sandwich shop. A trio of garbage cans overflowed their metal sides. The thick odor of rotting vegetables and old meat caused me to gag again.

Oh, God, please help me, I prayed. Frightening images spiked like electric currents through my mind. Break away, part of me said. *Run.* Wait, another part cautioned. It might be a gun. You could die.

"Take the money, please," I said, despising the begging tone in my voice. I reached for my pocket.

"Stop!" the voice said and jerked my neck. The wet rubber slipped against my skin. I bit my tongue. Tasted blood. White-hot anger burst out of me.

"No!" I yelled. I wasn't going to be killed or raped. Not without a fight. I twisted my body, tried to stomp the top of his instep and screamed from the bottom of my toes.

"No!" he echoed and grabbed my shoulders. We struggled in an awkward dance. I caught glimpses of a rainbow metallic wig and a grotesque rubber mask.

"Hey, what's going on back there?" a deep voice called from behind me.

The mugger shoved me into the trash cans. Something sharp scraped across my temple. I heard a rustle in the trash. Just before my head hit the pavement, I screamed again.

The grotesque mask loomed over me for a split second. "No more questions," the voice hissed. A thought flashed through my mind right before everything went black. That voice. I know it. I *know* that voice.

16

"Help's on the way," George Washington told me. His breath smelled like beer, but his watery eyes were kind.

"You're going to be fine." A woman wearing a red beret dabbed at my aching head with a dark scarf. A glittery painted spider spun a web on her cheek. I blinked my eyes and the spider crawled down her neck.

"I'm okay," I said, struggling up. A shotgun blast exploded in my head. I gasped and lay back down. The spider lady brushed back my hair and kept dabbing.

By the time the paramedics arrived, the whole world was spinning. They talked to me in their soothing, professional voices, hooking me up to plastic bags and carefully lifting me onto a gurney. In the gathered crowd of people, I listened for the voice of the person who mugged me, the voice I recognized but couldn't place. My head ached with the effort. A tiny involuntary groan rumbled deep in my throat. A deep shiver rippled through me. One of the paramedics tucked a blanket around me. Inhaling deeply, I gasped in pain.

"Easy there," he said, his friendly dark eyes smiling at me. "We'll get you to the hospital in no time."

"Benni?" Lieutenant Cleary's sharp tenor broke through the buzz of spectators. His worried face appeared behind the paramedic.

"Jim?" My voice sounded like a parrot's.

He pushed up to the side of the gurney and bent over me. "What happened?" He flashed his badge when the paramedic protested.

"Someone tried to mug me," I said, giving a small laugh. "I offered him ten bucks, but he wouldn't go away." Another hysterical laugh gurgled up. His warm hand squeezed my icy one.

"Did you get a good look at him?" Jim asked.

I lifted my head slightly. "He wore a mask, one of those monster kind. Gray-colored. And a wig. A rainbow metallic one." I grabbed Jim's arm. "Would you call Elvia Aragon, Miguel's sister? She's with the Blind Harry float. Tell her to call my gramma at home and tell her I'm okay. I don't want her to hear that I'm dead or something. You know this town." I dropped my head back down, exhausted.

"Yeah," he said, smiling. "I know this town. I'll take care of it. Do you want me to call Gabe over at the hospital?"

"No."

His brown eyes admonished me.

"He has enough to worry about with Aaron," I said. "Tell him tomorrow."

He shook his head and stood up. "Whatever you say. I'll get a call out on this guy, but with what little we have to go by, I don't anticipate finding him."

"He was probably just a junkie looking for some money," I said, turning my head. I knew that wasn't the case and I don't know why I didn't tell Jim that. But what could I tell him? That the voice sounded vaguely familiar? That he was telling me to quit asking questions I wasn't supposed to be asking to begin with? And what questions exactly did he mean? I had to think about it, try and place that voice. But I wasn't going to do it while I had this splitting headache.

The emergency room at San Celina County Hospital looked like a cast party of the Rocky Horror Picture Show. On the bed next to me, a turbaned man with a large gold ring in his nose held his stomach and moaned for a nurse.

His companion, Cat Woman, looking as uncaring as the animal she portrayed, patted his hand silently, an unlit cigarette dangling from her black lips.

"I know this sounds like a line," Malcolm's brother-in-law, Jon, said, about a half hour later—he peered into my eyes with his small flashlight—"but haven't we met somewhere before? Follow my finger." I did as I was told, then closed my eyes. My head felt like someone had set off a cherry bomb in it and I swore if someone didn't stop shaking my bed, I was going to really get mad.

"Benni Harper," I answered, groaning a little when he pressed gently on my stomach. "The folk art museum potluck . . . Malcolm . . ."

"Right," he said, pulling out his stethoscope and listening to my heart. "You're the lady who found the bodies in the museum a few months back. And a couple more recently, if I remember correctly."

"I prefer to think of myself as the museum's curator," I said.

"Well, you're my first mugging victim of the night," he said. "Brings back old memories, believe you me." He turned to the nurse who'd appeared beside him. "Get her into X-ray and let me know when they're through."

"Am I going to live?" I joked weakly.

"Got insurance?" he asked with sober brown eyes.

"Yes."

He wrote something on my chart, then looked up and grinned. "Then we'll do our best."

By the time I was X-rayed, brought back down to Emergency, then stitched and bandaged by an intern, Dove had arrived. From behind my curtained-off area, I could hear her strident voice arguing with an admitting nurse.

"It's very crowded tonight," a stern, edgy voice told her. "You can't go back there."

"I'd like to see the person who can stop me," she declared. Seconds later her voice reverberated through the emergency room, calling my name.

"Over here, Gramma," I croaked.

"Oh, honeybun," she said when she saw me. Her cool

hand touched the bandage on my forehead, smoothed my hair. The downy feel of her fingertips, the sweet almond scent of her Jergens hand lotion let loose the flood of tears I'd been holding back

"Now, you hush that bawling," she said, folding me into her cushiony chest. "Nobody's going to hurt you now."

Within minutes, we were joined by Daddy, Elvia, and Miguel. They surrounded my bed and were all talking at once when the curtain was flung back and Gabe loomed over us. His eyes were bright as marbles against his dark, angry face.

"What happened?" he demanded, looking straight at me.

"I told Jim not to tell you," I said.

"Fortunately he realizes who his commanding officer is. All he'd tell me over the phone was you were here in Emergency. I repeat, what happened?"

"She was mugged, young fella," Daddy said. "And you best be doin' something about it real quick." They stared at each other, challenge gleaming in both sets of eyes. Gabe broke away first and turned to Miguel.

"Tell me what you know and what's being done."

Miguel quickly told him the story as he'd heard it from Jim and what they'd found so far—nothing. Gabe turned back to me. "And?" he asked.

"And what?"

"What aren't you telling me?"

I buried my head into the crook of Dove's arm. "What makes you think I'm not telling you everything?"

"Benni, I swear I'll . . ." He threatened in his stern cop's voice.

Just tell him, a voice inside me said. Then everyone will leave you alone and you can beg a pain pill from the nurse and roll over and quietly let your head explode.

"I might know the voice," I whispered.

"What?" Gabe said, followed by echoes of similar words from everyone else.

"I said, *might*. It sounded familiar, but I just can't place it."

"What did he say?"

I mumbled into Dove's arm.

He bent over me. The spicy scent of his cologne mixed with the scent of coffee on his breath. "What was that?"

I looked him directly in the eyes. " 'No more questions.' He said, 'No more questions.' "

"*Hijo de . . .*" Gabe said under his breath. "That settles it. When they release you, you're coming home with me."

"I think not," Dove said. "*I'll* be going home with her tonight."

"I think I should take her out to the ranch," Daddy said.

"She can always come home with me," Elvia piped up.

"I've already decided," Gabe said. "No discussion."

Dove stood up, an indignant five feet one, and pointed a finger up at him. "Young man, if you think I'm letting her go home with you with the shape she's in and the shape you're in, you're out of your ever-lovin' gourd."

"The shape I'm in?" Gabe asked. "What do you mean by that?"

She narrowed one blue eye. "With her weak like this and with both of y'all's hormones all worked up like they have been the last few weeks, there's no way she's spending the night with the likes of you."

"Dove!" I protested, lifting my head. "I can't believe you'd . . ."

"You think I'd . . . ?" Gabe exclaimed. "What kind of a person do you think I am?"

"A man kind of person," Dove said, folding her arms across her chest.

Beside me, Elvia snickered. I sank back down into my pillow, wondering if it might not have been preferable for the mugger to have finished me off in the alley.

"You think I'd take advantage of her when she's this vulnerable?" Gabe asked.

"I have lived a lot longer than you, and I know what fear can do to people. And—" she eyed him fiercely—"I raised four sons. I know what's what. Besides, what do I really know about you anyway? I don't even know if you've got some of that blood disease that's killing everyone left and right. No, siree, Bob. I'll be taking care of her tonight.''

"Daddy, do something.'' I looked over at him helplessly. He just grinned at me and shrugged. He knew there was no stopping Dove once she got rolling.

"For your information,'' Gabe said in a low, even voice, "I've been tested.''

"Don't mean squat,'' she said. "I heard you can have one of them tests, then go out and kick up your heels afterward and get it just like that.'' She snapped her fingers.

"Look, it's been two years since . . .'' He clamped his lips shut, his face flushing a dark red.

"For pete's sake,'' I said, surprised. "You've gone longer than I have.''

Elvia snickered again. Miguel kept a straight face and studied the black and white tiles on the floor. Daddy's smile could have posed for a Halloween pumpkin.

Gabe scowled. Dove scowled back.

"Doesn't matter,'' she said, uncompromising. "She's still not going with you.''

"I told you I wouldn't . . .'' he started.

"Okay, that does it!'' I struggled up. In an upright position, my head felt like a balloon at the point of bursting, but I had to speak up. It was one thing to argue about where I was going to spend the night, but when my sex life suddenly became a topic for public debate, it was time to take control. Just as I was about to command everyone to clear out, Dr. Jon walked in.

"Your cheering section has arrived, I see,'' he said to me. "Got your verdict here.'' He rattled the X-rays in his hand.

"How is she?'' Dove asked.

"She has a couple of cracked ribs and will have a nasty headache for a day or two, but there's no indication of concussion. The head wound is superficial. The stitches should dissolve in a week or so. Shouldn't be too much of a scar.'' He smiled at me. "You were really lucky.''

"Yeah, right,'' I said, looking at Gabe and Dove who were still bristling at each other like two dogs squaring off for possession of a fire hydrant.

A thought broke through the pounding in my head. I grabbed Jon's white-coated arm. "Am I hurt enough to stay one night here?"

He gave me a curious look. "We've got empty beds. I can hold you one night for observation. Your insurance will probably accept that."

"Do it," I said.

Before a whine of protest commenced, I started giving orders. "Daddy, take Dove home. I'll be out tomorrow and will spend the night with you. Miguel, can you take my keys and somehow get my truck back to my house?"

"Sure," he said.

I looked up at Jon. "What time is checkout?"

"Noon."

"Be here at eleven-thirty," I instructed Elvia. "And bring me some clean clothes."

"Yes, ma'am," she said, giving me a small salute.

"And you." I zeroed in on Gabe. His jaw tensed, but he didn't say a word. "How's Aaron?"

His eyes clouded over. "He's still having tests."

"You need to go see how Rachel is doing. I'll be fine tonight and we can get this all straightened out tomorrow. Now go, all of you." I lay back against the pillow, exhausted and on the verge of tears.

With only minor protests from Dove, everyone did as they were told. Well, I thought, as they wheeled me upstairs, this taking control business is pretty simple once you get the hang of it. The nurse helped me into a hospital nightgown that, skimpy as it was, still felt better than my dirty clothes, and I sank into the clean sheets of the firm hospital bed. Fortunately, the other bed in my semi-private room was empty, so the only sounds audible were the subdued conversation of hospital personnel out in the hall. I dozed off and on, too nervous to fall into a deep sleep. At one point, I was wakened by a nurse with glossy auburn hair cut in a shag. She wore her eyeliner in the way they did in the sixties, like little bat wings flying out from the corners of her green eyes.

"How's your head?" she asked, taking my pulse with her cool fingers.

"Still hurts," I said.

"I could give you something for the pain. It'll probably help you sleep too."

"No, it's not that bad," I said. Maybe I'd watched too many movies, but after what happened tonight, the idea of being completely unconscious in a hospital room that anyone could walk into, made me a little edgy.

"Okey-doke," she said, adjusting my blankets. "You know, I told your boyfriend he could come in here and sit with you, but he insists on sitting there outside your door. Been out there for hours."

"Who?"

"I assumed that's who he was. Tall, dark-haired guy, gorgeous blue eyes. If he's not yours, can I have him?" Her round cheeks dimpled.

"Could you please tell him I want to see him?"

"Okey-doke."

A few minutes later, Gabe entered the room. His eyes, glazed with exhaustion, stared down at me defiantly.

"Gabe, what do you think you're doing?"

"My job."

I pulled the covers up over my chest. "How's Aaron?"

"Better. It was just a reaction to his new medication. He'll probably go home tomorrow or the next day."

"Well, if you're determined to stay, you may as well sit in here," I said. He walked over to the chair next to my bed and sat down, his posture as inflexible as the set of his jaw. "What about Rachel?"

"She's doing okay. She's staying in town with a friend."

We were silent for a moment. "Gabe, you look exhausted. Why don't you just go home? I'm sure whoever attacked me wouldn't try anything while I'm in here."

"I'm not leaving," he said, his voice thick. His anxiety seemed to have a physical presence in the air, like pollen. I knew I would never be able to talk him into leaving. I watched the tight line of his jaw, wanting to touch it, to run my finger down the clean length of it, smooth out its rigidity.

"Okay," I said. "As long as you're going to stay, you may as well make yourself useful. I can't sleep, so talk me to sleep."

"What?" He gave a puzzled look.

"Tell me a story. Didn't your mother ever tell you bedtime stories when you couldn't sleep? Dove used to tell me one about a calf named Boom-Boom who didn't know how to moo. He'd learned all the other animal sounds, but couldn't figure out how to moo. He was the Rich Little of the barnyard."

"My mother never told us stories. She's . . . well, you'd have to know her. She's a good person, but she's not the type to tell stories."

"But she was a schoolteacher."

"I don't know, maybe she was just tired of kids by the time she got home. Anyway, it was my father who told us stories, put us to bed every night. He was the funniest man I ever knew." His face relaxed slightly.

"So tell me one."

He ducked his head. I ached to stroke the top of his glossy, black hair. "I can't remember any."

"C'mon, Gabe, be fair. I told you about Boom-Boom."

He looked up and smiled. "When Dove and I are speaking again, I'm going to tease her about that."

"Oh, don't let her bamboozle you. She adores you."

"Could have fooled me."

I grinned. "Well, she adores me more. Now, out with your story, Friday, or I'll be forced to bring out the bright lights and rubber hoses."

He leaned back in the chair and crossed one leg over the other, tracing the maze of his hiking boot's tread with his finger. "Dad used to tell us, me and my sisters, this story about a turtle who had a blue shell. *Señor Azure,* he called him."

"Mr. Blue. Like the fifties song."

"Yeah, not very original, but we liked it."

"I think it's wonderful. Go on."

"Anyway, this turtle, he didn't fit in with the other turtles, because of his shell, but it didn't make him sad because . . ." He stopped, and cleared his throat. "I can't do this."

"You don't have to," I said softly.

"No, it's just that, he always told it to us in Spanish. It doesn't sound the same in English."

"Then tell it to me in Spanish. I know enough to pick out the major points."

He started over and the words flowed smoothly, soothing me like a low, humming song. The hard angles of his face smoothed out, making him appear to grow younger as he told the story of the lonely little turtle who didn't fit in, but was happy anyway because he had a secret—the blue shell that made him different also enabled him to fly. I fell asleep to the melodious sounds of what I assumed was *Señor Azure's* quest for a place to fit in somewhere between the earth and the sky.

Sometime during the night, while traveling through that deep murky canyon between sleep and the real world, a voice whispered in my ear, "Move over." Habit from years of marriage caused me to obey without hesitation. I remember thinking, I'll have to ask him how the new heifers are doing, did he lose any calves tonight. But the body that pulled me to him, my back resting against his solid chest, was different. The weight of the arm holding me was heavier, the warm male scent of him both foreign and familiar.

"Gabe?" I murmured.

"Yes," he answered, then fit himself around me, burying his face in my hair and I went back to sleep.

THE SOUND OF laughter outside my room woke me. One nurse was telling another about the kiss she'd gotten from her blind date last night. He apparently had some sort of excess saliva problem. I turned over and touched my face to the far side of my pillow. Gabe's faint scent lingered there. So it hadn't been a dream. Unsure about what exactly last night meant, I was staring at the ceiling when the nurse came in ten minutes later.

"About time you woke up." She was tiny with gray hair and a small mole next to her left eye. "Breakfast is on its way," she informed me, opening the blinds with a brisk efficiency. "Then I guess you'll be leaving us."

"Thanks," I said, sitting up and looking around. On the nightstand, a small message pad with the hospital's logo sat propped against my water glass.

"Elvia picking you up. I'll call you at the ranch. *Be careful.* L. Gabe."

L period Gabe. What did that mean? Like, love, later? Did not spelling it out have some sort of significant psychological message? Why can't men just say what they mean?

I contemplated the note the whole time I ate my breakfast, and came up with the usual conclusion—I had no idea what was going on in his mind.

By noon, I was on my way to the ranch, comfortably cradled in the passenger seat of Elvia's Austin-Healy.

"You scared us half to death, *gringa*," she said, speeding over Rosita Pass, one eye vigilant for Highway Patrol cars.

"Sorry," I said, looking out the window, wondering what the person who attacked me was doing right this minute.

"That was quite a little show Dove and Gabe put on last night in the emergency room." She laughed, whipped around an old farm truck hauling caged chickens and punched the accelerator. "At least you know he's safe now."

"If it matters," I said.

She looked at me curiously. "So, what do you think he's going to do about the job?"

"I have no idea." I told her about last night and the note he left.

She reached up and adjusted the rearview mirror, then slowed down slightly. "Well, I wish I could help you there, but the male mind has long eluded me with its inconsistencies."

"No kidding. And they say we're the illogical ones."

"Speaking of men, have you placed a name to that voice yet?"

"No," I said, sighing. "I'm beginning to wonder if I only imagined that I recognized it. I've been in such an emotional tizzy these last few days, I'm not sure I can trust any of my senses."

"Well, you can't deny that it had to do with the murders. That 'no more questions' business is just too coincidental, don't you think?"

"You're right. But . . ."

She looked at me, her mouth a straight line. "I know that 'but.' You're not going to stop, are you?"

I leaned my head against the window. "I don't know. Right now, all I want is a plate of Dove's chicken pot pie and to lie on the sofa and watch Oprah."

Beef stew was what Dove had actually made for lunch.

Elvia declined an invitation with the excuse the bookstore was a mess and she had to get back to it.

"Need a ride to town tomorrow?" she asked as I walked her down the long driveway to her car.

"No, thanks," I said. "I'll catch a ride into town with Daddy. He always has breakfast in town on Monday mornings. I've got to be at the museum early because that reporter from L.A. is supposed to be there by eight o'clock."

When I walked into the kitchen, Dove had an ironstone soup bowl of stew dished up for me.

"I can't eat all that," I said, my churning stomach already protesting the gravy-covered chunks of beef, potatoes and carrots.

"You need to get your strength back. I wish you would stay longer than one night. I'm worried about that man who tried to hurt you."

"Gee, and I thought you'd be worried about me," I said, sitting down and laying the checkered napkin across my lap.

"This is not something to joke about. Whatever it is you're doing to cause this man to attack you, I want you to stop it right now."

"Dove Ramsey telling me to back down," I said, sticking a juicy piece of beef in my mouth. "Somebody pinch me. I think I'm dreaming."

"Don't smart-mouth me, young lady. You're not too big to switch, you know." She turned around and started fiddling with the miniature television sitting on the counter. "Now, Ahmad's show is going to be on in ten minutes and I want you finished with your lunch and out of my hair before it starts."

I made a face at her back and continued eating. I was almost finished when Daddy walked into the kitchen. His faded blue eyes lit up when he saw what I was eating.

"Real food? There's some real, honest-to-Pete, American food being served in this kitchen?"

"None left," Dove said, dumping the rest of the stew down the garbage disposal and turning it on. The loud grinding drowned out Daddy's fiery comments.

Dove flipped off the disposal and turned around, a shameless smile on her face. "What was that, son?"

"Nothing," he growled and turned to me. "You've got company outside. Tell your gramma I'll be going to town for dinner. Until then, I'll be out in the barn waiting for my hay to come in."

"What's got his dander up?" Dove asked. I shook my head and didn't answer. I had enough problems of my own without getting in the middle of their little domestic spat.

Clay sat on the front porch swing holding a cellophane-wrapped bouquet of mixed flowers. "Heard you were sick," he said, handing me the flowers.

"Thanks," I said, bringing them to my face. "But actually, I was mugged."

"Yeah, well, they don't have cards for that, so I figured flowers would have to do."

"How'd you hear?"

"Here and there. You know this town. Are you feeling good enough to show me around? I haven't been here in a long time. Looks like you've made some changes."

"We have."

I set the flowers on the porch railing and led him out back toward the barn. After showing him all the improvements Daddy had made in the last seventeen years, we ended up on a bench underneath an old oak tree on a small rise overlooking our driveway. We'd picked up a couple of barn kittens along the way, a calico and a gray with white mittens, and were teasing them with long strands of hay while talking about Daddy's latest attempt to upgrade our stock with imported bull semen from Canada and my interview with the L.A. *Times* reporter the next morning.

"So, you're going back to town tomorrow," he said. "Do you think that's smart?"

"What does everyone expect me to do, stay out here for the rest of my life? I only came out here today to make Dove feel better. I'm perfectly safe in my house. I lock all the doors and windows. I have a gun and I know how to use it."

He pushed his hat back slightly. "I don't know, Benni.

Seems to me you're asking for—''

The roar of an engine coming up the driveway drowned out the rest of his sentence. Gabe, dressed in a dark suit and his customary snow-white shirt, pulled up close to the house and climbed out of his Corvette.

''Well, look who's here, Wyatt Earp,'' Clay said, sticking a piece of straw in his mouth. I didn't answer. This was not a good sign. Gabe told me he was going to call, not come out.

We watched him slip off his dark aviator glasses and toss them on the seat. Not noticing us, he walked up to the ranch house and knocked on the door, then stepped inside when Dove answered.

After a few minutes, they came out of the house and stared up toward Clay and me from the front porch.

''I'd better go see what he wants,'' I said. ''Why don't you go down to the barn and talk to my dad?'' I picked up the calico kitten and held it against my chest. Its claws pierced the thin cotton of my turtleneck and pricked me.

''I'll tell you what he wants,'' Clay said. ''For you to stay away from me. To quote a favorite singer of mine, let's give them something to talk about.'' He leaned over, grabbed me by the waist and gave me a swift, hard kiss. In between us, the kitten mewed in protest.

I pulled away, trying not to smile. ''You are such a troublemaker, Clay. You always were.''

He laughed and scooped up the gray kitten. ''Just trying to keep things lively. Think I'll go down to the barn and talk to your dad. By the way, I do believe you have company.''

''Thanks a lot,'' I said, handing him the other kitten.

We walked down to the porch, Dove's and Gabe's eyes following us the whole way.

''Miz Ramsey,'' Clay said. ''Nice to see you again.'' He paused. ''Hey, Chief.'' His voice gave a twist to Gabe's title that made it sound like an insult.

''O'Hara,'' Gabe said, nodding slightly. I searched his sober olive face for the man who told me the story of a flying blue turtle, the man who curled around me last night, his warm breath against my neck. This morning he was all business, a man who had questions and would demand answers.

"I'll talk to you later, Benni." Clay held up a kitten in salute and gave me a broad wink. "Don't let that old gomer bull there intimidate you too much." He strode off toward the barn.

Dove shook her head at his comment and shot me the same resigned but disapproving look she used to give me when, as a teenager, I missed curfew or insisted on spending my money or time on something she deemed foolish and wasteful. I sent back the same mind-your-own-business frown I gave her back then. An uncomfortable silence commenced until a crow, black as tar and big as a possum, let out a loud *scraw* before lifting off the white rail fence lining the driveway. Dove *hmphed* under her breath.

"I've got cooking to do," she said, slamming the screen door behind her.

I turned to Gabe and said in a calm and reasonable voice, "That wasn't what it looked like."

"Looked like he kissed you."

"Well, I guess it was what it looked like, it just wasn't . . ." What in the world was I doing? I didn't have to explain anything to him. The man who didn't even know how to spell the word love. "So, what's up?" I asked, my voice deliberately friendly and casual.

"I came by to see if you were okay. Obviously, you are."

Ignoring his sarcasm, I pointed at the porch swing. "Want to sit down?"

"No, I can't stay long." He stuck his hands in his pockets and looked out over my head. "What did he mean by that?"

"What?"

"Gomer bull. I take it that's some sort of inside lingo in the cattle business. What does it mean?"

"Oh." I chewed on the inside of my cheek. "You don't really want to know."

"If I'm being laughed at, I prefer to know why."

"Okay, you asked. A gomer bull is sort of a . . . warm-up act."

"Elaborate."

"Well, cows are mostly impregnated these days by artificial insemination. But sometimes cows come into heat at night when no one can see them. So there's these bulls that you buy for a couple of hundred dollars called 'gomer bulls' and their only job is to . . . well . . . be active. Except that we either give them a vasectomy or put a penile block on them so the inferior sperm won't, you know . . . take. Then we put a thing called a 'chin ball marker' on their heads. It's filled with STP motor oil and different color dyes, so we know which bulls are doing their job. Then we let them loose with the cows cause . . . well . . . the bulls know by odor which cows are in heat and they—"

"I get the drift," Gabe said, his voice cool.

"He was just teasing you," I said.

After a few minutes of silence he said, "Tell me everything you recall about last night, even if it doesn't seem relevant."

I repeated everything I could remember. He didn't write any of it down, but I knew it would be filed away in his memory, ready to be extracted exactly when he needed it. He thought for a moment. "The voice," he said. "Have you placed it yet?"

"No, and now I'm not even sure I was hearing right. It all happened so fast and I was so scared." An involuntary tremble shimmied through me. I crossed my arms and leaned against the porch railing. Admitting I was afraid made it seem real again, just as I was beginning to relegate it to the mythical-past segment of my memory. "Not many clues for you to follow, I'm afraid."

"Clues," he repeated absently. He pulled his keys out of his pocket and fiddled with the keychain, a piece of greenish turquoise set in silver, handmade for him by a Navajo friend he'd met in Vietnam. The stone was worn smooth from Gabe's nervous stroking. "Clues are only signs, Benni. In themselves, they're worth nothing. They can just as easily point to lies as to the truth. Like fingers pointing at fingers pointing at fingers." He paused and cleared his throat. "I know Mac isn't telling me the whole story. I suspect he's trying to protect his grandmother. I've put it off as long as I can. Unless you can shed some light on this . . ." He let his voice trail off.

I looked at the ground and didn't answer. If Mac hadn't told Gabe that Oralee was involved, I couldn't be the one to do it.

"I'm going to have to question her," he said softly.

"Good luck," I said under my breath.

"Well, apparently I'm going to need it. I have to get to work. When are you coming back to town?"

"Tomorrow morning."

"Just be careful. Don't go anywhere by yourself after dark, or really any time. Make sure the locks on your windows and doors are secure. I think I should come over and—"

I interrupted his safety list. "Would you cut me some slack here? I'm not a complete idiot, Gabe. I can cross the street without getting hit by a car."

"Fine," he said abruptly. "I'll have someone call you if we come up with anything."

"Fine," I repeated, watching him walk toward his car, his head held high. Suddenly, I remembered something.

"Wait," I called and ran down the steps after him. "I forgot to ask you something."

He opened the car door, then turned to look at me, his eyes slit against the early afternoon sun hanging yellow and warm overhead. "What is it?"

"How's Aaron?"

"Fine. They changed his medication. I drove Rachel and him home this morning. That's why I wasn't there when you woke up."

"I'm glad he's better."

"Me too."

I had started back toward the house when gravel crackled behind me and I felt his fingers tighten on my shoulder. I slowly turned around to face him, apprehensive when I saw the determined look on his face.

"This is crazy," he said.

"I agree."

"I don't know exactly what you've got going with O'Hara, but I think you're way over your head."

I pulled away from his hand. "That's not really your place to decide, now is it?"

"You saw his criminal record. He's a hothead and unpredictable."

I laughed, thinking those same adjectives could just as well describe Gabe. "Maybe there's just something about that type of guy that appeals to me."

His jaw pulled tight and a ribbon of uncertainty fluttered across my chest bone. He scrutinized me for a moment, then leaned over and grabbed my chin, jerking it up sharply. He kissed me hard, his tongue sweet, insistent and angry. I kissed back, but pulled away when he wouldn't stop.

"What was that, Friday?" I asked, trying to subtly gulp air. "Marking your territory?"

White ridges scarred both sides of his mouth. I took a shaky step backwards, certain I'd gone too far this time.

"Benni Harper," he said, his voice quiet and level, his eyes hard as two blue stones, "I'm warning you. You're dancing way too close to the base of the fire."

Five minutes later, I was still standing there watching the dust from his tires settle back down in the driveway. I chewed a thumbnail and considered his words. There was no doubt I wasn't the most experienced woman when it came to the opposite sex, but it certainly didn't take a genius to figure out he wasn't talking about the investigation. Or about Clay O'Hara.

18

THE COMFORTING SMELLS of fresh coffee, country sausage and baking bread woke me early the next day. I grunted at Dove's "Good morning" and headed straight for the coffeepot. She floured her hands and started kneading the huge lump of dough on the counter, all the while getting on my case about what happened at the parade.

"I don't want you going back to town." She smacked the white lump with a practiced hand. "There's absolutely no reason to until Gabe catches that crazy person." She always bakes when she's upset. A part of me contemplated extending my visit just to enjoy the fruits of her stress.

"Dove, that might not ever happen," I said, nibbling on a piece of sausage. "I can't hide out here forever. I have a life. I have a job. And—" I glanced at the kitchen clock. "I have an appointment. Where's Daddy?"

"He said he'd be here shortly. You just do what Gabe tells you and stay out of trouble." She wiped her hands on the large white towel pinned around her waist. "And you'd best be watching yourself with those two boys. You know you'd just as well be playing with lighted dynamite as getting into the middle of two bulls with their hormones all fired up."

"Please, no bovine analogies this early in the morning," I said, studying the milk swirls in my coffee.

She tugged at a strand of my hair. "You sour, mean thing. You are just too ornery to live. Have you ever listened to a word I've said?"

"Oh, I always *listen*," I said, laughing.

"Well, I've got some advice for you, honeybun." She pointed a flour-dusty finger at me. "Going around all feather-legged like you've been the last week or so, you might not see it, but how a man treats a woman tells you a heap more about the man than it does the woman."

"What's that supposed to mean?"

"Just what I said."

"I have no idea what you're trying to say. Why don't you just spell it out for me?"

"You want me to tell you what to do, who to choose and what to do with him after you've got him?"

"That would be nice, seeing as everywhere *I* turn it seems like there's a barbed-wire fence."

"Well, I'm not going to do it. You're a grownup woman who was married almost fifteen years and been widowed a year now. You got to make up your own mind and get on with your life."

"Great," I said, with a snort. "*Now's* a fine time to start treating me like an adult."

"Just remember," she said, pulling a warm loaf of bread out of the oven. "Familiar isn't necessarily good."

During the ride to town with Daddy, I was relieved that he was the one person who had no opinion at all about what I should do. Or if he did, he wisely kept it to himself. We talked about the new phase of cow-calf operation he was moving into, what poor quality barley hay he was having to supplement our feed with and how hard it was to find ranch hands who actually wanted to work these days.

"Everyone wants to play cowboy these days," he complained. "But most of 'em can't tell a sick cow from a rotten tree stump."

I declined keeping him company over his late breakfast, since by the time we reached my house I had only a half hour to change and get to my meeting with the *Times* reporter. He insisted on getting out and walking through all the rooms to make sure they were safe, though with Mr. Treton standing guard next door, I couldn't see how anyone could get past his diligent twenty-four-hour surveillance.

"Be careful, squirt," was all Daddy said before climbing into his truck.

While changing, I picked up Mr. O'Hara's wooden scrapbook sitting next to my bed and stuck it in my leather backpack, figuring I'd glance through it at lunch. At the museum, I was thrilled to see that Todd had arrived before me and followed last week's schedule as if he'd been working there for years. The quilt rack was set up and the large coffee maker cleaned out and ready to go for the Oak Terrace ladies.

"You are a dream come true," I said, when I found him in the kitchen putting on the small coffeepot. I handed him a twenty-dollar bill. "Why don't you go down to the Donut Corral and get about three dozen doughnuts? Then take a break. You've certainly earned it."

"Thanks," he said, looking down at his feet, embarrassed. He looked back up. "Uh . . . you okay and everything?"

My hand automatically went to the cut on my forehead. I'd managed to cover all but a small corner of the white bandage with my bangs. "Yeah, I'm doing fine. Just a little headache is all."

"Did they catch the guy?" he asked.

"No, and they probably won't. All I saw was a grotesque rubber mask and a rainbow wig. It was probably just some dopehead." An inward shiver ran through me when I said the words. I knew good and well that the person who mugged me wasn't a junkie, and the thought that he knew who I was and could be following my every move was too frightening to even contemplate. "Well, I survived," I said, laughing. "Takes more than a knock on the head to get me down. Now, get going, and really, thanks for doing all this so promptly."

"No problem," he said and pocketed the twenty.

The *Times* reporter, a Ms. Beth Atwood, walked in about two minutes after Todd left. Somewhere in her early twenties, she was thin as a birch tree and punctuated the end of each sentence with a laugh that sounded like the silver bracelets jangling on her wrist. She showed a lively interest in the exhibit and the goals of the museum and co-op. By the time the interview was over, I felt comfortable enough to answer her curious questions about the murders back in December, though she promised they wouldn't show up in her article. I introduced her to the ladies from Oak Terrace and she took a picture of them smiling and talking around the half-finished quilt. By ten o'clock she was gone and I sat with the ladies at the quilt rack, listening to the latest Oak Terrace gossip.

"No new clues," Thelma whispered to me as I helped her up into the bus at noon. "But Edwin's been snapping everyone's heads off for days. I bet they have a contract out on him."

"Be careful," I said, not even wanting to imagine who "they" were. "Don't do anything dangerous."

"Ha!" is all she said and I felt my heart sink. I was reluctantly beginning to understand how Gabe felt about me being involved in this.

After they left, I decided to drive out to Eola Beach and Port San Patricio to have lunch. The Blue Seal Inn, a small restaurant-bar at the end of the pier, served great shrimp and fries and was usually pretty empty this time of year. I needed a couple of undistracted hours to work on writing up the interviews interspersing the personal stories with the historical information I'd collected.

Up on the interstate, I rolled down the windows, cranked up KCOW and along with Alan Jackson laid a little rubber on the asphalt. The early spring air was as fresh and clean-tasting as one of Aunt Garnet's nonalcoholic mint juleps. For my own sanity, I firmly put the problems with Gabe and Clay and the murders on the back burners of my mind. I was determined to get a good start on my writing even if I had to sit there until the bar closed at two A.M. On the turnoff to Eola Beach, four miles away, the smell of the ocean became apparent, making me ravenous, as salt air always seems to do. Eola Beach, off to my left, was still hunkered down in its winter mode. During the winter months, the only businesses that seemed to be open were a windowless no-name bar, a grocery store with a screen door advertising "Fresh Bait" with a bright orange hand-painted poster, and a small sheriff's substation. Out on the damp sand, a hump-shouldered old man in a blue watch cap slowly worked his way down the beach, the metal detector he held in front of him swaying back and forth like an elephant's trunk.

I turned right, heading toward the pier, taking the treacherous curve out onto the peninsula slowly. More than one car had crashed through the flimsy metal guardrail and ended up in the bay ten feet below the road. The gray February ocean lapped against the black breakwater rocks, looking so cold it caused me to shiver even though the heater was turned to high in the truck. I passed the weather-beaten Bad Cat Cafe and the Port San Patricio Harbor Patrol office, a pseudo-Spanish-style building that also held the offices of the U.S. Army Corps of Engineers. In front of the building a small white Harbor Patrol truck was parked, and a man in a khaki uniform was pouring out a pot of coffee into some scraggly bushes. I drove to the nearest parking space on the land end of the pier, passing the dry docks where the *Little Lady, Triple Star, Li'l' Mac* and the *Alma T* waited patiently for loving hands to scrape their hulls and gloss their decks.

The bait and tackle shop, the Alley Cat Snack Bar and the Harbor Cruise buildings were all shut tight until April. Only the wholesale fish market next to the Blue Seal Inn was open. I glanced in the glass picture window. The room was painted pale green, the walls glossy and cold-looking. Amidst the sounds of Mexican folk music, the Latino workers sliced huge fish from head to tail, their long black-handled steel knives flashing quick as lizards. Across the fluorescent-lit room, I was surprised to see Mr. Morita and Todd talking to one of the workers. Todd looked up and caught my eye. I waved and met him at the open door.

"Hi," I said. "What're you doing here?" A breeze blew through the room from the door on the other side that opened directly onto the wooden pier. The workers tossed the guts and heads of the fish onto the pier where fat tourist-fed sea gulls and brown pelicans sat perched on the knee-high railing waiting.

Todd jerked his head in the direction of his grandfather. "I'm helping him talk with some of the workers. His Spanish is pretty bad."

"Do you buy your fish from here?"

"Yeah, most of it. Some of the more expensive stuff like lobster and shrimp we buy from a wholesaler in Santa Barbara. Grandfather owns half of this place. What are you doing here?"

"I'm going to have lunch at the Blue Seal and hopefully get some work done on those chapters for the Historical Society."

"Better you than me. Sounds too much like a term paper." He grinned at me.

I laughed. "I've had those exact thoughts myself. And even though I find the subject fascinating and I've enjoyed the reading and the interviewing, I've found myself avoiding the actual writing. You know how that goes."

"Boy, do I." He looked back over his shoulder, where his grandfather was staring in our direction, a slightly impatient look on his face. "I have to get back and help Grandfather. What time do you need me tomorrow?"

"Make it tenish," I said. "You're so efficient, I haven't had a chance to catch my breath and see what else we need done around there."

I settled down in one of the large black booths of the Blue Seal Inn, spreading out all my notes. When my shrimp and fries came, I decided to set aside my work and relax over my meal. I dug through my backpack for a paperback novel and came across Mr. O'Hara's wooden scrap book. Scanning the titles of the crinkled, yellowing newspaper articles he'd pasted onto the black pages, I looked for recognizable names or stories that sounded interesting. It seemed to be a collection of war-related articles about the residents of San Celina County. Many of the articles concerned people who had the last names of kids I went to school with. The boys in stiff uniforms and red-lipped girls in their ankle-strap shoes posed against old Chevys and Ford coupes, didn't seem like living, breathing human beings, but more like characters in a movie made in the forties. I tried to imagine San Celina during those years, but couldn't. With all the reading I'd been doing, I had all the technical details, but I just couldn't make it real. Everyone remained as flat and hazy as the thin newsprint their stories and pictures were printed on. I flipped through the last pages as I finished my lunch. At the end of the scrapbook there was a sealed, faded business-size envelope with the return address of O'Hara's Department Store. I hesitated for a moment before opening it, wondering if I had the right, then decided that as a representative of the Historical Society, I did. With my clean knife, I carefully slit it open and scanned the paper inside.

It was an old telegram addressed to "Brady O'Hara, San Celina, California, 14 Dec 1941." The kind that many people had received during that time. The kind that never brought good news. "We regret to inform you that your brother, Brian O'Hara . . ."

I read through the brief message quickly. Brian O'Hara, seaman second-class, had been missing since the day Pearl Harbor was bombed. All attempts had been made . . . more information to follow as soon as it became available. The name at the end of the telegram was Vice Admiral Louis Denfeld, Chief of Navy Personnel.

Something about it pricked at my subconcious. I lingered over my coffee trying to pry information from my brain cells. Finally, in frustration, I turned back to my notes.

"Get much done?" The waitress appeared and refilled my coffee cup.

"Not as much as I should have."

She laughed. "Story of my life. Never enough time in the day."

"Speaking of time," I said, glancing at my watch and gathering up my papers, "I'm late." I had less than a half hour before my appointment with Mrs. Yamaoka. After talking to her I'd swing by the library and go through the microfilmed back issues of the *Tribune*. I'd been meaning to look in the newspapers from about the first few weeks before and after Pearl Harbor anyway. Mentally, I added Mr. O'Hara and his brother to my list of things to read about.

Mariko's peach-colored, two-story house was in one of the newer housing tracts south of town. A thick blanket of ivy covered the left side, and a trio of slim birch trees dominated the square, green front yard. The gray concrete driveway was empty, but I parked on the street in front of the black metal mailbox. Mrs. Yamaoka answered on the third ring. She wore a dark flowered dress with long sleeves and white canvas tennis shoes. Behind large round glasses, her eyes seemed happy to see me.

"Come in, come in," she said, opening the door wide. "I've made some tea."

We walked through the spotless living room decorated in dark woods and navy and russet-red fabrics in a sort of staid, New England elegance. Her kitchen felt cozier with its white walls and natural pine cabinets. Cherry-red and yellow calico flowers splashed across the wallpaper, curtains and seat covers. In the small white and pine breakfast nook, Mrs. Yamaoka had a white china teapot steeping. She poured me a cup and sat across from me.

"Is in here all right?" she asked.

"It's great," I said, smiling. "I always feel more comfortable in kitchens."

"I thought it would be easier to show these." She touched the three photo albums sitting next to her. While I drank my tea, she turned the pages and started relating an involved story about her part in the Obon Festival at the Buddhist Temple in 1941.

"Excuse me. Could you hold that story just a minute?" I asked, pulling out my tape recorder. "Do you mind if I record this? It's easier than trying to take notes."

"Not at all," she said and began her story again. As we moved page by page further into the albums, the hostility against the Japanese-Americans progressed. The first pictures were of festivals and celebrations—an especially touching one was that of a Japanese-American float that won first place in the 1936 San Celina Fourth of July parade. Dozens of smiling Japanese children in all-white outfits waved at the camera from a float covered with flags and patriotic bunting. There was a photograph of the head of the San Celina Japanese-American League presenting twenty cherry trees to be planted in front of the city hall, and one of a smiling Japanese baseball team sitting in wooden bleachers somewhere, cleated shoes casually propped up on the seats in front of them.

She turned the page and pointed to a jagged-edged photograph of a teenage girl standing in front of O'Hara's Department Store. "This is my good friend Toshi Ikeda's daughter. She worked in the linens department. Only on call, of course, or for holidays. Japanese were not hired for full time back then. Mostly we worked in our family's fish businesses or picking fruits and vegetables in the fields. But Hati was so smart and so pretty, they had to hire her." She touched the picture tenderly.

By my third cup of tea, Mrs. Yamaoka had warmed up enough to me to start talking about the days right before the evacuation.

"At first," she said, "we'd heard only noncitizens would be sent away. It was a shock when the newspapers announced that all Japanese would have to leave. We couldn't believe it." Her face sagged slightly.

"What did you do?"

She gave me a perplexed look. "What could we do? We were good citizens. We would not break the law. We did as we were told."

Remembering Mr. Kuroda and the Sukami sisters and how they also seemed to passively give in when their rights were so blatantly taken away, I couldn't help but ask, "Didn't you say anything? Didn't you . . ." I paused, not knowing exactly how to put it.

She sighed and turned another page in the album. "You are like my grandsons. 'Why didn't you fight back, Granny?' they always ask. Fight back? Against who? The president of the country? The whole army? Our friends and neighbors? We just accepted it, I tell them—the law is the law and you've got to obey. Then they get angry, say we were weak, say they would have been different, fought back. I say you don't really know what you do until it happens. And I hope it doesn't ever again. To anyone.''

"I'm sorry," I said, embarrassed by the shallowness of my quick judgment. "What about your store? Mariko told me that you were helped by Mr. O'Hara. How did you know him? Were you friends?"

She gazed out the window behind me, a distant look in her dark eyes. "I think Mr. O'Hara probably have no friends. Not the happiest man. So sad how he died."

"Yes, it was," I said. "I'm sorry to be so forward but why would he loan you money, then?"

She poured another cup of tea and held it under her nose, inhaling deeply before she drank. The heat steamed her eyeglasses opaque. She removed them and wiped them off with the edge of her dress. "Toshi told us to ask him," she finally said.

"Did she tell you how she knew he was doing this?"

"All she say it was least he could do after what he stole. My husband was already gone, taken away to a camp. I went to Mr. O'Hara's store, and the lady at the desk there, when I told her Toshi's name, sent me to the office where they do the payroll and the man there arranged to buy our store. I signed some papers that I kept with me all through the camp, wrapped in a silk scarf of my mother's. When we get back, after the war, my husband looks at papers and goes to O'Hara. We get our store back next week. We kept it until my husband died ten years ago."

"Didn't you find it odd that he would help you, a stranger?"

"We didn't question. So many people were unkind that when someone wasn't, we didn't ask why."

I didn't know how to ask the next question. I spoke hesitantly. "Mrs. Yamaoka, your friend, Toshi . . .''

She reached over and patted my hand, the wisdom and kindness of her age rescuing me from embarrassment. "She is gone, my friend Toshi. For eight years now. Ah, how I miss her." She turned a page in the album and tapped her fingernail on a black-and-white photo. "Here we are, Toshi and me and Hati." The two women in their thirties linked arms and smiled widely in the bright sun. The teenage girl stood to the side, a slight distance between her mother and Mrs. Yamaoka, wearing the mysterious half-smile of youth. They all wore plain A-line skirts and flowered blouses. Behind them, a lilac bush bloomed.

"May I borrow this?" I asked. "I'd like to copy it for the book. I'll take good care of it."

"Yes," she said. We spent another half hour going through her albums with her telling the story behind each picture. I chose five more pictures for possible use for the book and thanked her for her time.

"Come back, please," she said, walking me to the door. "Not many people are interested in our old stories these days."

"Well, maybe more will be after this book comes out," I said.

A half hour later, I pulled my truck into the last row of San Celina's new library. The less-than-year-old building seemed to balance precariously on a bluff overlooking a knee-deep lake in Central Park that usually dried up and made a fine soccer field in August. Since it was a Monday, the two-story, gray concrete fortress whose design couldn't possibly inspire the urge to read in anyone except homesick ex-cons, was crowded with the usual crazed teenagers working on term papers due last Friday. With the help of a Snickers bar and two bucks, I persuaded a kid with kohl-rimmed eyes to sell me his spot at one of the microfilm machines. I checked out the reels of the *San Celina Tribune* from September 1941 through February 1942 and settled down to read. Almost two hours later, I had a sheaf of photocopied articles and an even stronger curiosity about Mr. O'Hara and his altruism. I'd skimmed most of the articles and discovered a strange twist in his story. Until the day Pearl Harbor was bombed, according to the papers, Mr. O'Hara was indeed, as Russell Hill had recalled, at the front of the pack for relocating the Japanese. He was, in fact, the president of two civic associations who were adamant about the perceived menace of the Japanese-Americans. They were the San Celina Farm Bureau and the San Celina Association of Retail Distributors. Oddly, though, two days after he received notification about his brother, the *Tribune* ran a short piece stating that Mr. O'Hara had resigned as president of both groups. And according to the ledgers, it wasn't long after that he started buying out Japanese businesses, legally guaranteeing they would be returned to the sellers after the war. Nothing I'd discovered made sense. His brother had been killed at Pearl Harbor. Mr. O'Hara was against the Japanese even before that. How could his brother's death cause him to suddenly become the Japanese-Americans' greatest patron? And there was something else, too, something nagging at the back of my mind. Something else about this particular time I'd heard about recently. On the way home, it occurred to me. Dr. Brownmiller's house call. That happened right around the same time. I'd have to call Sissy and see if she could give me the exact date on the medical record. But what connection could that have with Mr. O'Hara, except that Miss Violet and Oralee were involved with it and they were involved with him? It reminded me of the remark Gabe had made about fingers pointing at fingers. There was no doubt now that the three of them had been involved in something and that particular something changed all of their lives. And unless there was a record of it somewhere, the only person who knew what connected all of them was Oralee . . . and perhaps the killer. *If,* I said to myself, this has anything to do with their murders. I could just be making a story out of pieced-together facts because, except for Edwin, all the people I suspected were people I cared about. Even, a mocking little voice said, or maybe especially, Clay O'Hara.

I wanted so badly to call Gabe and run all this by him. I didn't realize until we'd started fighting about this case, how much I'd come to depend on his friendship. When we weren't arguing, he had a comfortable gentleness about him that made it hard to believe I'd only known him three months. I hated admitting it, but it would be hard to imagine my life without him now, and that thought frightened me. I wondered if it had anything to do with his never having known Jack. He knew me only as Benni Harper, single person, not part of a couple. Jack would never be a real person to Gabe and for some deep psychological reason that I knew I'd never figure out, it made it easier to be with him.

Not that you necessarily will be anymore, I told myself. But maybe that's the way it was supposed to be. Like when a person gets divorced—I'd had enough friends go through it—and there's the transition person, the person who helps you get back in the stream. Maybe that's what Gabe was, my transition person. And those relationships never work out. Everyone knew that.

I tried to convince myself of that as I pulled up in my driveway. I kept trying while calling Sissy and talking her into giving me the date on the old medical record—December 14th—the same day of the telegram telling Mr. O'Hara about his brother's death. And I almost had myself convinced when I pulled out the ledgers and noted that the date of the first loan was December 20th.

Compulsively, I glanced at the clock at eleven o'clock, Gabe's usual calling time, cursing myself as I watched the minutes tick past. You aren't right for each other, I told myself, you argue too much, you both want control, you grew up in completely different decades under entirely different circumstances, your lifestyles would never be compatible. Never. By eleven-thirty, I had completely convinced every part of my body and mind that it didn't matter, that it was for the best.

Well, every part except my tear ducts.

19

I STOOD SHIVERING in front of my closet the next morning in my long waffle-cotton underwear trying to decide what to wear to today's opening of the sampler exhibit. I finally chose a new pair of blue jeans and a moss-green wool sweater. After some consideration, I pulled on my Reeboks rather than boots. Opening days usually meant a long time on my feet.

Sure enough, I gave three impromptu tours to senior citizen groups in three hours. One good thing, it didn't leave me much time to think about either the murders or about Gabe. I brought all my notes, photocopies, tapes and pictures and threw them on top of my desk. Once I got the exhibit underway, I intended spending the rest of the afternoon really making progress on the book. If nothing else, I was going to decide which pictures I definitely wanted to use. I was shuffling through them when the phone rang.

"How's it going?" Elvia said.

"Okay, I guess. We opened the new exhibit today. Gave three tours and I haven't even eaten yet."

"Hungry?"

I glanced at my watch. It was almost noon. "I didn't realize it was so late. Yeah, I am. What's on Jose's menu today?"

"Corn and shrimp chowder. And he's baked your favorite sourdough biscuits."

"Pour me a bowl. I'll be there before it cools. Do you have time to join me?"

"I can fit it in. Any special reason, or you just miss my brilliant conversation?"

"You can help me choose the pictures for the book. They're all so good I'm having a hard time deciding." I almost brought up what happened with Gabe yesterday. No, I thought, biting the words back. Forget it. Just forget it.

Blind Harry's was back to normal after the weekend festivities, even though today was officially Mardi Gras. There were only four other customers in the coffee house for Tuesday's lunch special—a couple of students drinking foamy coffee drinks and eating baskets of crispy Cajun onion rings with Louisiana hot sauce, and an older couple in matching French berets arguing over whether they should split a ham or turkey sandwich.

I spread the pictures across the round table and tried to decide which would tell the Japanese people's story the best. Elvia joined me at the same time Jose brought over our soup and biscuits. She picked up the picture of Mrs. Yamaoka, her friend Toshi and Toshi's daughter, Hati.

"Look at those shoes," she said, pointing to the ankle-strapped platform heels both older women were wearing. "Classics."

"The lady in the dark skirt is in her eighties now," I said, trying to imagine myself at that age. "And that's her best friend and her daughter. During the relocation, they were sent to different camps and didn't see or write to each other for four years."

Elvia looked up at me, her dark eyes sober. I knew what she was thinking. She and I had never been apart for more than a few weeks since we were in second grade. How would we have felt if we'd been in Mrs. Yamaoka and her friend's position? It didn't seem possible that something like that would ever happen to us. But then, it probably hadn't seemed possible to Mrs. Yamaoka and Toshi either.

"How did these people survive?" Elvia said softly, holding the picture closer and studying it..

"With an incredible amount of courage," I said. "Some of them are bitter, but it's amazing how forgiving most of them are. Maybe there's something to learn there. It's as if they knew that if they were bitter, it would be like losing twice. That is certainly a wisdom beyond what I can understand."

"Perhaps," Elvia said. "But what happened to them seems unbelievable to me. I'd like to think I would have protested. Fought back somehow."

I didn't say anything. Who can understand why we act the way we do in certain situations? And who could, or should, judge someone else's reactions? Since talking to Mrs. Yamaoka, I not only realized it wasn't as simple as that but, also, that each of us has to make those decisions alone. Like my fighting back when I was mugged. I made that decision and it worked out okay, but it could have just as well ended in tragedy. Each situation is unique, as is each person. How we react is a perplexing product of our genetic structure, our environment, and that special, unidentifiable spark that makes each of us an individual soul. The part of us that loves when it should hate, forgives when it should blame, survives when it should die. The part of us that scientists will never be able to corral and tag in one of their little test tubes.

"Let's eat," Elvia said with a sigh, picking up her soup spoon. "As Mama says, at least when your stomach is full, you have one less problem."

During lunch Elvia and I perused the photographs, arguing about which ones we preferred. We were halfway finished with our meal when a familiar pair of Army boots came clumping down the stairway.

"Ramon," I called out. "Where have you been? I've been looking—"

The boots stopped and started backing slowly up the stairs.

I jumped up from my chair and stuck my hand through the railing, grabbing one large foot. "Hold it right there, buddy. The SWAT team's got you surrounded. Come out with your hands up.''

"Oh, geeze," he whined.

I walked around and stood at the bottom of the stairs, arms crossed. "Ramon Aragon, you get down here right now."

He slowly descended the stairs. "Look," he began, "I've been meaning to come by the museum, it's just that . . .''

"Get over there and sit down," I said, pointing at the table where his sister sat, a knowing grin on her face. "We have to talk about this history project that you're supposed to be helping me on. Where have you been? How can I honestly tell your teacher you worked on this project when I haven't seen you for days?"

"I swear I was going to call you today. It was on my list of things to do." He patted the pockets of his baggy jeans. "It's here somewhere, I swear. Maybe I left it in the car—I'll go—"

"Forget it," I said, pushing him down in an oak chair. "You and I have to make some plans here. I've got a list here of people who have agreed to be interviewed and they're all right here in town. Now, if you can find Todd . . ."

"He's at the pier today. At least that's where he said he was going. Hey, look at these funky old pictures," he said, ignoring my lecture. I gave Elvia a peeved look. She just shrugged her shoulders, with the same resignation expressed by her mother a few days ago.

"Ramon," I said. "You have got to take more responsibility. Now—"

"Hey, here's one of Todd's great-grandma and his grandma. He was real upset when his grandma died. She cooked the best noodles.''

"Let me see," I said. He handed me the picture.

"This is Todd's great-grandmother and grandmother?" I asked, looking intently at the picture. It was the one of Mrs. Yamaoka, Toshi and Toshi's daughter. "Are you sure?"

"Sure," he said, looking at me oddly. "I saw his grandmother lots of times. And she had this picture on the piano
at their house. Except it was bigger. She was always giving
Todd money. She was really cool. For an old lady, that is."

"What's wrong?" Elvia asked. "Your face looks
funny."

"Nothing," I said and turned to Ramon. "I want you in
my office tomorrow at nine o'clock sharp. If you're not
going to help on the interviews, then you're at least typing
this stuff into the word processor."

"Okay, okay," he said, holding up his hands. "Can I
go now, Officer?"

"I guess," I said, still peeved.

At that moment, more steps sounded on the stairway.
"What in the heck's keeping you, runt?" Miguel asked.
He wore his blue patrolman's uniform and an impatient
frown. "You were supposed to ask Elvia about Saturday
and get back up here. I'm not running a taxi service here."

"It's Benni's fault," Ramon said. "She's been keeping
me here against my will. Isn't that against the law? Isn't
that kidnaping?"

Miguel gave his brother's ponytail a hard tug. "I'm going to get you drunk one day and cut this thing off, *Señorita*
Aragon."

"The drunk part sounds good," Ramon said, pushing his
brother's hand away.

"What are you two up to?" Elvia asked.

"Mama asked me to drop him off at school," Miguel
answered. "His truck blew a head gasket last night."

"How's the crime business doing these days?" I asked
casually, tearing at one of the biscuits on my plate.

"Everyone's goofing off today, as you can imagine.
While *el gato grande's* away and all that . . ."

"Gabe's out of town?" Elvia asked and looked at me
curiously. I shrugged and continued to make bread crumbs.

"Got a call last night about his son. Kid apparently got
mixed up in some trouble down in Santa Barbara where he
goes to school. Chief was really pissed off when he left.
Things have been real tense around the station lately, since

there hasn't been any headway on the murders. The mayor called the chief four times yesterday. Cleary even pulled some patrol people off street duty to run down leads."

"I've gotta go," I said, scooping up the pictures. "Thanks for your input, Elvia. I'm going to go on home and try to paste up some kind of reasonable facsimile of a book." Besides, I had a phone call to make.

Elvia gave me an odd look. "What's going on, *gringa?*"

"I'll call you later," I said. I didn't want to start talking about the murders in front of Miguel and put him in the uncomfortable position of being caught between our friendship and his job.

On the way back to my house, all the information seemed to swirl around my head like cream in coffee. Passing by the city hall, a thought occurred to me and I swung into the municipal parking lot across the street. Thirty minutes and ten bucks later, I had a copy of Keiko Simmons' death certificate. It only took me a few seconds to count back from her birth date to the time when she was most likely conceived. Right around the middle of December 1941. Before Hatsumi—Hati—was sent to the assembly camp at Santa Anita. Before she married Mr. Morita in that same camp and had the illegal picture taken by the guard. Pregnant by a white man whose genes would eventually show up in Todd. Especially in his bright blue eyes.

THE MINUTE I pieced everything together, I knew I needed to tell someone. And the most logical someone, since Gabe wasn't here, was Mac. "He's visiting his grandmother," his secretary told me when I got to his office. "And then he has a meeting with the board of deacons." She eyed me suspiciously. I couldn't help but wonder how much she knew and how much she blamed me for Mac's dilemma.

I found him sitting next to Oralee's bed at Oak Terrace. He wore a pale blue button-down-collar shirt and a brown corduroy jacket. She looked as if she'd been ill. The color in her cheekbones was high and bright, like someone who had run a fever for a long time. They silently watched a talk show on the small television atop her chest of drawers.

"Well, look who's come to see you, Grandma," he said, standing up.

She looked at me without saying a word, her blue eyes narrow and watchful.

"Hi, Mac," I said, glancing up at him, then back at Oralee. "Oralee, you know we have to talk."

"I don't have to do anything," she said, her face hardening.

"No matter what happened, people can't be allowed to get away with murder. You know that."

"Benni, what's going on?" Mac asked, his voice low

and urgent. He sat back down and took his grandmother's hand.

"I think I know who killed Mr. O'Hara and Miss Violet. And I think I know why." I paused. "Oralee, you have to tell us about what happened fifty years ago."

She pulled her hand out of Mac's and touched her cheek. "Oh, Mac," she whispered. "I thought it was over. When they died, I thought it was laid to rest."

"It can't be until the murderer is caught," I said. "You know that."

She answered with a jagged voice. "We carried the burden for so long. Rose Ann and I never thought it would work, but it did. And justice was served. It was the only justice she would have ever got."

"Who?" Mac asked.

"Go ahead, Oralee," I said. "Tell Mac what happened, what he gave up his reputation and career for. He deserves at least that much."

Oralee gave a deep, bone-wrenching sigh and began. "At one time, Rose Ann and I were best friends, did you know that?"

"No, I didn't," Mac said.

"We'd known each other since we were five years old. It was funny, her and I ending up in the same room, two old ladies. We used to talk about going to live in the city— San Francisco or Los Angeles, and getting an apartment together. But neither of us ever left San Celina. It was all just girl talk. We read too many romance stories, I think." She laughed, her eyes glazed over remembering their plans.

"I loved him," she whispered. "He was such a handsome man and it was me he picked. Me." She looked up into Mac's face, her eyes bright and wondering. In them, I caught a glimpse of the young Oralee. I felt a cool dampness start to collect on my breastbone.

"Who, Grandma?"

"Brady." Her eyes closed. "Brady O'Hara. The catch of the town. He used to bring me yellow roses every Saturday night before we went to the picture show. Yellow roses and a silver box of chocolates he had sent from San

Francisco. I saved the boxes out in the barn for years.''

Mac turned to look at me, surprised. Apparently, he'd never heard about the engagement of his grandmother and Mr. O'Hara. "What happened?" he asked.

She opened her eyes and her face hardened. "I broke the engagement."

"Why?" Mac asked.

"I was there when he received the telegram, you know. December fourteenth, 1941. I'll never forget that day. I'd come to town because we were going to pick out our china. Me picking out china, can you imagine that? He made me feel like such a lady, me, this little old country girl.'' She paused for a moment and took a deep breath. "They came to his office at the store because that's where he always was. He was certain his brother was still alive. Other people had gotten telegrams already and he hadn't, so he figured his brother was still alive. But he wasn't. They didn't even find his body. It's there, on that ship in Hawaii. People have their pictures taken in front of it now.''

"Mr. O'Hara's brother was on the *Arizona?*" Mac said.

"Yes. And he hated the Japanese for that. He wanted to join up himself—go and kill them all. He ranted and raved about it all afternoon. But I talked him out of it. Said he was of more use here, that he was too old to go. But it was just selfishness on my part. I didn't want him to go. Maybe if he'd joined, his hate would have been better served. At least it wouldn't have hurt innocent people.''

"What innocent people?" Mac asked.

"He started drinking. He always kept a whiskey bottle in his drawer. He would read the telegram out loud to me, then take another drink. When I couldn't make him stop, I finally just left. I hated being around him when he drank, and he knew it. I should have told all his employees to leave so he would have to close the store, but I was too embarrassed. I figured he'd drink until he passed out. I hate admitting it, but he'd done that before. I was so giddy in love—I never really believed he would hurt anyone. I went back to the ranch and figured he'd be fine the next day. Later that night, Rose Ann called me.''

"What did she want?"

"She told me to get over to her place right away. The sound of her voice made me drive that old Ford pickup like a banshee over the pass. When I got there, they were both huddled on the sofa, crying. I remember I just stood as still as could be looking at them. She sounded like a bird, her head buried like that in Rose Ann's shoulder. 'What are you going to do about this?' Rose Ann asked me. I just stood there. I didn't know what to do."

"Who was with Rose Ann?"

She shook her head mutely.

"Hatsumi Morita," I answered for her, walking over to the side of Oralee's bed. "Only she was Hatsumi Ikeda then. Everyone called her Hati. She was a pretty sixteen-year-old, excited and proud about her part-time job at the town's only department store. The first Asian ever to be hired. Someone who was young and timid and taught to be obedient to authority. Even the authority of a drunken boss."

"Benni, what are you saying?" Mac asked. Oralee and I stared at each other.

"He raped her that night, didn't he?" I said to Oralee.

"I didn't know he'd do something like that," Oralee whispered. "He was so mad at the Japanese. She was too ashamed to go home, too afraid her parents would blame her. So she ran to the only person she felt safe with, a teacher who'd been her friend since she was a little girl." Oralee looked at me, her eyes dark in a face the color of bleached bones. "If I'd just taken the bottle of whiskey, told everyone to leave, if I'd stayed . . .". Her voice trailed off.

"Why didn't you call the police?" Mac said.

Oralee silently shook her head, so I answered. "Oralee called Dr. Brownmiller the night of the rape and he treated Hati, set her broken hand, prescribed pain pills. But they all knew one thing. There was no way that the word of a young Japanese girl would stand up in court against one of the town's leading citizens. Especially when feelings against the Japanese were already escalating out of control.

Think about what rape victims go through today, Mac, when our laws are supposedly in their favor. Imagine what Hatsumi would have had to endure. No, Rose Ann and Oralee knew they couldn't get justice from the authorities, so they decided to extract their own justice, and I suppose, in a way, they did.''

"What did they do?" Mac asked.

"Thanks to Mr. O'Hara's money, many of the Japanese-Americans were able to come back from the internment camps without having lost a single dime." I looked at Oralee. "I'm curious, though. How did you get him to agree to do that all those years?"

She gave a crafty smile, and the steel-backed Oralee that I'd always known replaced the frightened old woman. "We went to his house the next day. I held a shotgun on him while he handwrote the confession that Rose Ann dictated to him. It was one of the sweetest moments of my life."

"Is that what I took from the nightstand?" Mac asked.

"Yes," she said, disgusted. "Rose Ann, that stupid ninny, had her lawyer get it from her safety deposit box where she'd kept it all those years. She wasn't right in the head those last few months, was getting confused about things and people. She'd memorized the whole letter and would walk down the corridors reciting it. Most everyone took it for the rambling of an old woman, a soap opera she'd mixed up with real life. Only I knew she was telling a real story."

"You and Mr. O'Hara," I said.

Oralee's eyes widened. "When I went back to my room, I saw him there dead," she whispered. "And her too. I didn't think. All I could do was just get away as fast as I could. So I had to send Mac to get the confession. I couldn't let the police see it. I couldn't let anyone see it." She looked up at him, tears in her eyes. "I'm sorry, Mac. I never wanted you to get hurt."

"It's okay, Grandma," Mac said softly. "I'm a grown man. I made my own decision." He turned to me. "I still don't understand how this explains who killed Mr. O'Hara and Miss Violet."

"Though I have no idea how to prove it, I think Mr. Morita did it."

"No!" Oralee said, sitting upright. "He wouldn't have done that. He loved Rose Ann. He named his daughter after her."

"Yes, but he hated Mr. O'Hara. He raped his fiancée, the love of his life, and nine months later she gave birth to the only child she would ever bear, Todd's mother, Keiko. Legally, Mr. Morita's, but biologically, Mr. O'Hara's. Through the luck of the genetic draw, Mr. O'Hara's Caucasian blood didn't show up in her. That must have made it somewhat easier for her growing up. Unfortunately, it did show up a generation later in Todd."

"He loved Keiko," Oralee said, her voice harsh. "Like she was his own."

"Yes, he did, but I'll bet he never stopped hating Brady O'Hara. Fifty years is a long time to build up anger. I'm guessing that with the death of his wife and his daughter so close together something in him just snapped and he killed Mr. O'Hara on the spur of the moment. He could have easily sneaked in and out without anyone seeing him . . ."

"He didn't," Mac exclaimed.

"You don't know that. He could have easily . . ."

"No, I mean he didn't sneak in. I saw him that night. He delivered fish. You saw me putting it away."

"Well, that places him at the scene. This is all just theory, though. But we do have to tell the police. They may have physical evidence that could link him to it. I know they always pick up a lot of fingerprints that don't match anything. I doubt very seriously whether he spent much time, if any, planning this."

"No," Oralee said weakly. "I'll never believe he killed Rose Ann." She collapsed back on her pillow, breathing heavily.

"This is too much for her," Mac said, pouring a glass of water and holding it to her lips. "We have to stop."

I walked to the other side of her bed. "Oralee, I feel the way you do. It's hard to believe that Mr. Morita would kill

Rose Ann, but maybe he panicked. Grief and anger and bitterness can work on a person's mind until they aren't rational. You know that. Look what it drove Mr. O'Hara to do.''

"What now?" she finally said.

"Grandma, Benni's right. We have to tell the police," Mac answered. "It's time for this all to end. This time, we have to let the authorities decide what to do."

"He doesn't deserve to be punished," Oralee said. "He's been punished for so many years already."

"You need to rest right now." He pulled the covers up and tucked them around her. "Let Benni and me take care of things. I promise, we'll do our best to make sure Mr. Morita doesn't get hurt."

Outside a dense fog was starting to move in, bringing with it the kind of dampness that seeps into your skin and makes you feel there are ice crystals in your blood. I stood on the front steps of Oak Terrace, rubbing my hands up and down my arms, shivering from more than just the cold. "Well, I guess our first stop is the police station," I said.

Mac leaned against the stucco wall, his face gray and exhausted. "I'm still trying to take this all in. It seems too fantastic, this blackmail plot that spans over fifty years. My mind is trying to assimilate all these facts, discern what is right, what would have been the right thing to do back then, but I can't think. It's a big jumbled mess in my mind."

"I know," I said. "I wish I could tell you that I've got it all figured out. I only know that whatever happened fifty years ago, it wasn't right for Mr. Morita to kill Mr. O'Hara or Miss Violet. Maybe that's all we can do, look at each thing individually. Maybe that's the only fair way to judge things."

"I don't know," he said, rubbing his face. "It says in the Bible that the sins of the father carry on to the third generation. This is the first time I've actually seen evidence of that. The person I really feel bad for is Todd. What is he going to think when he hears all this and finds out his grandfather is a killer?"

"I know," I said. "I've been thinking about that and I

think you should go to the police station and tell them the story. Gabe's in Santa Barbara taking care of some personal business, so you'll have to talk to Lieutenant Cleary. I'm going to find Todd and tell him before he hears it from someone else. Or worse, on the radio or TV.''

Mac looked at me, his face shadowed. ''Do you know where he is?''

''Yes, Ramon told me he was working out at the pier today. I imagine his grandfather is running the store, so maybe I can get to Todd and talk with him before they pick up Mr. Morita for questioning.''

''It looks like everything I did to protect Grandma was for nothing now.'' He clenched his fists at his side, looking as if he wanted to hit something.

''Not for nothing,'' I said, touching his solid forearm. ''You did it out of love. That's never for nothing.''

''But what about truth? You want to tell me what's more important here? Or if it's possible to have one without the other?''

''Oh, Mac, I don't know. I wish I could tell you. A lot of good came out of that evil act. Whole generations were helped. I'm not saying it was a good thing it happened, but I've always believed that nothing happens without a reason. As a matter of fact, I think I've heard you say that once or twice.''

He shook his head wearily. ''I know you're right here.'' He pointed to his temple. ''I'm just having a hard time understanding here.'' He tapped his chest. ''Good luck with Todd.''

I watched him walk out to his Bronco, his shoulders slumped. The task set before both of us made me shudder and I desperately wished Gabe was here. My body suddenly felt as heavy and cold as iron.

''Looks like you could use some warmin' up,'' a voice said behind me.

''Clay,'' I said, turning around. He set down the pasteboard box in his hands and put his arms around me, hugging me gently. I closed my eyes and rested for a moment against his chest, absorbing his body heat. Reluctantly, I pulled out of his embrace. He kept his hands on my shoulders. "What are you doing here?" I asked.

"Picking up the rest of my uncle's stuff. I don't think there's anything the Historical Society would want, but you're welcome to look through it."

"Maybe later," I said. "I've really got to get going now."

"Where are you off to?"

I bit my lip and looked away, trying to hide my anxiety. "Just an errand."

"Honey, seems like you're always running away from me. You look troubled, and that guy who just left looked it too. I'm taking a wild guess here, but I'm thinking you two have figured out something about my uncle's death."

I stared at the yoke of his navy shirt and kept silent. His fingers tightened slightly. "If it's about my uncle, Benni, I have a right to know."

He was right, but I didn't want him involved. "Look, Clay, it's just a theory. Nothing concrete. I swear I'll tell you the whole story when we verify our facts."

"Well, I'm not letting you go until you tell me. You have a funny way of disappearing on me and then it takes me days to track you down."

I pulled away from him. "I really don't have time to spar with you." I turned and started down the steps. He followed me across the parking lot without saying a word. When I reached my truck, he calmly walked around to the passenger side and pulled the door open. Slamming the door behind me, I turned and faced him.

"Clay, get out. I don't have time for this."

"Nope. You can tell me everything while we drive to wherever it is you're going."

"You can't come with me. I won't allow it."

"You weigh, what, a hundred five, a hundred ten? I weigh one ninety. I do believe I'll go where I dang well please."

"I don't have time to argue with you." I cranked the ignition and slammed it into gear. He didn't speak again until we were up on the interstate heading for the turnoff to Port San Patricio.

"Why don't you just tell me what's going on?" he asked softly. "Brady was my uncle. If this is about him, I do have a right to know."

I inhaled deeply. He was right, and at that moment, my stomach rolling with worry, I knew I'd have to do something. Talking was certainly better than screaming . . . or crying. So, driving up the freeway, I told him the whole story. He didn't say a word, but I felt his eyes on me the whole time. My explanation ended as I slowly maneuvered the curve right before the pier. The silvery-gray ocean lapped against the breakwater and looked as cold as a nightmare. As the pier drew closer, the fog thickened, making everything seem slower and quieter. Even the truck's growl seemed to soften, its engine noises bouncing off air as thick as a feather mattress. In the Harbor Patrol office at the land end of the pier, a single office window shined bright yellow.

"That is the wildest story I've ever heard," Clay said. I parked the truck as close as possible to the fish market. Todd's car was among the few that were parked in the lot; hearty souls apparently having a drink at the Blue Seal Inn. I took a deep breath, licked my salty lips and undid my seat belt. With a sharp click, so did Clay.

"You can't come with me," I said. "Please, just wait here."

"I don't think you should do this alone," he said.

"I'll be okay. You know, it's actually good you came. He may be too upset to drive, and this way I can take him to the police station . . . or home, and you can drive his car. All of this is still just theory. They may not be able to prove anything. I'm not sure what evidence Gabe has."

"That's his job," Clay said. "Let him do it."

"I am. I just don't want Todd to hear about his grandfather third-hand. He's just a kid."

"Well, I'll be here if you need me." He leaned over and kissed my forehead. "Good luck."

"Thanks."

The air was pungent with a dank, brassy smell the ocean usually had only after an oil spill. As I walked across the damp wooden pier, listening to the bottoms of my Reeboks squeak, I pictured a tanker somewhere in the fog gushing oil onto the cold turquoise of the ocean floor. It reminded me of the *Arizona* and the members of the 442nd and all the young boys on both sides who never grew up, of the stupidity of war, of the futility of hatred. It reminded me of the blood pumping that minute in my heart, pumping rapidly out of excitement and sorrow and fear. The masts of docked sailboats were barely visible through the thick gray air. Off in the distance, a foghorn squalled a warning.

The blue neon RESTAURANT-BAR sign shined cheerfully over the entrance of the Blue Seal Inn. Next to it, the fish market was closed up tight. I knocked on the metal door and tried to peer into the filmy window. All the fish-cutting tables and deep sinks were clean and bare. Giant metal fish hooks dangled empty from the ceiling. I walked around the back to the ocean side of the building. Sea gulls and plump brown pelicans huddled on the knee-high railing waiting for a handout, their chests expanding every few seconds like feathery balloons. The concrete platform next to the back door of the fish market was slick with water. I stepped in a deep puddle and water soaked my Reeboks. The back door was locked too. I stood for a moment, hands on hips, trying to figure out what to do next. Todd's car was definitely here. Where was he? I looked up to the second floor of the wooden building. One of the small windows was lit. Those were probably the offices. I started toward the steep outside staircase, when the door at the top opened and Todd stepped onto the landing.

"Todd," I called out.

He peered down into the fog. "Benni? What are you doing here?" In seconds, he was at the bottom of the stairs. He carried a box full of loose metal objects. Whatever it was rattled like silverware in a drawer.

"I have something important I need to tell you about your grandfather. I'm sorry, but they—"

In the middle of my sentence, someone else came down

the stairs and appeared behind Todd. I stopped and involuntarily took a step backward. "Mr. Morita," I choked out.

My face must have told the whole story. Mr. Morita and I stared at each other for a long moment. His face was as still as marble.

"Shit," Todd said, walking slowly toward me. "She knows, Grandfather. I told you she knows."

"Todd," I said. "You . . . you know?"

He gave me a disgusted look and threw the box down. "Why couldn't you just mind your own business?" he asked. Mr. Morita stood silently behind him on the bottom step.

"Todd, the police only want to question your grandfather. There's no proof—" I clamped my lips shut when his face contracted in anger.

"I won't let them take him," he said. "He couldn't help what happened. That stupid old man deserved what he got."

"Maybe," I said. "Maybe he did. But what your grandfather did wasn't right. He should have gone to the police. Killing Mr. O'Hara and Miss Violet wasn't the way to handle it."

"No!" Mr. Morita cried, reaching a hand out to me. "Not Rose Ann. I didn't . . . not Rose Ann. I . . . he . . ." Tears streamed down his sagging cheeks.

"He didn't kill Miss Violet," Todd said harshly. "He'd never do that. He loved her."

"But who . . . ?" Then it dawned on me. "Mr. O'Hara?"

Todd gave a sarcastic snort. "She finally sees the light. Did you really think my grandfather would kill someone in cold blood?"

"Todd, what happened?"

"He went to see Mr. O'Hara, that wonderful man whose disgusting blood I have in my veins, to ask for another loan, just to get us through this bad time with all the bills from my mother's and grandmother's funerals. He hadn't asked him for money for a long time. He hated doing it, but he was so afraid he would lose the fish store and"—he swallowed convulsively—"he wanted to send me to the best college he could. When he went looking for Mr. O'Hara and couldn't find him, he heard voices down the hall. He followed them, and when he found them in Miss Violet's room, Mr. O'Hara had the pillow over her face."

"He's evil man," Mr. Morita said. "I protect Rose Ann like she protect my Hatsumi. My hands are strong hands still." He held up his square, clean hands.

I stared at them for a moment, feeling like I couldn't take a breath. "Todd," I finally said, "Oralee told Mac and me everything. Mac went to the police. They're probably looking for your grandfather now."

"Shit!" Todd hit the side of his leg. He turned to his grandfather and grabbed his arm. "We have to get out of here."

"Where are you going to go, Todd?" I asked, trying to keep my voice calm and soothing. "Your grandfather is almost seventy years old. You're not even eighteen yet. Where are you going to go?" My ears roared as if a wave had crashed inside them.

"I have some money saved," he said, his eyes desperate. "We'll go to Mexico. They can't get us in Mexico." He dug his fist into his thigh, desperate tears shining in his eyes.

"Son," a voice said through the fog behind him, "you watch too much television." Clay walked up, tall and comforting, and I exhaled in relief. "You wouldn't last five minutes south of the border. Shoot, I'm not even sure if they get MTV down there yet." He came up and stood beside me. "Now, why don't we all just go on down to the police station and get this straightened out."

"No!" Todd said. "They'll put him in jail. I won't let them do that. Mr. O'Hara deserved to die. He deserved to die fifty years ago."

"We go with them," Mr. Morita said, touching his grandson's shoulder. "They are right. . . ."

"No!" Todd turned and grabbed his grandfather's arm. "You can't go to prison, Grandfather. Not for him. We have to run."

Mr. Morita's face became confused. It was obvious a battle was taking place within him. I'm sure he was thinking of the one thing that Todd wasn't. That Todd himself could be held as an accessory. "I don't know," he said.

"You're not going anywhere, son," Clay said, making the decision. "Your grandfather is too old to go on the run and you're too young and stupid. Now, just come along with Benni and me...."

Todd bent over and grabbed something from the box at his feet. He pulled out a long steel-bladed fish-cleaning knife. "I'm not your son," he said tightly. "And we're not going anywhere with you." He took his grandfather's arm and started inching past us.

"Put that away before you hurt someone, more'n likely yourself." Clay's voice was lazy and calm. I stood frozen, not certain how serious Todd was.

"No!" Todd said, holding tightly to his grandfather's arm and backing away. Mr. Morita looked confused and slightly frightened.

Clay started walking toward them.

"Stop right there," Todd said, holding the knife out in front of him, pushing Mr. Morita behind him. "I'll use this. I swear I will." His hand trembled so much it looked as if he were shaking the knife at Clay.

"Be careful," I said as Clay inched forward. "I think he will."

Clay held up his hand to me and kept walking. His boots made a sucking sound on the wet concrete platform.

"Kid, I'm getting tired of this game. You give me that knife right now." Clay reached out his hand. In a flash, Todd reached over and slashed it.

"Shit!" Clay jerked his hand back. "Why, you little—" He lunged at Todd. He caught him by surprise and grasped his wrist. Mr. Morita and I both jumped back and watched them grapple for the knife.

They twirled and grunted, the sounds of combat muffled by the thick fog. Clay was bigger than Todd and a more experienced fighter, but Todd had youth on his side and the adrenaline produced by fear. Mr. Morita pressed himself against the side of the building, his face a yellowish-gray against the dark wet wood. He looked ready to pass out and I started to go to him, but stopped, afraid of what it might set off in Todd.

They wrestled closer to me. I moved back, the back of my thighs hitting the low railing of the pier. Todd broke away from Clay. He slashed at Clay's thigh. Red instantly soaked Clay's jeans.

"You little asshole," Clay roared. The back of his hand collided with Todd's jaw.

The knife clattered to the concrete in front of me. I dived for it.

"Benni, stay back!" Clay shouted.

Todd broke away from Clay and reached the knife the moment I did. I grabbed the smooth handle and stood up. My triumph lasted only a second. He slammed his fist down on my wrist. I screamed in pain and surprise. The knife clattered to the ground. He kicked it away and shoved me hard. I felt the back of my thighs hit the low pilings. Then I went over.

It was like that dream. The one where you're falling, falling, and before you hit the ground, you wake up in your safe, warm bed, trembling with excitement and relief. I'd heard it said if a person ever hit the ground in that dream, they would die. But it wasn't a dream. I hit the water backwards. Pain shot up my spine and the cold water enveloped me like a giant's fist. For a second, I went under and everything was black and freezing and all I'd ever imagined hell would be. I kicked my legs and pushed to the surface. Tread water, my mind commanded. The voice of my junior lifeguard instructor, Miss Marion, screamed in my head. "Don't thrash about so, Benni. Slowly, slowly. Remember, the proper way to tread water could some day save your life."

No. It was impossible. My legs were too heavy. Then there was no feeling at all. Pictures flashed through my mind—my mother lying in bed the last day of her life, face as smooth and white as her bleached sheets; Dove's hand on my shoulder waking me to tell me my life as a married woman was over; Jack's face in his coffin, the bruising only faintly visible under the pinkish makeup; Gabe's face the first time he kissed me, that mixture of longing and fear that had permeated our relationship.

I went under again, my mouth open. I pushed my head back over the edge of the water, gulping air and salt water. "Jack," I cried. "Mama. Help me." Far away, the foghorn moaned again. *Swim toward it,* my mind irrationally cried. I started moving my arms, stroking my way into the gray nothingness. Gabe's face exploded in my mind. Gabe's face, his voice, calling me.

"Benni!" The voice came from my right. "Swim toward my voice. If you can hear me, swim toward my voice." The sound was muffled, like someone yelling through a thick wall.

"Gabe?" I choked out, swallowing more water. I inhaled a large gulp of air. "Gabe! Help me!" I screamed.

"You can do it," he yelled. "Swim toward my voice."

My arms started pumping of their own accord, following the familiar sound of his voice, toward warmth and safety. His voice called encouragement with each stroke.

"Answer me," he'd yell every so often and I'd take a big gulp of air and call out his name. "Keep going," he'd yell and kept up his loud patter as a beacon for me to follow. I pictured him in my mind, his sharp, high cheekbones, his crazy blue eyes, his large gentle hands. Gabe, who I would always feel safe with. Gabe, who I loved.

After what seemed like hours, in the cloying fog, a figure emerged, standing at the bottom of one of the metal ladders attached to the side of the pier for the commercial fishermen. I swam toward him, toward the outstretched hand. With each stroke, I said his name over and over in my mind.

"Gotcha," he said, grabbing my hand and pulling me to the metal ladder. The strength and solidness of his hand made me whimper in relief. "Good girl," he praised and pulled me up out of the water. "You'll have to climb the ladder by yourself. Can you do it?" Through my water-clogged ears, his words sounded like someone yelling from miles away.

"Yes," I said, holding onto the metal with a grip that bit into my numb hands. "Yes, I can do it." Through the wet hair clinging to my face, veiling my eyes, I watched his jean-clad legs climb up ahead of me. I pulled myself up the ladder, thanking God for each rung.

When I reached the top, strong arms pulled me over the low railing. We collapsed on the cold concrete. His arms encircled me and I buried my face in his warm chest. His breath came in short, hard gasps, and I could feel the comforting warmth of it on the top of my head.

"Gabe," I said, my voice catching in a sob. "How did you find me? Todd? Clay? What happened? I thought I was going to die. I saw Jack in his coffin and my mother. I felt Dove's hands. Gabe, you found me. I love you."

He sighed underneath me, his chest inflating like a blowfish.

"Well," Clay said. "I guess I could consider changing my name."

21

I COULDN'T GET warm. The heat from the small electric heater in the Harbor Patrol office couldn't seem to penetrate my chilled skin. One of the officers brought me a scratchy wool blanket that smelled faintly of beer and a small white hand towel to dry my hair. But even under the blanket, my wet clothes felt like ice. When the paramedics arrived, they checked me over and concluded I was all right but suggested that I should see my own doctor soon. The mug of coffee one of the sheriff's deputies had kindly poured for me sat on the desk growing cold. With the amount of salt water I'd swallowed, I knew that anything that touched my stomach would come right back up. Puking into a trash can was an embarrassment I just couldn't deal with at the moment. I huddled in the chair and shivered while Clay answered the deputies' questions for both of us. They had reached Gabe on his cellular phone. He was already on his way back from Santa Barbara when he received the call, and was currently about a half an hour away. I heard enough of the conversations between the various emergency personnel milling about to know that Todd and his grandfather never made it around that curve. In Todd's haste, he apparently took it too fast and spun his little Toyota out of control. They crashed through the flimsy guardrail into the ocean. I still didn't know how badly they were hurt.

I watched in a haze as a trim, fresh-faced young paramedic cut Clay's jeans up to his thigh where the knife had sliced into his leg. As they worked on him, Clay caught my eye and gave me an encouraging wink, as if to say "This'll be one to tell the boys in the bunkhouse, won't it?" So like him to treat even something this serious as a lark. But then, each of us deals with trauma differently. For all I knew, he was eating a hole in his stomach the size of a baseball.

Everything and everyone seemed to be moving so slowly. I pulled the blanket closer around me and watched the front door of the Harbor Patrol offices with confused feelings of yearning and dread. Gabe arrived twenty minutes later. His face held that expressionless look I'd come to dread.

"Chief Ortiz, San Celina Police," he said in a terse voice when one of the deputies asked him if he needed help. His eyes scanned the room like radar and I felt tears well up in my eyes when they finally found me. He crossed the small office in seconds and stood in front of me, his eyes smoky gray with anger. He didn't say a word to me, but turned back to the sheriff's deputy. "Fill me in."

They led him over to where Clay sat, his leg wrapped in a trauma bandage and propped on a small box, and the murmur of explanations started. I closed my eyes and leaned back in the chair, calm for the first time in hours. I didn't want to think about what would happen when Gabe and I were finally alone; it was enough that he was here, taking care of things, here to eventually take me home. That we cared about each other was painfully obvious. That we could ever reconcile those feelings with how we lived our lives seemed doubtful.

I'm not sure how much time had passed when I sensed someone standing in front of me. I opened my eyes to Clay's brown, smiling gaze.

"They're taking me to the hospital," he said, leaning on the desk for a support. "I told them I'd been chewed up worse at a two-bit rodeo, but they insisted."

"Does it hurt much?"

"Not as much as a renegade cow's hoof that broke my knee once." He reached down and touched the bandage. "I reckon I'll walk again, though I doubt if I'll ever play the organ quite as well."

I gave a weak smile. "You don't play the organ."

Grinning, he made a gun with his finger and thumb and shot at me. He shifted and his face went bone-white and I knew the leg was hurting him more than he let on. "How are you?" he asked.

"Cold," I said. "Tired. Sad. I feel like I failed Todd somehow." A tear sneaked down my cheek. Before I could unwrap myself from my woolly cocoon to wipe it away, he reached over and captured it with a rough finger.

"Oh, honey," he said. "There wasn't anything anyone could do. That story started long before you ever came into the picture."

"I know. Logically, I know that. But I still feel like I could have done something."

"You did. You cared enough to try. That's as much as anyone can ask these days."

"Thanks." I snuggled deeper into the blanket. "You're a good friend for saying that. Maybe someday I'll even believe it."

"Friend, huh?" He shook his head sadly. Hatless, with his coarse blond hair all wavy and wild from the humidity, he looked like a teenager. Just like the Clay O'Hara who seventeen years ago strolled into the Senior Dance and stole me away right from under Jack Harper's nose. "Oh, Benni Harper," he said. "We could have had fun, you know."

I couldn't help smiling. "Yeah, I bet we could have."

"You'd love the Triple Ought. Two thousand acres of the most beautiful pasture land east of the Rockies. Air like the best Chablis you ever drank. More cattle than you can count. I'm telling you, the smell of sagebrush there would break your heart."

"Sounds like heaven." I sighed.

"Just not yours."

"Just not mine."

"What's he got?" He jerked his thumb in Gabe's direction. "A job that'll kill him someday, one way or another. A pension if he's lucky. An old Corvette."

"He's got one thing." I pulled a hand out and laid it over my heart.

Clay gave a dramatic groan. "You're takin' all the slack out of my rope, Widow Harper."

I laughed out loud this time. It echoed across the room and I noted with satisfaction Gabe's spine straighten slightly. "I imagine somehow you'll survive, Clay O'Hara."

"Well, I guess we've started us a tradition now."

"What's that?"

"I have to come back to San Celina every seventeen years and get my heart broke by you."

I swallowed hard, willing myself not to cry. What he was offering me was all I thought I ever wanted. But as Dove would say, "Wants are like a dog barking at a knothole; just because you think there's something there you'd like to have, doesn't mean there is. Sometimes what you really want is sitting right there in your own food dish."

"Well then," Clay said, "I've got a gift for you. You know that quilt that was being made for my uncle? I want you to have it. I'll send a letter to the co-op. That's on one condition though."

"What's that?"

He lifted one eyebrow and gave a crooked smile. "Everytime you and Wyatt Earp snuggle under it, I want you to think of poor old lonely me."

I laughed. "I'm going to miss you, you randy old cowboy."

"Likewise." He leaned over and kissed me lightly on the lips. "Drop by the Triple Ought some day. I got a pretty little buckskin you'd decorate just fine."

"Better watch it, O'Hara. I might take you up on that some day."

He turned and walked toward the waiting paramedics,

the limp from his wound still not covering that slight swagger I'd almost gotten used to.

Gabe appeared in front of me. "Ready to go?" His voice was cool, noncommittal.

"Yes. Do I need to sign anything? I didn't really talk to anyone. And what about my truck and my purse?"

"I've arranged for you to give your statement tomorrow. O'Hara filled them in on most of the details. I'll send an officer out to pick up your truck. Your purse is in my car."

"What . . . what happened with Todd and Mr. Morita?" I stood up, unwrapping myself from the blanket. Stars danced in front of my eyes and I felt the room sway, the ground loom up in front of me. Gabe's arm caught me and I leaned into him, trying to ignore his rigidity.

"Mr. Morita's dead," Gabe said bluntly. "Todd's got a broken back."

Hearing that, my legs did buckle; Gabe gripped my shoulders tighter and kept me from falling.

"Am I going to have to carry you?" he said in a low voice.

"No!" I said in a panic, forcing my knees to lock, to take one step, then another. No way was I going to be carried out of there in front of all those men like some kind of weak-kneed Victorian damsel.

"Just a minute," he said when we reached his Corvette. From behind the driver's seat, he pulled out an old gray sweatshirt. Without a word, he led me behind the building. Then, as if I were a child, he pulled off my soaked sweater and tugged the sweatshirt over my head. His hand accidentally brushed my cheek and it seemed, for a split second, that his face softened.

"Gabe . . ." I started.

"Let's go." He took my upper arm in a firm grasp and steered me toward the car.

He turned the heater on full blast as we drove out of the pier parking lot onto the small access road leading back to the highway. When we made the curve, we could see the county fire engines and a large tow truck struggling to pull the Toyota out of the bay.

"How's your son?" I asked, my teeth chattering slightly.

"Fine."

"What happened?"

"He's gotten involved with a gang of kids I don't like. They tore up someone's place after a party and the landlord took names."

"What did you do?"

"Paid damages. Talked the owner out of pressing charges. Told Sam he was an idiot to screw up his life hanging around scum like that. He wants to quit school, but I convinced him to stay through June."

"Think he'll listen?"

His eyes remained glued to the highway. The jaw muscle underneath his ear jumped. "I don't know. My advice doesn't seem to affect people much. Guess I'll just have to wait and see."

We didn't speak the rest of the way back to San Celina. The drone of the car's engine and the warm air from the heater made me nod with sleepiness. My head drooped, leaning toward Gabe's shoulder until I forced it the other way and laid it against the cold window. I awoke with a start when the engine stopped.

"We're home," he said. He got out and came around to the passenger side. With a leaden feeling, I swung my legs around. He reached down to help me and I jerked away from his outstretched hand. "I can walk just fine. Thanks for the ride." I made it to the front door under my own steam, Gabe close behind, dug in my purse and found my keys. After three unsuccessful attempts at getting the key in the lock, Gabe calmly took it out of my hands and unlocked the door. The phone started ringing when we walked into the living room.

"Get out of those wet clothes," he said, picking it up. "Take a hot shower." Part of me was irritated that he so arrogantly took control and part of me was so tired and sad, I didn't care. I stood waiting to see who the caller was. He carried on a brief conversation, his back to me, then hung up and looked at me, his face still and unreadable.

"Go on, do what I told you," he said.

"Who was that?" I crossed my arms and tried to control my shivering.

"Dove."

"What did she want?" As if I didn't know. And how does she find out about these things so quickly?

"To beat you black and blue for doing such a stupid thing."

"What did you say to her?" I clenched my teeth in anger.

"To save her poor old arm, that I'd be happy to do it for her. Now go get those clothes off like I told you."

"Quit telling me what to do. You know, I—" The look on his face stopped my words. I closed my eyes for a moment. I was going to say my piece, that was certain, but not in cold, soggy clothes and not until I had it perfectly clear in my mind what I wanted to say. I went into the bedroom and slammed the door. I stood in the shower a long time, letting the hot water stream warmth into me, using more shampoo than necessary to wash my hair. My mind kept picturing that little car sinking in the ocean. More than once I had to lean against the tiled walls of the shower stall for support.

After dressing in old jeans, a blue sweatshirt and my warmest pair of wool socks, I toweled my hair to semi-dryness, feeling almost up to the emotional battle that was about to take place.

Gabe sat on the edge of the brown leather recliner, his head bowed over clenched fists, staring at the floor. I stopped dead, not sure what to do. He raised his head when he heard me walk in. The raw, vulnerable look on his face scared me more than any anger I'd ever seen in him.

"Gabe," I said in a wavering voice. "I'm sorry. I didn't mean for it to happen like this. I only did what I thought was right."

"You should have waited," he said, his voice thick. "You should have trusted me."

"Yes." He was right and I knew it.

"You could have died."

"I know."

"Do you realize what that would have done to me? Do you?"

I didn't answer. I couldn't. My voice seemed to be frozen somewhere deep inside me. Tears slowly filled my eyes.

His face turned hard. "I should have known it was him. If I'd done my job right, this wouldn't have happened."

"That's ridiculous, Gabe. I won't let you take the blame for this."

"If I'd been there, I would have killed Todd, you know. He isn't any older than my own son, but for what he did to you in the alley, what he did to you tonight, I would have killed him."

"He thought he was protecting his grandfather, Gabe. People sometimes do crazy things in the name of protecting people they love."

We stood silently contemplating each other, waiting.

"I took the job," he finally said.

"Why?"

"You know why."

"I want to hear you say it."

"I won't ever leave you, Benni."

"That's not a promise that you . . . that anyone can make."

"I love you."

I smiled. "That's one you can." I walked over to him, and his arms closed around me and for the first time all day, I felt warm.

"So, Mr. Official Chief of Police," I said, my words muffled against his chest. "What do we do now?"

His embrace tightened, and though my ribs ached, I didn't tell him to stop. "Well, *querida,* in my opinion, it appears there's only one thing we can do."

Three Days Later

"YOU'RE WHERE?" DOVE made a sound similar to one of her geese when someone walked too close to its pen. "You did what? Oh, my lord, is it legal?"

"The last time I checked, Las Vegas was still a legitimate part of the United States," I replied calmly. I leaned back against the padded chintz headboard of the king-sized bed. Through some connection with a police buddy from his L.A. days who was now head of hotel security, Gabe had managed to land us a suite at the Tropicana. I tightened the belt of the thick white terry cloth robe that came with the room and sank down into the rumpled sheets next to my drowsing, soap-scented husband. "Hey, just be thankful I called you."

"Hmph," Dove said, apparently speechless for once. I guess it took me eloping to pull off that miracle. She clicked her tongue irritably.

"I'm just taking your advice and deciding what to do with my life and getting on with it." I reached over and gently traced the grayish-green tattoo on Gabe's smooth olive back, a permanent souvenir from Vietnam. A snarling bulldog wearing an oversized helmet and the words

"USMC—First in, Last out." I wondered what other things I didn't know about this man.

"Since when did you start listening to me?" she complained. "And I meant in its proper time. With an engagement and a real wedding. In a church. By a man of God."

"We were engaged for three days, even if no one knew about it. And the place where we got married sort of looked like a church. It had a steeple. Well, a pointy roof anyway. The minister was very nice, though a bit tipsy, I think."

Dove groaned. "You didn't get married by one of them Elvis impersonators, did you? Garnet is never going to let me live this down after I ragged on her about your cousin Rita running away with that cowboy."

I couldn't help giggling. "Actually, he bore a remarkable resemblance to Wayne Newton."

"Well, missy, I suppose you think this is real funny. I'm telling you, you're putting your boots on before your socks. Your daddy is going to have a fit."

"I guess you two will *have* to speak to each other now just so you can complain about me."

"I'm going to call Mac."

"Why? There's nothing he can do about it."

"You're getting married in a proper church, young lady, by a *real* minister. Next Saturday. We'll have the reception at the ranch. Maybe we'll have Gormeh Sabzi and maybe some Ghemeii Bademjan. Or, I know, Albalo Polo, since Gabe doesn't eat beef."

"What's all that?"

"A few of Ahmad's specialties. I'll just need to go down to the Persian market in Santa Barbara and get—"

"I think we'd be better off just having a good old-fashioned barbecue," I interrupted.

"We'll talk," she replied.

"Dove . . ."

"Hold on, I'm making a list. First, call Mac . . ."

"Speaking of Mac, what happened at the church meeting last night?"

"Oh, that. Not much. He's staying." Her voice had that sneaky sound I knew as well as my own name.

"Dove, what happened?"

"What do you mean?"

"Don't give me that. What did the church do? Were people really mean?" My heart went out to Mac. He was such a good minister, but people could be cruel and judgmental.

"We had a vote, like I told you we would, and even though we said it would be majority ruled, Mac said if there was even one person who didn't think he should stay, he would leave. Then he left the room and we took a vote."

"And?"

"Most everyone voted he should stay, of course."

"Most?"

"We all had to admit that in the same circumstances we probably would have done the same thing. People aren't as unforgiving as you'd think." She sniffed. "At least, *some* people."

"I know that tone. Tell me the rest of the story."

"Sissy Brownmiller."

I groaned. "I should have known. What did she do?"

"Well, she voted he should be fired. I was so mad at that pointy nose of hers twitching like a cranky old possum that I just couldn't help myself."

"Dove, *what* did you do?" I briefly wondered if relatives of the police chief were given cut rates on bail bonds.

"I threw a rock at her."

"You did what?"

"Well," Dove said, her voice calm. "I was just doing what Jesus said to do. Cast the first stone."

"I think you got that story twisted, Dove. It's supposed to be those who are *without* sin cast the first stone. I'm pretty sure you don't qualify. I can't believe you threw a rock at Sissy Brownmiller. In church, yet."

"Well, it was actually a roll of Life Savers," she admitted. "And we were in the fellowship hall, not the sanctuary. But, I made my point."

"Then what happened?"

"Well, what do you think happened? She changed her

vote, of course. By the way, I stopped by and saw Oralee today.''

''You did? How is she?''

''Right as rain. Guess what's going on at Oak Terrace.''

''I haven't the foggiest.''

''Auditors. A whole mess of them. Apparently the home office got some kind of anonymous phone call. I think Oralee knows more about that than she's saying. Anyway, old Edwin is about ready to pee his pants. Guess he won't be playing the ponies for a while.''

''I guess not.'' Thinking about Edwin made me think of Mr. O'Hara and Miss Violet and Todd and Mr. Morita. Todd was still in Intensive Care, but the Japanese community as well as his college friends had started a fund to pay for his medical expenses and any legal help he was going to need. Between his injuries and doing what he did for his grandfather, he was going to have a tough row to hoe.

''Now, don't you be worrying about any of that sad stuff right now,'' Dove scolded. It's uncanny how sometimes she knows just what I'm thinking. ''You got plenty of time for that. Now's the time to be happy. What's my new grandson-in-law up to?''

''He's lying here asleep. I think I exhausted him, poor old guy.''

A hand snaked out and grabbed me around the waist causing me to squeal. He turned his head and grinned at me. ''Ask Dove if I can call her *Abuelita* now.''

''What's he saying?'' Dove asked.

''He wants to know if he can call you *Abuelita*.''

''What's that mean?''

''Granny, basically.''

''You tell him if he can manage to keep you out of trouble, he can call me the man in the moon.''

I covered the receiver with my hand. ''She says yes.''

''Well, you'd better get off and take care of that husband of yours. Lord knows you're going to have a rocky road ahead of you the way y'all squabble all the time.''

''We haven't fought for three whole days,'' I protested.

"We'll see how things go when you two crawl out from under the sheets," she said. "Call me when you get home."

"I will."

"And, honeybun . . ."

"Yes, Dove?"

"I'm real proud for you both." If it had been anyone other than Dove, I would have sworn there was a catch in her voice.

Warm tears pricked at my eyes. "Thanks, Gramma. You know I love you."

"Oh, pshaw," she said and hung up.

I had no more set the phone down when Gabe rolled over on top of me and pinned my arms back. "Wore me out?" he said. "Old guy? I'll show you old guy." He bent his head and kissed me, long and deep, and I thought, I'll never get enough of this, not if I live to be ninety. He let go of my arms and I ran my hands across his damp back, tracing his vertebrae. He relaxed his weight, causing me to let out a yelp.

"Watch it," I said. "I still have cracked ribs, you know."

He nuzzled my neck and pushed himself up slightly, resting his weight on his forearms. "I didn't hear you complaining a half hour ago."

"Sometimes," I said with dignity, "there are things more pressing than pain."

He laughed and rolled over, pulling me on top of him.

"That's better," I said.

"Well, don't get used to it. I like being on top."

I slapped the side of his thigh sharply. "Why doesn't that surprise me, Friday?" I laid my head on his chest and sighed.

"What's wrong, *querida?*"

"I was thinking about Mac. And you."

"What about us?"

"Gabe, he did what he thought was right. You really need a friend and so does he, and besides, you probably would have—" He stopped my words with a finger.

"I have a date to play racquet ball with him next week, okay? I still don't agree with what he did, but I understand it. Tell me, is this a sign you're going to be one of those wives who interferes in every little aspect of my life?"

I rested my chin on his chest and looked at him. "Probably. Why?"

He laughed. "Just checking."

"Gabe, doesn't it worry you that we got married and we hardly know anything about each other?"

"For example?"

"Like who your favorite actor is . . ."

"Robert Duvall."

"And, I don't know, who your first girlfriend was, how many cavities you've had . . ."

"Cindy Jean Evans. I was ten years old. And none."

"None? Ever?"

"That's right. Good genes. Now, my turn. Do you realize you have never cooked a meal for me? I don't even know if you can cook."

"I've cooked for you. I'm sure I've cooked for you."

"When?"

I searched my memories. "A pizza. I distinctly remember making you a pizza."

"One of those bake-your-own-pizzas doesn't count."

"Well, I *can* cook. Problem for you is I cook mostly beef dishes. As a matter of fact, this time of year is when I cook my specialty. People come to the Ramsey Ranch from all over the county for it."

"What's that?"

"You do know Spring Roundup is coming."

"Actually no, I didn't mark that particular event on my calendar. What's that got to do with you cooking?"

"You've heard of prairie oysters, haven't you? You'd love the way I prepare them—after they're freshly cut, you peel off the surplus tissue, then split them open, wash them thoroughly—I like using a little salt in the water—then deep-fat fry . . ."

He groaned and shifted under me. "Do we have to talk about this right at this moment?"

"I use a little pinch of garlic powder and red pepper in the batter, but that's my secret, don't give it away."

"I wouldn't think of it. Remind me to give you a full description of my first floater the next time we go out for sea food."

I sat up, straddling his stomach. "Ah, c'mon, I was just kidding. Really, you should come to the roundup. You can get acquainted with my herd."

"*Your* herd? You have a herd?"

"Yep. A hundred head. I run them with Daddy's cattle. Got my own personal brand too, so you'd better watch out. I like marking things that are mine. Anyway, they started with my first heifer when I was seven years old. No matter how hard up the ranch got, Jack would never let me add them to the Harper stock. And he would never let me make them community property. He said they were my insurance policy if anything happened to the Harper Ranch ... or him." I was surprised to find I could say it without a lump in my throat.

He reached up and stroked my cheek. "He sounds like he was a good man."

"He was, Gabe. He really was."

"Well, I didn't know I was marrying a cattle baroness." I laughed. "There's a lot about me you don't know."

"Sounds ominous."

"You don't know the half of it."

He laced his fingers behind his head and grinned up at me. "Now you've got me nervous. Looks like I might be in for a rough ride."

Grinning back, I started untying my bathrobe. "Chief Ortiz, you have no idea."